FREEZE FRAME

By Marjorie Dorner

FREEZE FRAME
FAMILY CLOSETS
NIGHTMARE

Marjorie Dorner

FREEZE
FRAME

William Morrow

and Company, Inc.

New York

Recognizing the importance of preserving what has been written, it is the policy of William Morrow and Company, Inc., and its imprints and affiliates to have the books it publishes printed on acid-free paper, and we exert our best efforts to that end.

Library of Congress Cataloging-in-Publication Data

Dorner, Marjorie.
    Freeze Frame / Marjorie Dorner.
        p.   cm.
    ISBN 0-688-09530-5
    I. Title.
    PS3554.O667F74   1990
    813'.54—dc20   89-49722
                                                             CIP

Printed in the United States of America

First Edition

1 2 3 4 5 6 7 8 9 10

BOOK DESIGN BY RICHARD ORIOLO

For Roger, Mary Ann, Tom, Nita, Lori, and Diane:
the best bunch of natural storytellers any writer
ever had the good luck to grow up with

Acknowledgments

I would like to thank Judith Weber for her patient and sensitive help with the manuscript of this book, Kristi Lane, Ph.D., for her expert advice on the psychopathology of one character, and Sumitra Dorner for thinking up the title.

FREEZE FRAME

They were hiding the girls now.
Keeping them inside, off the streets. Or else other
people went everywhere with them or sent them off in groups, so they
were never alone, and he couldn't talk to them, couldn't just walk
up and start a casual conversation the way he used to. It had been so
easy once, even a few months ago, because the girls still trusted him,
hadn't been scared yet. But now he didn't have many chances, at
least not in the villages, because *any* stranger would be immediately
suspected, watched, reported if he even looked sideways at their pre-

cious girls. He hated to be watched, lived in fear that someone would make a mental note of his face and then be able to describe it afterward, or even help the police to make one of those drawings.

It was the bloody newspapers, of course. Those sensational rags like the *Daily Mirror* and the *Evening Standard* with headlines trumpeting about the "Cambridgeshire Strangler," and running those pictures of the girls—school photos, probably—grainy reproductions of the smiling faces. Silly smiles. Silly girls. All the faces alike. Girls like that looked like each other. Of course, he cut the pictures out, followed the stories carefully, looking for any indication of what the police might know. But the police held things back from the papers, he knew, details, so the papers weren't the surest way to tell what was really going on.

One thing the papers had let him know though; after the girl in St. Ives, Scotland Yard had been called in to "aid local police in the investigation of what appears to be a series of related killings," so the papers were good for something. He had his countrymen's awe of Scotland Yard, had it deeply ingrained in his psyche, along with all the other baggage from his childhood. Once when he was eight or nine he had told his father he wanted to work for Scotland Yard when he grew up, and his father had said, "Don't be so daft. You have to be clever to work for the Yard, and clever isn't your long suit, is it?" But there's clever, and then there's clever, isn't there? Fat lot the old man knew. But still, with Scotland Yard on the case, he knew he'd have to be more careful than ever. Much more careful.

But the papers, those stories, were scaring people all over the county, and they had started hiding the girls. It drove him almost mad with frustration that he could never find any girls walking alone by themselves anymore. No, not mad. That was just an expression, "It's driving me mad." It didn't really mean that he was going crazy like the old man. "Madness in the family." That's what people would say if they ever found out about him and the girls. But, of course, he wasn't mad, functioned quite normally, shaved every day, dressed carefully, ate regular meals. His father had gone to pieces completely toward the end, before they took him away to the hospital. Hadn't eaten at all anymore, looked like a street bum, his eyes hollow and red-rimmed. *That* was madness. But the face in his own mirror was a

nice, normal face—good-looking even, he didn't mind thinking. So,
it clearly wasn't a question of madness.

He was frustrated, certainly. Impatient with a world so full of
stupid and venal people. Why hadn't those idiotic parents taken care
of their daughters properly from the beginning, seen to it that they
wouldn't look like that, wouldn't act like that, wouldn't swing their
skirts like that when they walked? It was a little past time now for
them to be locking the doors. Even in the villages, where life was
supposed to be so pure and simple, those girls would toss their heads
and laugh in that provocative way, flirt with boys outside the schools.
He had watched them. He had been watching them for years.

Even at Christmas, those girls couldn't pretend a little modesty.
The girl in Haslingsfield had been wearing some sort of skating costume, a skimpy little skirt over purple tights, just a short jacket and
nothing on her head at all. Hair flying in the breeze as she walked
along, going to spend Boxing Day with her grandmother, she'd said.
Likely story. He tried to make her tell the truth later along the roadside, to make her admit that she'd been going to meet some man, but
she would only cry. Once she tried to scream, though he'd warned
her about that, but she wouldn't admit anything. When he first walked
up to her, he could hardly believe it was so easy. A smile, a quick
story about visiting from Scotland and looking for the Collingsworth
house—he had noted the house the day before, outside the village
along a wooded road—and the silly little cow was charmed. She even
believed in the accent. Of course, he was good at putting on all sorts
of accents, had an ear for it. He'd always been good at voices, even
as a child. "I suppose you think that's clever," his father would say.
"But it's just a parrot's trick." But other times, the old man would
wake him up in the middle of the night and make him do voice
impressions for drunken guests, would praise him and give him sweets
for doing well. That was the worst about his father, never knowing
which one would be there—Father Christmas or Father Dreadful.

But the girl believed. So easily. "Can you show me the way? Just
walk with me a bit and point out the house?" And she had come right
along. Silly bitch. If they were going to be both provocative *and* stupid
. . . If their parents couldn't control them *or* teach them . . . Well,
whose fault was it, anyway? That hair. It should have been covered.

Never mind that it had been a mild winter. They should have made her cover her hair, wear proper clothes. Then she would have been all right.

Now the villages were out of the question. Too easy to be noticed. Even the bigger towns had the wind up since the girl in Caxton. Just last week, in Bury St. Edmunds, he had actually seen a girl carrying a knife! He had begun to breathe fast with hope when she'd come out of the library at dusk and started alone across the market square. But when he began to quicken his pace a little to catch up to her, she had reached inside her parka and produced the knife—one of those small kitchen knives used for paring vegetables. He had turned off quickly to the right, pretending that his destination had been in that direction all along. He'd ended up leaning against the church, clenching his fists in rage, breathing hard, and listening to the grinding of his own teeth.

The teeth grinding had begun even before he was a teenager. He knew all about it now, had read up on it in medical books. Hillary had once told him that it was called bruxism. She always thought she was so much more clever than he was just because she was three years older and because their father always praised her brainpower. Flattered her always. In everything. "My girl is so much brighter than the boy," his father would say—to anyone, to tradespeople—not caring who might overhear. There was so much in that sentence to explain how things were: "*my* girl," but "*the* boy." And, of course, Hillary *was* clever. He knew that, wasn't even angry most of the time when she lorded it over him.

But she was wrong about bruxism. The medical dictionary said that bruxism was the grinding of the teeth in the sleeping state, and that wasn't what he did. No, his condition was called bruxomania. It didn't mean he was a maniac, didn't mean he was crazy. It was just one of those medical terms, like "kleptomaniac"—shoplifters didn't belong in mental wards, for Christ's sake! He had copied out the definition to show to Hillary. "Bruxomania—the neurotic grinding of the teeth during the waking state." Neurotic. Not psychotic. It was fashionable to have a neurosis or two, after all.

Later, when he was at the boarding school where he'd been sent after the old man went into hospital, he'd tried hard to hide his quirk from the other boys. And it *had* been better those first months at the school because he'd been more numb than anxious. But, of course, that couldn't last. When he began to take notice of things again, he inevitably found himself in situations where humiliation was possible, and then he couldn't help himself. The boys whispered and the masters exchanged looks; he could tell what they were thinking. At last they sent him to doctors. Incompetent fools, most of them. But one had been at least kind, had given him a book to read about his "condition." "Perhaps this will reassure you. Perhaps reassurance is all you need."

The book said that "sufferers" couldn't control the grinding when they were under a great deal of stress, often weren't even aware that they were doing it. And he knew this was true. Sometimes he would notice the sound and wonder where it was coming from, feel outraged that such a noise should be bothering him when he was already so upset—that awful grating and scraping amplified inside his head until he thought he might scream. The books said that in "severe cases" the sound could be heard several feet away from "the sufferer." That part scared him, worried him. If he couldn't stop it, didn't even know he was doing it . . . "Madness in the family." But he had learned to adapt, to recognize when his anxiety level was rising; then he made excuses, got well away from other people.

But he knew it was getting worse. Everything was getting worse. There had been a time when he could go for ages without getting upset like that, months and months without thinking about the girls and what he wanted to do with them. There had been times when he'd felt almost happy, could forget about his father and Hillary, could begin to hope again for a normal life, just as he'd planned and hoped in his boyhood. When the old man had been taken away, he'd thought, "That's the end of it. I'm through with all that now. I'll go to university, get a job like other people, find a wife, settle down." He had seen models of normal families on the telly, after all. He knew what it was supposed to be like, looked at himself in the mirror and saw a face rather like those faces on the screen, so it must be possible.

But there was no university, of course—not possible after what had happened. And lately, it had been getting bad again, and he didn't know why. He'd lost another job, was "at leisure," as his father used to say with a sneer whenever he thought the boy was being lazy.

17

Too much leisure. He didn't need money, really, never had. The checks came regularly from the solicitors. Money had never been the problem in his family. But a job—even a boring job—occupied the mind, made it seem possible that he could be like other people, built up his hopes.

He was moving around too much, he knew. He should settle in one place, maybe buy a flat somewhere. The house was sold, of course, and he was glad of it because he never wanted to go near it again; the solicitors had said he could use the money to buy a house. But while his father lived—(Lived? Was that called "living," what the old man was doing now?)—he couldn't have the estate free and clear. But he didn't really care about having pots and pots of money. He just knew that it would be better for him to settle somewhere. But he couldn't make himself do it. And everything was getting worse.

So, he'd come into Cambridge, despite all his best intentions to stay away from here forever. He'd never been able to make himself leave the county altogether, but he'd stayed away from the city ever since Hillary— But the girls in the towns had gone into hiding, had been locked away from him, and Cambridge was a big place, had lots of girls, at the University as well as in the town, and very soon would have many more. Girls from all over the world who hadn't read the *Daily Mirror* or the *Evening Standard*, who would walk along in the spring sunshine or ride bicycles with their bare legs flashing, who would appreciate kindness from an Englishman. He had grown up seeing them and their male counterparts—French, Belgian, Swiss, German, Spanish—all chattering in their foreign tongues, flocking to Cambridge's famous "languages schools" to perfect their "school English"—teenagers on holiday, really, but all dutifully enrolled in schools. "Ridiculous foreigners," Father Dreadful used to say.

He'd moved into a shabby room in a converted worker's cottage near the Grafton Center, the gleaming new shopping mall which had been built since his departure from Cambridge. He'd followed the controversy in the newspaper, preservationists battling the business interests. He didn't think the shoppers of the area cared a rap about preserving historical buildings; they were probably overjoyed to have the mall, considered it a splendid addition to the neighborhood. And why shouldn't they? A convenient place to stop for a packet of biscuits on the way home from work meant more to that lot than the "historical integrity of the neighborhood."

Now on this first really warm day of the spring, he'd found his way to the University's Botanic Gardens at the foot of Trumpington Street. He didn't care much for gardens himself; that had been Hillary's passion. He could remember the way she used to bury her face in flowers as if she meant to eat them instead of just smelling them. Girls were dotty about flowers, about gardens. Girls might easily wander about alone in the Botanic Gardens on a warm day in May.

He walked slowly along the tree-lined paths, hardly seeing the magnificent Cedars of Lebanon, the exotic fir trees, the dazzling display of flowering shrubs. In his years as a "watcher," he'd learned to observe other things, special conditions. Were there many people around? Which direction did other people walk? Who else was walking alone? But it was teatime and the park was almost deserted. He was beginning to think he'd better leave. But as he approached the rock garden, he saw her, just a glimpse at first from behind some trees, but then more clearly as he moved quietly closer. She was standing with her back to him, gazing out over a pond. She was a slim girl in a yellow dress, and her golden hair tumbled free down her back. She was alone.

As he was quickly rehearsing his speech, what he would say as he approached her, he saw her stoop into a crouch and lift a camera that had been dangling around her slim neck. He followed the line of her glance and saw a black duck cruising slowly across the pond from left to right followed by a string of perfectly matched baby ducks, mottled and fluffy, hardly looking as if they could belong to such a sleek mother. The girl was focusing her shot as he stepped from the cover of the trees, his smile already fixed, his stride relaxed, his hands clasped behind his back in a gesture of nonthreatening self-effacement—the way Prince Philip walked, he remembered from the films.

Chapter **2**

Beth Conroy was enjoying the feeling of the sunshine against the back of her neck. Wisconsin's hard winter had given way to a wet, chilly spring, and her first weeks in England had merely confirmed all the warnings she'd ever heard or read about English weather—"Carry an umbrella at all times," her friend Charlotte had warned her. So this delicious warmth was particularly welcome; it must be in the mid-seventies, but local weather broadcasts always gave the temperature in Celsius and she was still not able to make the mental conversion easily.

She had deliberately waited for this kind of day to make her pilgrimage to the Botanic Gardens, even though she knew many things had bloomed earlier. Her passion for formal gardens had led her to read all about the University's collection long before coming to England, and she had already enjoyed the gorgeous flower beds which studded the "pieces" of the University's various colleges, those open fields which gave the illusion that the University was in the country instead of inside a bustling city. Christ's Pieces next to the Drummer Street bus station had circular flower beds with blooms in the rich, jeweled colors of stained-glass windows. She wondered what flowers those were that had such deep purple blooms, but she was an amateur at identifying flowers and could only admire in a generalized way. And she had "saved" the Botanic Gardens themselves for just such a day as this, a sunny Sunday afternoon, the first day of May.

It had been worth the wait, she reflected, as she wandered along through the rows of flowering shrubs. She'd already taken several pictures of some varieties of lilac that she recognized only because of the smell, so different did they look from the lilacs she knew at home. A few exposures of this film had already been used up on the pieces and at the lovely Clare College garden which she'd stumbled on as she was crossing Clare Bridge to get from the library back into the city one day, but she had bought only thirty-six-exposure films, so she could still take many more pictures, didn't have to worry about running out. That feeling of luxury, of almost limitless possibility, had been with her for some time now.

Beth had been in England for three weeks, having spent the first week playing tourist in London before coming up to Cambridge for her "work." A lifelong Anglophile, she had never considered any other place for her sabbatical trip, the long-awaited reward for all those years of school, both as student and later as teacher, all those years of scraping and saving. She'd postponed a sabbatical application until she was promoted to associate professor, so this trip to England was part of the luxurious feeling—her first taste of London was just exactly what she'd expected it to be, and she was planning several other trips to wallow even more deeply in her fantasies. She had almost two months left before the plane would take her back across the Atlantic, and that seemed all the time in the world. Once, she would have considered two and a half *weeks* in England a dream come true, but two and a half (almost three) months—well, that was like being a Rockefeller or a Carnegie. Anything under a month would later be discussed as "my trip to England," but three months meant that she could afterward say, "When I lived in England . . ." She'd actually practiced the phrase a few times, laughing at her own pretentiousness as soon as she'd done it.

But the sense of luxury, almost of license, had another, deeper source. Here where no one knew her, Beth felt she could relax in ways she hadn't been able to relax in fifteen years. Through college and graduate school, in all the years of building her academic career, she had battled a handicap that most people didn't even see as a handicap: At the age of thirty-seven, Beth Conroy still looked like a perky child. She was only five feet three, so slim as to appear almost boyish of figure. Of course, an adult-looking face would have overcome that impression—many dignified-looking women are slight in build, after all. But Beth had always regarded her face as a curse: widely spaced, cornflower-blue eyes looked out from under a high forehead and flanked a snubby nose sprinkled with freckles that became stubbornly darker and more numerous whenever the sun touched her skin. Her mouth was small and the space between her upper lip and her nose was marked by a deep indentation, almost like a dimple. Her cheeks rounded above a pointed chin, cheeks that would not look fashionably hollow no matter how carefully she followed makeup instructions, cheeks that showed bright circles of pink whenever she blushed, a frequent occurrence that she seemed unable to control.

Her hair, white-blond in her girlhood, was still pale and baby fine, resisting all efforts to curl or "style" it; she had finally concluded, after years of struggle, that the only practical way to wear her hair was to allow it to fall straight to her jawline from the slightly off-center natural part and to have it cut slightly longer on the sides than in the back. She had developed a habit of trying periodically to sweep her hair behind her ears with her fingers—a distracting habit some of her students had commented on in class-evaluations—but the silky strands would almost immediately slip back out again; it was the same with ponytails, French twists, "buns"—every style she had ever affected in an effort to look more sophisticated. Hopeless.

In an undergraduate art class, Beth had looked at the demonstration sketches meant to show the basic differences between a baby's face and an adult's face and had instantly recognized her own features in one sketch: the bulging upper head, the chief facial features crowded into the lower half of the face, the almost total dominance of curved lines over angled lines. Of course, it was the baby sketch she was looking at. And her voice, too, had always remained girlish, high and somewhat breathless, a quality exaggerated whenever she felt self-conscious, and she had a disconcerting tendency to giggle when she was amused or embarrassed.

Beth knew that her physical characteristics would have been definite assets if her ambition had been to marry a protective man and then settle into the life of a spoiled and pampered doll-wife. But from early childhood she'd set her sights on a different kind of life. Bright even as a little girl, she'd been encouraged toward academic ambitions by her parents, both teachers in the local school district— her mother still taught fifth grade and her father had recently retired after a long career as a high school chemistry teacher and tennis coach. But Beth had soon expanded her goals beyond even her parents' expectations, sailing straight on to graduate school after her undergraduate English major and then teaching at a community college for only three years before going back to get a Ph.D. Teaching, research, and writing—all three delighted her, called on her strengths in ways that gave her deep satisfaction.

And yet she always felt she was fighting to make people take her seriously. She felt she could hear condescension in her professors' voices, could see it in their faces. Later, when she began her teaching career again as an assistant professor at a university, even colleagues her own age showed a distinct tendency to patronize her, to talk down to her whenever department business or pedagogical issues were being discussed. She would have been inclined to believe that this was simply a response to a woman in a profession formerly regarded as a male preserve—unlike elementary schools where female teachers predominated, university faculties were still overwhelmingly male—except that even some of the other women professors took this tone to her. Many of her colleagues treated her as if she were a precocious child who had wandered in off the street to eavesdrop on the grown-ups.

The worst of it was that Beth couldn't stop *feeling* like a child whenever she was treated in this way. Her confidence in her own opinions, even in her own knowledge, would rush downward whenever someone got that "look," that tone of voice. Once, at a faculty party, she had been quoting from *Macbeth*—"Screw your courage to the sticking place"—when one of the other young profs had said with the usual smile, "That's 'sticking point,' my dear." And she was instantly sure he must be right, could feel her cheeks reddening as she looked down at her drink. Later that night, when she had looked up the line at home and discovered it was, indeed, "sticking place," she was overcome by a wave of intense anger, almost as much at herself as at the smug colleague who had found it so easy to "correct" her in public: Why *couldn't* she have the courage of her own convictions?

So, over the years, Beth had built up her arsenal of weapons against being treated like a child. She bought only the most tailored and businesslike clothes for "work." She wore makeup chosen to minimize her babyish features as much as possible, to hide her freckles. For two years in graduate school, she had even dyed her hair auburn in the mistaken belief that it made her look older. She affected a "learned" vocabulary, so formal and stiff that it made her seem "professorial" in the most negative sense of the term. Only gradually had she come to see that the effects of her campaign to be taken seriously had backfired. She had been aiming for a polished and calm assertiveness, but had achieved only a brittle stiffness that put people off, especially men.

Most men were either puzzled or repulsed by Beth's manner; few were willing to investigate what might be behind the brittle armor she'd so carefully built up. Fortunately, she'd been lucky in her women friends at Lawrence University, a handful of bright, energetic professionals who looked past the girlish face and the hard mask to discover the woman inside Beth struggling to define herself. Most of these women were married, some were mothers—Charlotte Empson, in her own department, even had grown children—but most were independent enough to have a social life apart from their families, and they included Beth, listened to her ideas, encouraged her scholarship. They were sympathetic sounding boards for her insecurities, both personal and professional. It was Charlotte who had "fixed her up" with George

Bachman from the philosophy department, and the other women had warmly approved. "Confident enough to let you be smart," Charlotte had characterized George during one of the weekly lunches the women enjoyed together, and the others had nodded agreement.

And they had been quite right. George was warm, good-looking in a rumpled sort of way, patient with her defensiveness, a relaxed and thoughtful man who cherished her without diminishing her. With him, Beth began to relax, to shed some of her uncertainty, and, with it, the stiff mannerisms she'd acquired over the years. To this man, softness didn't seem to mean weakness or childish dependence.

But after two years, George had wanted to get married and start a family; he was seven years older than Beth and had one failed, childless marriage behind him. She knew what such a step would mean; she would be putting her career on hold, perhaps even ending her career. After some agonizing, she'd realized that she just didn't love George enough to make that sacrifice; she was even uncertain about whether she wanted children, ever. One of only two children, she didn't have any experience with younger siblings as George had had, no strong impulse to "mother" anyone.

"Don't get married just because everybody expects it," Jill Hendricks had said emphatically over coffee one day when Beth voiced her doubts. Jill was in the psychology department and was very happily married herself. "Get married only if you can't stand *not* to."

Finally, Beth had decided to say no to George's proposal. The next year, he had taken a new position in Colorado and she missed him even now after two years had passed. And there had been no one to take his place in her life. The progress toward balance in her own self-definition seemed to have stagnated. "Just be yourself," Charlotte would say, but Beth had begun to feel that she no longer knew who that was.

So Beth's sabbatical year had been rather lonely without her classes to teach, holed up in the library and in her apartment working on her research; the sabbatical was intended to give her the chance to finish her book on E. M. Forster. Of course, the other women would periodically call her up and take her out to lunch, voicing their envy over her "vacation," helping her to plan the trip. It was Charlotte who had helped Beth arrange inexpensive lodging in Cambridge, who had simply handed over all her travel books so Beth could prepare in advance for the last phase of her project—research at the Cambridge University Library; Forster had been an undergraduate and an honorary fellow at King's College. Getting away from Lawrence, from Wisconsin, was just what Beth needed, Charlotte had insisted.

And she'd been right, as usual. In England, Beth felt no need to impress anyone, no need to compensate—perhaps overcompensate—for her girlish appearance. She could abandon makeup altogether, wear casual clothes, indulge her taste for junk food, run off to plays and gardens whenever she felt like it—no fear that someone would think her appearance or her behavior frivolous, at least not anyone who was making tenure or promotion decisions. She could have some fun without feeling she was being watched, judged. It was a wonderful, liberating feeling, and in the past three weeks, she'd even begun to walk differently, striding in a confident natural way, throwing her head back and swinging her hips a little. Some of the undergraduates at the library had been giving her appreciative glances—she looked younger than many of them—and she'd begun to think it might be fun to have a relationship with a man who didn't know her as Dr. Conroy, who didn't see her as a professional or personal threat. It would be almost like making up a new version of herself, starting over on new terms.

And now spring was cooperating with her newfound optimism, warming her body and cheering her spirit as she moved around in this beautiful place, smelling the wonderful bouquet of the gardens—there was one spot given over completely to herbs—and feasting her eyes on the shapes and colors of plants brought here from all over the world. She had tied her sweater around her waist and was swinging her large bag as she walked, glancing occasionally at her map as she looked for the famous rock garden. When she found it at last, it more than lived up to its advance publicity, gorgeously terraced and already in radiant bloom.

In one of the pools, she spotted a black duck, cruising placidly along with a string of babies in tow behind her. She remembered her camera, suspended as usual from her neck, and brought it up to focus the shot. Her old book bag, used as a purse here because of its size and cunningly placed compartments, slid from her shoulder to her elbow and jerked the camera out of focus. She put the bag down at her feet and quickly refocused, meaning to capture the ducks before they sailed out of the bright center of the pool. Just as she was about to trip the shutter, she noticed something in the background of the image in her viewfinder: a woman crouching on the other side of the pond, a blonde in a yellow skirt, who was aiming a camera at her, a camera that totally obscured her face. "Oh," Beth thought idly. "There's somebody taking a picture of me taking a picture of her taking a picture of me. . . ." And then she concentrated on the ducks once again, moved the camera a fraction of an inch to place the little feathered parade in the center of the frame, and then clicked the shutter.

As she was leaving the gardens more than an hour later, Beth came across an old woman offering popcorn to a squirrel under one of the immense cedar trees. The squirrel approached boldly and took the kernels one by one, retreating only a few paces to eat before advancing for another treat.

"How tame he is!" Beth exclaimed spontaneously.

The old woman stood upright—she had been bending over almost touching the ground with the back of her outstretched hand, a surprisingly limber position for someone of her age. Now she turned her leathery face at Beth and smiled slowly, a sweet, tolerant smile.

"Oh, he's a wild squirrel, right enough," she said in her rich Cambridge accent. "But I come here every day to feed them and they know me. Know I won't harm them, I mean."

"May I try?" Beth asked, leaving the path to approach the squirrel.

"Certainly," the old woman said, handing some popcorn to Beth. "Don't make any quick movements, but don't be disappointed if he's too frightened of you to come forward."

Beth bent over with the popcorn, her camera swinging beneath her as she stooped, and held her hand toward the squirrel, who twitched his impressive tail and skipped away a few more paces. From this safe distance, he stood upright and chattered in a scolding voice for a few seconds. Beth and the old woman laughed together and the squirrel retreated even farther from the sound.

"Maybe he's not hungry anymore," Beth said ruefully.

"Go back to the path and watch," the older woman said with a twinkle; clearly, she knew this beast's capacity for popcorn.

Sure enough. As soon as Beth had withdrawn and the old woman had bent over again, the little scolder skipped forward to accept the popcorn. Quietly, Beth raised her camera, moved the zoom lens into place, and caught the beggar sitting bolt upright, reaching forward with his tiny paw toward the wrinkled hand that he knew offered no threat. It was this charming picture that pushed from Beth's mind the picture in the rock garden: the pond, the ducks, the girl in the yellow dress with a camera where her face should have been.

Chapter 3

The clicking of the camera's shutter was the only sound for a few minutes. Chief Superintendent Michael Wilson of Scotland Yard stood in the long grass, deep in thought, swatting absently at the bugs that rose like clouds from the river's edge whenever someone moved. He was waiting for the police photographer to finish the last pictures of the scene. The Cambridge police had telephoned to Caxton as soon as the body was discovered—an undergraduate who was trying to tie up his punt at this isolated bend in the Cam had found her—and Wilson had left immediately, racing over the twenty kilometers from Caxton to Cambridge. He had carefully instructed the local police to wait for his arrival before beginning the investigation.

Of course, the perimeter of the scene had already been trampled a bit—the boy who'd found the body, the first spectators who'd responded to police presence, the police constables themselves. Just getting to the body meant walking across some of the paths the killer might have used. Yet Wilson had supervised the forensics team as carefully as he always did, seeing to it that potential evidence was collected, bagged, and labeled after the photographer had first recorded its location on film. The police ambulance was standing by now to take away the body itself after some last close-ups. Wilson waited without impatience, his years with the Yard having accustomed him to painstaking detail. He was never really inactive, though, because he'd learned to use moments like these for reflection, for "totting up," as he would say, the material he'd just been observing.

Only eleven days since the girl in Caxton. This was bad. Between the first murder and the second, it had been almost two months, from December 26 to February 24; between the second and the third murders a bit more than a month, from February 24 to March 30; from the third to the fourth only twenty-one days, from March 30 to April 20. And now just eleven days between numbers four and five. The psychiatrists had been right, it seemed: This was a psychotic whose illness was accelerating, spinning out of control. And now he was in the city itself, just as Wilson had feared. Haslingsfield, Huntingdon, St. Ives, Caxton, and now Cambridge. A killer who wouldn't stay still, who could strike anywhere—though apparently partial to only one county. And Cambridge was full of young blond girls, all prey to a maniac whose killing tempo was speeding up. They could expect another victim at any time, and preventing it here was much harder than it would have been in the villages or towns.

The photographer had finished now and was walking away toward the row of cars at the top of the embankment. Wilson turned to the local inspector, one Christopher Mulgrave, who'd met him when he'd first arrived. Mulgrave had waited quietly for the Scotland Yard detective's face to lose its abstracted look. Now he coughed politely and spoke.

"Is it the same as the others, do you think?"

"No question about it," Wilson answered. "Almost identical to the case in St. Ives, down to the riverbank setting. And now I think we can add another detail to our profile of this bloke."

"What's that?" Mulgrave asked when Wilson fell silent. At first, the local policeman had been somewhat in awe of the chief superintendent from the famous Murder Squad of Scotland Yard, but it was hard to remain so in the presence of the man himself. Wilson was so unimposing, so downright grandfatherly in appearance and manner that Mulgrave was quickly at ease. It didn't occur to him that this mild persona was one of the things that made Wilson so successful, exactly that bland and open manner that induced people to confide in him. Ironically, murderers were seldom hardened criminals—the truly cynical crooks were too careful to commit murder. More ordinary folk, moved to violence by sudden storms of passion, often craved a chance to explain, to be understood, even forgiven. Faced with this sweet-looking, round-faced little man, they frequently broke down into complete confessions almost as soon as he said, "Wouldn't you like to tell me about it, then?" Very few of them knew about the shrewd intelligence that lay behind the kindly eyes, and fewer still understood the ambivalence Wilson felt about his own skills: One side of him loathed the need to pretend sympathetic understanding in order to extract a confession, while the other was coldly determined to solve the crime by any means that worked.

"What?" he said now, turning his pale blue eyes toward the local policeman.

"What detail can you add to the profile?" Mulgrave prompted.

"She was wearing that yellow sundress," Wilson said, gesturing at the clear plastic bag that now held all of the victim's scattered clothes. "So all of the victims were wearing some sort of skirt or dress when they were taken off—no trousers or jeans. It would appear that this lunatic prefers his victims to be feminine in an old-fashioned way. Part of his fixation, apparently."

"Have you searched her bag yet?" Mulgrave asked.

"Yes, yes," Wilson replied. "After the fingerprinting crew showed there was nothing useful on the outside, of course. Everything inside seems intact. Robbery isn't what this is about, of course. Here's her passport." And he held out the document he'd been holding in his left hand with his thumb against the page bearing the photograph. "Greta Keller, a Swiss national from Zurich."

"I thought it might be," Mulgrave interjected. "The people at her lodging reported her missing when she didn't come back last evening. She came to Cambridge only last week for her language course. It was to have begun today."

Wilson looked down into the young face in the photo, a flawless face framed by long pale hair. She looked serious, a little affected, but still just a baby. And she looked like the other victims. The psychiatrist had been right about that, too. A "fixation," he'd called it. The killer preyed on fair-haired, slim girls in their mid-teens. Two of the victims had been fifteen, two had been sixteen, and this one was seventeen.

"God, the language schools," Wilson sighed. "The city will be crawling with kids who barely speak the language. Lots of blondes, too. We'll have to see to it that warnings are issued at every school, and issued in a dozen languages."

"We can handle that, Chief Superintendent," Mulgrave said, drawing himself up, aggrieved at Wilson's hopeless tone. "I'll get somebody on it right away."

A uniformed police constable trotted down the embankment toward them and then paused, uncertain about which of these two men he should report to. Finally, he focused on a patch of sky about halfway between his own officer and the stranger from London.

"Found a bicycle up the road a bit, sir," he said.

"A bicycle?" Wilson asked.

"Rental, by the look of it," the policeman said.

"Yes," Wilson said speculatively. "He would have to get her here somehow, too far from the city to walk. I'd assumed a car, but bicycles would do it. Probably she wouldn't think a bicycle ride was dangerous, not like getting into a car with someone. Nobody's touched it?"

Both of the Cambridge policemen looked wounded.

"No, sir," the uniformed officer said. "We're dusting it for fingerprints."

"We know how to gather evidence, Chief Superintendent," Mulgrave said.

"Sorry," Wilson said, looking away. "Get the girl's passport photo copied and start at once showing it round to all the places that rent bicycles. Find out who might remember the girl and the man who was with her at the time. Put two PCs on it."

The constable scrambled back up to the road and Mulgrave signaled to two other men who were standing by with a stretcher.

"Did you look closely at the body, Chief Superintendent?" the inspector asked.

"Of course I did," Wilson said evenly. "It's my job."

"Yes, certainly, sir," Mulgrave said, blushing a bit. "I meant, isn't it horrible? I've never seen anything like that before."

"I know," Wilson said softly. "The mutilation happens after they're dead, though. The pathologists can tell that from the way the blood behaves. So at least we don't have to imagine them suffering from it."

"But she was raped and then strangled, too," the inspector said. "That's suffering enough, I should think."

"Yes, of course," Wilson sighed. "The medical people think the strangling goes on during the rape. It stops them screaming."

"Horrible," Mulgrave shuddered. "I've got a girl about that age myself."

The two other men had moved into the long grass now and were lifting the body onto the blanket-draped stretcher. One of the pale legs flashed into view before being lowered onto the khaki-colored cloth.

"Those wounds," the inspector said. "Does he really—?" And he broke off.

"Yes," Wilson said harshly. "He does it with his teeth. Tears the face and the breasts that way. Sometimes the arms as well. If we ever find a suspect, we'll be able to tell whether he's guilty or not by taking a mold of his teeth. Distinctive as fingerprints."

"I didn't know a human bite could do that sort of damage," the other man said.

"Not normally," Wilson replied. "But this is no normal kind of biting. This lunatic is in some kind of frenzy when he does that, uncontrollable. Driven by adrenaline, the doctors say. Afterward he must be exhausted."

"And covered with blood, I should think."

"Yes. It's one of our puzzles. All of the victims were murdered outdoors, and all except one in daylight hours. Perhaps that one, too, but we don't really know when she died. Yet somehow, this devil manages to make off to a safe haven somewhere without anyone seeing him when he must be soaked in blood. In St. Ives the body was found along the banks of the Ouse, and here we have another river, of course. So these two are easy. He has the river to clean up in, perhaps just enough to make himself presentable for a bicycle ride back into the city where he can have a real bath somewhere. But the other victims were not found near water. So how did he get back to cover? It's a puzzle, as I say."

Wilson turned his face from the scene of the body-wrapping. He'd taken a good look, several good looks, when he'd first arrived and now had no desire to see this poor child again. He had never got used to it, knew now that he never would. It was the smell that was the worst. This girl had died only yesterday, but the warm weather had already begun the work of putrefaction, a sickly-sweet smell just beginning to replace the slightly rusty smell of dried blood. And her poor little face. Hardly recognizable anymore as a human face. Her parents in Zurich would have to be told. It made him tired to think of them. Thirty years he'd been at this, ten of those on the Murder Squad, and his species was still capable of surprising, even shocking, him in its capacity for depravity and ugly violence. The police in Caxton had called this killer an animal, but Wilson knew that the label was a slander on all other creatures. This was a peculiarly human act.

"Why do you think the girls go off with him, Chief Superintendent?" the inspector was asking. "Do you think he forces them, threatens them with a pistol or a knife?"

"That seems unlikely," Wilson answered, coming back out of his reverie to look at his fellow law officer. "He might have tried that once or twice and had it go completely unnoticed, but not five times. No, he probably just strikes up a conversation, charms them, persuades them to walk off with him quite willingly. No one would get the wind up over that. Could have been several witnesses who never knew what they were witnessing. Don't know it even now."

"But this sort of man . . . Wouldn't they take fright, run away from him?" Mulgrave was clearly troubled about this issue.

"What do you mean 'this sort of man'?" Wilson asked, raising his shaggy eyebrows. "You mustn't imagine that he's some sort of slobbering degenerate that would strike terror into people on sight. On the contrary. The psychiatrists all agree that there is a sort of 'profile' for killers like this, those who keep on getting away with it, that is. Most of the time they are completely in control, function quite normally. This man is probably very charming in a manipulative sort of way, intelligent, well-spoken, well-dressed. Handsome, quite likely. Butter wouldn't melt. It's that charm that makes it easy for him, makes him think he can't fail. And it's that intelligence that keeps him from being caught. The sickness is another side of him altogether."

"Does he plan it all out, do you think? Pick a girl out ahead of time and then follow her around?"

"The doctors don't think so." Wilson started up the embankment now, following the heavily laden stretcher-bearers. "They describe him as 'impulsive.' He sees a particular girl, someone who resembles his fixation, and then he acts at once. If the girl's alone, that is, and if she's outdoors. One psychiatrist said that a combination of circum-stances has to be present in order to trigger the impulse. He might see lots of girls every day who look like the victims and feel no impulse to attack them unless the triggering circumstances have come to-gether."

"But surely he can't be so bloody charming that every girl he approaches will just walk off with him." The inspector sounded ex-asperated.

"No, of course not." Wilson smiled patiently. "Ever since the papers started putting the murders together as a series, the police have been getting reports of strangers bothering girls all over the county. Surely some of those girls were approached by our man and just walked away from him. Walked away and lived. Trouble is we don't know which ones are reporting on this lunatic and which ones are being approached by more normal wolves. We've had descriptions of every imaginable variety all the way from a twelve-year-old delivery boy to a babbling old man. I'd be willing to wager that we've already got his description, but we can't tell which one it is. No help there."

"And what do the head doctors think about the probable age of this monster?" They had reached their cars now and were watching the ambulance doors close on Greta Keller.

"Hard to say. He could be quite young. The victims might be attracted to him as a potential beau, someone nice who seems near their own age, or maybe just a little older so they would feel flattered that he paid them any attention at all, wanted to walk with them. Or he might be quite a bit older and so might appeal to the girls as a sort of fatherly type, seemingly harmless. But the doctors are sure that he must have good looks of one kind or another going for him. And lots of charm. We don't know how many girls walked away from him, but we know that five of them went with him willingly. Five in as many months."

"Do you think he'll stay in Cambridge? He hasn't done two in any one place before."

"I don't know, Inspector," Wilson sighed. "If I could figure him out so easily, he'd be in custody by now." And Greta Keller wouldn't be dead, he thought as he turned toward his own car. He was thinking too, about the parents in Zurich, picking up the phone, listening, their faces freezing into shock and horror. He'd seen faces do that, had often had to be the one who broke the news. And soon enough they would begin to ask for details, insist on knowing things that would only add to their pain. So someone would have to tell them, if they asked to see the body, that they wouldn't be able to recognize her, that her face had been torn away.

Chapter 4

Nobody knew what the panic was like. Nobody could understand. And it had been going on for four days now. He always felt some panic afterward anyway, of course, that breathless fear that he'd made some mistake, left behind some identifying sign that would bring the police to his door the next day. But usually he could regain the feeling that sustained him, the conviction that he was much more clever than any police, even Scotland Yard. He had learned how to be careful, how to protect himself.

After the first girl, the one in Haslingsfield, he had almost choked with panic. When he first approached her, he hadn't known what he intended to do. He'd only thought that he wanted to speak to her, to get her to walk with him a bit. It had been so long since he'd spoken with a girl; watching was suddenly not enough anymore. His normal caution had given way finally to an overwhelming impulse to have her very near, to smell her hair. He'd been cautious for almost two years, just looking on from a distance, trailing after girls he felt compelled to watch, the fair ones, the ones in skirts and dresses. Two years since the girl in Italy, the one he'd found alone on the beach, the one who'd lied to him when he told her he knew what she was.

But it was an accident that he'd killed her. He had to stop her noise, had to make her stop struggling. As if he were actually hurting her. It was absurd—pretense. But she was dead, all right; when he finally pulled himself up onto his elbows to look down at her face, she was ugly, distorted, her eyes bulging. So he'd run away, cut his holiday short, and fled back to Cambridgeshire, where he should have stayed in the first place—a bad mistake to go to places like Italy. Such places made you think there were no barriers, no rules; they encouraged a sense of license.

Once he was back in England again, he had made himself keep his distance. But the watching made him so agitated, so angry. Because, of course, he saw how the girls flirted, how they laughed, how they let boys touch them, hold their arms, even stroke their hair. So when he saw the girl in Haslingsfield striding along all alone, swinging that long blond hair and smiling as if she'd told herself a joke, he had found himself talking to her even before he knew he was going to do it.

But this time, it was the blood that had scared him so badly. That was new. When he stood up, he had been surprised by the blood on his shirt, his hands, his arms, had thought for a moment that he was bleeding himself. But then he looked down at the girl, forced himself to remember. The biting, the tearing—it was horrible, and she looked so awful now, so gruesome, that he didn't want to think about it. But remembering made him calm down a bit, stop the terrible shaking. It wasn't his own blood; he was all right. But then he began to look around himself at the gray winter landscape, the trees and, beyond them, the road. It was daylight, midafternoon, and he was a long way from where he'd left his car. How could he get back there? What if someone saw him? All this blood! It was on his clothes, soaked in, on his face probably. Instinctively, he lifted his sleeve and wiped it across his face. The red stain appeared at once along the gray fabric, soaking in and darkening as he watched it.

The panic had flooded his brain, making his insides tremble, his legs weaken. They would catch him, lock him up. Prison, a hospital. Madness in the family. Closed in—the door wouldn't open—locked—pounding on it wouldn't help. His father used to say that from the other side: "Pounding doesn't help, you little idiot. You're staying there for the whole hour and if you pound again, I'll add another hour." In the dark, locked in.

He ran blindly, crashing through the brush, scraping his shoulder against a tree. At last he stumbled and fell, slamming his side against the exposed roots of a maple tree. It knocked the wind out of him and, for a few seconds, he was really afraid he would die, that the universe had run out of air and he was suffocating. When he began to breathe again, to calm down a little, he made himself lie still for a long time. If he kept this up, he would hurt himself, scratch himself against the shrubs, and then some of the blood *would* be his, like leaving a trail behind himself. Already, he had brushed some of *her* blood against things, had made a clear path for someone to follow when she was found. They would find her, he knew, because he hadn't taken the time to hide or cover the body, and her clothes were scattered around in open sight. So he had to calm down, had to think. He would have to get back to his car without anyone seeing him. Then he could drive to his rooming house, sneak inside, and get cleaned up.

Gradually his breathing had steadied, his brain had begun to clear. When he stood up again, he began to move slowly and carefully, watching where he set his feet, holding his body away from bushes and trees as he passed them. The road was off to his right, he knew, and if he stayed among the trees, he could go along parallel to the road, make his way past the village, and then wait for dark—darkness came so early at this time of the year. Why, it was only a few days ago that it had been the shortest day of the year. In the dark, he could get into his car and drive off. Then he could have a nice bath—"Wouldn't a nice hot bath be a lark?" Hillary used to say. "You'll feel like sleeping then, won't you?" She was always nicer to him after Father Dreadful had locked him up in the pantry. Yes, a nice hot bath would get rid of the blood, and then he would burn these clothes, even the shoes. The check would come at the end of the week and he could get new clothes.

After that scare, he'd thought everything over carefully. He felt sickened with disgust whenever he thought about the biting, what the girl had looked like afterward. But he soon realized that it was just another one of those things he couldn't help. People shouldn't upset him, make him so angry that he lost control like that. What frightened him most was that it might happen again. He hadn't meant to bite the girl, hadn't even meant to speak to her in the first place. If the feelings came over him again, what might happen? He would have to be ready, just in case. He would have to adapt. He'd always done that, hadn't he? Make certain things habitual and then you'll make yourself safe. If you never lock the door to your room at night, you won't be trapped if you wake in a panic and feel you have to run. If you always keep your things arranged just so, you can grab what you need quickly when you need to get out. "You're so damned rigid," one of the masters at the school had said. "I'm amazed that you don't just break in half." But he was a fool, after all, mistaking intelligent planning for rigidity.

So he had bought the sport bag. It looked harmless enough, even added to his casual good looks, he thought. "Adidas," it said, and spoke of squash or tennis or some other trendy sport. No one would know to look at him that he'd never been good at any sports. He looked so fit. Genetics, that. The old man had always cut a dashing figure and his mother was once a field-hockey standout. He'd never seen her, but he had seen the photos—the slim girl in those silly school bloomers, her face like Hillary's, though the hair was much darker, of course. So he came by his athletic looks honestly, no matter what Father Dreadful said. "You," the old man would sometimes say to him, "you don't look like anyone else in the family. Sometimes it makes me wonder about your mother." And it was true, of course, that his coloring was quite different from theirs, but he could see the old man's eyes when he looked in the mirror, could trace something of Hillary's jawline in his own.

The bag held a complete change of clothes, even shoes, and towels, one of them very damp and wrapped inside a plastic bag. He made sure that any room he rented had a working fireplace. If he had to burn something, it would not do to have to search for somewhere to do it. After Boxing Day, he had burned everything up and raked through the ashes to take away the metal eyelets from the shoes. They were called "grommets," those eyelets. He'd read that once and looked it up. Words stayed in his mind, and he liked knowing things like the meaning of "grommet." He'd read once that a killer in Yorkshire had been caught because he'd left those grommets behind in his fireplace and the police had used them to break the wife: "He came home that day and burned his clothes, didn't he?" they'd asked her, and the silly bitch had burst into tears and told them everything.

Better not to have a wife, to be wholly free. Still, it got so lonely, so quiet at night in the strange rooms, no one to talk to, no human face to look into—only the blinking eye of the telly where people looked happy, where beautiful women were good—usually—not sluts, where mothers stayed with their babies and held them close against their cheeks. There was a picture like that of his mother holding Hillary, Hillary as a bald, pink-faced baby. Was it *his* fault that his mother had died having him? The old man had never said it, never actually used those words, but that's what he *meant*, that's what his face said whenever it scowled down like that. "You have to be punished," he would say whenever there was a broken lamp or a bad mark on a school report, but the rest of the sentence hung in the air, followed him into the pantry, and was closed in with him when the door swung shut: "You have to be punished for killing her." "Pay him no mind," Hillary would say. "He's mad as a hatter." But, of course, *she* had been held against the motherly cheek; she didn't really know what it was like.

The sport bag had caught the eye of the girl in the Botanic Gardens. "Adidas," she had exclaimed when he brought it forward from behind his back. "Did you know that this is a German product? It is everywhere now, of course, but first it came from Germany." She sounded as if she were reciting for her English class.

"Are you German, then?" he'd said.

"No, Swiss," she answered. "From Zurich. I am staying in—in —how do I say it?—in 'digs' on the Mill Road." And when she pointed, the draped sweater fell away from her pale, slender arm. The tricolored strap around her neck made a sharp V to the camera that hung between her breasts.

He'd strolled next to her down the deserted lanes of the gardens, chatting with her, avoiding body contact because he knew that might frighten her; even brushing against an arm had once made a girl pull away and rejoin the friends she'd left a few minutes before. That had been last month sometime. It was absurdly easy to make friends with this Swiss girl, though. She seemed hungry for someone to talk to— probably just wanted to show off her English. Had her host family shown her around Cambridge? Not much as yet. Did she know that the best way to see the city was along the river? Did she know about punting, a famous way to get about here in Cambridge? She had seen punts, but was afraid of them; they seemed to her to be so—groping for the word—"tippy," and she didn't swim well. Well, what about bicycles, then? She wasn't afraid of bicycles, was she? A toss of the golden hair and a laugh. No, of course, she wasn't afraid of bicycles. Little fool!

And later, when she'd been ready to turn back toward the city, he'd had no trouble talking her out of it. Just a bit farther; there was such a pretty spot he'd like to show her; such wild flowers as no one in Switzerland had ever seen; she could take a picture. And she had gone on with him without a blink, swinging back up onto the pedals with a dazzling smile. Such stupidity made his blood boil. And then when she'd finally pretended to be alarmed, that had made him even angrier. Why did they always pretend to be so innocent when he touched them? Why did they act as if they were afraid? That was just pretense, lies. "I'm afraid of him," Hillary had said. "Can't you understand that I'm afraid of him?" Lies. All lies. And she had cried, too, tears sliding down those porcelain shepherdess's cheeks of hers. That was the next thing from the Swiss girl, too, the crying. So predictable. And all part of the act. It enraged him, whipped him into a fury. "Stop that crying, bitch! It's not going to help you. And don't try to scream. That would be a big mistake."

But she kept struggling, of course. They always did that. Just as if this were all something new to them. Thrashing around, fighting him. And the faces. That was the worst. Contorted, ugly, eyes accusing him, looking at him as if he were some kind of monster. It drove him wild, made a kind of red fog come into his brain, made his teeth begin to grind. "Stop that, stop that. I'll have to make you stop that." But he knew he wasn't actually saying that out loud—only his mind was saying that—but he didn't know if he was saying it to the girl or to his own teeth. And the sound inside his head, the sound of his own panting and the grating sound—that was always the last thing he was consciously aware of until everything was still again and he became aware of the wet, of the blood.

Then he had to swallow the panic, take the rest of his clothes off, get out the damp towel, and wash himself. Careful, careful—he had to wipe his whole head. In Huntingdon, when he'd got back to his room and looked in the mirror, he had seen blood in his hair. After that, he put a small hand mirror in the bag. If you're prepared, you'll be safe. Pack up everything, leave nothing behind that could be traced, nothing that could have a fingerprint on it. Wrap the old clothes in the plastic bag—there must be no blood inside the sport bag later. Watch where the feet were placed when he had the new shoes on; mustn't leave footprints for anyone to make molds of. Wipe down the handlebars of her bicycle where he'd touched it to lean it against the tree—"The flowers are just down here, along the bank." He would wipe his own bicycle thoroughly before he abandoned it just inside the city.

But this time he'd taken something that belonged to the girl. He had taken the camera. Just before starting back toward the bicycles, he'd caught a glimpse of the camera's strap in the long grass. It was a nice camera, a 35mm—Japanese, by the look of it. He was struck by a notion that it would be interesting to see what pictures she'd taken. He had no intention of keeping the camera. That would be really stupid—just the sort of thing to give him away. In fact, he had thrown it into the river the next day. But the pictures interested him. She had asked, in the gardens, if she could take a picture of him, but he'd dismissed the notion with an elaborate show of modesty. Such an aggressive photographer might have photographed the other men, though. Of course, he knew there were other men. If he saw the photos, that would prove he was right, had been right all along about her, no matter how hard she tried to deny it when he had his hands on her throat. So he had stooped, caught up the camera, and slipped it inside the sport bag. He had never before taken anything from the girls and it gave him a little thrill of alarm to carry it around with him. Back at his room, he'd rewound the film—it was about half used up—and taken it the next day to a "While-U-Wait" kiosk next to Boots on St. Andrew's Street.

Two hours later, he'd sat down in his room with a cup of tea and opened the envelope with the photos in it. Most of the pictures were standard tourist shots—the changing of the guard at Buckingham Palace, flowers in St. James's Park, a yeoman warden at the Tower of London; apparently, the girl had done a predictable and boring tour of London before coming up to Cambridge. He'd been right to think her stupid. There was nothing in these snaps that showed any imaginative spark. He flipped through the scenes of the Botanic Gardens and, finally, recognized the very last picture she'd taken—the ducks in the rock garden—the picture she had been taking when he'd come up to her and said, "Lovely little family, isn't it?"

He'd almost put the picture behind the others, had started to move it, when he noticed something in the background, on the other side of the pond: a girl in dark trousers and a white blouse, a girl holding a camera. She'd obviously been taking a picture of the ducks, too. A dizzying wave of fear swept over him as he realized what would be in the background of *her* photo of those ducks—a girl in a yellow dress with a man just coming up behind her! He sprang to his feet, jarring the table; tea sloshed out of the cup and ran across the cracked surface of the table toward the hot plate. Good God! This bitch had a picture of him and that Swiss girl together. It was only a matter of time before she had the pictures developed. Already the papers were babbling about "the Strangler's latest victim," about "the girl in the yellow dress." This girl would read about it, put the facts together, go to the police. They would have his bloody picture!

He paced to the small fireplace and back to the table, over and over again, trying to force himself to be calm, trying to focus his attention on what to do next. He kept looking at the picture in his hand, trying to control the shaking enough so that he could see it clearly, study it. If he could find the girl, get the film *before* it was developed, he would be safe. But how? How could he find one girl in all of Cambridge when he couldn't even see her face in the photo? The damned camera was hiding her face. He dropped the picture onto the table and sat down, rocking himself back and forth and gulping air. The walls of the squalid room were closing in on him; he had to get outside—there was more air outside; he would feel better outside. But he couldn't run; he had to think. He wrapped his arms tightly and concentrated on his breathing—slowly, slowly—too much was as bad as too little—too much oxygen could make you faint. Gradually, he calmed himself enough to concentrate on the picture. Without touching it, he brought his face down to within five inches of the shiny surface, squinting to focus on the background alone.

The girl was small, slight, had pale hair almost to her shoulders; the camera obscured most of her face, but he could make out a pointed chin. Her clothes were no help, plain, unornamented. Why hadn't he noticed her there? He was usually so careful to make sure no one else was around. He *had* looked, had swept his glance in all directions before stepping out from behind the trees. This stupid bitch must have come up suddenly, out of nowhere, when he was concentrating on the crouching figure before him. His eyes were beginning to burn from staring so hard. He blinked, left the lids closed for a second, and then studied the photo again. There was something at the girl's feet, a black mass—a bag.

He stood up now, picked up the picture, and carried it to the one window where a grayish light came through the dust-streaked glass. There was something on the bag, something white. Without pausing to think, he ran downstairs and knocked on the low door to his landlord's room; just that morning, he'd seen the old man bending over a newspaper with a magnifying glass. It took a few minutes of forced charm to persuade the old man to lend the glass—"Just for a moment, really; I'll bring it right back down to you." Suspicious old fool! As if he would want to steal his cheesy magnifying glass—or anything else belonging to him. But the glass did the job, all right.

It showed him that the tiny white marks must be letters, words. But he couldn't make out what they were. This was his only clue and he couldn't read it. His mind reeled in terror again.

But good film could produce clear enlargements, he thought suddenly. He'd read once that 35mm film could be blown up without much distortion. It might work. It *had* to work. And there was no time to waste.

So the next morning, he'd gone at once to a photo lab, insisted on getting an enlargement the same day. "It's for my sister's birthday," he lied when the technician protested. "I'd forgotten until it's almost too late. I'll pay what you ask. Just say what you want." The money didn't matter, of course. He hadn't even blinked when the arrogant young man had said, "Twenty-five pounds, then." "Of course," he'd said smoothly. "My sister is worth it." He kept himself studiedly calm. It wouldn't do to have this fool think him too desperate—he might remember that later, might tell: "Some idiot gave me twenty-five quid for one bloody enlargement—foaming at the mouth, practically." Luckily, it was an attractive photo—the flowers, the pond—nicely composed. It wasn't an outrageous idea that someone might want to have it enlarged for a gift. In fact, he thought idly, Hillary *would* have liked the photo.

When he carried the enlargement away later in the big envelope, he was afraid to look at it in the street, afraid it might not show him anything useful. So he clutched it against himself all the way back to his car and then lifted the flap carefully, sliding the shiny photograph out into the daylight pouring through the driver's side window.

The figure in the background was much bigger now. He could see more details of the partially hidden face, could half convince himself that he might recognize it if he saw it in the street. He moved his eyes down toward the bag, holding his breath, bracing himself for disappointment. He wasn't good at disappointment—he knew that, dreaded the depression he was already anticipating.

The bag, now swollen in size and only slightly grainier than the original picture, was folded inward at the center and obscured at its right side by the girl's leg, but there were clear letters on either side of the fold. The left side said LAW with a vertical bar after the w—

the first half of the next letter, probably. On the right side of the fold, the lettering said IVERSI before the dark pant leg cut off the rest of the word.

He let his breath out in a ragged sigh. It wasn't much of a clue, after all. The second word was obviously "university," but the first word was an enigma. The word was not just "law"—that was clear. It was a longer word, probably a name. The bag was a book bag with the name of some university on it, but he couldn't think of any British university that began with those letters.

But how could it help him, even if he could figure out the whole name? It was not a local institution, so even finding the place wouldn't help him to find this interfering bitch, this goddamned tourist with her bloody camera. What could he do? His jaw was beginning to ache from clenching it so tightly. He was fighting hard against the impulse to grind his teeth. Mustn't lose control. Must keep thinking calmly.

He stared back at the girl herself, at the pale hair flying back from her left cheek—breezy day, he remembered—the slim hands, the girlish body hidden inside the ugly, shapeless clothes. She must be a student. Not at the language schools—no one came from a university to the Cambridge language schools. Then at the University itself. Finding her seemed almost impossible. But he couldn't just chuck it. Running away wouldn't help—not if there was a picture of him with that other bitch. He would have to try.

He could start at the usual University haunts, the places where the students went to eat and sit about. And the library. It was May and the students were studying for their examinations, so she might use the library quite a lot just now. If she carried the bag with her often, he might spot that before he even spotted her. What he might do if he did see her was not something he could think about right now. One thing at a time. Thinking too far ahead might bring on a panic attack and he couldn't afford that now. Mustn't give way to the gasping, the terror of suffocating. Just get back to the room and store this huge picture where snooping landlords wouldn't find it. He put the enlargement on the seat next to him and started the car.

Chapter 5

Beth Conroy trotted down the shallow front steps of the library, squinting up at the sky with a worried frown. It was late afternoon, growing dark already, and the sky was darkened further by heavy banks of low clouds. Looked like rain any minute, and she'd forgotten her umbrella. It was much cooler than it had been five days ago when Beth had strolled in the sunshine through the Botanic Gardens—the air was crisp against her face, but very still. She had made herself pay for that day in the gardens by working extra hours since then, filling up pages in her notebook and staying inside the library through long afternoons.

The Cambridge University Library was located across the Cam River from the "Backs," those wide and lovely grounds that swept from the college buildings to the river's edge. By Cambridge standards, it was a fairly new building (built in the thirties), massive and stark, looking on the outside like a prison, Beth thought. But inside, it was the most civilized library she'd ever been in: beautiful tiled floors, splendid woodwork, a tearoom, softly echoing rooms through which "fetchers" moved quickly to bring the books that card-holding patrons had requested.

When Beth had first arrived in Cambridge, she'd come to the library bearing her letter of introduction from Lawrence University's president. Charlotte had warned her that this was the only way she would be allowed to use library facilities. She'd been ushered into a small office on the ground floor (she was learning to say "ground floor" rather then "first floor," which, in England, meant second floor) where a solemn-faced, graying gentleman had examined her letter, taken her photograph, and issued her a temporary card clearly stamped with its expiration date, June 30. She had to present this card every time she wanted to ascend the long flight of marble stairs that gave access to library holdings. And every time she left, she had to turn over her bag to the man on the other side of the lobby, who would search carefully inside—this was not a lending library and its books did not circulate. One of the most charming features of the library was that a patron could simply leave material at a carrel or desk with a note saying she was not yet finished with it, and it would be there waiting for her on the next day.

Beth had been tickled to discover one day that the scrutiny she underwent daily was not reserved only for "foreigners." A tall undergraduate complete with the scarf of his college had been ahead of her in line that morning waiting to enter the library as it opened. As he approached the uniformed admittance guard, he discovered that he didn't have his identification card.

"I have left my card in my rooms," he said. "But you know me.

I come here every day. I'm at Clare." And he had lifted the scarf as if it were a substitute for his library card.

The small man behind the desk remained impassive.

"Well, then," he said quietly. "You shan't have far to go to get your card, shall you, sir?" Clare was one of the colleges closest to the library. Defeated and blushing, the boy gave up his place in line and left the building.

By this time, Beth had almost got over feeling intimidated and was enjoying her sense of being "one of the young people" moving easily in and out of this great seat of learning. She looked enough like the undergraduates to be treated as one of them by the library staff. Today, she was wearing jeans and a sweatshirt and had just slipped her bare feet inside a pair of tennis shoes before she left her apartment in the morning; she hoped she wouldn't get wet feet before she got back there. She turned right now and headed for the fence where she'd chained up her bicycle.

One of the reasons she had chosen the flat she was living in was that its advertisement had announced in small print: "bicycles available for rental." She didn't feel confident enough—or rich enough— to rent a car because it would have meant learning to drive on the "wrong" side of the road at the same time she was learning her way around in completely strange surroundings. But she also didn't want to be wholly dependent on public transportation; her American sense of independence called for the freedom to go when she wanted to go. The bicycle was a good compromise.

But Beth hadn't counted on bicycle traffic in Cambridge. She'd never seen so many bicycles concentrated in one place before in her life and the narrow streets of the ancient city left no margin— literally—for error. Undergraduates would fairly fly along on their bikes, staying ahead of buses and cars which had barely enough room to meet each other. There were no traffic lights and, in many of the smaller lanes, no sidewalks. Getting from place to place on a bicycle was a constant adventure requiring steady nerves, a lot of daring, and strong legs. Beth knew she was still a bit too timid, but she was learning, and she had bought a bicycle bell at Marks and Spencer ("Marks and Sparks," the locals called it) to warn inattentive pedestrians to leap out of the way as she came shooting out of winding lanes and one-way "passages," slipping between the august splendor of twelfth-century chapels on one side and the striped awnings of the bustling Cambridge market on the other.

The first part of her ride today wouldn't be so harrowing; she had to walk her bicycle across Queens' Road at the pedestrian crossing, mount up, and ride along Garret Hostel Lane, up the steep pitch of the little bridge, and down to Senate House Passage. All of this route was open only to pedestrians and other cyclists. But Senate House Passage opened onto King's Parade very near the magnificent King's College Chapel, her favorite building in Cambridge, and here, Beth knew, the traffic would be frantic. She would have to cross King's Parade, fly down Market Street to Sidney Street, and turn left (easier in British traffic than in American) to get to Sainsbury's, a delightful market where she planned to pick up a few pieces of chicken and some fresh broccoli for her dinner. As long as she bought only a few items, she could stuff them into her all-purpose book bag and suspend it from the handlebars; the bicycle didn't have a basket. She hoped she could get it all done before the skies opened.

The wrought-iron fence where Beth had chained her bicycle looked almost bare now compared to its appearance when she'd arrived. It had taken her almost twenty minutes to find a vertical bar to which she could attach the chain and padlock. The University put signs everywhere saying, "Please do not chain bicycles to the fences. Use the racks provided." But, of course, there were never enough racks to accommodate the thousands of bicycles teeming through the narrow streets of this ancient institution. Students cheerfully ignored the signs, attaching their bicycles to anything stationary. As far as Beth could tell, no one ever made an effort to enforce the warnings anyway, so she soon joined the crowds of petty lawbreakers. After all, she literally could not afford to have this bicycle stolen.

There were days when she had trouble finding her bicycle again among the crowd when she meant to leave a place, but now she spotted it at once, leaning precariously to one side with no other bikes near it; apparently most Cambridge undergraduates were less diligent than she was about spending a long Friday afternoon in the library. Beth shifted her bag to her left shoulder, dug into the pocket of her jeans for the padlock key, and reached for the chain. One of the twigs protruding through the fence scratched the soft pad of skin between her thumb and forefinger, and Beth lifted the hand reflexively to suck on the afflicted area.

The British never seemed to consider *one* fence enough to protect their precious privacy, she thought irritably. They were forever placing dense hedges just inside iron and wooden fences to provide a second barrier, and an opaque one at that. Often, passersby saw only the upper floors and roofs of English buildings and glimpsed lawns and flowers only through gates. This particular fence was doubly fortified by a towering hedge which was only imperfectly trimmed so that, earlier, Beth had even noticed bicycles chained to hedge branches that poked into the street through the bars.

Just as Beth was taking her hand from her mouth, she heard, very close to her, a strange hissing sound, almost like air escaping from a tire. She even glanced down at the front wheel of her bicycle before her brain registered the fact that the sound was coming from a point level with her own head. She turned to squint at the thick foliage of the hedge. A breeze coming through the leaves? Could that be it? But there was no breeze. The air was almost unnaturally still. The roar of a passing car on Queens' Road startled her, and she began to fumble nervously with the padlock.

The silence that fell in the wake of the car seemed ominous somehow. Beth realized that, before today, she'd never seen this area so nearly deserted. The shadow of the hedge made this part of the road almost as dark as night and the sky seemed so close overhead that she might have reached up and touched it. The sound of the padlock opening seemed as loud as a gunshot, and Beth paused, almost dreading the noise the chain would make being pulled through iron and shrubbery and bicycle wheel.

In the pause, she heard again the sound from the hedge, a sound like a gasp this time, muffled but audible. It sent a shiver of fear down Beth's spine—it was so near, so close to her face. What could be in the hedge, or behind it, making that sound? Some animal? She ripped at the chain now, the sound it made exaggerated along her tensed nerves, and rolled it quickly into a mass she could stuff into her bag.

Just before she pulled backward on the bicycle to position it for mounting, she paused again, alert, listening. Now the sound was clearer, repeated, no longer intermittent. It was the sound of breathing. A gasping and shallow sort of breathing, the kind that comes after some quick exertion or after prolonged holding of the breath. And whatever was breathing that way was not small, not a small animal hiding in the dense foliage—nothing little could need that much air.

Beth sprang away from the hedge, banging the bicycle against her hip, a sudden panic closing her throat. She flung herself onto the seat, her bag clutched against her ribs, and pedaled furiously out into the road, fleeing from that sound of strangled breathing, riding under the blackening sky toward the light of the old city.

Chapter 6

He had lost her! How could he have been so stupid? He knew better than this, was more clever than this. After the incredible luck he'd had this morning, how could he have let the chance slip away? But it wasn't his fault, not really. Who could suffer as he'd suffered these past few days and remain calm? Even the most rational planner could be unsettled by this kind of stress. Not knowing was the worst, not knowing where she might be, what she might be doing. Was the film used up?

Was she taking other photos? Would she have the film developed? Perhaps she'd already done it.

He could picture that snapshot in his mind's eye—the crouching body of the Swiss girl, the soft lines of her shoulders and arms and, just behind her, a man in plain, sober clothes, a man with his hands clasped behind his back, just the edges of a dark sport bag showing at the left side of his body. He couldn't stop himself from seeing the picture, couldn't stop himself from hearing the voices of arrogant policemen: "Oh, yes. We'll have no trouble finding this chap once we distribute copies of the photo. There will be posters everywhere and someone is bound to come forward. It's a small island, after all." Who could wonder that he was so upset!

He had scoured the neighborhood of the University, risking his life in the car because he wasn't watching traffic very carefully, but was scanning the pedestrians looking for a small, blond girl carrying a large black bag. Two days of that, with panic growing every minute. And despair. The conviction that he would never find her. So today he'd just parked the car on Queens' Road very early and positioned himself to watch the front of the library. The street filled up with young people, a blur of moving bicycles and hurrying pedestrians, until he was half blind from staring. He hadn't been sleeping and the strain was beginning to tell on his vision. The headaches were back, too.

But then a miracle happened. At 10:30, he spotted a girl approaching from the east on a bicycle, a blond girl with a pointed chin. And suspended from the handlebars of her bicycle was a black bag. As she passed in front of him, he read the lettering: LAWRENCE UNIVERSITY. He moved quickly so he could see where she chained the bicycle, make a clear mental note of which one it was. When she came walking back toward him, he pretended to be fiddling with one of the other bicycles chained to the fence, but he focused carefully on her face as she passed within a few feet of him. From that distance, he could see that she wasn't as young as she looked in the photograph. She wasn't a girl at all, but a woman, in her mid-twenties, perhaps —there were fans of small lines around her eyes.

Of course he couldn't follow her into the library—universities had slammed doors in his face before this. "We have the knowledge, the pass to success and approval, but we're not letting *you* in." Who needed them, anyway? But now the waiting wasn't so hard. She would have to come out by one of those doors, would have to come out eventually, and he would be waiting to follow; he would have the car to follow her. What he meant to do then was not something he had turned to yet in his mind. Find out where she lived? Get at the film somehow? Not yet. One thing at a time.

But he couldn't go on waiting in the open—it made him too nervous. People looked at him, seemed to take notice of his face, of his clothes. He'd read a book once about spying. It gave advice to spies in enemy country, in the presence of enemies: "Don't hide in the haystack. Pick up a fork and start pitching hay." But he would never be able to do that; he would funk it, start to run if anyone came near him. So now he'd begun to panic when students started pouring out of the library as the afternoon wore down to a close. What if he missed her in the crowd? He should watch the bicycle, that's what he should do. She couldn't go anywhere without it, and even if she did so briefly, she would have to come back for it eventually.

So he found the bicycle, stayed near it as students loosened bicycles from all around it. Some students looked at him strangely, as if he were some common loiterer they feared might tamper with the bicycles. Idiots! But he hated to be stared at, was afraid someone would say later, "Yes, that's the fellow. Hanging about the library, ogling the girls." And she might remember him herself if he were hanging about when she came back for her bicycle, might have noticed him in the morning when she passed so close to him. That wouldn't do.

So he'd found a way to get to the other side of the fence, to hide himself along the hedge just opposite the bicycle—so close that he might have touched it if the foliage hadn't been so thick. And he waited. Such a long time, with his head hurting more with every passing minute. Waited while the sky darkened and the threat of rain pressed down on his head.

Finally, she arrived—he could hear her rather better than he could see her, though he'd hunted a long time to find an opening in the hedge that allowed him to see one of the handlebars. And he could hear the pauses in her actions, could sense that she was alarmed in some way. Was he making some noise? He was holding his breath; he was sure of that. Surely nobody could hear the soft sound of pulling that little bit of air into his lungs when he needed some.

But she'd taken fright, he could tell, and now he couldn't stop his own terror—the fear of exposure was so terrible that he couldn't prevent the panting, though he was trying to be as quiet about it as he could. When she started away on the bicycle, he'd sprinted for his car—he could catch up with her in the car easily enough. And he could keep the bicycle in sight as he ran.

When he saw the bicycle turn into Garret Hostel Lane, he'd almost dropped from panic. He couldn't follow there with the car! Pedestrian traffic only. And by the time he got to the other side, to Trinity Lane, it would be too late to see where she was going from there. Why had he assumed that she would stay on Queens' Road just because she'd *arrived* by that route? Why hadn't he remembered that, in Cambridge, a bicycle has certain advantages over a car? Why hadn't he planned better? But it was *her* fault! Where was the stupid bitch going? Why was she so unpredictable?

So the miracle was for nothing. To have found her and then to have lost her again almost at once! The usual course of fate where he was concerned—hold out hope, promise, and then snatch it back—laughing, mocking him. When had that ever been different? Because fate was just like the old man, just like Father Dreadful. He stood next to his car now, pounding the heel of his hand against his forehead, squeezing his aching eyes shut.

But, at last, he left off, turned his face up at the mocking sky. Not yet; you don't have me yet, he was thinking. I know now that she's a hardworking student—staying later than almost all the others at the library. She's likely to come back here again soon—Monday perhaps. It would be hell on earth to wait all weekend—he wouldn't be able just to wait, of course, would have to keep hunting around Cambridge for a glimpse of her, however hopeless it was to expect such a coincidence. And he wouldn't have any idea what she was doing, how many photos she might be taking. Let it rain! If it rained all weekend, she wouldn't be likely to use the camera. And then Monday might be time enough to find her again, to follow her, to get at that damned picture.

He didn't yet consider how. The thought that this woman had got away from him made his jaws ache with suppressed rage, made him want to tear at her, to—but he mustn't let that come up in his mind, mustn't let it take hold of him. He had to stay calm, to plan. The important thing was to prevent that snapshot from falling into the wrong hands. Then he would consider what would have to happen to the blonde. Not now. Not yet. One thing at a time.

Chapter 7

Beth was bicycling home along
damp streets thinking with some amusement about
an incident that had happened in the library tearoom this afternoon
while she was taking a break from her reading. After a weekend spent
mostly inside her apartment watching the rain that had caught her
on Friday and then kept up intermittently ever since, she'd returned
gratefully to the library both yesterday and today. Right in the middle
of her tea, while she was reading her newspaper, a gangling young
man had asked if he might join her at the long table where she'd

carried her little snack. There were plenty of other places to sit in the room, many empty tables. So Beth suspected that this fellow had meant to flirt with her. She had discouraged him by her firm attention to the newspaper.

If only they weren't such boys, she thought with a sigh. Were there no older scholars taking advantage of the fact that the library contained a copy of every book published in Great Britain? Without makeup and with her hair held away from her books by a pair of close-fitting barrettes, she knew she must look like a teenager, so any potential suitors of her own age probably wouldn't look twice at her anyway. It was an interesting predicament, having to choose between cradle robbing and being left strictly alone.

Now Sidney Street did what so many streets in Cambridge did, much to the confusion of anyone accustomed to the city planning of American midwestern towns: Without changing direction or even curving much, Sidney Street became Bridge Street and then Magdalene Street before intersecting with Northampton Street, where another left turn brought Beth to the Madingley Road. This was a major highway once it got out of the city, the A-25, and the traffic was always heavy, so she maneuvered carefully on the slippery pavement. She'd gotten over her scare on Friday afternoon; "nerves," she told herself. There might very well have been a flasher behind that hedge, but that could hardly have been very dangerous; he couldn't have got at her through all that shrubbery. It might even have been a horse. After all, she had no idea what was behind that barrier and she'd often seen horses in this city, near her own apartment, as a matter of fact. Her flat was located about a mile from Cambridge, just past the University's Veterinary School where the open fields and livestock were an almost instant change from the bustle of the city— no intervening suburbs here.

Beth sped along the Madingley Road in high gear, glad of the cool breeze in her hair, enjoying the sweet aroma of the fields. It was Tuesday, more than a week since her day at the Botanic Gardens, and temperatures had cooled again to near-normal for early May. She was getting accustomed to British traffic, proud of being able to negotiate the roundabouts, familiar now with the triangular signs that said GIVE WAY rather than YIELD as they did at home. She liked the fact that her flat was "in the country," had made friends with some of the beasts that were her nearest neighbors to the east.

Her flat was in an odd-looking building set back from the road in a tight circle of trees. Viewed straight on, it looked like a big, squat box with a much smaller box perched atop it like the top layer on a wedding cake. But the building had almost no depth; it reminded Beth of the Hollywood sets she had once visited, where an impressive facade had only a shallow little building behind it. There were only five "units" in the building, two on the ground floor, two on the first floor, and one, much smaller, in the little box at the top. Each of the four big units stretched away from a central staircase in a line of rooms: first a living room/dining room with a very narrow kitchen off to one side, then a bedroom, and then a bathroom that was divided into two smaller rooms, one with a tub and one with a toilet and sink. Living room and bedroom each had a small electric fireplace, coin-operated, and the little room with the tub had a baseboard electric heater, which could be turned on "for free." There was no central heating in the building. The kitchen had a tiny electric stove and an even tinier refrigerator on one side, and a narrow sink and cupboard on the other. It was the sort of accommodation that Charlotte Empson described as "shabby-genteel."

During her first week in Cambridge, Beth had felt depressed by the flat—it was such a comedown from her tasteful and cozy apartment in Appleton—and the weather had been so wet and chilly that she never felt comfortable unless she was sitting almost on top of one of the little electric heaters. But she'd grown quite used to the place by now, had made a series of little purchases to both personalize the place and make it more convenient—a faucet adapter from Marks and Sparks made it possible to wash her hair in the sink, which had a cold tap on one side and a hot tap on the other. As the weather warmed, she was able to open windows even at night and the flat began to take on a cheery aspect that rather reminded her of summer camp. There was only one phone in the building, a pay phone in the ground-floor lobby, but Beth reflected that she had no one to call in England anyway. Sometimes, when she heard the odd, two-toned ring of the phone muffled by the intervening floor, she would think with a sigh that of course it could not possibly be for her. In fact, it was usually for the Colombian student who had the ground-floor flat on the opposite side of the building. She would often see him, when she was going in and out, lounging against the stained wallpaper, chattering on the phone in Spanish. The landlord had told her that the boy's father was "fabulously wealthy" and had rented the flat for the whole spring term so that the boy could have "a place of his own" with a parking space for his Ferrari while he spent half a year at the University.

The landlord was an Indian named Mr. Chatterjee, who lived in a cottage next to the building. He had the disconcerting habit of calling Beth "Missy" as if it were her name. At home, she would have corrected him, insisted on a more respectful form of address, but here in England, she never knew what to expect, was never sure what was customary or acceptable, so she kept quiet. Actually, Mr. Chatterjee was a fine landlord, helpful, friendly, full of gossip about the other tenants. Apparently, the Colombian and Beth were much more "long-term" than usual for this building. The flats, Mr. Chatterjee said, often rented for only two weeks at a time to people who were "on holiday," or to scholars coming to the University for a short "project." Since Beth's arrival, the couple in the flat directly beneath hers had been replaced by a woman whose mother, Mr. Chatterjee said, was dying in the local hospital. At the moment, only the topmost unit was vacant and when summer finally arrived, Mr. Chatterjee assured her in his confidential voice, there would be no vacancies for three months. "Tourist season," he said. "All booked up into September. You're lucky to be in residence, or you wouldn't find a place."

Beth watched now for an opening in the traffic so she could make the right turn into the circular drive that would bring her to the bicycle rack in front of her building. Cars and trucks—she was learning to say "lorries"—whizzed past her at speeds surely in excess of the legal limit. Finally, she was able to make her turn, chain up her bicycle, and climb the stairs toward her own door. At the head of the stairs there were two doors; the one on the left opened directly into the apartment currently occupied by an elderly couple from Scotland, and the one on the right opened into a short hallway that corresponded spatially to the downstairs lobby. The hallway had three doors in it: one led to a small utility closet with brooms, dustpans, and an ancient vacuum cleaner ready for use by all tenants; one led to a staircase that ended in the little top-floor flat; and the third led to Beth's flat. All of the doors had handles rather than knobs, handles that moved up and down like those on antique cars.

When Beth let herself into the hallway, she saw at once that something was wrong. The door to her flat was standing slightly ajar, and as she moved closer to it, she could see that the wood around the lock was splintered. A chill raced up Beth's spine. She paused with her bag dragging at the end of her arm, debating with herself about whether to advance or flee. She listened intently for a moment, but there were no sounds coming from the apartment. She crossed the hall steathily, her tennis shoes making no sound on the flowered carpet. With her arm straight out in front of her, she pushed against the damaged door, which swung open to reveal the mess that had been made of her small living room: papers and books scattered on the floor, a small bookshelf overturned.

It was enough for Beth. She turned and ran, out of the hall and down the stairs, straight back out the front door and across the little flower garden to the cottage. Mr. Chatterjee responded to her knock almost at once, his cheerful face lapsing at once into a concerned frown as soon as he saw Beth's face.

"What is it, Missy?" he said. "There is some problem?"

"Someone has broken into my apartment," Beth said, a little surprised at the pitch of her own voice. "The living room is trashed."

"Broken in?" Mr. Chatterjee cried, his own voice sliding up half an octave. "But this has never happened, ever, not since I am here. When did this occur?"

"Beats me," Beth said, swallowing to get her breathing under control. "I've been in the city since breakfast. Have you been here all day?"

"No, no," he said, wringing his hands. "My wife and I went into town ourselves after luncheon. We were away, perhaps two hours. It must have happened then because I would surely have seen or heard something if I'd been here."

"And the woman downstairs was probably with her mother all afternoon," Beth said. "Easy enough for a burglar."

"What is burgled, Missy?" Chatterjee asked, his sweet face creased with concern. "I hope nothing valuable."

"I didn't go in," Beth said. "I couldn't tell if whoever did it had left, so I came straight over here. I think we should wait for the police."

"Of course," he said, bowing her into the cottage. "I'll telephone at once."

The constable who arrived forty minutes later was young, earnest, a little nervous about entering the flat, but "correct" in his attitude toward Beth and Mr. Chatterjee.

"Wait here until I've determined whether the perpetrator is still inside," he said.

It took no more than five minutes for him to summon them upstairs. The "perpetrator" was, apparently, long gone. The constable and Mr. Chatterjee checked the doors of the other flats and then followed silently behind while Beth walked from room to room, her small lower jaw setting more and more grimly shut as she surveyed the damage. Kitchen drawers had been emptied onto the floor, the contents of the bathroom cabinet spilled into the sink, towels scattered everywhere. The bedroom was the worst. Clothes, jewelry, perfume, shoes—all tumbled out of drawers and wardrobe, scattered over the bed and the floor. Films had been pulled from their canisters and draped like dark confetti streamers over the clothes and bottles. Traveler's checks, which Beth had hidden under the paper lining of a dresser drawer, were scattered everywhere.

"Can you tell if anything is missing, Miss?" the constable asked at last. Despite his own youth, he seemed to take it for granted that Beth was his junior.

"I don't know," Beth replied. "I'd have to clean everything up, take inventory. But the only valuable things I had were my garnet earrings and there they are." She pointed at a gleaming spot showing through the spilled powder near her pillow. "And the traveler's checks, but there they are. What the hell could he have been looking for?"

"Burglars usually look for currency, jewelry, or firearms," the young constable said. He sounded as if he were reciting a school lesson. "Things that can be easily concealed and carried away."

"Well, I didn't have any of those things," Beth said, and she sounded angry now. "So why me? Were any of the other apartments entered?"

"Apparently not," the policeman said. "There are no signs of tampering anywhere else in the building."

"It looks more like vandalism than burglary," Beth insisted. "My powder dumped out, perfume spilled. And my films. Look at that. All my films ruined. I had taken two whole rolls in London when I first came to England and now they're all spoiled. And even the unused rolls, all pulled out. Who would do something like that? It's just mean." Her outrage was bringing tears to her eyes and she could feel a shaking sensation in her stomach. Mr. Chatterjee was making sympathetic clucking sounds.

"It does seem odd that you were the only target," the constable said reflectively. "Do you know of anyone who might be angry at you for some reason?"

"Angry at me?" Beth paused in her pacing to stare at him. "I don't know anyone in England. How could anyone be angry with me?"

"Absurd," Mr. Chatterjee sputtered. "Miss Conroy is a teacher and a scholar. She does not go about causing people to be angry with her."

The young policeman blushed, but went on resolutely.

"Forgive me, Miss. But it could be because you are American. Have you sensed any hostility from anyone based on your being from America?"

Beth was quiet for a moment, thinking. Anti-American sentiment? She'd read that there was some hostility toward Americans even in England, but she had certainly not encountered anything overt.

"No. Everyone has been so nice to me," she said. "I don't even think many people know I'm from America."

"But the accent would give it away whenever you could be overheard," the policeman said. "Might it be someone else in the building?" And he looked at Mr. Chatterjee for an answer.

Beth and Mr. Chatterjee exchanged glances. She could tell that he, too, was thinking of the young student from Colombia.

"I don't think it could be," Mr. Chatterjee said at last. "The only possible candidate is a Spanish-speaking boy, but he is quite harmless, I think. More interested in friends and parties than in politics. Wouldn't you agree, Missy?"

"Yes, yes," Beth nodded. "I think you're right. He's always quite friendly to me when I see him."

"Well, it *could* be just a burglar who found nothing," the constable sighed. He seemed discouraged. "If you can look carefully to see if anything is missing—anything at all—when you clean up, I mean— that would help us to track down whoever did this. We know the usual places where stolen goods are passed."

"Yes," Beth said absently. "Yes, I'll let you know."

"That wasn't much of a lock," the constable said to Mr. Chatterjee. "It probably took only one moderate kick to break it. You should have a locksmith out." His voice somehow conveyed simultaneously his disapproval of faulty crime prevention and his distrust of Indian property owners; he almost made it sound as if Mr. Chatterjee himself were in imminent danger of arrest for the break-in.

"Certainly," Mr. Chatterjee said, drawing himself up. "My only concern is the well-being of my guests."

When the young constable had left, Mr. Chatterjee offered to help Beth clean up.

"No, thanks," she said wearily. "It's probably better if I sort through everything myself, for taking inventory, I mean."

"Perhaps you are right," he said gently. "I cannot get a locksmith here until tomorrow, so you must be our guest at the cottage tonight. It would be too frightening for you to remain here alone."

Beth could see the genuine concern and kindness in his brown eyes.

"No, don't worry about me," she said. "Since there's no tenant upstairs, I'll just lock the stairwell door from the inside. Nobody else will need the hallway entrance tonight. I'll be all right. Honest." She knew that the cottage had only one bedroom and felt sure that the Chatterjees would insist on her having it if she accepted his invitation, so she would swallow her fear and stay alone.

It took several hours to tidy the flat. Beth forgot about dinner. It was after ten when she tried to go over her notes, digging them out of her book bag. In addition to her notebook, she found her camera, remembered her intention. She had popped it into the bag that morning, thinking she might take a break from the library and just take pictures of college gates, each so distinctive, but the sky had never brightened enough to make picture taking an appealing prospect. Well, another day.

She couldn't concentrate on the notes, couldn't stop wondering about this awful break-in. Nothing was missing. All the traveler's checks were still there. No jewelry had been taken. Whoever had kicked her door in had found nothing to his liking. Beth had locked the stairwell door and had shoved an upholstered chair against the door of her flat. She sat up very late, sipping tea and listening to the night sounds drifting up through the half-opened window over the table.

Everything seemed spoiled now. Her growing feeling of relaxation with England and herself *in* England, all the enjoyment of finding her sabbatical trip even more interesting and satisfying than she'd imagined it would be—all that seemed kicked away by one blow to her front door. Like so many Americans, she'd always thought of England as a place where everyone was somehow *safer* than in other "foreign" places, a country where even criminals were, somehow, sort of civilized. And now this shockingly personal exposure to violence and crime. She had simply bundled up all of her scattered clothes for the Laundromat, couldn't bear to think of wearing them after they'd been touched in that way.

And only this morning, she'd been reading more details about that awful series of murders. The victim last week was right here in Cambridge. Somehow it was much worse in her imagination, because so unexpected, than if she'd read of it happening in Dallas or San Francisco. Her vision of England had never had room in it for anything sordid, anything truly horrible. She sat on the lumpy sofa with her small feet drawn up under her, her wide blue eyes staring at the door.

Chapter 8

**The room was too small. Just too bloody small. And it smelled bad. He could feel his lungs coating with whatever was floating around in the stale air, with whatever it was that smelled like that. Not healthy to have to live in a place like this. He shouldn't be here—*wouldn't* be here if it were not for that damned photograph. And his head was banging so; aspirin wouldn't touch the pain, not really—only dull the edges of it a bit.

He had no idea how late it might be. No good trying to sleep—

too worried, too upset. Because, of course, once again he'd been offered a solution, had it dangled temptingly before his desperate eyes, only to have it snatched away. Life was never going to be easy because, of course, everything was against him, everything conspired to keep him down, to thwart and hamper him.

He'd spent a horrible weekend, driving past lecture halls and concert sites, coffee houses and movie theaters, with the windscreen wipers thumping, sweeping against the rain. No sign of her. She might just as well have vanished off the planet. Not much sleep. Bad dreams. But Monday had offered the chance, held it out to him with a deceptively benign face.

The rain had let up and the air felt good in his lungs—cold, but clean. And his vigil at the University library had paid off almost at once. The blond woman with the black bag had appeared only a little after the opening hour, had spent only three hours inside before starting off again. He'd rented a bicycle of his own this time, kept her in sight easily as she went to the post office, to the chemist's, to lunch at a Greek restaurant. When she left the city in the midafternoon, he stayed well behind her so she wouldn't notice him, and when he saw her turn into a drive, he stopped, dropped the bicycle onto the roadside, and followed on foot.

It took the rest of the day and well into the night to discover what he needed to know—which flat was hers, which of the other flats were occupied. He'd checked the mail on the lobby table, found her name and the return address in America—so Lawrence University was somewhere in America, then; no wonder he'd never heard of it. He even made friends with the dog at the cottage next to the main building. In the films, dangerous people were always killing dogs before going after people or property, but he knew that was absurd. The British selected dogs for their sweet temperaments, and it was never much trouble to make friends with a dog—he didn't even have to turn the charm up to medium.

And today, he'd watched the cars clear out—one was a red Ferrari driven by the foreigner in the ground-floor flat on the left; mail on the lobby table had a foreign return address. The woman who had the other ground-floor flat left early, too. And he'd seen the fair young woman carry her bag to her bicycle and shove off before noon. An elderly couple waited until after a brief cloudburst to walk up to the road and turn left toward Cambridge—brisk, athletic types by the look of them.

Then an incredible stroke of luck. The Indian couple from the cottage got into their car and drove off. He was already inside the main building by then, examining the door of the flat he knew was occupied by the blonde, debating how much noise he could afford to make. When he'd heard voices outside, he dashed to the lobby, poised for escape, but then he saw that what was happening was a sort of gift. Only the dog remained, staring mournfully after the retreating car. He was alone, and it wouldn't matter how much noise he made.

Still, the sound of cracking wood had scared him when he kicked in the door of the flat. The idea of doing something illegal inside a building where he could be trapped, unable to run, made the hyper-ventilation start even before he went inside the flat. He found the films almost immediately, five of them lined up in a neat row along the mirror of the dresser, each inside a plastic canister. He put all of them them into his pockets, not at all sure how to tell if they had been used or not.

Then he began to search in earnest, looking for snapshots. If she were only a tourist, she might wait until she went back home to have her films developed. But if she were a long-term student, she might want to see her photos while she was still in England. If she'd had any films developed, he had to know about it. He began in the living room, hurrying because, of course, he couldn't tell when someone might come back. He just spilled things onto the floor, shook out the books to make sure nothing was inside. The kitchen took only a few minutes; he didn't think anyone would keep snapshots in a kitchen, but he had to be sure.

The bedroom was harder because all of her intimate things were there. The lingerie made him think about things he couldn't afford to think about right now. The smell of perfume in her clothes was terribly distracting; he held one blouse against his face for a few seconds before throwing it onto the floor with the other things. Once, when he thrust his gloved hand into the wardrobe, he came out with a dark blue bathrobe, and that was a shock. He stood there, holding it away from himself, staring at the belt that dangled loose at both sides. The color was just the same as Hillary's robe, the one—but he made himself stop remembering, flung the robe away without looking at it very carefully. No time to waste. Mustn't remember. Not now.

He turned drawers upside down onto the bed, pawed through their contents as quickly as he could. He opened all the suitcases, ran his hands inside the empty compartments. He even emptied the small jewelry box, attracted for a few seconds by the sparkle of garnets— garnets were the color of blood. He wrenched his mind away from such thoughts and went on to the bathroom, another unlikely place to keep photos, but it was best to make absolutely certain. By the time he'd finished, he was panting and sweat was pouring down his face, though it was by no means warm in the little flat. It was no more than fifteen minutes since he'd kicked in the door.

There were no photos in the flat, none at all. So she hadn't developed any of her films. That was an immense relief. He could have the films developed himself, find the photo from the Botanic Gardens, and shred it along with the negative. Then he would be safe. Then he could leave Cambridge, go on to some other town.

He was halfway out of the flat when it occured to him that it might not do to steal something as odd as films—just films and nothing else. That would arouse suspicion, make the police ask what she'd been photographing lately that someone might want to see; where had she been Sunday week when the Swiss girl had disappeared? Taken any photos that day? And she might have *seen* him there in the park as well as photographed him; questions about films might be just enough to trigger her memory. No, no; it would be better to destroy the films, all of them, so as to be sure to get rid of that one picture, and then just leave them here.

He turned back to look at the flat. It certainly looked like a case of simple vandalism. He paused, listening. There was no sound from outside except the gentle hiss of rain—another shower. He ran back to the bedroom, fumbled in his pockets, and brought out the canisters. He had to take off his gloves to get at the narrow edge of film still showing in the slot of each cylinder, but he could wipe them carefully afterward—mustn't leave fingerprints; he'd learned to be careful about that.

Carrying the films to the window so that the light would ruin them, he carefully pulled each strip out until it would unroll no farther and then tossed it onto the mess already heaped on the bed. When he finished the last film, he pulled his gloves back on, took a box of powder from the dresser, and emptied it over the bed in a strewing motion, careful not to get any onto himself. He picked up a lipstick and began to consider what he might scrawl on the mirror—in the films, vandals were always leaving such messages as a sort of signature.

There was a sound now, voices surely! He dropped the lipstick and raced for the door, pausing at the head of the stairs, his breath held. Yes, someone was approaching the front of the house, a man and a woman by the sound of the voices. He ducked back inside the upstairs hallway and closed the stairwell door to a narrow crack. The couple came into the lobby, then started up the stairs. He could see them in their tweeds and their rain boots as they unlocked their flat—just a scant few feet away from where he was standing—and went inside. The pressure in his head and lungs was excruciating.

Finally, he was able to open the door enough to let himself out, close it again behind him, and creep down the stairs. Outside, the dog gave only one little whine of greeting before subsiding, so he was able to leave the yard without danger of being noticed—by staying close up to the front of the building, he could avoid being seen even if one of those old fools should look out a window.

It was not until he'd reached his bicycle—hidden since dawn next to a field of sheep—that he realized for the first time that he hadn't found the camera in the flat. He'd been so desperate, so focused on films and snapshots, that he hadn't even thought of the camera itself. She must have the camera with her like the bloody American she was. If the film was still in the camera, he'd taken this awful risk for nothing. She would still have the picture. There was no telling how many photos she had left to take before that film was used up. It had been cloudy and cold since that day in the gardens, so she might not have taken many photos, but he couldn't be sure. He would have to get the camera itself and get it soon, because she might, at any time, replace the present film with a new one and he wouldn't know it. He kicked at the bicycle in pure rage, his teeth beginning to grind without his even knowing it.

It was very late at night now and he was pacing up and down in this cage of a room, thinking. He would get the camera by stealth if he could—that would be cleaner, less risky. He would have to get closer to her somehow so he could watch her without arousing suspicion. He would have to move again, leave this room and take one near to her building, even *in* her building, if there was a vacancy. Then, if he had to, he would initiate an acquaintance with her; it might be necessary to get access to the camera. Another break-in was out of the question—too dangerous. Who could tell what traps might be set? The thought of exposing himself by actually approaching this woman was terrifying; he would have to call on all his resources, his ability to "act the part." He was good at acting, but it was such a dreadful strain.

He must get that camera soon. Perhaps force would be necessary. If this young woman tried to interfere, he would have to kill her. It would be a pity, of course, because she seemed nice enough, rather pretty. But she must not develop that film. He would have to put a stop to that, no matter what risk it took. He hated feeling rushed, hated the desperate feeling that he had no time to plan. As he paced, from the window to the table to the fireplace to the window again, a faint grating sound, intermittent but growing more insistent as the night wore on, filled the little room.

C h a p t e r 9

Beth sat in the small office at police headquarters, waiting for the officer she had
been assured would be able to answer her questions and listen to her
concerns. It was a rainy afternoon three days after the break-in at her
flat; it had, in fact, been raining almost nonstop since that day, and
the gloom was getting on Beth's nerves. The gloom and other things.
She had come to the police station ostensibly to inquire about the
progress of the investigation into her burglary, but really to sound out

the local police about her growing fears. Since the morning after the break-in, she had felt she was being watched, followed.

There was nothing definite, no single incident she could point to as certain evidence that her fears were well based in fact. At first, she herself had dismissed her feelings as an understandable paranoia brought on by the vandalism in her flat, by the fact that no one else in the building had attracted such attention. On her way into the city the day after the break-in, she'd imagined that a small, pale-colored car driving much more slowly than the other traffic on the Madingley Road was following her. With only occasional glances, she couldn't tell if the car was some shade of beige or an unwashed white. At the roundabout, the car had gone left as she went right, so she had, temporarily, dismissed it from her mind. She'd spent that morning supervising the installation of two sturdy locks on her door and listening to Mr. Chatterjee's assurances. "No one will soon again get past me. I will be watching like the hawks."

So she didn't think she was feeling particularly vulnerable when she sensed that someone was staring at her in the tearoom at the library—one could go to the tearoom as soon as the main doors opened and need not be admitted to the stacks to do so. Yet every time she turned around to look at the occupant of the table behind her, his face was hidden behind a raised newspaper, and when she finally stood up to leave, he was already gone. So, once again, she had shrugged off her suspicion as "nerves," bound to settle down once the shock of the break-in began to wear off.

But the feeling had stayed with her, had grown more acute as the days passed. And she remembered the incident at the library last Friday, the sound of breathing behind the hedge. Had someone been watching her as early as that, following her? When she was walking through the market, or stopping at the post office to mail a letter to her brother in Maine, or waiting with her bicycle to cross King's Parade, she would feel the crawling sensation at the back of her neck. When she turned to look into the crowd, to scan the cars along the curb, everyone looked quite normal, quite ordinary—young people on bicycles, housewives doing some shopping, men in suits hurrying along to some appointment—all with that self-contained reserve she had come to expect of the British. No eye contact, no apparent interest in her.

Yesterday, while she was having some lunch at the Italian Kitchen, a nice little upstairs restaurant just opposite King's Chapel, she had seen on the sidewalk below the young Colombian student from her building—Ramón was his name, Mr. Chatterjee had said. He was just standing there, a bag slung over his shoulder, but the sight of him made Beth's chest tighten in fear. Had he followed her here? Was he waiting for her to come outside again so he could go on following her? She scarcely glanced at the young waiter when he brought her pasta, so intent was she on watching Ramón. And then, a dark-haired girl came walking up the sidewalk, Ramón sprang to attention to greet her, and the two of them walked away with their arms around each other. A harmless liaison between two young students. He *was*, after all, a student here, so there was nothing sinister about his showing up on one of Cambridge's busiest streets, the street nearest to the University's major buildings. Jumpy, she told herself; she was just being unreasonably jumpy.

And Beth had begun to feel acutely alone. If she'd been back in Wisconsin, she would have talked about her fears and suspicions with Charlotte, with Jill, with her other friends. Charlotte would have said, "Of *course* you're feeling persecuted. Quite natural under the circumstances. But you'll get over it, don't worry." Jill, with her more active imagination, would have turned it into a game. "I'll walk with you and be your spotter," she would have said. "If any creeper is after you, we'll jump him together." And she would have laughed her wonderful cackling laugh, so that Beth would have felt at once that no real danger existed.

Here in Cambridge, she had no real friends, had met very few women at all. The library staff was largely composed of men, many of whom exuded that cool, superior aura that Americans often associate with the British. At her apartment building, there was the quiet and somber Miss Chalmers, who was away at the hospital most of the time, keeping a deathwatch over her mother; and there was Mrs. Chatterjee, who was a traditional Indian wife, so much in the background that she was virtually invisible, while her energetic and talkative husband dealt with the tenants. So Beth was struggling on her own to determine if her feelings of being watched had some basis in fact or were only the result of an overheated imagination.

But the incident today at Auntie's had been too much for her. Auntie's had quickly become one of her favorite places in Cambridge. It was a tea shop on St. Mary's Passage, just off King's Parade, a wonderful little place redolent with mouth-watering smells, where people shared tables in the cramped quarters even if they didn't know each other, where one could sit for an hour over a feast of sweet, milky tea, huge scones, bowls of raspberry jam, and thick whipped cream for a topping. For Beth it was exactly the sort of place she had always conjured up in her imagination when she thought about England, about places where authentic British people would "hang out." Since her arrival in Cambridge, she'd struck up more friendly conversations while sipping tea in Auntie's than in any other setting.

Today, she'd taken a break from her research at two-thirty, left a "reserve" note on her books, and biked through the drizzle to Auntie's. She'd been hoping to strike up a conversation with a friendly-looking customer, preferably another woman, but it was not a very busy time of the day for tea, so she had a table to herself near the sweets table, a surface lined with the cakes, pastries, and tortes so dear to British palates. She became so engrossed in the newspaper she'd picked up on the way over that she hardly noticed the man who came in and sat at the table next to hers. When she *did* finally look up, she saw only the back of a tweed jacket—he was facing away from her toward the door, holding his own newspaper in front of his face. It struck Beth that this was exactly the pose of the man in the library tearoom a few days earlier. Again, she felt the crawling sensation at the back of her neck, the fear that someone was shadowing her movements, waiting—waiting. For what? For her to be quite alone so that he could attack her? The headline of her own newspaper stared up at her from next to her teacup: POLICE NO NEARER TO IDENTIFYING STRANGLER.

She stood quickly, scooping her big bag up from the floor, and the man at the next table sprang almost simultaneously to his feet, his shoulder banging up under her elbow. She staggered backward and sat down hard on the edge of the chair from which she'd just risen;

her bag went flying and landed upside down under the sweets table. She could see pencils and scraps of notes beginning to spill out, a lipstick rolling down the slightly inclined surface of the floor. The man had whirled toward her and was already exclaiming his apologies.

"So sorry. Are you all right? So clumsy of me. Oh, look at all your things."

Beth saw that he was a young man, tall, with reddish-blond hair and a long, ruddy face—a sort of "homely-cute" young man who looked decidedly familiar. Was it, Beth wondered, that he looked quintessentially English and so resembled half the population of Cambridge? Or had she seen him, specifically *this* man, before? At the library? In a crowd behind her in the market? She was frozen, immobile, looking up at him without speaking. The longer she stared, the more certain she became that she'd seen this young man somewhere before.

He blushed and fell to his knees, his hair flopping forward over his eyebrows as he bent to begin scooping up her things. He crawled forward and pulled her bag out from under the table, dragging it toward himself with both of his big hands. He kept snatching at the scattered contents, dragging them over to the bag which he now held against his chest. Suddenly, Beth found herself moving, sinking from the chair to the floor to reach for her bag; she found that she couldn't bear to have this young man touching her things.

"Don't, please," she panted, finding herself suddenly breathless. "Let me." And she took hold of one corner of the bag, just under the Y on the word UNIVERSITY.

"No, no," he insisted, actually pulling on the bag to get it from her grasp. "My fault. Clumsy fool. Just sit down and I'll get these things right up for you."

Now Beth felt angry, a hot rush of color coming up into her face.

"Give me my bag," she said, and her voice was sharp. He lifted his shaggy head, his pale eyes registering surprise, and then he let go of the bag very suddenly. Beth almost toppled backward—she'd been balancing on her heels—and the boy began apologizing again.

"Sorry. So sorry. I didn't mean anything—I was only intending to help." And then he stood up suddenly, turned, and fled from the shop.

"He didn't pay!" This from the young waitress who was just coming down the two little steps that led to the back room of the shop. "That wretch has run off without paying."

Beth crouched on the floor with her book bag clutched against her stomach, shaking and swallowing the acid taste of fear. At last, she was able to collect her scattered belongings, pay for her tea, and leave, pausing long enough to retrieve her newspaper, fold it carefully, and slip it into her bag.

Now, sitting here in this tidy little room, she was beginning to wonder what the Cambridge police were going to make of her suspicions. Would they think they were dealing with a paranoid foreigner, a hysterical woman? Beth was just beginning to think it had been a mistake to come here when the door opened and a balding, sharp-featured man came into the room.

"Miss Conroy," he said briskly. "I'm Evans, the station sergeant. PC Baines tells me you have some new concerns over the break-in at your flat."

So she took a deep breath, assumed her "professor voice," and told him just what had given rise to those concerns. He listened impassively, leaning against the table that faced Beth's chair. When she finished, he was silent for a moment, stroking his bony jaw as if deep in thought.

"You've never actually *seen* anyone following you?" he said at last.

"No." Beth sighed. "It's just a feeling I have, a very strong feeling."

"I see," the sergeant said impassively. "A feeling. And just since the break-in at your flat?"

"Once before that," Beth said, remembering. "At the library just before a storm, I felt someone was watching me from behind a hedge. I didn't see anyone, but I thought I heard something—" She fell silent before the skeptical expression on Sergeant Evans' face.

"I can understand that you've been upset, Miss Conroy," he said, and Beth instantly recognized the tone, the unspoken "There, there, little girl" that lay behind it. She wanted to snap at him, to make him see an adult, professional person who was not to be trifled with; "No one calls me Miss Conroy," she wanted to say. "Professor Conroy, or Ms. Conroy would be fine." If she were at home, she would say it. But here she felt intimidated by British custom, could remember the announcers at broadcasts of Wimbledon tennis matches carefully labeling Chris Evert as "Mrs. Lloyd" until her divorce, when they went back to calling her "Miss Evert." In the face of such "correctness," Beth kept silent.

"Nothing you've told me seems very sinister," the sergeant was saying. "All of it has a perfectly ordinary explanation. You were made jumpy by the break-in at your flat, and you're likely to imagine all sorts of things in that state. The young man in the tea shop was probably an undergraduate who suffered such an acute attack of embarrassment over his clumsiness and your reaction that he just funked it and ran off. Very likely, he's already remembered about the bill and gone back to pay for his tea."

It sounded so reasonable when she heard him saying it that Beth could feel herself beginning to blush. But she pulled herself up and reached inside her bag for the newspaper.

"I've been thinking that these things are not only connected to each other, but to something else as well," she said, opening the newspaper and spreading it out on the table next to the sergeant's hip. The faces of five blond teenagers were arranged in a row across the bottom of the front page, the five victims of the Cambridgeshire Strangler. Beth put her right index finger under the row of photographs.

"These girls all look like each other," she said. "They all look like me."

The sergeant squinted a moment at the newspaper and then up at Beth's face.

"I beg your pardon, Miss Conroy," he said at last. "But these girls are all teenagers."

Beth could feel her blush deepening.

"And I, of course, am not," she said, her voice as controlled as she could manage to make it. "But I *look* much younger than I am. It hasn't always been an advantage, I assure you. Just now, when I'm dressed in very casual clothes, and not wearing makeup, I look like these girls. Especially this one."

And she put her finger under the picture of Sally Wright, the third victim, the sixteen-year-old from St. Ives. The face had haunted her from the first time she'd seen the photo in the papers: the wide eyes, the tip-tilted nose, the rounded cheeks. It was like looking in a mirror, or at one of her college-yearbook pictures.

The sergeant picked up the newspaper now and peered at the photographs. Then he looked hard at Beth, his sharp eyes narrowing.

"Yes, I *do* see it," he said. "But this is surely just a coincidence. What do you think it has to do with your break-in, with your concerns about being followed?"

"Don't you see?" Beth said, leaning forward eagerly. "The papers are saying it's so uncanny that these girls just disappear without anyone seeing them being taken off, without any witnesses. Suppose this maniac follows them around for a long time, finds out where they live, learns their habits, when they're likely to be alone. Then he would know when it was safe to—to—strike."

"Oh, I see," the sergeant said. "And you're afraid he might be doing that to you now." Then he shook his head, even smiled faintly. "No, no. You mustn't worry about that. The man from the Yard has given us a briefing straight from the police psychiatrist. Our lunatic is an opportunist. He strikes on the spur of the moment when a teenage girl of the right physical type presents herself in a vulnerable circumstance. He doesn't break into people's rooms; he doesn't 'case the joint,' as you Americans would say."

Beth's face was stony.

"Please don't patronize me, Sergeant," she said in an icy voice. "If the police can't find this monster, how can they be sure that they know what makes him tick?"

Beth saw a flash of anger pass over the narrow features opposite her; apparently, he was not used to anyone, particularly a woman, speaking to him in that tone.

"These profiles are not just idle speculation, Miss Conroy," he said tightly. "They have years of police experience behind them."

Beth sighed. It was a familiar situation for her, this struggle to be taken seriously. But she realized that, this time, there might be a life-and-death urgency in the struggle. So she composed her features into a smile, a sideways glance, the traditional grimaces of submissiveness.

"I'm sure that's true, Sergeant," she said softly. "All I want is for someone to consider the *possibility* that this killer might be following me. This last victim was a foreigner and so am I. I'm afraid and I would like to feel more safe."

It worked like a charm. The sergeant was instantly a protective man, solicitous, serious.

"Of course you would," he said. "I'll be happy to pass your concerns along to the investigating team, to Chief Superintendent Wilson himself. He asked to be told about all potential leads, especially about any girls—young women—being pestered by strangers. So try to put it out of your mind. No doubt the vandalism at your flat was an isolated incident that made you nervous enough to misinterpret these other little occurrences. But we'll follow up on them nonetheless."

Ass! Beth thought irritably. Why couldn't he have told her right at the beginning that he was instructed to pass along all potential leads about the serial killings? Why did men like this feel obliged to play everything so close to the vest? Did it augment their own sense of importance to put down the theories of "amateurs" like her? Surely Scotland Yard investigators would be grateful for any leads in a case the newspapers were calling "baffling."

"Could I see this Wilson person myself?" Beth said at last, standing up and trying to maintain the demeanor of a cooperative woman.

"Oh, that won't be possible," the sergeant replied, moving toward the door. "He's terribly overloaded with the details of this case—with all five cases, as a matter of fact. But he'll be informed of your concerns, as I said."

"Is there someone I can telephone directly if there's a sudden problem?" She wanted to impress him with her determination.

"Just ring nine-nine-nine," he said smoothly. "It's the emergency number for all of Great Britain. You don't even need a coin to dial from a phone box."

Outside, Beth opened her still-sodden umbrella against the drizzle and made her way to her bicycle. The streets were not very crowded at the moment—the *real* teatime was in full swing at four-thirty—but she found herself looking nervously around just the same. She decided against returning to the library; it would be impossible to concentrate now anyway. She swung up onto the damp bicycle seat and hung the book bag from the handlebars. Balancing the umbrella with one hand and steering with the other, she made her way out toward the Madingley Road, glancing into the occasional group of pedestrians and even into passing cars, looking for a tall redhead in a tweed jacket.

Chapter 10

Chief Superintendent Wilson
watched the rain trickling down the window of
the office the Cambridge police had set aside for his use. Spread out
in front of him was the forensics report on Greta Keller. It contained
no surprises for him. The girl had died of asphyxiation, her windpipe
crushed by human hands, the same cause of death as for the other
four. She had been raped, and the semen sample revealed that her
attacker had type AB-negative blood, the same rare type as the rapist
in the other murders. Her face and breasts and right shoulder had

been mutilated, torn by the same teeth whose marks had already been photographed and measured four times before; the mutilation had occurred after death. All signs of struggle and flight stopped after a contained area no larger than ten meters across. Once again, the killer had seemed to lift himself out of the crime scene without leaving a trail.

The abandoned bicycle hadn't yielded any fingerprints at all, not even the dead girl's. Someone had wiped it carefully. Wilson sighed as he thought about how rapidly a promising lead had disappointed. The bicycle-rental place had been found very quickly, the day after the discovery of the body, as a matter of fact. Yes, the owner remembered the girl quite clearly—a looker and that foreign accent, well, who wouldn't remember? But there had been no man with her when she rented the bicycles. He'd teased her about needing two bicycles and she'd told him her "friend" had given her money, but then had to use the WC, the public one across the street, so she would just bring the bikes over there. The owner had offered to help her by wheeling one of the bicycles across the street, but she had insisted she could manage, and off she went. He'd watched her for a few minutes, waiting on the other side, but then another customer had come along and he got distracted, didn't see the foreign girl and her friend ride off. And the day after that interview, Wilson was told that the other bicycle had been found, abandoned, on Maid's Causeway; it, too, had been wiped clean.

Wilson didn't like the feeling of being stymied in this way; he'd developed a reputation on the Murder Squad for getting cases cleared up quickly. In his experience, most criminals were rather stupid, tripped themselves up in rather obvious ways. Some were luckier than others, of course, and so local police forces sometimes had to turn to the Yard for help. But, usually, it was only a matter of a few days after that when the criminal was arrested; often the local police had a pretty good idea about the identity of the culprit but needed the resources of the Yard to make the evidence foolproof. But this nasty chap was a clever one, Wilson would give him that. Clever and unpredictable. It was almost impossible to guess where he might strike next.

Wilson had been on the phone to the police psychiatrist only yesterday. The doctor confirmed his suspicion that the compulsion must be accelerating. Yes, the doctor would have predicted another attempt by this time—going on for a fortnight since the Swiss girl had died. The killer's anxiety level must be building terrifically. Perhaps there had been failed attempts to lure another girl to her death, attempts that *hadn't* been reported to the police. Or perhaps something was distracting the killer, some other preoccupation, and he had, temporarily, given up on blond teenagers. But the doctor was quite sure that the lull was only temporary; such compulsions did not go away. Unless he was caught, this one would kill again.

"Got a few minutes?" a voice said from the doorway behind Wilson. The chief superintendent looked up to see the moon-shaped, freckled face of Edward Timmings, the sergeant who had been assigned to him for three years now. Timmings had finished up the investigation in Caxton and had come over on Saturday to join Wilson in Cambridge.

"What is it, Sergeant?" Wilson said.

"I've got a good citizen out here I think you should see," Timmings said without coming into the room. "Good citizen" was the young sergeant's term for a volunteer witness who came forward with information; part of his job was to screen such witnesses through preliminary questioning and sort out the crackpots from the potentially helpful ones.

"Bring him in," Wilson said, sitting up straight.

"Her, Superintendent," Timmings said with a smile. "It's a woman."

The old woman Timmings brought into the office was wearing Wellington boots; she was also clutching in both hands a sodden bundle made up of her plastic rain slicker, her umbrella, and her handbag. She looked, as so many good citizens did, afraid to be in the presence of the police. Wilson showed her to a chair, his manner—gruff with Timmings—instantly softened to the nonthreatening, cajoling tone he had learned over the years of taking evidence. Yet today, he didn't feel insincere; his usual low opinion of the human race always made exceptions for people like this, genuine salt-of-the-earth folk who really wanted to help. After introductions and an exchange about the filthy weather, Wilson said calmly, "Sergeant Timmings tells me you have information that might help us in our inquiries."

"Yes, I believe I do," the old woman said. "I've been looking at the photos in the newspapers, the ones of the murdered girls. I saw that poor Swiss girl last week on the day the papers say she disappeared. I saw her in the Botanic Gardens. I go there quite often, you see, to take food to the little animals, and I saw her there."

"Are you sure of this?" Wilson said, trying to mask his eagerness. "Are you sure of the day?"

"Yes, I'm sure," she said, nodding vigorously. "It was on Sunday, about four o'clock. She was wearing a yellow dress with a white sweater tied round her shoulders, like this, by the sleeves," and she made a gesture of wrapping herself in a shawl. "Such a pretty girl, friendly, smiling. She was carrying a camera, I remember; it had a wide strap in several colors—red and white, perhaps some other color, too."

Wilson became still, extra attentive now, because he had heard a detail which made him know that the old woman had actually seen Greta Keller on the day of her death.

"Yes," he said softly. "We knew about the camera. The girl's landlady said she'd gone out with it in the morning, but we haven't found it—it wasn't at the scene of the crime. But we didn't know where she'd been all day, so this is helpful, indeed."

"Oh, I'm glad," the old woman murmured. "I've wanted to help."

"Now this is very important," Wilson said leaning forward. "Did you see anyone else with the girl? Anyone at all?"

"No, no," the old woman said, her eyes widening in the leathery face. "She was quite alone. Just wandering about in the sunshine, taking snapshots. It was very sunny that day."

"Yes, I know," Wilson sighed, trying to hide his disappointment. "It helps us, of course, to piece together the girl's movements on that day. Do you have any idea if she left the gardens after you saw her?"

"I couldn't say," she answered. "I stayed for quite a while longer. There are plenty of hungry squirrels there you know. I talked to another girl for a bit, but I never saw that poor child again."

"Sergeant Timmings will show you out," he said, moving toward the door. "Please accept my thanks for coming forward with your information. You've been very helpful."

But not helpful enough, he thought, as he turned back into the office. Now we know she was in the Botanic Gardens, but we don't know if our man approached her there or somewhere else. The girl had given her hostess no itinerary of her plans for the day: "She just said she wanted to look about, to take photos because it was such a lovely day. We didn't want her to feel she was a prisoner here, accountable to us for every move. We were sure she'd be all right."

The business of the missing camera was intriguing, a puzzle. It made the case of Greta Keller different from the others. There was no evidence that the killer had ever taken anything from the first four victims; robbery, as Wilson had told Inspector Mulgrave, was not a motive. Of course, they couldn't be sure that the killer had taken the camera; the girl might have accidentally dropped it somewhere while they were riding around on the bicycles. But there had been a concerted effort to find the camera, PCs combing the roadside all along the probable route the pair had taken out of the city; nothing had been turned up. So it seemed likely that the killer had made off with the camera. But why? What was that all about?

Timmings had come back and was looking at him from the doorway.

"Not as much as I'd like," Wilson said in answer to the sergeant's quizzical look; they had worked together long enough to communicate with a minimum of words. "But something, something at least."

"This one's going pretty slowly, isn't it?" Timmings said, coming into the room.

"Yes," Wison sighed. "But he'll make a slip. Bound to."

"Local police are being pestered by relatives of the victims, too. Some want to get through to us, it seems, find out what's going on."

"The Keller parents?" Wilson couldn't get them out of his mind.

"No, no. They came for the remains, but nothing else. No, it's the Cambridgeshire folks, of course. Want to know what they pay taxes for if the police can't catch this fellow."

"Well, we have to let the inspector deal with them. We have enough to do without handling public relations." Wilson was thoughtful for a moment before he spoke again. "Ask Mulgrave if he can spare a few men to go round to photo-developing places, will you? I've a notion that our boyo might have had some pics developed. Now I don't suppose those photo chaps pay much attention to what's in the pictures they're developing, much less to the people who bring them in, but it's a chance. Have our fellows tell them that we're interested in a film with pictures from London and from Cambridge, the last ones taken in the Botanic Gardens. And the film may not have been completed. Have them say that, as well."

"Right away, sir," Timmings said, turning to leave. "Oh, by the way," he added, pausing to turn around again. "There's one other bit that might interest you. The station sergeant just interviewed an American woman who thinks she's being followed."

"Details, please," Wilson said wearily.

"She's doing research at the University, living in a flat on the Madingley Road. Her place was broken into three days ago and since then she feels someone has been shadowing her."

"What's the point?" Wilson said impatiently. "Our man's no burglar."

"Station sergeant says this woman looks like the victims."

"How's that?" Wilson was interested now.

"She's older, but small and fair. Bears a strong resemblance to the Wright girl especially. Her flat is out near the Veterinary School, isolated, in the country, just what our boy looks for, eh? And the sergeant says she doesn't seem like a crackpot . . . some sort of teacher back in the States."

"What makes her think she's being followed?"

"Lots of little things, she told the sergeant. But he's pretty sure there's nothing to it."

Wilson frowned. He didn't like the idea of the local station sergeant making such judgments on his own.

"Well, copy her file and bring it to me," he said. "I'll arrange an interview. Have the PCs reported in for today?"

"Just now," Timmings said. "Shall I bring them here or will you go to them?"

"I'll go to them," Wilson said, heaving himself up, thinking for the hundredth time in the past few months that he really ought to lose some weight. If he was going to keep on running about the kingdom chasing after maniacs, he'd better get himself in better shape for it. Either that, or retire the way his wife wanted him to. Damned rain didn't help the aching joints, either.

Chapter 11

Beth had almost reached the roundabout at the edge of Cambridge when she realized that she wasn't wearing her jacket. The interview with Sergeant Evans had been occupying her mind ever since she'd left the station. His reassurance had sounded plausible while she was listening to him, but now she was having her doubts again. It made her furious to discover that her hard-won self-confidence was apparently so fragile that she would allow a smug, condescending man like Evans to make her doubt herself almost at once. If only she knew some people here in Cambridge, some like-minded friends who could listen to her concerns and reinforce her judgments. But being so alone had the disconcerting effect of making her increasingly forgetful of who she was, increasingly susceptible to the assessment of strangers.

She'd been thinking as she waited in the rain to cross Sidney Street that this was the other side of "making up a new version of herself, starting over on new terms"; she shook her head in disbelief that she could have had such thoughts only ten days ago, been confidently loping around the Botanic Gardens imagining that she didn't have to impress people in England with her maturity. Now she was beginning to fear that she would have to start all over again to establish herself as a credible adult.

She realized for the first time as she pedaled along toward the Magdalene Bridge that the American awe in the face of British mannerisms, the conviction that a British accent automatically conferred intelligence on whoever possessed it, might have its converse: British people might, just possibly, believe that an American accent automatically lowered the IQ of anyone who spoke with it. That expression on Sergeant Evans's face conveyed his dubiousness that a slip of a girl, and an American at that, should have theories about English serial killers. It outraged Beth to think this might be so, but it also daunted her, made her nervous about the impression she was making, self-conscious and unusually sensitive to the danger of looking like a fool. It was like being a first-year graduate student all over again, and Beth hated the feeling.

As she shifted her umbrella, balancing the bicycle for the turn onto Northhampton Street, she felt a stream of water from the edge of the umbrella slip down inside the neckline of her sweatshirt. Only then did she realize that her jacket collar should have been preventing this soaking. She skidded the bicycle to a stop. Where had she left the jacket? At the police station? No. She hadn't been wearing it there, either. At the library? But no, she remembered tying its sleeves around her waist before unchaining the bike. Auntie's. That was it. She'd run out of there in such a hurry, so determined to get to the police station, that she'd forgotten her jacket. Sighing, Beth turned the bike around, waited for an opening to cross the street, and headed back into Cambridge.

It had almost stopped raining by the time Beth arrived at Auntie's. She was chaining up her bicycle when she saw a familiar figure coming out of the tea shop. It was the tall redhead in the tweed jacket. Beth froze for a second, half poised to flee, but then she set her jaw firmly and walked straight up to the man.

"Hello," she said, her voice wavering only a little. "We keep meeting, don't we?" She was not at all sure what she hoped to accomplish by the confrontation, only knew she was tired of feeling stupid, of feeling wrong.

The young man had blushed instantly as soon as he recognized Beth, his eyes darting sideways, away from her face.

"Yes, yes, we seem to be," he stammered, pulling at his own lapel and looking up at the sky. "Rain appears to be stopping."

"Yes," Beth said more firmly, her own confidence rising as she watched his apparent discomfort. "But could we step back inside for a moment? I'd like to talk to you about our earlier collision."

"Sorry about that," he said, glancing back at her for a second and then away again. "Bloody clumsy of me. I acted like an ass."

"Well, I didn't behave very well myself, I guess," Beth said soothingly. "Could we just step inside? I forgot my jacket when I—when *we* were here earlier."

"Yes, I forgot something, too," he said, moving to hold the door for her. "I ran off without paying, like the ass I am, and I've just come back to set things right."

Beth remembered Evans saying, "Very likely, he's already remembered about the bill and gone back to pay." She fiercely did not want Evans to be right about anything, wanted to question this young man inside a building where there were plenty of people around to protect her. Inside the shop they came to a halt at the coatrack—the tables were still crowded with customers and there was no place to sit down.

"I overreacted to being bumped like that," Beth said, looking up intently into the boyish face which was still averted from her gaze.

He was holding on to the coatrack now with his big right hand, as if he were afraid the tea shop might begin to pitch and roll. "It's just that I've been feeling jumpy, and I thought I'd seen you somewhere before. You look very familiar to me. That seemed somehow threatening to me, I guess."

He looked down at her quickly, his face reddening again.

"Well, you *have* seen me before," he said. "At the library. I remembered you from the tearoom in the library. Do you recall that I asked to sit at your table just a few days ago? You read a newspaper the whole time."

Of course! That was it. This was the undergraduate she had imagined was flirting with her at the library.

"Seeing you here today was just a coincidence, then," she blurted out.

"Well, not exactly," he said with a half smile. "I saw you on King's Parade, recognized you, and followed you here. I hoped I could strike up a conversation with you, but you were so engrossed in your newspaper again that I lost my nerve."

"Hoped you could strike up a conversation?" Beth repeated, alarmed again now that he'd admitted to following her. "Why?"

"Same reason I spoke to you in the library," he murmured, looking away from her again. "I thought you looked nice and I wanted to— to make your acquaintance."

"How old are you?" Beth asked and found herself using her "teacher voice" in spite of herself.

"Twenty-one," he said in a confused stammer. "Twenty-two in July."

"I'm thirty-seven," she said flatly.

His eyes grew immense.

"Gosh!" he exclaimed, the boyish word surprised out of him. "You don't—I mean to say, I wouldn't have—" And he fell silent, overcome by embarrassment.

"Look," Beth sighed. "Did you follow me around at any other times during the past week? I've had a sense that someone was following me."

"No," he gasped, looking at her directly now. "Honestly, I haven't. Just today when I saw you on King's Parade."

"And you haven't been hiding behind newspapers in the library tearoom watching me?" she asked rather severely.

"No, I haven't," he insisted. "Really. There was just that one time when I asked to sit at your table. It was on Tuesday, I think. And then I saw you again today. That's all, I swear."

"Tuesday," Beth said musingly. "This past Tuesday." Yes, she remembered—the day of the break-in at her apartment. She'd been thinking about the flirtatious young man on her way home that day, a last pleasant ride before the trauma brought on by what she'd discovered when she got to the flat. This boy had been sitting in the library tearoom with her while someone was breaking into her rooms and vandalizing them. He couldn't be connected with that event.

"You're sure you haven't been following me?" she said, reluctant to admit that she had been so wrong about everything. "It would be all right to tell me about it. I wouldn't be angry."

"I would tell you if I had," he said, and his boyish face looked impressively sincere. "Truly I would. You can check on me if you want to. I'm at Christ's College and my name is Peter Hollings. I'm most sincerely sorry if I've alarmed you, but I assure you it was quite inadvertent." Now that he'd learned her age, he was being much more formal, more diffident.

"Well, I'm inclined to believe you," Beth said with a wry smile.

"Thanks awfully," he said, and his nice, country boy's face broke into an appealing grin.

"You should stop traipsing around after us senior citizens," she said in a mock-serious tone as she lifted her jacket from the coatrack.

"Oh, I will," he breathed, turning toward the door to hold it for her again, and his tone was heartfelt.

Beth stood next to her bicycle and watched him walk away along the damp street. She knew she ought to be feeling some relief, should be glad that this boy had not been stalking her, after all. But what she felt was acute embarrassment. She'd gone to the police station to report on a sinister encounter with someone she believed might be a serial killer, and he'd turned out to be a calfish undergraduate trying to pick up a "girl" in a tea shop. Sergeant Evans had been right. She had been wrong. Paranoid. Silly.

As she mounted her bicycle, Beth wondered if she had been

wrong about everything else, too. Probably no one was following her at all. The break-in, an isolated incident, had combined with her sense of being foreign here, alone and vulnerable, to produce an illusion of persecution. She couldn't trust her own judgment; she had made a fool of herself.

Dodging traffic along Sidney Street once again, Beth made a firm resolution. She would shake off this paranoia as fast as she could. And if she couldn't wholly shake her fears, she could at least keep them strictly to herself. She would have to have concrete evidence of a very convincing sort before she would ever face a Sergeant Evans again. Indeed, she would need hard evidence before she could face even her own self-doubts.

Chapter 12

It was raining again three days later when Beth was leaving the library and she was fed up with it, fed up with "England's green and pleasant land." She'd been warned about the weather, but nothing could really prepare anyone for this. The rain here was just not like the rain in Wisconsin; at home, the rain came in definable waves from the west, pelted out of the sky for a limited amount of time—sometimes minutes and sometimes hours—and then went somewhere else, somewhere to the east. But here, the rain could just keep leaking out of the sky for days, sometimes steadily insinuating its chill between neck and collar, some-times falling so softly as to make only a faint whispering sound in the leaves overhead, barely visible in the air—but always *there*, always turning everything into unpleasant clamminess: clothes, furniture, bicycle seats. Nothing ever felt dry.

Beth's nerves were in a bad state for other reasons, as well. Since her conversation with Peter Hollings, she'd turned her conscious at-tention to ridding herself of paranoia. She had stopped herself from looking around in crowds, from peering at passing cars—had resolutely gone about her business with "eyes front." Yet she couldn't shake off the feeling of being watched. It persisted, a stubborn and intractable sensation that all the reason in the world seemed unable to change. When she was safe inside the library or behind the new locks of her little flat, she would tell herself that it was all in her imagination. A maniac attracted to teenagers would not have broken into her apart-ment, would have no reason to follow her around Cambridge. Any observation of her activities would show him that she was not a teenager, and if Sergeant Evans was right, the killer was interested only in teenagers.

Yet the fear persisted. Whenever she was outside, making her way around Cambridge, or biking back and forth to her apartment, the feeling would come over her again, the eerie sensation that eyes she couldn't see were watching her every move. Her feelings of iso-lation and vulnerability were growing. For the first time in many years, Beth was feeling acutely homesick—for her own apartment and friends in Wisconsin, for her parents only a short trip away in Minnesota, for the comfort of familiar ways. She even missed her car.

As she biked along in the rain, balancing her soggy umbrella over her head, Beth was grateful that she had planned a theater trip to London for the next day—she had booked a fourth-row ticket to the new comedy that was opening at the Theatre Royal, Drury Lane. Getting out of Cambridge was just what she needed at this point. As the lights along the Madingley Road winked and danced in the late-afternoon gloom, she decided that she would get up early and go into London even before the express train, just make a whole day of it. She could replace some of the photos that had been ruined by her burglar, play tourist again before the play. She'd read that there were some very posh restaurants in the area around the theaters, so she would treat herself to a nice meal, too—for one day, a break from the bland and inexpensive meals she cooked on the tiny stove whose oven couldn't seem to heat up to any more than 350 degrees.

Beth was stepping off her bicycle in front of her apartment building when she saw a man coming out of the lobby and into the parking lot—a man she had never seen before. She turned toward him, her umbrella poised over her head, and he came to a halt to look at her, framed in the light from the lobby door. He was a man of medium height, trim, well-dressed in a subdued, English sort of way. His dark hair appeared to have a few traces of gray at the sides. Even at a distance of twenty feet, Beth could tell that he was a very good-looking man of her own age, perhaps a few years older. Slowly he stretched his right hand out in front of him, palm up; then he raised his whole face toward the sky, looked back at her, and shook his head gravely back and forth, a little smile turning up the corners of his mouth. The entire pantomime was immediately clear; he was signaling that the rain had stopped, that she didn't need the umbrella.

Beth snatched the umbrella down and gave it an impatient shake. Indeed the rain had stopped. She looked back at the stranger whose smile had widened; he gave a little shrug.

"Damned English rain," Beth grumbled, but she could feel herself beginning to smile in spite of herself. "You can't even tell when it's stopped."

"You're an American," the stranger said, coming toward her.

"Does it show that much?" Beth asked, releasing the mechanism that kept the umbrella taut.

"The accent," he said pleasantly. "It's a dead giveaway." His own accent was the refined, upper-middle-class British accent of Cambridge.

"We colonials have fallen a long way from grace, haven't we?" Beth said with a bit of an edge in her voice. She had only recently been thinking how easily she herself fell into that American assumption that sophistication went along with a British accent, and she felt suddenly defensive about her Americanism.

"Oh, I find the American accent quite charming," he said, his smile growing even more broad, revealing a row of slightly crooked but very white teeth. Up close, Beth could see that his eyes were pale gray, edged by a fine rim of darker gray.

"Do you live here?" he was saying.

"Yes, since the end of April. I'm doing some research at the University Library."

"I as well," he said. "Live here, that is, *not* the bit about the library. Up there." And he pointed at the box that perched on the top of the building. "Just getting settled in. Now I have to go out and get some things for the kitchen."

"Are you on business in Cambridge?" Beth asked, feeling almost immediately embarrassed at having asked the question. "Intrusiveness" was a word that the British often offered as a criticism of American curiosity, she knew.

"No, on holiday, actually," he said, not seeming to mind the question at all. "I'm an 'old boy'—a graduate of the University, that is—and it's the first time I've had a chance to revisit old haunts. I live in Birmingham now."

Beth thought this an unusually long speech for an Englishman to make to a stranger.

"I think the University is quite wonderful," she said. "All of Cambridge."

"Well, I'm glad we Brits have made you feel at home," he said and began walking toward the row of parked cars. "We'll probably see each other again, going in and out. Bound to. My name's Carmichael. Andrew Carmichael."

"I'm Elizabeth Conroy," she said, feeling almost at once that it was absurd to give her formal name like that. "Beth, actually."

"Well, cheerio then," he said and turned away.

Beth almost laughed aloud. British people actually *did* say "Cheerio." She had for years imagined that this was an affectation made up for American movies. The man who searched bags at the library said, "Righto," whenever he finished a bag, and that was another word she'd thought was just some Hollywood writer's idea of the way Englishmen talked. She was still smiling as she watched Andrew Carmichael climb into his small, light-colored car. Then she turned her attention to the business of chaining up her bicycle.

Inside, over a pot of tea, Beth realized that she felt much more cheerful than she had in days. It had stopped raining and a very attractive man, on holiday with no wife in sight, had just moved into the building—a man who was emphatically not a callow undergraduate. This was much more like her fantasies about this sabbatical trip, fantasies nurtured through a cold and lonely winter in Wisconsin. It had been a long time since she'd felt such an instant attraction for a man.

The train for London left exactly on time the next morning. It was still overcast, but there was no rain. Of course, Beth carried her umbrella anyway and wore an all-weather coat over her blue dress; it would not do to get soaked before going off to a London play. The train car Beth settled into was one of the old-fashioned ones with the compartments on one side and a narrow corridor down the other. Inside the compartment, plush benches faced each other, three seats to a side. This early train was not crowded and Beth had the compartment to herself. She raised the arms that divided the seats from each other, put her feet up, and watched the countryside roll past the window.

The stops along the way had the sort of names Beth imagined small British towns should have, names like Bishop's Stortford and Audley End. The train kept up a rattling pace through the lush green of the farmlands; Beth reflected that this rich shade of green was paid for by getting rained on throughout the spring. And she thought, too, how wonderful it was that an island as crowded as this one could still have such unspoiled open fields, surrounded by quaint stone walls, dotted with small clumps of trees. It seemed that just ten minutes on a train could take a person back into a George Eliot novel. The train pulled into Liverpool Street station only a minute late, an hour and a half after leaving Cambridge—the express would have taken only an hour—and Beth prepared herself to encounter the great city whose grimier outskirts she'd been viewing through the train window for the last fifteen minutes of the trip.

As Beth crossed the platform from the railroad side of the station to the underground side, she marveled once again that she, who would never have dreamed of taking on the New York subway system on her own, should feel so comfortable about getting around in London on the tube. But from the first day back in April, she'd found this form of mass transit easy to learn, orderly, "sensible." Color-coded maps were everywhere, in the stations and on the trains themselves; if she made a mistake, she could correct it at the next stop with very little loss of time and no loss of money. Her London street map had a "London Underground" map on its reverse side. Only occasionally, when she noted how old some of the escalators were, did she feel a twinge of fear about being so deep inside the earth, using a system that was built mostly before the twentieth century; she remembered reading about the terrible fire of a few years ago which had taken so many lives at King's Cross station. Most of the time, however, she shared the same confidence and sense of well-being that most Londoners seemed to feel when using the tube.

Beth got onto a Circle Line train and got off again two stops later at Tower Hill. Here she intended not only to replace some of her photographs of the Tower of London but also to visit the nearby St. Katharine's Dock with its historic-ships collection; she had the landlubber's awe of ships and an acquired love of British history. When she came aboveground at Tower Hill, she was delighted to find that the skies had brightened into what promised to be a rather nice spring day. She felt a surge of good cheer as she stripped off her coat, pulled her camera out of her bag, and checked the little window that displayed the number of exposures. She'd taken only twelve pictures, a long way to go before the number 36 would signal that it was time to change films.

Yet, as the day wore on, Beth became so absorbed in what she was seeing that she only occasionally remembered to take pictures; the camera suspended from her neck became obvious to her only when it thumped against her chest as she was standing up or sitting down and, as this happened mostly on the trains where there was nothing to photograph, she began to think wryly that she had saddled herself with a clumsy necklace that it would have been better to leave in Cambridge. At St. Paul's Cathedral, which she had visited in April, she noticed for the first time the "American Chapel" behind the main altar where a simple and moving inscription in the floor expressed Britain's gratitude for the American dead of the two world wars. Behind the National Portrait Gallery, she watched with fascination as the street artists created remarkably true likenesses of tourists, who "for only eight pounds!" would later have a priceless souvenir of London. It didn't occur to her to try to record such things on film. But she did take one nicely ironic photo at Trafalgar Square: in the background the ceremonial propriety of Nelson's Column and in the foreground the irreverent gaudiness of two men with green spiked hair and painted faces.

All day she felt a wonderful sense of anonymity in this huge city. She knew, absolutely, that the only familiar face she would see would be her own reflection in a shop window. The fear of being followed, shadowed by someone who had singled her out for some terrible reason, had stayed behind in Cambridge. Flying along on the trains underground, watching the wonderful names pass by in the stations—Mansion House, Blackfriars, Leicester Square (she loved to say the names over in her mind)—gave her the feeling of being invisible, and therefore invincible. No one was interested in her and so she was safe.

She saved for late afternoon a part of London she hadn't seen in April and had only read about—Covent Garden. Here, the huge glass and steel enclosure of the old flower stalls had been converted into a series of very smart little shops and restaurants, and the forecourt had been preserved as a place for market stalls and street entertainers—buskers they were called in England. Between buying a pair of silver earrings for herself and a hand-knit sweater for her nephew, Beth paused to watch an acrobat-juggler and a string quartet, all four musicians dressed in tuxedos with swallowtail coats.

As the dinner hour approached, the crowds began to swell and Beth turned her attention to where she would eat before walking the three blocks to the Theatre Royal. She paused at the edge of the market stalls; people crowded around her on all sides and she couldn't decide which direction might be best to begin hunting for a place to eat. Well, this was as good a time as any to dig out her guide book and check on the location of the recommended restaurants. She bent over her bag and began to dig around near the bottom where the guide book had surely sunk.

Suddenly she felt herself wrenched sharply to the left, her head dragged even farther downward. The shock made her drop her bag; she could see it falling at her feet, its contents spilling out. She'd thrown her arms out instinctively to try to restore her balance. Only now did she realize that the impact was not a blow, as she'd first assumed, but a sharp pull. Someone was pulling at the strap of her camera, someone whose body she'd struck with her left arm as she'd thrown it outward. She tried to lift her head to look, but the strap had caught behind her ears and the force of the attacker's motion—moving forward to strip the camera on the way past—kept her bent over, in danger of being spilled forward onto the pavement. Beth instinctively grabbed for the strap with her right hand and hung on fiercely.

Her eyes had popped wide at the first sense of danger; she must have blinked suddenly, too, because one of her contact lenses had been dislodged, moved off of the cornea, so her vision was instantly blurred. She could see her own feet, trying to plant themselves to resist being dragged forward over the maps and papers that had spilled out of her bag. And she could see the feet of the person just to her left, feet shod in black men's shoes, dark trousers above the shoes. She struggled to turn her head, partly to release it from this powerful drag and partly to see who was doing the dragging. The most she was able to see was a tan jacket with its right sleeve extended above her straining face. Her impression was that it wasn't a suit jacket but some kind of windbreaker, cotton chino with a buckle at the side of the waistband.

By now she could hear shouts of "Here! Stop that!" and "Thief! Stop him, someone!" A burning sensation at the back of her neck and behind her right ear was bringing tears of pain to her eyes. She knew the pain was more than just on the skin surface; it was in the muscles. Suddenly the dragging force simply stopped and Beth staggered backward, would have fallen if she hadn't crashed into people who caught her, held her elbows, set her back upright.

As Beth closed her eyes, blinking deeply to move her contact back where it belonged, she could hear a man's voice talking urgently next to her left ear, a voice speaking in a language she didn't recognize. She opened her eyes, found her vision restored, and began gingerly to turn her head to look around. The foreign man was dark-skinned, a Mediterranean of some sort, and his concerned face showed him to be a rescuer, not an attacker. All around her, she could now see, were solicitous faces, voices murmuring, "Are you all right?" someone assuring her, "My husband has gone for the police." Beth began to respond: Yes, she was all right, she thought; yes, she could stand on her own; had anyone seen what had happened? A barrage of voices responded and from the confusion Beth could gather that someone had tried to snatch her camera; that no one had got a good look at him; that he had "medium" coloring, pale stringy hair, sunglasses; that no one could agree on approximate age or even height; that he had run off when the Mediterranean-looking man made a lunge at him.

Beth raised her right hand to the burning sensation on her neck and encountered the strap of her camera; she looked down and saw the camera dangling in front of her. Only now did she begin to look around for her other possessions, her coat, her bag, her umbrella.

"My bag," she said, making a helpless gesture.

"Here it is, dearie," a small, round woman said kindly, handing her the black bag. "I think people have caught most of the things that spilled out," and she looked around at the others who, sure enough, were holding her wallet, her maps, her compact, her package with the sweater for her nephew. They began at once to hand the things over for Beth to put back inside her bag.

"Thank you," she kept murmuring. "You're so kind. Thank you."

Suddenly the crowd divided, as if on a signal, to make way for a tall bobby, his distinctive hat towering above the pedestrians around him.

"What's the trouble here?" he asked; Beth thought he looked about fifteen years old despite the uniform that was meant to confer a sense of authority.

Again, everyone began to speak at once. When the bobby had managed to quiet the others, he turned to Beth.

"Are you the victim, madam?" he asked, very stiff, very formal.

"Yes," Beth whispered. "I think I'm going to have to sit down now."

The young bobby's face immediately changed to a look of genuine concern. A nearby stall proprietor sprang forward with a wooden chair.

" 'Ere you are, little lady," he said. "You 'ave a seat right there." And he patted the chair, took Beth's arm, and guided her to a seat.

It took a few minutes for Beth to feel that she wouldn't faint or throw up, both of which alternatives had seemed imminent before she sat down. She'd reached the age of thirty-seven without ever having been assaulted, without ever having been personally touched by violence; now that it had happened, she understood completely why people passed out from the trauma, locked themselves inside their houses for weeks afterward. There was something fundamentally horrifying in the experience, a horror that the body reacted against with a revulsion that was itself almost violent.

Gradually, the young policeman elicited all the details that could be remembered. When he was finished, he thanked all the witnesses who had volunteered information. Then he bent to speak to Beth.

"I'm sorry to have to tell you, madam, that it's unlikely we'll be able to apprehend this chap. Covent Garden is a favorite haunt for pickpockets and snatch-and-flee thieves of all sorts. We've had several incidents this week alone."

"Why didn't he grab my purse?" Beth asked, looking up at the earnest young face. "I've got money, traveler's checks, my passport. It doesn't make sense that he would make a grab for my camera."

"But it does, madam," he replied. "These modern thieves are specialists, you know. This one probably has a fence that specializes in cameras, won't take other things at all. Your snatcher probably thinks he could get more lolly for the camera than you're carrying in your handbag."

"I see," Beth murmured. "But he could have got the bag so much more easily. I didn't have it around my neck."

"Are you sure you're not hurt?" the bobby asked, for the fourth time. "I could get you some medical attention. There's a nasty red patch behind your ear."

"No, really," Beth sighed. "Some minor whiplash, I suppose, but nothing serious." She stood up resolutely.

"All right then, madam," he said, raising his hand to his hat in a kind of salute. "Be watchful. These thieves prey on dawdlers, people who seem unsure of their destination."

"Yes, of course," Beth said, remembering what she'd been doing when the would-be thief struck. "Thank you."

As the bobby walked off, Beth returned the smiles of the few witnesses who were still hanging around, reluctant, she supposed, to let go of the bit of excitement that had involved them for a moment. Suddenly she remembered the dark man who had scared off her attacker. She scanned the crowd to find him, to thank him for being ready to take such a risk, but he was nowhere in sight. A stranger who didn't even speak the language had sprung instinctively to her aid and then had moved along, not demanding or even expecting thanks. She sent out into the crowd the fervent wish that her old pastor in Minnesota had often expressed for anonymous donors: May God return your kindness a thousandfold.

Beth walked quickly to the near-
est café, hurried inside, and sat down to survey
the damage. Her umbrella was fine, but her coat was streaked with
street dirt, had obviously been trampled. The contents of her bag were
jumbled, in the wrong compartments; her compact had come apart
into two pieces, the hinge broken. She explored the back of her neck
and head with the fingers of her right hand. The skin under and
behind her right ear felt very tender and the burning in her neck
indicated more injured tissue.

"A menu, madam?" a waiter next to her said, and Beth jumped with alarm; she hadn't seen him approach.

"Just some coffee," she said, half apologetic. The thought of trying to eat made the nausea return briefly. As the waiter went off for the coffee, Beth looked down at her watch. It was still more than an hour before curtain time, and she suddenly wondered if she could actually sit through a comedy after what had happened. She felt a strong urge to just go straight back to Cambridge, to lock herself inside her flat. No, sir! she said to herself. She would *not* run, not be driven off by some petty thief. She had come to London for a play, had paid handsomely for a ticket. A good comedy was probably just what the doctor ordered, anyway.

When the waiter had set the coffee down in front of her, Beth began to organize the contents of her bag: lipstick and comb on this side of the partition, wallet and maps on that side. After a few minutes, she realized that her guidebook was missing. Then she thought of the theater ticket; she had tucked it inside the cover of the guidebook to keep it safe. When all those people were retrieving her belongings, somebody had just missed the guidebook. Or, she suddenly realized, somebody had picked up the guidebook, noticed the ticket inside, and thought a night at the Theatre Royal might be fun, especially in the fourth row. That a person might have subjected her to this secondary victimization after witnessing the attack on her was too much for Beth, seemed somehow worse than an attempt to snatch her camera, meaner. She began to cry, tears spilling down her face, her chest heaving with suppressed sobs.

Heads at nearby tables began to turn. The waiter came back, slowly at first, then hurrying up to her.

"Are you ill?" he asked, bending over her. "Can I do something?"

Beth shook her head, unable to speak, helpless against the gusts of weeping that continued to shake her. She reflected that she not only looked like a child; she cried like one, too, with the sort of abandon that feeds on itself and makes the crying worse—it had always been one of the things about herself that she regretted, "worked on" in an effort to change it. All to no avail. The waiter stood helplessly by for a few more minutes until Beth was finally able to get herself under control and mop her face with the napkin.

"I've just been robbed," Beth said, and she didn't mean the attempt at her camera. "Out there. I'll be all right now. How much for the coffee?"

"If you have no money," he said sympathetically, "it's all right about the coffee."

"No, no," Beth exclaimed, and, incongruously, found herself laughing. "I have money. People don't seem much interested in taking my money."

When she'd paid for the coffee, she went to the Covent Garden station, clutching her coat and bag against her stomach as she walked, got on a Central Line train, and went straight to Liverpool Street. The next train for Cambridge didn't leave for twenty minutes, but she stood on the platform right next to the attendant until it was time to board the train. Beth deliberately looked for a compartment that had a young family inside, and then she sat with them, staring at the window. This time she didn't really notice what was outside as the train gained speed and left London behind.

In Cambridge, the taxi left her off at the door of her building and she hurried inside. The lobby door had been standing wide open and she could already hear the racket before she got into the building—the blare of rock music, the sound of excited voices, many voices. Apparently, a large party was in full swing in Ramón's flat. The distinctive smell of marijuana hung in the air, drifted up the stairs with Beth as she began to climb toward her own apartment. Wonderful, she thought; just wonderful! This was exactly what she needed after the day she'd had: a raucous, drugged-out party to keep her awake and to threaten the building with fire.

Locked inside her own flat, Beth found herself too restless to read. After picking at some leftover chicken curry that she'd brought back from a take-away place two days before, she tried to watch television, but could find only a soccer match and reruns of American nighttime soaps. It was getting late by this time, but she felt no impulse toward sleep. On the contrary, she found herself very much awake, strung out from the excitement of the day, annoyed by the noise from downstairs, and worried. The smell of marijuana had made her think of fire and now she was thinking what a firetrap this place was. There were no smoke alarms anywhere, no sprinkler system, no fire escapes. She walked into the bathroom to see how far it was from the window to the tree outside—a good seven or eight feet. If she had to jump for it, she would probably miss and break both legs on the driveway below. But it would be a better chance than plunging from her dining-room window to the parking lot, and the kitchen windows, with their access to nice soft shrubbery and back lawn, were too small for her to get through.

Just as Beth sat down again, she heard a shout and a shattering of glass from the ground-floor front. By standing on a chair, she could get the right angle out of her own dining-room window to see the scene in front of Ramón's flat: glass strewn in a four-foot arc on the white cement of the parking lot; Ramón and some other young men standing in the midst of this arc shouting and gesticulating. Where was Mr. Chatterjee? Beth wondered. She had to go into the bathroom again to look at the cottage where the Chatterjees lived; it was dark and there was no car in the little parking space next to it. Beth wondered if she should go downstairs and call the police. But she immediately dismissed this notion; the phone was directly across from Ramón's door and she didn't want to think what might happen if hot-blooded Latins, drunk and drugged, already angry about something, should overhear her turning them in to the law.

Suddenly Beth remembered Andrew Carmichael, the nice man she'd met only yesterday; that event now seemed to have happened weeks ago. He should be right over her head if he was home. Perhaps he could intervene, tell the partygoers that enough was enough, maybe even call the police. But then she realized that if he'd been home, she would have noticed lights up there when the cab was pulling into the drive, and if he'd come in since then, she would have heard him. So it was apparent that both the Chatterjees and their newest tenant were out for the evening, leaving her, one other woman, and an elderly couple from Scotland to cower behind closed doors while hooligans trashed the building.

Beth realized that there was one slight precaution she could take; she could go out and close the stairwell door at the end of the upstairs hall. If a fire started on the ground floor at the other end of the building, this extra door could keep it away from her for a bit longer.

And closing that door could help a little to muffle the noise. If she was going to get any sleep at all, she would have to do something about that racket. She fumbled with the new locks, still unfamiliar with how to make them work; one was a spring lock which worked automatically when the door closed and the other, above it, was a sturdy deadbolt lock. Beth finally got them both open and pushed down on the handle.

As the door swung toward her, Beth noticed at once that the hallway was dark. The overhead light, which had been on when she came in—its switch was at the bottom of the stairs—was not working now. Burned out, she thought, hesitating at the prospect of crossing that dark space. There were no windows in this hallway and her own kitchen light was so far to the right that it did little to help. Another burst of laughter from the floor below made up Beth's mind for her, though, and she swung the door open a little wider.

But just then, she heard another sound, not loud, but closer than the party noises, a sound very near to her, to the right where the utility closet was located. It was an odd grating sound, a scraping noise as if someone were rubbing stones together. It sent a chill through Beth, a sudden shiver that made her shoulders shake. She didn't know why such a faint sound should seem more sinister than the noises from below, but it did; it seemed to convey a sort of concentrated menace. Beth swung the door shut with a bang and twisted the knob of the deadbolt lock sharply to the right. Noise or no noise, fire or no fire —she was not going out into that hallway.

Chapter 14

Chief Superintendent Wilson and Sergeant Timmings were driving along the Madingley Road, Timmings at the wheel. As usual, Wilson felt that his young assistant was driving too fast, but he resolved to ignore it and concentrate instead on the progress of the investigation—or, rather, the lack of progress. There were no substantial clues as to who might have killed Greta Keller. Every day the police constables assigned to the case brought him tips they had collected: a woman had seen a blond teenager being "dragged" along the street by a middle-aged man, but the man turned out to be the girl's father propelling her into their house to help with the cleaning; someone had reported a pool of blood in an alleyway, but it was discovered to be cat blood, obviously the result of some unusually ferocious feline battle; an old man had reported that his tenant, who made "strange noises" and "acted funny," had moved out of a paid-up room, saying he had to return to Cornwall, only to be spotted by this same landlord "twice now" still in Cambridge—didn't the police find it peculiar that someone would "up sticks and leave," not even asking for his money back, and then stay in the same city where he must be paying for another place to sleep?

Well, yes, Wilson thought; some people were certainly peculiar, but that was no proof of criminal activity—if it were, the prisons would be chock-full. But there was nothing much for the police to connect with their investigation. He was beginning to be afraid that his quarry had left Cambridge. It had been more than two weeks since the Swiss girl's death, and the psychiatrist he consulted with by phone agreed with him that it was odd the killer had made no attempt at another crime in that interim. It could mean that he was "in transit" to a new location where there might still be young girls who hadn't been frightened by the publicity. Certainly it would be growing more difficult, in *any* location in Great Britain, for this killer to use methods of persuasion in order to lure girls to their deaths, and he was, apparently, too cautious to use force at the outset. But, the psychiatrist believed, that caution would erode as the psychic tension continued to build; with someone this ill, that tension must already be growing almost unbearable. He was a ticking bomb. And Wilson was very much afraid that he might explode before he could be found and permanently defused.

So the chief superintendent had decided it might be worthwhile to follow up on earlier leads, among them an American woman who thought she was being followed. Timmings didn't see the turnoff to the apartment building until he was almost past it. He had to brake suddenly, turn into the next road, and then swing around to execute a left turn back onto the A-25. Wilson made no comment other than a baleful stare at Timmings's reddened face, which remained resolutely "in profile" during these maneuvers.

They had to wait for a few minutes after knocking at Elizabeth Conroy's door, and when she finally answered it, it was clear that they had awakened her; she was wearing a dark blue robe and her fine hair was matted.

"Sorry to wake you," Wilson said after introducing himself and showing her his identification. "This is Sergeant Timmings, my assistant."

The woman looked at him blankly, as if unable to absorb that they were from Scotland Yard. Wilson studied the small face, the wide blue eyes. Yes, he could see it; she looked like the girl in St. Ives, like Sally Wright. And, of course, Sally Wright looked a lot like the other victims.

"What time is it?" the woman said at last.

"About ten-thirty," Wilson answered.

"Did you come about the party?" she asked leading the way into the small living room.

"What party?"

"The wild party last night," she said. "Downstairs. I didn't get to sleep until very late. That's why I was still in bed."

"Oh, no," Wilson said wryly. "We normally allow the local police to handle rows of that sort. We've come about your break-in and your feeling that you'd been followed after that."

"I see," she said, waving them to seats on the overstuffed sofa before sitting in the chair facing them. She was beginning to look more alert now, the eyes behind the big glasses eager. "I'd begun to think no one was taking that very seriously—no one except me, that is."

"Have you had any more trouble with anyone poking round your flat?" Wilson asked. In these interviews, it was Timmings's job to take notes, so he sat back and opened his notebook.

"No. Not since the new locks. And nothing was taken the first time. It looked like sheer vandalism, as if someone were angry with me for some reason and wanted to devil me. But I don't know for the life of me who that could be." She raised a hand to smooth her hair as if she had just realized what it must look like.

"You told the station sergeant that a young man had frightened you at a tea shop," Wilson said, already feeling a surge of protectiveness for this small, vulnerable-looking woman. "Have you seen him since that time? Have you still had the feeling you were being shadowed?"

He noticed that she'd begun to blush at the first mention of the young man in the tea shop.

"I was wrong about that young man at Auntie's," she said, looking away from him. "I've spoken to him since and I'm convinced he's harmless." She seemed suddenly very stiff, almost cold. "But, to answer your second question, I *have* continued to feel watched, as if someone were waiting—I don't know for what. Waiting for me to do something, make some mistake that he can take advantage of. I suppose it sounds silly. I've sometimes thought that I'm just feeling paranoid because somebody felt hostile enough toward me to do what he did to my things." She said the last part almost as a question, as if she expected him to confirm what she was saying.

Wilson was unsure what to make of all this. The young woman didn't seem like a crackpot, though he cautioned himself against snap judgments, especially where young, vulnerable-looking women were concerned. She was practically admitting that the suspicions that had brought her into the station were groundless, yet she still seemed frightened, uncertain.

"Yes, that must have been a nasty shock for you," Wilson said, expressing the genuine sympathy he was feeling. "You're in a strange country and you've done nothing to merit such treatment. Bound to make you feel a bit edgy."

"After what happened in London yesterday, I'm beginning to consider just going home," she said, and he could see fear in her eyes. "It's as if the gods are trying to tell me that I don't belong here."

"Why don't you tell us about it." This might explain her present distress, apparently unconnected to her earlier fears about being "stalked" in Cambridge.

"Well, there's not much to tell," she sighed, sitting back in the chair. "Some man tried to steal my camera. He wrenched my neck pretty badly and I can feel it this morning."

"Steal your camera?" Wilson said, sitting forward a bit. He and Timmings exchanged a glance. The detail of the Swiss girl's missing camera had been withheld from the press, so Timmings would understand that they were not to mention the coincidence here.

"At Covent Garden," she went on. "The bobby said there are lots of thieves who hang out there. This one is a specialist, apparently, who finds it easier to turn cameras into cash than other sorts of valuables. I didn't get a look at his face and none of the witnesses could agree on a description. He didn't get my camera, but it was so—so unpleasant."

"I'm sure it was," Wilson said soothingly. "Tell me, Miss Conroy. Did you have the feeling of being followed in London, or on the way to London?"

He saw the remarkable eyes widen in surprise. The notion had obviously not occurred to her until this moment.

"No, on the contrary," she said at last. "I felt completely safe in London, anonymous. Do you think it's possible that someone from Cambridge could have followed me to London just to attack me?"

"No, no," he said. "I think that's highly unlikely. I was just wondering if the feeling persisted when you left here."

"Well, as I said, it didn't," she said, but her face still looked troubled.

"I think the London PC is dead-on in what he told you," Wilson said, eager now to reassure her. "That area of London is notorious for snatch-and-run activities especially targeted at tourists."

"And you don't think my troubles could be connected to this ghastly series of murders?" she said, her gaze clear and direct.

"Again, highly unlikely," he said. "We don't believe this killer does any sort of stalking prior to his attacks on girls. No victim has ever had her house burgled in advance, either. This killer suffers from a fierce and very narrow fixation on blond girls in their mid-teens. The psychiatrist says it's certain that he would not be interested in, would probably not even notice, a woman in her twenties, no matter how much she might otherwise resemble the victims."

"I'm thirty-seven," she said, almost absently. Wilson was genuinely shocked. She looked quite a lot like a teenager, sitting there without makeup, her feet drawn up under her in the big chair; he would have guessed her as being twenty-five or twenty-six at the outside, and then largely because he'd been told that she was a schoolteacher in America.

"Of course, you look much younger," Wilson said hurriedly. "So

I can understand your concern. But I believe that our killer is a very clever fellow indeed. He has a rather uncanny sense of age; all the victims have been fifteen, sixteen, or seventeen—and we suspect that the one seventeen-year-old, who was also rather taller than the others, may just have been a matter of growing desperation on his part. So many young girls have been warned off now. But the psychiatrist feels sure he isn't much interested—sexually, that is—in anyone outside that rather narrow range."

Wilson found Timmings staring at him, the young man apparently surprised at this long speech, more accustomed to businesslike brevity in his superior.

"I don't suppose," the young woman was saying pensively, "that one could tell by looking at him that this man is a lunatic."

"On the contrary," Wilson sighed. "He probably looks quite ordinary, perhaps even attractive. I imagine he'd be sort of chameleonlike, able to become anything his victims appeared to need, something he's good at guessing. And he'd be an accomplished liar, too, very convincing. Young girls should resist overtures from *anybody* unless they've had a long-standing relationship with him."

"Well, let's hope he has no more success," she said.

"So say we all, Miss Conroy," Wilson said, standing up. "I think the original assessment of your case by the local police is probably accurate. Of course, I urge you to take all normal precautions; commonsense things like locking your doors, that sort of thing. And here is my card. I've written on it the local police number where I can be reached if there's anything you need to tell me, anything of a suspicious nature."

She took the card, a beautiful smile spreading over her face, revealing her small, regular teeth. Smashing-looking woman, Wilson thought, as she walked with them to the door.

"Well, what do you think, sir?" Timmings asked as the car hurtled up onto the Madingley Road.

"It looks like the locals were right," Wilson growled. "This doesn't seem to have anything to do with our man. Still, I'd bet there's *something* going on. That's not an hysteric up there. Sensible, intelligent woman."

"Good-looking, too," Timmings said with more than his usual amount of enthusiasm. Wilson eyed the freckled profile.

"Slow down, will you, Timmings?" he snapped. "It wouldn't do for two of the Yard's finest detectives to be squashed to death in Cambridge." In truth, Wilson was feeling rather protective toward Elizabeth Conroy, and felt somewhat shocked that Timmings was reacting toward her as a "pretty bird." Despite his appearance, Wilson was not a grandfather, not even a father, and occasionally some young person would appeal to the frustrated parent in him.

"Yes, sir," Timmings said and slowed the car just a little. "What do you make of that business in Covent Garden?"

"Sounded interesting for a moment, didn't it?" Wilson answered, mollified by this swing back to business. "But it must be a coincidence, of course. The London bobby is quite right about that area and the thieves there. There'd be no reason for somebody to follow the woman to London to snatch her camera. He could grab it right here in Cambridge, if he wanted it for some reason, couldn't he?"

Wilson paused for a moment, thoughtful.

"Still. It *does* seem strange, doesn't it? All this interest in cameras. Odd."

Chapter **15**

It was not until Beth heard the car driving away that she remembered about the strange noise in the hallway and wondered if she should have mentioned it to the Scotland Yard men. But what could she have said? That she'd heard a funny scraping sound and that it had frightened her? What would these professionals have made of something that seemed, even to her in the light of day, so silly? The superintendent seemed much more sympathetic than Sergeant Evans had been, but still, she didn't think she was ready to risk mockery by complaining of "funny noises." She sighed and went into the narrow kitchen to make herself a cup of coffee.

She found herself smiling a little as she thought about Wilson and his sergeant. Another stereotype exploded. She'd unconsciously been carrying around a mental picture of what a Scotland Yard detective looked like: tall, lean, hawkish; sort of like Basil Rathbone as Sherlock Holmes. This man Wilson looked like somebody's grandfather: short and stocky with a rather sweet-looking moon of a face, tufts of gray hair sticking out above his ears. And the other one, the sergeant, looked like a slightly superannuated Huckleberry Finn. Still, Wilson sounded very professional, was very reassuring. She felt obscurely relieved that the local police had really passed her theories along to Scotland Yard, even if the upshot was that the theories were discounted. After all, she wanted very much for her theories to be wrong, had recently made a resolution to abandon theories altogether. It was just that the attempt on her camera in London had shaken her again, made her feel targeted in some way that she couldn't explain.

Now she carried her coffee out of the kitchen and turned her attention to the events of last night. A glance out her bathroom window showed that the Chatterjees' car was in its accustomed place. She would have to speak to her landlord about that awful party, about the smashed glass, and about the hallway light. It wasn't something Beth relished doing, but she'd practiced long and hard to assert herself in the face of intimidating people and circumstances and it was time to stop herself from backsliding. She got dressed quickly, exchanged her glasses for her contact lenses, and trotted down the stairs.

In the lobby below she saw a man bending over the little table that stood under the telephone, a man who looked away quickly from her sharp glance. Beth recognized in his face, in the quick movement of his shoulders, the effort, unsuccessful, to look casual, as if he had *not* been staring at her all the time she was descending the stairs. She'd never seen the man before. He was slim, of medium height, dark in his coloring: dark hair, tanned skin, dark lashes curling out extravagantly from his profile. Beth was immediately struck with an impression that he didn't look English; something about that profile, even something about the way his clothes hung, looked foreign, continental. Greek? Italian? The way he kept right on pretending that he didn't know she was there—she'd stopped on the last step—was unsettling. Beth took a long breath and walked past him to the door.

Mr. Chatterjee was on his knees working among the flowers in his lovely little garden. The dog, a rather dopey-looking Brittany spaniel, was lying next to him. Mr. Chatterjee stood up quickly when he saw Beth, his brilliant smile managing to combine greeting with apology.

"You are coming to complain of those thugs last night," he said, wagging his head back and forth. "I have already heard of it, I assure you. Miss Chalmers was quite terrified. That boy is out, gone. I won't have such goings-on, no matter how much money the boy's father offers. He has broken the law and he is gone. Packing even as we speak."

"Well, that's reassuring to hear," Beth said evenly. "I was worried about the fire hazard, too. They were smoking."

"Yes," he said, and his eyes grew even larger. "Smoking drugs, Miss Chalmers says, though how she would know I'm sure I cannot say. Does she seem to you to be the sort of person who would have experience in that line?"

"Hardly," Beth said, smiling slightly. "There's a strange man in the lobby, Mr. Chatterjee. What do you know about him?"

"Mr. Carmichael, Missy?"

"No, not Mr. Carmichael. I met him two days ago. Somebody else."

"Ah. Mr. Tate, then. A man with dark hair and eyes?"

"Yes, that's the one."

"Mr. Adam Tate. A scholar like yourself. He has come from Leeds University to work at the observatories. He is an astronomer on the staff up there, he tells me. A bachelor, I believe." He raised his shaggy eyebrows significantly.

"Is he going to have Ramón's flat?" Beth asked, ignoring the eyebrows.

"Oh, no, Missy. He has been your neighbor upstairs for several days already."

"Upstairs?!"

"The McDonalds left on Saturday and Mr. Tate had already inquired for a flat."

"Why didn't I know he was there?" Beth felt obscurely alarmed.

"He's very quiet. Shy, I think."

"And he hadn't booked the flat ahead of time?" Beth asked, her suspicions now aroused.

"No, just came in off the road to ask if we had an opening," Mr. Chatterjee said, cheerfully willing to impart what he knew. "Just like Mr. Carmichael. I'm grateful, I can tell you. It doesn't do to have vacancies for very long. Now that June is coming, of course, things will pick up; we'll have booked guests straight through till the autumn."

"Mr. Carmichael, too?" she asked pensively. "He had no advance booking?"

"That's right, Missy. Another nice gentleman. A solicitor on a short holiday from Birmingham."

Beth's frown deepened.

"I should think a lawyer would earn enough to afford a hotel in the city," she said.

Mr. Chatterjee drew himself up, looking slightly injured.

"Some persons do not like hotels, I think," he said. "And, for a holiday, they might prefer a refuge from the noises of the city."

Beth thought of the wild row of the night before and smiled slightly at the irony.

"No doubt you're right," she said soothingly. "I'll leave you to your flowers. I'm relieved to know that we won't have a repeat of last night." Her own words suddenly reminded her. "Oh, by the way. The upstairs hall light seems to have burned out."

"I have already been informed," he said, his cheerful smile returning. "Mr. Carmichael told me this morning that it would not come on for him when he got back late last night. But the bulb was fine. It wanted only a bit of tightening and it worked again quite beautifully."

"Could it get loose by itself like that?" Beth said, feeling her breath tightening a bit in her chest.

"Hard to say," he replied with an elaborate shrug. "These old houses, Missy. Who can say?"

Beth walked slowly back into the building, the frown still fixed between her eyes. Adam Tate was no longer in the lobby. When Beth got to the top of the stairs—she found that she was almost tiptoeing—she saw that the door to the left was closed. So, he'd already been there behind that door for three days when she'd imagined that those sweet little people from Scotland were still sharing the floor with her. Though they'd done little more than nod on the stairs, occasionally murmuring things like "Beastly rain" at each other, she felt almost as if they were friends, felt a little hurt that they'd gone away without saying good-bye.

Inside the hallway to the right, Beth looked up at the light bulb—it had no shade over it—and wondered again if it was possible for it to loosen by itself. That noise in the hallway last night. Could someone have been waiting there, someone who had loosened the bulb? But why? To cover another break-in attempt just in case someone should hear over that terrible racket? Someone frightened off when she'd momentarily opened her door? A shiver ran over her arms as she unlocked the door of her flat. She must stop imagining things, she told herself. The new locks were very sturdy, even if someone *should* try to get in. She was perfectly safe. But when she'd locked herself inside, Beth found that she was trembling. The shivering made her aware of the strained muscles in her neck and she raised a shaking hand to rub the painful tissue. Half the day was gone already, she told herself; it was hardly worth going into the city now. Better to stay here and get some reading done. Here behind two strong locks.

By evening, Beth was growing restless, tired of being cooped up in the little apartment. It had started to rain again and she felt even more closed in by the darkened sky which seemed to press against the windows. Her tiny refrigerator had only a few leftovers in it and her cupboards only two cans of soup. She'd begun to have a craving for steak, reminded herself that she hadn't had a steak dinner since leaving Wisconsin. Charlotte had warned her that the British "didn't do very well with steak," having a pronounced tendency to overcook it, but Beth had taken note of a restaurant about a quarter mile from her building, a place called Churchill's, that advertised itself as specializing in steak. When she'd mentioned it to Mr. Chatterjee, he had assured her that it was "lovely," one of a chain of Churchill's restaurants. It was "moderately priced," the landlord had told her in his nice, avuncular way, so Beth made up her mind to give it a try.

Even more than hunger and restlessness, though, Beth was motivated by a newfound determination, born of a long afternoon of thinking. In the morning, she'd actually found herself considering a quick departure from Cambridge, just packing up and going home. Her next thought had been one of disgust that she could even think of such a thing. She'd saved for years for this trip, had earned it. She was finally in the place she'd admired and fantasized about for years. Her research was coming along nicely, and she could see pretty clearly now how it was all going to work in the book. And that book was important to her academic career, a career she'd worked like a slave to establish and advance. No, sir, she would not be run off by ghosties and ghoulies and things that go bump in the night. Scotland Yard was on the job, and she was determined now to be reassured by that fact. A short walk to a neighborhood restaurant was a normal activity she would never have thought twice about two weeks ago, so now she was going to *treat* it as normal.

At seven-thirty, Beth got out her umbrella and her bag, checked to make sure she had her new keys, and strode out of the building. On the way past, she noted the closed doors of both Andrew Carmichael's flat—she'd heard no noises above her all day—and Adam Tate's flat—no sign of him since the morning encounter. She marched up the short drive, crossed the road at the zebra crossing, and went striding along in the light rain, her umbrella poised over her head. She realized that she was probably walking faster than necessary, but she reminded herself that decisive movement was a recommended strategy for women alone. She resolutely refused to look at passing cars or to listen to any little noises that drifted up from the grass at the roadside; insects, she told herself firmly. Still, she felt inordinately relieved when Churchill's sign came into view, still more relieved when its door had swung shut behind her.

The maître d' kept his face impassive when Beth asked for a table for one, and the waiter looked only mildly surprised when she asked for ice in her drink; she'd learned that liquor was regularly served without ice unless ice was specifically requested. She was just looking up from her second sip of scotch when she saw Andrew Carmichael coming into the dining room. In bright light, he looked even more handsome than he had in the gloomy parking lot; he was wearing a charcoal-colored jacket over pale gray slacks. When he turned his head, Beth could see some dark hair curling above the open collar of his shirt, and she felt a little shiver pass over her own neck and shoulders. She found it remarkable that the "chemistry" she felt in this man's presence was so strong. She was just beginning to wonder if such chemistry was to be trusted when Andrew Carmichael turned his head and noticed her. He smiled at once, spoke to the maître d', and then came walking over to Beth's table.

"Is madam dining alone?" he asked, and his face had the same playful expression she remembered from the parking lot when he'd indicated that the rain had stopped.

"Yes, I am," she answered, stirring her drink in a nervous gesture.

"I as well," he said. "Would you mind awfully if I joined you? I do so hate to eat alone in restaurants."

"Of course not," Beth said. "Please do sit down. I haven't ordered yet except for a drink." She was a little startled by this direct friendliness, having grown to expect Englishmen to be much more reticent.

"I'm not used to eating alone yet," he explained, lowering himself onto the chair next to her. "I'm recently divorced." And he looked down, reddening a little as he said this. "This is my first holiday by myself, as a matter of fact."

"Should I be sorry?" Beth said, eyeing him speculatively. "About the divorce, I mean." He smelled nice and it occurred to her that few of the Englishmen she'd met wore cologne.

"Not really," he sighed, taking the menu the waiter offered him. "Best thing all round, I suppose. Tell me a bit about you."

Beth gave him a small autobiography, keeping the details general, reluctant to seem even slightly self-important in front of this attractive man. Then she deftly turned the conversation.

"Mr. Chatterjee tells me you're a lawyer."

"A solicitor, yes. In Britain, we have solicitors and barristers, and barristers are much the grander of the two. I do wills and contracts, that sort of thing. None of the courtroom pyrotechnics one sees on the telly. Are you seeing anything of Cambridge besides the library? It's a grand old city."

"Some of it," she laughed, thinking how quickly he'd deflected the conversation from himself. "Not as much as I'd like, but I'll correct that before I leave. Now that the colleges are about to open again, I'd like to visit each one." May was the month students studied for their final examinations and all college grounds were closed to visitors. And now there were not even two weeks left in May.

"Have you been to the Fitzwilliam Museum?"

"No, not yet."

"Oh, you must go soon. The Fitz has a splendid collection of medieval armor and weaponry. It's an interest of mine, that period of military history. You would hardly believe the things they got up to in those days, the really cunning ways they found to kill each other, and the even more cunning ways to protect themselves from a gruesome death." His face had brightened with enthusiasm; he looked boyishly excited and happy.

"Are there other things I might look at? If I find armor and antique weapons a bit daunting after a while, I mean."

"Oh, heavens, yes. There are rooms of ceramics, several hundred illuminated manuscripts. They should be very interesting to someone literary such as you."

"The modern period is more my speed," Beth laughed, touched by his eagerness to please. "I've been enjoying Cambridge's wonderful gardens, by the way. I *do* have an interest in porcelain, but I prefer real flowers to painted ones. In fact, I have a genuine passion for gardens."

"You must go to Kew then," he exclaimed. "I don't think it's an idle boast to say it's the finest botanic gardens in the world. The very next fine day, you should take the train up to London and go out to Kew. Take the boat upriver; it's ever so much nicer than the tube train."

"Yes, I've read all about Kew," Beth said, twitching a little at the suggestion of another trip to London. "I plan to go there, of course. It's a treat I'm saving for a reward when I get a little further along in my research."

The waiter came to take their order and Beth realized that she'd scarcely glanced at the menu. She did so quickly now after urging

Andrew Carmichael to order first, and then asked for the first steak she'd seen listed. When it came, it was as bad as she'd been warned—thin, overcooked, and tough as shoe leather. But somehow, Beth didn't mind one bit. She found, as the meal went along, that she was enjoying herself immensely. Andrew (he had soon insisted on her calling him that) was a delightful conversationalist, pleased whenever he discovered that they shared a common interest. He didn't laugh easily, she noticed, but when he did, it was a deep, rich laugh that made the gray eyes twinkle. Beth began to feel decidedly feminine and charming in his company. He was an appreciative listener, and she hardly noticed that he wasn't revealing very much of a personal nature about himself. She, on the other hand, became more expansive as the evening wore on—expansive and just a bit tipsy. Andrew ordered wine with dinner and insisted on their having a drink afterward.

Beth never drank much, had learned over the years that she would stay in control much better if she limited herself to two or three drinks. And, of course, she valued control, thought it was necessary to remain watchful and alert even in social situations if she wanted people to treat her with respect. "Loosen up," a colleague had once said to her in an exasperated tone, but Beth was sure that any "loosening" would make her appear childish—one giggle and she would seem twelve years old. But tonight she found herself giggling often and discovering that this good-looking, grown-up man seemed to regard her as a peer in spite of the giggle.

When the checks came, Andrew insisted on paying for both meals.

"No, no," Beth protested. "I can't let you do that. We'll go dutch. Do you have that expression here?" She was already lifting her bag to hunt for her credit card. Before she knew what was happening, Andrew had simply reached over and taken the bag from her hands. He set it on the table in front of himself, holding it in both of his large, well-shaped hands. The gesture reminded Beth uncomfortably of the incident at Auntie's when another man had handled her bag like that.

"I insist," Andrew was saying, leaning toward her with his nice smile. "I invited myself to join you and I forced you to listen to my nonsense, so the least I can do is pay for your meal."

"Well, all right then," she said, and noted that he was turning her bag in his hands. Was that just a nervous gesture? His smile widened and he handed the bag back to her. Silly, she told herself. She'd just developed a ridiculous hypersensitivity to having anyone touch her possessions, some aftershock of seeing that mess in her flat, no doubt.

When they finally got to the door, Andrew cupped his hand under her elbow as they walked down the short flight of steps to the pavement.

"I have my car," he said, "so milady can be driven back to her flat."

Beth hesitated. It was dark now, very overcast even though the rain had stopped. Once she stepped into a car, she would be at the mercy of the driver. Part of her hesitation was her recent experience, and part of it was the result of every woman's set of self-protective measures, especially a woman as tiny as Beth was. A person of her size was bound to internalize an awareness of her own physical vulnerability—it could never be very far from her consciousness. But now she looked up at Andrew Carmichael and saw nothing to fear in his nice, open face.

"That would be nice," she said, smiling back at him.

His car was small and, to Beth, looked like every other British car; she had developed no skill at differentiating between models. Perhaps, she thought as the car moved out onto the Madingley Road, this is the very same phenomenon that makes all the people in a foreign culture look alike—it is simply the inexperience of the be-holder who, within his own culture, has come to take minute differences for granted. Beth knew she would have been able to tell a Pontiac from a Chevrolet from a Ford quite easily if she were in Wisconsin, even if all three were exactly the same color, the same approximate size, the same general shape.

Andrew chatted easily during the brief trip to the apartment building, but seemed to grow more awkward as they approached Beth's door. When she turned to look up at him, he looked rather embarrassed, had lifted his hand to his mouth and was passing his index finger over his lips.

"Well," he said at last. "Could I perhaps come in for a coffee or something?"

The question was so much in contrast to his body language that Beth was startled. On the way back in the car, she'd considered asking him in for a nightcap—she had some cognac in the cupboard—but was now knocked off balance by having him bring it up himself. As she hesitated, thinking, she saw his hand cover his mouth completely for a few seconds, almost as if he were trying to gag himself. She felt suddenly that it was best to slow things down a bit, give herself a chance to reflect.

"Oh, another time, I think," she said, smiling warmly to convey that this was definitely *not* a brush-off. "It's rather late and I had a bad night last night."

"Yes, I heard about those hooligans," he said, dropping his arm to his side. His face looked—what? Disappointed? Offended? Irritated? Beth was suddenly finding him very hard to read. "I missed it all, luckily. I didn't get in until quite late." Beth noted that he didn't seem eager to volunteer where he'd been until so very late. "I hope you weren't frightened." And now Beth saw the face opposite her resume its pleasant expression.

"Oh, a little, I suppose," she said. "My flat was broken into last week and I suppose I haven't got over it yet."

"I see," he murmured, lifting his hand to his mouth again, almost seeming to tug at his upper lip. "So sorry. I can see how that would make one feel a bit jumpy."

He had begun to edge away from her toward his own door. Beth waited until they'd exchanged "good nights" and he'd started upstairs before unlocking her own door and going inside. Odd, she thought. The man blows hot and cold. Very much more direct than the average Brit, but then seemingly shy and easily embarrassed. Had she been too abrupt with him at the door? Had her sudden qualm at his asking to come in for coffee translated into rejection in his mind? Beth sighed as she tossed her bag onto the table. How tiresome to always be trying to analyze the nuances of a man's reactions! Did men do this kind of thing? Was Andrew Carmichael upstairs even now thinking to himself, "Did I come on too strong? Was she frightened off? Will she be coolly polite the next time I see her?"

Not much seemed to change over the years, she decided as she got ready for bed. It was the same old dance—advance-retreat, flirt-withdraw—the same dance in Wisconsin or in England, the same at seventeen and thirty-seven; probably at sixty-seven, too. Well, never mind. She'd had a nice evening, a definite improvement over last evening, and she was beginning to regard the Covent Garden incident as something firmly in the past—nasty, but over.

Chapter **16**

It was raining again, but he hardly noticed. The clammy feeling at the back of his neck, the smell of the pavement as it got wet, the hissing sound of car tires heard at a distance—these things impinged vaguely on his consciousness, but he didn't feel uncomfortable or cold. He was walking so much lately, at all hours. It must be near three-thirty in the morning, he knew, but he felt no desire to sleep. He hadn't been sleeping very much for the past few days. Panic, that. And he could hardly bear to be inside a building anymore, had to discipline himself to behave normally when he was around other people. But when he was alone, closed inside, he felt he was sucking all the oxygen out of the air. Surely there was less oxygen inside buildings. So he had to go outside again, even in the middle of the night. Tonight, for instance, he'd been unable to bear the close quarters of his new place when he got back from dinner, had to flee out into the rain.

He'd hated being indoors for as long as he could remember. Never had been able to understand the phrase "safe as houses." To him, houses weren't very safe places; they were positively dangerous places. Not public buildings; he didn't mind those. Libraries, museums, churches—they were all right. Everybody going in and out, high ceilings, sounds echoing across big spaces. Lots of air, too. And so much to learn at libraries, at museums. The old man said he was dull, but that wasn't true at all. If they left him alone to find out about things for himself, he could learn like anything. At the boarding school, he'd been a superb student—the masters all said so. And he could remember everything, too. Yes, he remembered everything. Remembered the old man ripping up his books, remembered the wild rages, the icy silences that went on for weeks. And the pantry. No light. No air.

So he'd learned to hide his things outside where he could get to them when he was allowed out again. The wall at the end of the garden, the shrubs along the drive, the bins behind the tool shed—all places for his books, his toy soldiers. And when the old man had his quiet periods, those days when he slept a lot, then there were long walks right out into the countryside, and sometimes Hillary would go along. Not often. She said she liked the house and the garden, the flowers, of course, and she said he was just a kid and "a bloody bore"—she would talk like that when she knew the old man couldn't hear. Because he would never let her say "bloody" if he was there. But she would walk sometimes and talk to him kindly. Sometimes.

And walking, it turned out, could be useful. If he hadn't been out walking so early yesterday morning—or was it two days ago now?—he never would have seen the taxi; if he had been able to sleep, he might have been asleep when she left the building and went to the train station. He'd had to sprint for his car in order to follow the taxi, had almost lost it in the traffic on the Madingley Road. Be prepared and then you'll be safe. But now it seemed that being prepared meant never sleeping, having to watch all the time, and he was getting so tired. It would be over now if it hadn't been for that bloody foreigner jumping at him like that at Covent Garden. He would have the camera, have the bloody film, if that babbling wog hadn't tried to be a hero. Father Dreadful was right about foreigners; ruining England, that's what they were doing. Ruining everything.

How much had people in the crowd seen? Could anyone describe him? It was all a blur to him, a kind of agonizing slow-motion blur, but it could only have been a few seconds in all—surely, no more than ten or fifteen seconds. And he'd been wearing the wig and sunglasses—the wig had slipped slightly over one ear, but it hadn't come off. That was another instance of how important it was to be prepared, to consider all eventualities.

He'd bought the wig and sunglasses—several pairs of sunglasses, in fact—after the girl in Caxton. He'd stuffed them into the sport bag along with the other new things after he'd burned the old things. It had occurred to him that he might want to go back to some of the places where he'd already—where he had lived for short periods of time. The newspapers had been speculating that the Strangler was always moving on to new places, so no one would be expecting him to return to the villages. But if he went back, he had thought then, he couldn't look the same; someone might remember him. So he must be ready, just in case he ever found himself in one of those places again. The sport bag was getting fuller all the time. And he always had it with him; that was the beauty of being so cleverly prepared. It was always locked up in the boot of his car. Always ready. Just in case. Like this morning.

Still, disguise or no disguise, it scared him badly to take such a risk, expose himself to notice in a crowd. He was usually so careful to keep from drawing attention to himself, so certain that people weren't aware of his presence. Why, he even selected his clothes to be unobtrusive: neutral colors, simple designs, never anything flashy or distinctive. Years of practice had made it possible for him to fade into almost any background. But now he'd done something very obtrusive indeed, and the worst of it was that it had been for nothing.

Of course, it had happened in London and that was some comfort to him. He felt anonymous in London where nobody knew him. And even if someone did get a good look at him there, it wouldn't matter because he would be gone in a matter of minutes, right out of the city. Elizabeth Conroy herself would never connect a London incident with anything that she was worried about in Cambridge—it would seem like a random theft. He never saw the camera while he was following her in Cambridge. Of course, she might have it inside that damned book bag, but he was afraid that grabbing that would produce no result and would expose him to recognition on his home ground. And another break-in at her flat was out of the question. That was why the trip to London had been such a good chance, such a lucky chance. And it had failed, failed miserably.

She still had the camera and now he'd lost count of how many photos she'd taken. How many were left on the bloody film? When the film was finished, what would she do with it? She would probably take it out and put it in her bedroom as she'd done with the others. But he couldn't get at it there. He'd already checked the door one day while she was out. The new locks were good and he couldn't risk noise trying to kick the door in again. People would be more on the lookout now because of the other time. Ready to catch him. *Happy* to catch him and put him in jail. He knew that expression, that "Got you, now!" face, glowing with joy at having another chance to punish, to humiliate. Oh, yes, he had seen that face. Many times.

And the humiliation of what happened later in the hallway was still too horrible to think about very much. But it wasn't his fault that he'd been unable to go through with it, unable to just leap at her in the dark when she'd opened the door. He'd developed one of his headaches in the train on the way back to Cambridge—and who could wonder after what he'd been through at Covent Garden? And headaches frightened him because the old man had had headaches; when they came to take him to hospital, he'd been screaming from pain. So there was the headache already, and then the dark. It was necessary, of course, to loosen the bulb, just in case one of those noisy boys from downstairs should hear something and try to interfere; he could run then and no one would be able to describe him. But still it was terrible, with his head hurting so dreadfully, to have to wait in the dark, to

house, got them sent down. The other boys stopped calling him "poof" after that, but they stayed away from him all the same.

But solitude was what he wanted anyway. He studied hard, worked at his courses with the sort of dedication that was bound to impress the masters. When they praised his progress, he could see quite clearly that they were covering for their own incompetence—it was not *they* who taught him anything. He taught himself, as always. It was just that the school environment hadn't placed obstacles in his way as Father Dreadful had done. There was no pantry at the school. So his natural intelligence was at last able to thrive.

And he had developed a real fondness for the stage, was in all the school plays. He was quite good at it, really, fading into a character so completely that the drama master said he had "professional polish." His natural gift for mimickry was a great advantage, too, and he was always selected to send up the masters in the annual "Follies"—it was almost enough to make some of the boys admire him. But they were jealous, of course, and that went a long way to explain why they all leagued against him. He took most of the academic prizes the last year of school and was assured of a brilliant university career—the headmaster himself had said so.

Why, he wondered even now, had he been so surprised, then, that they would treat him as they did? And why had he ever allowed himself to believe that they wanted to be friendly, all grinning together there in his rooms on that Saturday? "Come on, Weed," they all chorused together. "Weed" was the one nickname that had stuck all through his years at the school. "We deserve a treat because we've finished our A-levels and you, no doubt, will get the highest marks ever recorded. So give yourself a break and come out on the town with us." They were always breaking bounds, always flirting with disciplinary action. But they had seemed so bloody sincere that day, and he *was* feeling the need to mark the end of exams with some sort of ceremony. "Where are you going?" he'd asked. "To have a few drinks, is all," Ian Webster had said, deadpan. "We know somebody who can get us into a club." Ian Webster was the most popular boy in their form at the school.

He still could hardly bear to remember how long it had taken him to figure out what kind of club it was. The place was smoky and noisy, as he'd imagined bars were, and the others were actually bringing drinks to the table. The liquor had a very quick effect on him; he wasn't used to anything except an occasional glass of mild wine. When two of the others hoisted him onto his feet and walked him across the dim room, he was sure they had noticed his dizziness and were taking him out for air. The little room they took him into was even darker than the barroom.

"Here you are, old Weed," Webster said, thumping him on the back, making his stomach lurch and his head hurt. "We've pooled all our shillings to buy you a treat."

His eyes had adapted to the gloom by now and he could see he was in a bedroom—in fact, a bed was the only furniture in the room. Next to it stood a narrow floor lamp with a purplish shade. The light was just bright enough to show that the bed was not empty. He had tried to turn around, to get out of the little room, but Ian and the others dragged him forward and plopped him into a sitting position at the edge of the bed. He could hear the springs groaning as he tried to jump up, but they forced him down again. He kept his eyes averted from the figure on the bed next to him.

"Now, Weed, old sod." Ian leered down at him. "We've gone to a lot of trouble to arrange this treat for you, so don't you funk it on us. Show us what a man you are. We'd all like to be proud of you, wouldn't we, fellows?"

When they let go of him to leave, he tried to get up again, but someone else had hold of him now, someone surprisingly strong. He couldn't find his voice, couldn't protest, couldn't stop the boys from leaving him there.

"Just relax, little man," the woman said. "Nobody's going to bite you." He could hear the springs groaning again as she pulled herself closer to him. He made himself look at her, turned in her grasp to face her. She was blond, florid, fat. Her exposed breasts were huge, sagging to one side as she hoisted herself up onto one elbow. Her mouth was a dark slash across the bottom of her face and she smelled of tobacco and liquor.

"What do you like?" she asked in a throaty voice. "Maybe you don't know what you like yet? Is that it? Do you need some help finding out what you like, little matey? I'm a good teacher."

Her free hand was beginning to move toward him; her whole body was rolling over in his direction. He felt certain he was going to be sick. Yet he couldn't seem to move, was almost mesmerized by those movements in the dim, lurid light. She wasn't holding him down anymore. Both of her hands were on him now, moving, touching him, pulling at his clothes. He hated it, hated the way it made him feel. He put out one of his own hands to keep himself from being pulled over; the hand came down on the flesh of the woman's back, a pillowy mass of flesh that seemed viscous. It felt as if it might swallow his entire arm. She had loosened his belt now, was moving her right hand down inside the front of his trousers.

Later, Ian Webster had told the police that he and the other boys had no idea what would happen, would never have tried such a thing if they'd had an inkling. Just the sort of boy people believed in—so sincere, the little shit. They'd all gone back to the liquor, of course, but they came running soon enough in response to the screams—everyone came running eventually. When the door burst open, there had been enough light for him to see the blood on her face, but it didn't stop him from hitting her. Some men had grabbed his arms, had pulled him off the bed. Later, he had a dim memory of biting one of them. Then someone hit him, knocked him to the floor, kicked the breath out of him.

When he finally looked up, he saw Ian Webster's pale moon of a face hovering over him, blank eyes wide and shocked. "What are you doing?" he kept saying. "What in bloody hell do you think you're doing?" But he'd made no sound in response, just stared up at Ian until he backed off. He didn't like to think what he must have looked like, crouching in that filthy room with the purple light streaming down on him.

They had to take the miserable old cow to the hospital, so even a place like that couldn't keep the coppers out of it. Besides, the bitch was determined to press charges. It had taken most of the summer for the family solicitors to smooth everything over, to keep it out of the courts. There had been a sizable settlement—probably all she really wanted all along. Had found out about the family money, of course.

But it was too late for him to go to university by that time; things like that have to be planned and he'd been distracted by this silly business all summer. He might have gone later, of course, started a year later. He had no police record by the time his solicitors got finished, so that wasn't an issue. But somehow, university was spoiled—as an idea—for him. He realized now, of course, that university education wasn't necessary after all. He had gone right on reading and studying, just as he'd always done. So he'd got as good an education as anyone with a degree—better because he didn't have to slavishly follow someone else's idea of a "course of study." Fools like Ian Webster got degrees, so what could they be worth, really?

The only trouble was that he didn't have a profession as he would have had if he'd taken a degree. Not that he needed the money. But a profession was something to do, a source of identity and pride. A profession wouldn't be boring like a job, either. And in most professions, you got to work with people like yourself—you wouldn't have to be alone. Most people were bloody fools—and jealous, spiteful fools, at that, always trying to bring him down to their level—but still, it was hard to be alone so much.

The rain had become a fine mist now, and he circled back toward the Madingley Road. It was almost dawn. He might be able to sleep now, for a few hours at least. If he could find someone of his own, he wouldn't have to be always alone. He was glad that he'd decided on a more direct approach to his problem about the camera. Hanging back, following from a distance with the hope of getting the camera by snatching it, had been a dismal failure, after all. So now he would have to get at it by another means. After all, he'd been able to use his acting skills to his advantage before, hadn't he? Of course, those girls were easy marks, falling for his line with little effort on his part. This woman was brighter, more experienced. But he was very good at acting, very talented. She could be convinced, too.

Sometimes when he was following Elizabeth Conroy around Cambridge, the place where he'd grown up, he thought how much she was like Hillary. Would Hillary have come to be more like this? More serious? Calmer? Of course, she would have gone on looking young, too; she would have kept her figure, and the light step, the athletic spring. Elizabeth Conroy was slim but shapely, with small breasts, a narrow waist, softly rounded hips. What he felt when he looked at her brought on all the old confusions: desire, guilt, tenderness, anger.

Half the time, he wanted to hold her, sleep with his head in her lap, and half the time— Well, he had good reason to be angry with her, didn't he? Good, specific reasons that had nothing to do with Hillary. Hadn't she brought him all this trouble now? Taking that damned photo! Carrying it around in that camera. If she'd just left it in her flat that day when he'd pulled the other films out of their canisters, this would be over. Because, of course, he would have smashed the camera and the dangerous photo would *certainly* have been destroyed.

He didn't want to have to kill Elizabeth Conroy. If she ever made a connection between him and that Swiss girl, he would have to do it, of course. But maybe it would never come to that. If she could get to know him, to trust him, perhaps he could get the film away from her by stealth, destroy it without her knowing about it. Maybe it was not too much to hope that she would come to love him. That would put a stop to the other thing, he was sure. If he could have a good, loving wife who stayed at home with him all the time, he wouldn't look at other girls, wouldn't think about them in that way, wouldn't do those things. Wouldn't have to be so afraid that he might be going mad like the old man.

Paranoid schizophrenia, the doctors had told him. "Your father suffers from paranoid schizophrenia. He will never be well again." *He* suffers! Who else suffers? He makes others suffer. The awful room, bars on the windows—"for the dangerous patients only"—the smell of hospital. The doctors said it was the most serious kind of mental disease, that it meant the old man was a danger to others, to those he thought were trying to hurt him. Well, what difference did it make if he was a danger to those other people? It had only mattered that he was a danger to them, to him and Hillary. And now that she was gone—too late to lock the bastard up now, wasn't it?—he didn't care if Father Dreadful was a threat to the whole bleeding world. "I'm afraid of him. Can't you see that I'm afraid of him?" Then why didn't you run? Why did you stay there, make me stay there? Why did you say you loved the house? Because you didn't want to run away from him. Because you loved him. Not me. Only him. Loved him to death.

Chapter 17

On the morning after her dinner with Andrew Carmichael, Beth got up early, shampooed her hair, ate a good English breakfast, and checked through her last set of notes from the library. She was feeling less fearful, less alone. The Scotland Yard superintendent had been so reassuring, had seemed genuinely concerned about her. And she'd spent some of her falling-asleep time fantasizing about her handsome new neighbor up-stairs. But it was clear to her that she had to get back to work on her research, and there was nothing in the flat that she hadn't looked over pretty thoroughly. So it was back to the library once again. She gathered up her things, got out a light jacket—it was chilly in the flat though it wasn't raining anymore—and walked downstairs.

At the front door, she met Adam Tate coming into the building; they literally blocked each other's way, making it necessary for one of them to yield. Tate, looking both startled and embarrassed, immediately backed away, his gaze directed out across the yard. He was wearing a dark jacket bunched up around his ears and he looked chilled through. Now that Beth could see him this close, she was impressed by his good looks, the regular features, the gorgeously lashed dark eyes. He was perhaps a little younger than she was, maybe thirty-four or thirty-five. He looked tired as well as wary. But she was determined to avoid a repeat of their first encounter, that silent pretense of not seeing each other; it was absurd with them both living in the same building, on the same floor.

"Good morning," Beth said firmly, stopping in the doorway.

He looked back at her quickly, then dropped his eyes again.

"Good morning," he said, his voice barely above a whisper.

"You're out even earlier than I am," she went on.

"Yes," he said, focusing now on a point just to the right of her face. "Early walk, always part of my regimen. Went to see the old observatories."

Beth reflected that his accent didn't square with the impression of foreignness that he so strongly projected by his appearance. It was pure Southern Received Pronunciation, like the voices on the BBC. That curiously clipped way of leaving off the personal pronouns added even more to the effect of being British, even old-fashionedly British.

"I'm your neighbor from upstairs," Beth went on, eager now to engage this man in more conversation, to draw him out, to take his measure, so she could decide whether she ought to go on being suspicious about him.

"Yes, I know," he said, and his eyes flicked over to meet her gaze, then away again. "Looks like it's going to be fine today. No more rain. Hard to tell, though."

"I'm Beth Conroy," she said, feeling relentless; the conversation that descended almost immediately into a discussion of the weather was not going anywhere.

"Tate," he murmured. "Adam Tate." Again, that flick of the eyes.

What on earth was making him so uncomfortable? Beth wondered.

"Mr. Chatterjee tells me you're an astronomer," she said, making one last effort.

"Yes, yes, I am," he said, and now Beth could see him making an effort, looking straight at her, pulling himself up, almost as if he'd made a conscious decision to overcome his discomfort. "Cambridge has one of the finest observatories in the world, you know."

"No, I didn't know," she said, smiling to encourage him.

"Do the stars interest you at all?" he asked, his soft mouth relaxing into a shadow of a smile.

"Well, I took a course in college once, but science isn't my strength, I'm afraid."

"Mr. Chatterjee tells me that you come from America." Now his smile had broadened to show a row of even, gleaming teeth. "A professor in your own right, he says."

"Mr. Chatterjee won't let us keep any secrets from each other, will he?" Beth laughed, noticing that the laugh seemed to have a further relaxing effect on Adam Tate.

"He does seem to be aptly named, doesn't he?" he said with a little laugh of his own. "What's your speciality, then?"

"English literature," Beth answered, encouraged by the way the conversation was picking up. Tate looked very different when he was animated like this. How could she have thought he looked tired, she wondered now. Surely that had been only tension. "I'm studying E. M. Forster at the University library."

"Oh, indeed. Forster's very good, isn't he? *Passage to India* is a special favorite of mine."

"Mine is *Room with a View*," Beth said, heartened at finding a scientist who liked literature, a rarity in her American experience. "But I suppose that's because it's more a woman's book than *Passage* is."

Tate seemed to have no reply for this. An awkward silence made Beth think she'd better find a graceful way to end the conversation she'd worked so hard to start.

"And speaking of Forster, I'd better get going. I have a lot of work left to do at the library." And she moved out into the parking lot, literally backing Tate up as she did so.

"Will you be in Britain long?" he asked, his shy look back again. He had seemed slightly alarmed by her movement toward him.

"Until the end of June," Beth replied, recognizing that he seemed now to want the discussion to go on.

"You must see more of the country before you go," he said, smiling again. "Most Americans never go to the north of England, but it's really lovely this time of year. Yorkshire has some very famous moors, you know."

"So I've heard," Beth said, pausing with her hand on her bicycle seat. "I'm planning some travel at the end of my research. When the work is done, I can be just a tourist."

"Get lots of photos, I suppose," he said, looking back full into her face with his extraordinary eyes, so dark that they seemed almost opaque.

Beth felt a twitch of discomfort at this reference because it reminded her at once of the last time she'd used her camera in London.

"Yes, I suppose we Americans are rather notorious for running around clicking away at everything," she said.

"You needn't be defensive about it," he said, his smile broadening again. "If I were in America, I'm sure I'd be photographing everything I saw. I rather enjoy photography, really I do. I have one of those cameras that produces the snap on the spot. Instant gratification." Now that he was more relaxed, the personal pronoun seemed to have returned to his vocabulary.

"A Polaroid." Beth nodded. "My father has one of those. I'm afraid I have to wait to see my pictures until someone else develops my films. In fact, I haven't seen any that I've taken since I came to England. Some of my films were ruined."

"Yes, I know," he said.

Beth looked at him sharply, but he smiled and went on.

"I'm afraid our good landlord has told me all about your business. He's so upset about the break-in. Has instructed me to be 'ever so careful about locking things up.'"

Beth smiled at his imitation of Mr. Chatterjee's charming accent.

"Yes," she said. "He goes on about it every time I see him. I'd really better get going now."

"Perhaps I'll see you again," Tate said, his shy smile in place once more.

"Certainly," Beth replied. "You'll be here for how long?"

"Indefinite," he murmured, and now he looked embarrassed again. "I can't tell how long it might take to finish the project." He walked past her now toward the lobby door.

"It was nice to finally meet you," Beth said toward his back.

"Finally?" he said, turning back toward her with his brow wrinkled into a frown.

"Well, yes," Beth said. "We've been neighbors for almost a week now, according to Mr. Chatterjee. Though I didn't even know you were in the building until yesterday."

"Ah, I see," he said in a vague tone. "It's nice to finally meet you, too." And he turned away from her into the building.

On her way into the city, Beth thought over her conversation with Adam Tate. Once he had warmed up, he'd seemed less suspicious to her. He was even charming and very good-looking when he smiled. His learning and culture were obvious every time he spoke; he even seemed to have a subdued sense of humor. Just the sort of man Charlotte Empson would declare "a find" if she were here to observe. Alas, Beth reminded herself, Adam Tate might also be the sort of man Chief Superintendent Wilson had described when he was talking about the serial killer; his words came back to her now as she pedaled along. The Scotland Yard detective had said the killer might be "attractive," "sort of chameleonlike, able to become anything his victims appeared to need," and "an accomplished liar." If she was interested in literature, he would be, too. If she was a university professor, he might pretend to be one, too. If she was unattached and lonely, he might pretend to be the same.

It occurred to Beth with alarming suddenness that all of those things, with only slight modification, could also be true of Andrew Carmichael. Yet she had set aside all her fears last night, had enjoyed dinner with him, had even got into a car with him. She had to admit to herself that her caution had given way rather easily in the presence of the man himself; her powerful attraction toward Andrew had banished her common sense and now, in the light of day and out of his presence, she felt almost embarrassed about it. It wouldn't do for a sensible woman to be done in by chemistry, would it? And she had to face the fact that her continuing unease about Adam Tate could at least in part be traced to the fact that she felt almost none of the same chemistry toward him. He was certainly handsome—in some ways better-looking than Andrew—and he was the right age, the right profession, seemingly the right everything. Yet she felt there was no spark between them.

If Charlotte were here, Beth knew, she would say, "Forget that spark stuff, honey. Just gets you in trouble. Go for steady quality and the fire will get started in its own time." And Jill, subversive as always, would chime in, "If there's ever going to be a fire, there has to be at least a little smoldering at the beginning." Beth felt a powerful urge to talk this over with her friends, find out what they would make of all of it, and she regretted that her budget wouldn't allow for transatlantic calls. She was on her own without clear signals to guide her.

Of course, she thought as she waited at the roundabout, the problem was that her present worries precluded accepting *any* new man at face value—chemistry or no chemistry. If she couldn't shake this fear that she had somehow got caught up in something sinister —and the noises in the hallway the other night still haunted her— then suspicion must be part of her response to anybody she would meet. Only women seemed safe and she couldn't seem to meet any women. So apparently she would have to choose between risk on the one hand or complete emotional isolation on the other.

She had lately altered her route into the city, thinking that Queens' Road was too remote from other pedestrian and bicycle traffic; it made her feel vulnerable. So now she planned to turn left at the roundabout instead of right and bike down Magdalene Street to St. John's Street which later became King's Parade. By this time of the day, these streets were teeming with students, walking and biking, and, while she felt it was easier for someone to follow her unobtrusively in this crowd, she also felt it was less likely that she could be pounced on and carried off; it was a trade-off she was willing to make. Just as she negotiated her turn, it started to drizzle. She'd left her umbrella in the flat, had forgotten Charlotte's sensible advice about carrying it all the time, had been lulled into overconfidence by the chill brightness of the sky when she'd first got up.

Oh, damn, damn, she thought as the drizzle turned into steady light rain. She pedaled faster, heading for King's College Chapel, one of the few university buildings open to the public during May and a favorite haunt of hers anyway. She made it inside before she was completely soaked. Even in her present discomfort, she felt once again the sense of awe that King's Chapel had inspired in her the first time she saw it: the soaring columns of white limestone, the dazzling stained-glass windows in all four walls, the elegance of the fan-vaulted ceiling, and yet a breathtaking simplicity of overall design—just a rectangle, a single room bisected by the magnificently carved wooden screen that divided the ante-chapel from the choir stalls.

Beth preferred the ante-chapel, its sense of vertical spaciousness, almost an airy quality despite the weight of stone she knew was mounted above her in those spreading fans. She sat down on one of the folding chairs set up for a concert that was scheduled for the next day—she'd tried to get a ticket, but the concert had been sold out for weeks. She breathed deeply now, giving her hair a little shake and trying to ignore the clammy feeling of her rain-soaked shoulders. Other people who had taken refuge from the rain were strolling around or examining the souvenirs at the small stand along the west wall, but Beth blocked them out as best she could, concentrating on the soothing beauty of the chapel itself.

She often came here for Evensong now, before leaving Cambridge at the end of the day. She would come early to watch the arrival of the choristers, boys in Eton collars and tall silk hats, the costume carried forward from the nineteenth century and required of the boys when they appeared in public as a group. Inside they would change into their red and white surplices and take their places in the stalls. When those voices were raised in the traditional songs, the almost impossibly high and clear soprano of the youngest boys soaring above the other ranges, Beth could hardly keep the tears from her eyes. She had long ago dissociated herself from formal religious practice, but something about this place and those sounds called to a deeply buried sense of awe, of mysticism, whose existence she would have denied in herself a few weeks ago. The anxieties that had plagued her ever since the break-in at her flat were lifted here, put into a larger perspective somehow, so they seemed less important.

Some twenty minutes had passed before Beth began to notice a brightening of the windows and then, quite suddenly, sunshine pouring through the jeweled colors of the ancient glass, flooding the interior of the chapel with a quality of light she was seeing for the first time. She stood up, turning slowly to take in every surface and angle of the now radiant building. As she completed her turn, she saw a face among a group of people at the back of the chapel, a face looking right at her. She saw the face register her glance and then turn quickly away.

Beth blinked her contacts clear and then stared hard. Even at this distance, she felt that the face looked familiar. He was a young man, perhaps twenty-five years old, face almost bland. So why did it look familiar? Had she turned nervously in a crowd and seen it? Had she seen it perhaps more than once? A little chill ran down her arms at the thought. The young man looked back at her now and this time there was no mistaking the expression she saw just before he looked hurriedly away again: It was the embarrassed look of someone "caught." He began to walk now, against the flow of the group he was in and toward the exit.

Beth drew a deep breath and marched to cut him off. She was determined to confront anyone who seemed suspicious as long as she could do it in surroundings where she was safe. The young man glanced at her again and then picked up his own pace, really hurrying now. Beth was almost trotting when she intersected his path just before he reached the side door of the chapel.

"Excuse me," Beth said firmly, stepping almost literally in front of him.

He stopped abruptly and turned halfway toward her.

"Do you mean me?" he asked in a quiet voice.

"Yes," she answered. "I feel sure I recognize you from somewhere."

He turned full face toward her now and she saw a broad, boyish face, a corona of tightly curled dark brown hair, a snubbed nose, widely spaced hazel eyes. Her impression of familiarity was confirmed.

"I don't see how that can be," he said, looking nervously around and speaking in a tone that sounded as if he feared being overheard.

"Still, I'm almost sure I recognize you," Beth insisted, trying to get him to make eye contact.

"You mustn't be seen talking to me, Miss Conroy," he said, looking right at her at last, his expression a strange combination of irritation and chagrin.

Beth gasped at the sound of her own name, took half a step backward.

"Don't be alarmed," he said, glancing around the chapel again. "I'm a police constable. You saw me last Friday at the police station, though we weren't introduced at the time." Beth recognized the working-class Cambridge accent, its edges slightly polished.

"A cop?" she said, still dubious.

"Yes," he said, shushing her with a quick gesture. "But do be quiet, please. No one is supposed to know I'm watching you. It's part of the plan for me to remain unobtrusive. So, you see, we mustn't speak like this."

"But I want to talk to you," Beth insisted. "Why am I being watched by the police?"

"Not here," he said, glancing around nervously again. "It's too open. We could talk someplace less public." He had actually turned from her now and was talking out of the side of his mouth like some bad imitation of a movie gangster.

Beth glanced around now, too; his nervousness seemed contagious. There were perhaps twenty people in the chapel, some alone, some in groups. No one seemed to be looking in their direction, yet she felt uncomfortable.

"I'm on my way to the University library," Beth said, her own voice now almost a whisper. "I could meet you in the tearoom."

"Fine," he said. "You go ahead and I'll meet you in just a bit. I don't think Inspector Mulgrave is going to like this, but if you insist . . ."

"I insist," Beth said, moving toward the door. "You're not just going to disappear, are you? I've had a good look at you now."

"I can't disappear," he said, glancing back at her ruefully. "This is my assignment."

Beth waited at a long table in the tearoom for just a few minutes before she saw the curly-headed young man come in, buy tea and scones, and make his way across the room toward her. When he sat down, he did so not across from her but facing in the same direction with a chair left vacant between them.

"I know this will seem a bit cloak-and-dagger," he said, looking embarrassed again, "but I'm going to pretend to read this newspaper so we can speak without appearing to do so." And he lifted the paper up in front of his face. "Just look away from me."

Beth felt decidedly silly following this instruction, but the young man was so earnest in his game that she complied with an impatient sigh.

"I'm Constable Timothy Woods," he said into his teacup. "This is my first plainclothes assignment, and I seemed to have bungled it already."

"Bungled in what way?" She found herself taking peeks at the snubbed profile.

"Well, you spotted me straightaway, didn't you?"

"How long have you been following me?"

"This is my first day," he said miserably.

"But you said I saw you last Friday."

"You did, when you were at the station, but I was in uniform then. I didn't get this job until yesterday."

"But why were you assigned to me at all?" Beth asked. "And why now? When I complained last Friday that I thought I was being followed, no one seemed to take me seriously. Sergeant Evans almost laughed at me. Has anything changed?"

"I couldn't say, Miss," he said, rustling the newspaper, but it sounded as if he *wouldn't* say. "And you mustn't mind Evans. He's like that with everyone. Inspector Mulgrave—he's my superior officer—has formed a new surveillance squad because of the murders. We're all stymied now—not much in the way of new leads. So all the older leads are getting new attention. Your complaint of being followed is one the inspector pulled up. There was your break-in, too, of course."

"Has your inspector consulted with the Scotland Yard men who came to see me yesterday?" Beth said, glancing again at the averted profile. "Is that what this is all about?"

He gave her a quick sidelong glance.

"Yes, Miss Conroy," he said. "It was their idea. They've pooled all the existing leads and suggested this new undercover squad. Other constables are watching the language schools, walking in the parks, that sort of thing. You know, just in case."

"But Superintendent Wilson didn't tell me I would be getting police protection. He was very nice, but he seemed sure I was in no danger."

"Well, he didn't want you to *know* you were being shadowed, Miss," he said, and the sheepish look had come back. "He was afraid you might give it away, accidentally like, if you knew, and the game would be up. Superintendent Wilson commented how much you looked like the victims—those poor girls. So I'm assigned to see if anyone actually is shadowing you as you feared. Then we'd have at him, wouldn't we?"

"So, Scotland Yard isn't so sure I was wrong," Beth said musingly, looking front again. "He and that sergeant of his *did* keep exchanging glances when I was talking to them."

"It's probably nothing definite that you said," Woods said soothingly. "I'm not even assigned to you full time. 'Spot-checking' is what Inspector Mulgrave calls it. I was to watch for your bicycle this morning at the roundabout; you reported that you go to the library almost every day, so someone could have learned your habits, of course. If that someone is dogging you about, I might be able to tell who it is by watching the people around you. The hunter becomes the hunted— that sort of thing." And he smiled a broad smile, obviously pleased with his turn of phrase.

"And how am I supposed to behave, now that I know you'll be around watching every now and then?"

"Well, you must go about your business in the usual way," he said, and he looked rueful again. "I shouldn't like my superiors to know that you tumbled to me so quickly. They'll think me a right bumbler."

"Don't worry, Constable Woods," Beth said with a little smile. "I won't tell on you. But suppose I want to contact *you*, to tell you something? Could that be arranged?"

"I don't know," he said skeptically. "Not part of my orders. Mulgrave wouldn't like it." And he looked very young, indeed, when he said Mulgrave's name.

"Can't you show a little initiative?" Beth felt like a teacher again. "Wouldn't they appreciate that more in the long run than 'following orders'? Besides, I know about you now, so what's the harm?"

"Well, you can't count on me being about all the time, mind," he said, glancing at her with a little smile, "but if you tumble to something, you should tell me about it, I suppose. We could arrange a signal of some sort." He was like a child arranging the rules of some game now, enjoying himself immensely, Beth could tell.

"All right," Beth said, smiling back at him. "What do you suggest?"

He furrowed his wide brow for a moment, sipping at his tea while he glanced around the room.

"I know," he said at last. "When you're out in public like this, you could just put your hand to the back of your head as if you were arranging your hair. Do it several times, so I'll know you mean it for the signal. If I'm on duty at the time, I'll find a way to talk to you privately. I'll try to stay out of sight when I'm watching you—that rain this morning sent me inside when I didn't mean to do it, or you might not have spotted me. But if you do see me about, take no notice of me, pretend you don't know me. I hope no one's seen us together today—that is, no one who shouldn't." And he looked nervously around the tearoom again.

"The only people who came in since I arrived have left again," Beth said, following his eyes. "The others were all here when I got here."

"At King's, though," he said with a worried frown. "Someone might have seen you speak to me there." He put the paper down and turned to face her now.

"I was planning to go to London in a few days," Beth said, lifting her own tea to her mouth; it was almost cold. "Just take the train down for the day. Would that be a problem?"

"No, not necessarily," he said, but he was frowning again. "I should know about it ahead of time so I could see you safely onto the train—from a watchful distance, of course. Just name the day and time."

"Well, I didn't have a definite plan," Beth said, somewhat embarrassed herself now. She was thinking of Andrew Carmichael's suggestion that she should visit Kew Gardens and had hoped she might find some opportunity to ask Andrew if he would like to go along and show the gardens to her. "And I might not go alone, either," she finished quietly.

"Oh," he said, raising his eyebrows. "Inspector Mulgrave didn't say you had friends in Cambridge."

"Well, not friends exactly," she said lamely. "New acquaintances."

Now the top of the snubbed nose wrinkled into a disapproving frown.

"May I just caution you, Miss Conroy, to be careful of new acquaintances. Any male acquaintance, I mean. If someone is shadowing you, he may try to get closer to you by striking up an acquaintance. And this could be someone quite ordinary-seeming, somebody you wouldn't suspect."

"That's what Wilson said."

"Of course he did. It would be best for you to avoid association with any stranger until this matter is cleared up."

"But everybody is a stranger to me here."

"Of course, Miss." His voice sounded genuinely sympathetic. "It must be very hard on you, but I think caution is the better part. If any man seems especially friendly, tries to persuade you to go somewhere with him where you would be unprotected, you must avoid him. And, of course, you mustn't tell any new acquaintance about my assignment. You can never know when you might be talking to precisely the wrong person. I'm saying this for your own good, mind."

"I know you are," Beth sighed. "Very well, then, Monday."

"Monday?" He looked confused again.

"I'll go to London Monday morning on the express," she ex-

plained, laughing. "And I'll go alone. Unless *you* want to tag along."
She was only half teasing.

"I don't think I could be spared for a whole day." It was clear
from his blush that he had taken her very seriously. "But I'll see to
it that I watch you onto the train. As a general rule, you know, you
shouldn't do much out of the ordinary until something develops in
this case."

Beth laughed again at his fussing.

"Don't worry so much," she said. "I'll be a very good girl and go
about my business in the usual way. Stick to routine. All that stuff.
Okay?"

"Okay," he said, smiling gratefully. "I wouldn't want to have to
explain myself to Inspector Mulgrave if something should happen to
you while I'm on duty."

"Neither would I want you to," Beth said. "I'm going to go upstairs
now and work like the good scholar I am for the next four hours, so
you can do your surveillance somewhere else for a while."

"Well, good," he said. "I'll tell the inspector I can take one of
the language schools for the rest of the day, then. You go ahead. I'll
leave when you're at your books."

Beth looked back from the doorway at the earnest young face
bent over a raisin scone, giving that treat the same serious consid-
eration he had so recently shown her. His curly hair formed a halo
effect around his head. She smiled to herself and shook her own head
slightly: not exactly the bodyguard she would have chosen for herself,
but certainly a nice boy and better, surely, than no bodyguard at all.

Chapter 18

For the next three days, Beth went about her normal routine without seeing any sign of Constable Woods. Either he'd got better at being unobtrusive or he was on another assignment. She felt much better, though, just knowing he was on the job, if only occasionally, to "spot-check." She was relieved to know that she hadn't been consigned to the police "nut file," as she'd feared she might be after her mistake about Peter Hollings. Chief Superintendent Wilson *had* noticed her resemblance to the dead girls and had advised a follow-up. If she followed Constable

Woods's advice about avoiding any situation where she could be trapped, she would be all right. If someone *was* following her, Woods might eventually spot him and take him into custody. Of course, she told herself, there might be nothing at all to discover—there might be no substance to her fears. But then Woods might find that out, too, and she would be wholly reassured at last.

During these three days, Beth didn't see Andrew Carmichael, either. She didn't pass him on the stairs, didn't see him in the lobby, didn't even glimpse him driving off in his little car. In fact, the car was seldom in the parking lot. Occasionally, at night, she would hear movement overhead, the sound of the door in the hallway opening and closing, and once she smelled the distinct aroma of cooked cabbage coming from his door as she passed.

She could only conclude that the man was deliberately avoiding her, that her reluctance to invite him in for coffee last Wednesday night had sent him running. Try as she might to tell herself that she could hardly have expected commitment from a man she had spoken to exactly twice, a man who shared a table with her in a restaurant only because he happened to see her there, she felt keenly disappointed. She'd seen such possibilities in Andrew Carmichael, and now she seemed to have scared him off. Well, that was *his* problem, after all. She certainly hadn't been *trying* to reject him, to dump him.

She *did* see Adam Tate, several times, going in and out. Each time, he was friendly, forthcoming, having put his shyness aside apparently. In fact, he seemed eager to continue their conversations longer than she wanted to. With Constable Woods's warning still echoing in her mind, Beth was reluctant to encourage anyone who now seemed "especially friendly." On Saturday afternoon, though, she couldn't think of an excuse for running off when he came out to where she was hanging some damp towels on the washline behind the apartment building. The sunshine that had broken through when she was inside King's College Chapel had persisted; the temperature gradually warmed until she was beginning to understand why poets fell in love with England in the spring.

"Aren't the azaleas nice?" Tate said, gesturing at the back of the yard as she turned to watch his approach. "We used to have azaleas in the garden at home when I was a boy."

"In Yorkshire?" Beth asked as she put a clothespin at the edge of one of her beige towels.

"No, no," he said with a dry chuckle. "I wasn't raised in Yorkshire. You'd hear it in my accent if I had been."

"Where then?" Beth asked, called upon, it seemed, to be pleasant.

"London," he said shortly. "Everyone in England has a garden of some sort, I think."

"Yes, everything is quite colorful," Beth answered, turning to look at him now. He was dressed in simple cotton slacks and a short-sleeved pale blue shirt. Despite the casual attire, he seemed formal, somehow unable to make his lean body adopt a wholly relaxed stance.

"How is your work going?" Beth asked now because he had fallen silent as soon as she looked into his eyes.

"Oh, quite well," he answered. "And yours?"

"Coming along nicely," Beth said. "What exactly is your project?"

"I thought you weren't very interested in science," he said mildly with a little smile. "It would bore you to have me explain it, I'm sure. Besides, it's the weekend now, and we should be able to leave our work behind for a couple of days, shouldn't we?"

"I guess so," Beth said, wondering if she should press the subject of the project, test his authenticity further.

"Do you like music?" he said suddenly.

"Why, yes," she said, puzzled by this tack. "Some kinds of music."

"A friend at the University has passed along some tickets to a chamber concert at the University Music School on West Road," he said, looking away from her now, his hands jammed into his pockets. "I was wondering if you might like to go. It's tonight."

Beth looked hard at Adam Tate. She was being asked out on a date, a seemingly normal event, and being asked by a man she *should* find eminently suitable. This was, after all, one of the fantasies about her sabbatical leave she had nurtured through a cold Wisconsin winter. A handsome and cultured Englishman—single, of course—would find her irresistibly charming and sweep her off to plays and concerts, courting her in a delightful Old World style. But all she could think of now was that she mustn't allow herself to be alone with a man she hardly knew because he might turn out to be a psychotic killer who had been stalking her for almost two weeks—perhaps longer.

And her biggest problem was that she had no convenient excuse for saying no.

"A chamber concert," she stammered, trying to make her brain work. "That sounds as if it might be very nice, but I—I really have to consolidate this week's research over the weekend—write it up in some coherent form before I lose the thread."

He'd turned his immense dark eyes full on her now and the expression on his face made her realize at once how lame her excuse was. She felt the nervous need to verify what she'd said, to be more convincing.

"I won't be able to finish my work on time unless I keep to a pretty tight schedule." She knew with appalling certainty that her cheeks were flame red by now, could hear her already girlish voice sliding up even higher in pitch. "It's best for me to work all weekend because I'm going out of town on Monday." She realized at once that she shouldn't have said this, had been betrayed into saying it by her growing desperation. "Just for the day, but still—it's a break in my routine, and I can't afford too many of those."

She had been staring at the clothesline as she babbled on, but now she turned to look at Adam Tate. His handsome face had darkened into something very like a scowl; the thick lashes had half closed over his eyes, giving him a hooded, sinister look, she thought.

"I see," he murmured, his rich, correct voice more controlled than his face. "Demands of scholarship, of course. Short notice, anyway. I understand." And he was already turning to leave.

"Perhaps another time," Beth said weakly, hoping that this cliché was not as hackneyed in England as it was in America.

"Yes, perhaps," he said without turning back toward her. The lean body was stiff inside the carefully pressed clothes; the pace was swift, determined. Before Beth could decide whether she would say anything else, Adam Tate had disappeared around the corner of the building.

Beth stood for a long time, tapping a clothespin against the point of her chin. She was thinking how shy and closed in Tate had seemed when she'd first seen him, first begun to speak with him a few days ago. Now there was all this attention from him, almost as if he'd deliberately planned some of the "accidental" meetings on the stairs in the past few days. Constable Woods had warned her that someone might "try to get closer to you by striking up an acquaintance," that someone might "try to persuade you to go somewhere with him where you would be unprotected." Was that what Tate was trying to do? Or was he just a nice man trying to get a date with a woman he felt he wanted to know better? She sighed and picked up her little basket. It was a dilemma she had to resolve on the side of caution, though, so she'd done the right thing in refusing Tate, no matter how badly she'd handled it.

As she walked back toward the front of the building, Beth reflected that at least she couldn't accuse Andrew Carmichael of trying to "get close to her." He'd gone in the opposite direction, apparently, and was fleeing from her acquaintance. So, perhaps she could at least eliminate him from the suspicion of being a crazed killer. Unless— Beth stopped short on the drive at the side of the house, struck suddenly by the realization that Andrew Carmichael's disappearing act might have some other cause than being refused a cup of coffee. What if he had followed her into Cambridge the day after their meal together at Churchill's? What if he'd seen her talking to Constable Woods at King's Chapel? That might have scared him off. Beth shook her head sharply. The worst of her present situation was that it was almost impossible to tell what was simply paranoia on her part and what was justifiable suspicion. It was best to stop idle speculation and *act* in the most cautious way possible.

In the lobby, Beth met Mr. Chatterjee coming from the empty flat where Ramón had lived before his eviction.

"Hello, Missy," he said in his cheerful voice. "Are you delighting in the good weather? We can only hope that the rain has left off for the rest of the spring. A veritable monsoon until now."

"Hello," Beth said, laughing a little at this bumptious outburst. "Yes, it's been lovely since Thursday, hasn't it? Are you getting that flat ready for a new tenant?"

"Not really," he answered. "I've boarded up the window on the outside as you can see when you approach the front, but the repair people can't come out for a few days yet, and I couldn't advertise the flat before the window is restored. No, I was just checking inside because Miss Chalmers has been complaining of 'sounds' coming from this flat when she passes it. She couldn't say what sort of sounds, but it is making her nervous because, of course, no one is living here since Thursday morning. Well, the place is quite dirty, but there is nothing inside to make 'sounds.' Do you suppose Miss Chalmers is one to imagine things?"

"I couldn't say," Beth answered. "I hardly ever see her and I've never spoken to her at all. She's always at the hospital, I believe."

"Yes, most of the time," Mr. Chatterjee said, furrowing his brow into a parody of sadness. "It's very morose for her, I'm sure, to have her mother so ill. Perhaps it's unsettling her mind, making her jumpy."

"Well, I wouldn't hazard an opinion about it," Beth said, shifting her basket and fishing her apartment keys out of her jeans. "Jumpy is something I can identify . . ."

She broke off because Andrew Carmichael had come striding into the lobby and then stopped short, frozen at the sight of them there.

"Hullo," he said, taking a half step backward, his surprise looking almost like alarm.

"Hello, Mr. Carmichael," Mr. Chatterjee exclaimed happily, forgetting that he had only seconds before been speaking in somber tones about poor, "morose" Miss Chalmers. "Are you having a nice walk on such a lovely afternoon? You enjoy walking, don't you? I see you so often going in and out."

"Yes, yes," Andrew murmured, sneaking glances at Beth. She couldn't help noticing how nice he looked in his oxford shirt and jeans. But she also noticed that his embarrassment, or surprise, seemed excessive, almost as if he had been waiting to come into the building until after he believed she had gone upstairs and was now taken aback at finding that she hadn't.

"Did you retrieve your bag?" Mr. Chatterjee burbled, seemingly unaware of the tension between Beth and Andrew.

"My bag?" Andrew said, and his dark brows came together in a frown.

"Didn't you leave your sport bag on the parking lot for a bit last evening?" Mr. Chatterjee lifted his arm to gesture at the door. "Right next to the place where the broken glass was before I cleared it up? I was going to get a glass of milk to help me get back to sleep and I glanced out the window to see it. I would have come out to look at it myself, except that it was so late. When I looked out this morning, it was gone."

"No," Andrew said shortly. "I didn't leave any bag outside. Why would you think it was mine?"

Beth was staring at Andrew's profile, trying to read his expression as he was talking to their landlord. She thought he looked irritated somehow, as if he'd been accused of something unjustly; perhaps it was just that he felt trapped here by a conversation he didn't want to have, in front of a witness whose presence was embarrassing him. Or was it just weariness she saw in his face? There were circles under his eyes, a sagging of the skin around his mouth that made him look tired.

"Well, I don't know," Mr. Chatterjee was saying. "I thought I saw a bag like that one in your car when you were moving in—a small, dark bag for taking to gymnasiums, I believe. Perhaps it was Mr. Tate's."

"I *have* a gym bag," Andrew said after a pause, "but it's been upstairs since I got here. I haven't taken it out at all." Then he turned to Beth with a little smile. "I haven't had the time for swimming that I thought I would have."

"Then it couldn't have been yours," Mr. Chatterjee said decisively. "You must forgive my concern, but ever since the break-in at Miss Conroy's flat, I've been very watchful and concerned about the property of our guests."

"Yes, of course," Andrew said, looking back at him. "Carelessness is a serious matter. But the bag wasn't mine. I'm sure the rightful owner has it back again."

Beth had begun to smart under the sense of being ignored in this conversation, convinced that Andrew was covering his embarrassment at finding her here by talking with the landlord about trivialities. Who cared, anyway, whose bag it was?

"Mr. Chatterjee," she said firmly. "Why don't you show me your garden? I've been admiring the flowers and wondering what some of them are called."

The landlord's face was radiant with happiness.

"I should love to show you, Missy," he exclaimed. "Come right along. And you, Mr. Carmichael, are you interested in flowers?"

"That's all right," Andrew murmured. "I'll just be getting upstairs.

You go along." And he stepped well to one side of the lobby to allow them to pass.

Beth walked past him and out to the yard without a backward glance, hearing Mr. Chatterjee uttering farewells behind her. She walked stiff-legged toward the bright little garden, thinking with considerable irritation that she was living in a building with two good-looking men—one too eager and the other not nearly eager enough. And her sad plight was that she was forced to regard both reactions with fearful suspicion.

Wilson was pacing in the corridor outside his little office. The office itself didn't provide him with the necessary room to pace properly, so he'd come outside where he could still hear the phone. He was waiting for Timmings to ring up with the new lab results. It had taken all the clout of a Scotland Yard chief superintendent to get the lab technicians to come in on a Saturday afternoon—a nice, sunny afternoon, at that. Normally he would have waited until Monday but his hunch was that this time they had something important, not just cat blood in an alleyway. No amount of experience had ever been able to make him patient with clerical or scientific delays when he could smell a break-through in a case.

The first inkling had come almost casually two days ago when Evans had popped in to say that one of the good citizens in the case was certainly a "persistent old bird." Wilson had prompted only with one of his stares, and the station sergeant had reminded him of the landlord whose suspicions were aroused by the tenant who moved out of a paid-up room only to remain in Cambridge. This landlord had come back to the police station to announce that while he was cleaning up the fireplace in the vacated room, he'd found bits of charred fabric and something that looked like part of a shoe sole. What kind of a person is it, he wanted to know, who burns up clothes in a rented room and then moves out? Not to another town, look you, but stays right here, probably burning up clothes in another room.

Wilson's eyebrows went up; he and Timmings exchanged a glance, the only communication necessary between them. Burning clothes was indeed a significant detail, and burning clothes in a re-cently rented room in Cambridge—well, this was more promising than anything they'd stumbled on recently.

"Is he here now?" Wilson asked.

"Yes, sir," Evans answered. "Right outside."

"Bring him in for a chat" was Wilson's only rejoinder, though his heart was beating a bit faster than usual.

The landlord appeared in the doorway, old and stooped, peering owlishly from behind thick glasses. He even perched on the edge of his chair like a nervous bird, ready to rise at any alarm.

"Mr. Caldwell," Wilson said gently. "Have you saved the things you told the station sergeant about, the things you found in the grate?"

"Certainly," the old man said, his voice thin and cranky. "I've got them at home in a polythene bag, if anyone's interested at all. Coppers should have listened to me the first time."

"Can you tell us something about this tenant of yours?" Wilson asked, sitting down behind his desk, and keeping his voice studiedly neutral. Timmings had his note pad at the ready.

"Called himself Smith," Caldwell said and then gave a dry cackle. "I get lots of Smiths. Peculiar sort, this one, though. Made sounds

ith his teeth. I heard him when he was coming in late one night.
ust stopped in the foyer and made this noise; thought I was asleep,
suppose. Don't need much sleep when you get to be my age."

"Anything else seem 'peculiar' about him?" Wilson cut in before
he old man could digress any more on the characteristics of aging.

"Well, what about this burning of clothes, then?" Caldwell
eemed still sore about not having been taken seriously originally.
"Whole days of chill and rain, and this chap never has a fire. 'No,
thank you,' he says, all mincing like when I offer him some coal. And
then on the warmest day, he has a fire in his grate. A fine, sunny day
it was and he takes coal without asking and has a fire."

Wilson and Timmings exchanged a long look.

"Can you remember what day that was, Mr. Caldwell?" Wilson
said softly. "The date, I mean."

"No, not the date." The old man seemed annoyed by being asked
about such details. "But it was that one fine day we've had this spring.
You know, when it was like summer, before all that bloody rain came
back. More than a fortnight ago, I should think."

"Was it the same night you heard Smith making the sounds with
his mouth?" Wilson was leaning forward now.

"No, no, that was later. It wasn't night when he had the fire. It
was late afternoon. I knocked at the door to ask about it, and he says
he's taken a chill. Barmy. A chill on a day like that. And he won't
let me in the room; in my own house, and he keeps the door locked,
talking to me through the door."

"Did you notice anything else unusual about him on that day?"

"Not that day, but the next. He went out with his camera, but
he came back without it. Now, mind you, I'd never seen him with
the camera before. Didn't seem the tourist type to me. We get tourists
in the summer, of course, lots of them, but—"

"Mr. Caldwell," Wilson interrupted as gently as he could under
the circumstances. "Could you describe the camera?"

"Well, it was a camera, wasn't it?" Caldwell seemed annoyed
again, swinging his watery eyes, enlarged behind the glasses, to gaze
at Wilson. "Cameras are black. They're cameras, that's all. This one
had a colored strap, bright colors in stripes."

Timmings had now become so agitated that he seemed about to

bounce out of his chair. Wilson shot him a sharp glance and he subsided.

"And no one has lived in the room since this Smith person moved out?" Wilson asked.

"What have I been telling you people all along?" The old man was whining now. "He moved out and I don't have another booking until mid-June."

"And you clean a room pretty thoroughly, do you, when someone moves out?"

"Naturally. I keep a nice place. Not like the pokey holes some people offer to let, I can tell you."

"Would you mind if we sent some people to look over that room?"

"They won't find anything. Nothing more than what I've found." He looked proud of his own powers of detection.

"Well, we'd like them to try," Wilson said patiently. "Would that be all right?"

"Well, it's past time, I think, for you to get so interested. But all right, come ahead."

When the old man had left, Wilson found himself reflecting that his work brought him into contact with such types rather more often than the average: nosy, cranky people who distrusted the world, who felt it their task in life to spy on their neighbors, to collect details that would confirm their worst suspicions, and to inform—to squeal. He knew he needed such people to do his job properly, was genuinely grateful when, as now, they gave him the information he was desperate for. Yet, if he were not a policeman, he would never associate with such people, for he found them distasteful, even repulsive. Whenever he was around the Caldwells of this world, he couldn't stop himself from feeling a shamefaced sympathy for the people they informed on. It made him secretly furious that they should be right, that their judgments about their neighbors should so often be well-founded. Because, of course, he knew better than most people the varieties of mischief one's neighbors could get up to. But he didn't like it, felt somehow dirtied by dealing with informants, spies, Caldwells.

The forensics team had been dispatched the next morning, armed with their bag of tricks. Wilson and Timmings had gone along. At first there had seemed nothing in the shabby room that could yield clues about its most recent occupant. The grate was swept clean now, the threadbare carpet had been vacuumed, the bedclothes had been laundered. But at last the mirrored cabinet in the bathroom yielded two discarded razor blades which had been slipped into a slot designed for the purpose. Asked whether these blades could have been used by some other tenant, Mr. Caldwell had insisted in his aggrieved voice that he had cleaned out that little box just before Mr. Smith had taken the room.

"You don't have to empty it every time," he whined, as if apologizing for having neglected this housekeeping detail. "But I remember cleaning it out after the Italian fellow moved out last month—he made quite a mess."

The razor blades were lifted out with elaborate care—good source of fingerprints—and slipped into sealed bags. They were not very clean. Dust clung to bits of dried shaving cream and there were darker specks that might, Wilson hoped mightily, be blood—Mr. Smith's blood. The laboratory technicians had been on the job for more than two hours this afternoon, but Wilson had finally lost patience and sent Timmings over to "hurry them along." When the phone rang at last, Wilson half ran into the little office to pick it up.

"Good pair of prints, thumb and forefinger," Timmings reported. "But no match in the records. So we know that our boyo doesn't have a criminal record. Not yet."

"Anything else?" Wilson knew his sergeant's tendency to save news in order to present it for dramatic effect at the end of a list.

"Bloodstains along the edge of one blade, all right," Timmings said triumphantly. "Type AB negative."

So, Wilson thought as he hung up the phone, this was their man. They had a set of fingerprints now. And thanks to the careful observations of a snooping landlord, who seemed to see everything despite his rheumy old eyes, they had a very detailed physical description. Monday, a sketch artist would arrive from London and, with Mr. Caldwell's help, they would have a composite drawing to distribute to the surveillance men who were undercover on strategic assignments all over Cambridge.

Let it be in time, Wilson thought; let it be enough to spot this lunatic and stop him before he can strike again. Because Wilson had a bad feeling that their man must be near an explosion of some sort. The psychiatrist he'd spoken with yesterday had been speculating that someone like this killer, thwarted from acting for such a long time, might lose his usual cunning under the pressure of his psychosis, might finally precipitate his own destruction by an incautious outbreak of violence—perhaps more than one victim this time. They would have to get him first, Wilson thought, as he began to pace again; they would have to stop him.

Chapter **20**

Monday morning dawned clear and bright, though a bit cooler than it had been on the weekend. Beth had made up her mind to follow through on her plan to go to London and out to Kew Gardens. It was ridiculous that she should avoid the place, a place she'd intended all along to visit, just because a trip there had been suggested by that man upstairs. She could enjoy the gardens on her own and for her own reasons. Besides, she wanted very much to be out of Cambridge just now, wanted to be anywhere where Andrew Carmichael was not. She called a cab and made it to the station twenty minutes before the train was to leave.

Remembering Constable Woods's assurance that he would see her safely onto the train, she scanned the crowds looking for his curly head, but she couldn't spot him anywhere. Of course, that didn't necessarily mean that he wasn't around somewhere; the station was very crowded and there were plenty of places for concealment. She smiled at the thought of this eager young policeman having learned more about staying undercover than he'd apparently known five days ago. After a last look around, she boarded the train and found a place to sit.

The train was crowded with commuters, mostly business types in gray suits and narrow ties, and Beth felt rather underdressed in her denim skirt and sandals. In her glasses and sailor blouse, she thought with a smile, she must look like some owlish little waif separated by accident from a school group. She'd left her contact lenses in Cambridge, remembering the grit stirred up in the tube stations by the rush of air that was pushed ahead of the trains as they raced along in their tunnels. The express arrived in London exactly on time.

On the tube ride from Liverpool Street to Westminster, there was an unpleasant incident, rather more unsettling than frightening. At the Cannon Street stop, two teenage boys got on the train, running through the car and flopping down on the bench seat opposite Beth. They were done up in a sort of modified punk style, all white and black. One of them had black hair—probably dyed, for that monochromatic look was seldom natural—and black clothes, complete with silver-studded black leather jacket. His companion had very blond, almost white, hair and was wearing black denim, including a sleeveless denim vest festooned with pins and buttons, among them a swastika. Both boys had painted their eyebrows black. The boys were shouting everything they said to each other, though they seemed more hilarious than angry, sprawling back with their booted feet extended toward Beth. They were shouting in that lower-class London accent which, to Beth, was unintelligible even when spoken in normal tones and which sounded absolutely menacing when it was screamed as it was now being screamed. The boys were carrying aluminum cans labeled Heineken and Watney's Red Barrel. While the train jerked back into motion, they opened the pop-top lids, spraying themselves, Beth, and other nearby passengers with the ale. Instead of apologizing, they screamed with laughter.

Two passengers, both elderly women, got up to move to other seats, but Beth simply turned away and looked out the window. She adopted the pretense of indifference that "straight" people usually affect in such circumstances, not wishing to encourage further demonstrations of outrageous behavior by showing disapproval or even looking at the boys. Teenagers, and drinking in the morning! The "good Midwestern girl" in Beth was aroused—and the schoolteacher in her as well. Why weren't they in school where they belonged? They made her remember A Clockwork Orange, the novel that had so fascinated and horrified her when she was a college student; it was about a future time when the decadence of British society had produced a particularly violent strain of youth gangs. Was that time now? she wondered, staring fixedly past the boys to the other end of the car.

In the far corner sat a man with his whole upper body hidden behind a newspaper, a man in neatly pressed trousers and highly polished shoes. A dark bag labeled ADIDAS was held firmly between his feet. He was, Beth now realized, the only other man in the car. So, she thought with a mental shrug, this is "proper" Britain's response to hooliganism on the streets—pretend that you don't know that women are being terrorized; hide and hope it won't involve you. But then she reminded herself that, to be fair, there would probably have been no different response from most men in Appleton, Wisconsin. Then she looked back at the boys, caught the glance of the blond one who was momentarily quiet. She saw that he was wearing round, black-framed glasses, probably the same glasses he'd had in grammar school. And his face in repose looked startlingly childlike, the expression slightly sheepish, as if he knew he was "acting up." And Beth realized at once that her fears were almost certainly exaggerated; she smiled at the boy, and he reddened before looking away. In just a few seconds, he was shouting again, quaffing his Watney's Red Barrel. At Blackfriars station, they both jumped up and left the car, jostling each other in the doorway as they went.

Beth got off at the Westminster stop, crossed teeming Victoria Embankment, and trotted down the long flight of stairs to Westminster

Pier. Motor launches, most of them rather grubby-looking, bobbed up and down on the slate-colored river. She bought a ticket for Kew and was told that the next launch left in fifteen minutes. A Wall's Ice Cream stand caught her eye and she decided that a snack was in order despite the fact that she'd had breakfast less than two hours ago. She fished out enough coins to buy a Cornette, a wonderful combination of ice cream, chocolate, and nuts inside a sugar cone. Then she wandered up and down the crowded pier munching away happily. A man with a camera and two capuchin monkeys was trolling for customers to be photographed with the monkeys; he would, Beth heard him saying, send the pictures "anywhere in the world" when they were developed—for a small fee, of course. When Beth got to the bottom of her cone, she was delighted to find the tip filled with a generous chunk of solid milk chocolate; how like the British, who so loved their sweets, to save that delicious surprise for when you thought the treat was almost over.

At last the crowd began to move forward and Beth joined in the sweep toward the launch. She headed as quickly as she could for the chairs she'd seen on the upper deck, wanting to get as close to the prow as possible, so she could get the most panoramic view. She needn't have hurried. Most of the passengers headed for the doors that led to the lower deck with its enclosed lounge. Her chair was the lead chair in a V-shaped wedge, so she sat precisely in the point of the boat's prow. The sun was bright but not particularly warm. The breeze was coming straight downriver, right into Beth's face and it was definitely bracing in its chill. The launch engines began to rev up, making a raucous noise as the boat moved away from the pier.

As the launch emerged from under the shadow of the bridge, Beth found herself looking straight up at the Houses of Parliament, towering up from the river in all their ornate splendor. She snatched up her bag, found her camera, and took two pictures; this was a view of the historic buildings that she had seldom seen in photographs. The launch picked up speed now and made its way into the center of the river. Beth just watched now as the bridges approached and receded: Lambeth, Vauxhall, Chelsea, Albert, Battersea—all in different architectural styles. She began to be impressed by how ugly the underbelly of the great city could be, especially along the south bank where the warehouses looked particularly grimy. Later, when she saw one warehouse labeled HARROD'S FURNITURE DEPOSITORY, she jumped up and ran to the railing to get a broadside shot of it as the launch chugged on by; Charlotte, the mad shopper, would get a kick out of that picture.

On her way back to her seat, Beth passed the door to the lower deck and glanced down, thinking that a cup of hot tea would be nice; it really was quite chilly outside. At that angle, she could see the lounge patrons only from the waist down, just legs and feet milling around. The lounge looked so crowded that she dismissed the idea of trying to wade through it. As she turned away toward the prow, she scarcely noticed the figure that remained unmoving at the bottom of the sharply pitched stairs: a man in carefully pressed trousers and highly polished shoes, a man with a newspaper folded neatly under his left arm.

The river began to narrow now, imperceptibly at first, but more definitely after the launch made its one interim stop at Putney Bridge pier. Above Putney Bridge, the Thames became not much more than a big stream. At last the launch tied up at Kew, and Beth was the first passenger off, her camera suspended from her neck, her face already set in the direction of the fabled gardens. She paid no attention to the other passengers disembarking behind her.

The two hundred and eighty acres of Kew Gardens—or the Royal Botanic Gardens at Kew, as they were officially known—were too much for Beth to take in on one visit and she knew it. She'd made her plans the night before, listing the exhibits she wanted to see; the guidebook was one of Charlotte's and not very current, so she would have to wait until she was on the grounds to discover which parts had been destroyed by the terrible windstorm of a few years ago, a storm so unusual and so devastating that it had been reported in all the American newspapers. But she knew she would begin at Kew Palace, one of the few royal residences not actually used by a member of the royal family—it was only a museum now. A large part of the launch crowd had the same idea, apparently, and because of Beth's short stride, many of them overtook her and even passed her up before she reached the surprisingly modest-looking palace.

She enjoyed Kew Palace immensely; after the awesome dimensions of Windsor and the elegance of Kensington—both of which she'd seen in April—Kew seemed much more like a house someone might actually live in. It was constructed on a human scale. Next she went to the Orangery, now a gift shop, and saw firsthand how the principles of the passive solar greenhouse could be applied on a grand scale, a technology well known, apparently, long before the twentieth century. Here, too, there was a crowd of other gawkers. After the Orangery, Beth set out on her own down the wide paths of the gardens themselves. Ordered, carefully labeled sections of plants studded close-cropped lawns, everything so emerald bright and well tended that it reminded her of putting greens. After the seemingly random jumble of the Cambridge Botanic Gardens, this orderliness gave the impression of august formality.

Beth strolled in the chilled sunshine, drinking in the colors, the shapes, almost the textures of the exhibits. In the rose garden, she was one among many admirers. But along many of the walks, she found herself quite alone. While she was photographing a display of rhododendrons, she thought she heard footsteps in the grass behind her, but when she turned, no one was there. A little chill of the old fear, the one she thought she'd left behind her in Cambridge, swept up her neck and into her scalp. Nonsense, she told herself. It's just imagination. Sounds were distorted here in this artificially constructed bit of nature. But every time she was away from other pedestrians now, she heard some odd noise, sometimes very near—behind a hedge or massive shrub—and sometimes farther away: a rustle, a little thump, the sound made when the legs of trousers rub together as the wearer is walking quickly.

Beth found herself whirling around, jumping away from shrubs in alarm, making sharp turns to see what was behind hedges. She'd stopped looking at the displays now, had stopped taking pictures. She'd had eleven exposures left on this film, had taken five photos on the trip so far. At one spectacular reddish-purple shrub that towered some fifteen feet and was at least twenty feet wide, Beth literally ran around the foliage after she was certain she heard someone walking parallel with her on the other side. If she could just catch somebody skulking there, she thought, she wouldn't have to feel like a skittish horse, shying at imagined threats. At last, she gave it up, overwhelmed by a sudden need to have other people around her.

Walking very quickly now, Beth headed for the nearest group of people and found herself about to enter Queen Charlotte's Cottage. But the crowd didn't provide the comfort she'd hoped for. She made the tour almost completely oblivious to what she was seeing, turning from the charming interior to look outside, to scan the crowd around her. Could somebody be following her here? And why? Why was every innocent tour spoiled by this terrible sense of menace? She felt that she was simply doomed to have her first experiences in England ruined. When the tour emptied out onto the grounds again, she headed straight back toward the main entrance to the park, walking as fast as she could and looking neither to right nor left.

She remembered that the path she'd come along at that end of the grounds had a sharp bend in it just before one of the famous weeping beech trees, a bizarre tree whose enormous canopy, twisted and gnarled and very thick, drooped all the way to the ground, creating the odd illusion of a huge tree which had had its trunk removed without killing it. On the curve of the path, she increased her speed even more, panting from the effort. When she felt she was screened from the view of anyone on the path behind her, she began to run, off the path, across the short expanse of finely trimmed lawn, and into the canopy of the beech tree. From inside this screen, which would hide her completely even two feet back from its outer edge, she would be able to watch the path, notice who was hurrying, who might suddenly look confused by her disappearance.

Seconds passed, then minutes. Three people engaged in animated conversation strolled past. A young couple, arms linked, followed some twenty paces later. Then no one for a long time. Then a group of five people. When they, too, had strolled back in the direction of the palace, Beth was ready to give up on her plan, had even begun to think again that she'd imagined her pursuit. Just at that moment, she caught the sound of faint rustling in the foliage behind her—not at the edge of the canopy where the breeze could stir the leaves, but toward the center of the tree, a center she couldn't see, where the wind couldn't penetrate.

She whirled around, making a considerable racket herself in the dense foliage. Then she stood very still, her breath held, listening intently. Her vision could penetrate no farther than three feet in any direction; the branches were so thickly leaved, so crisscrossed, that somebody could have been almost near enough to touch her before she would have seen him. She was beginning to feel faint from holding her breath. But then she heard a sound—in front of her and slightly to the right—a very faint noise that was not the sound of the moving branches. Beth thought the noise sounded familiar, but at first, she couldn't place it: a scraping, grating noise like—like stones—And then she remembered and her panic was so instantaneous that she burst into motion even before she drew the first gasping breath. Arms flailing against the branches, she came rushing out of the tree and ran wildly, not even looking which direction she was going.

A woman pushing a child's stroller snatched back on the handle as Beth flew past her; other people became wide-eyed blurs as she intersected their paths. Only when she could see a whole line of people did Beth change from random to purposeful flight. A queue was moving into a large glass-enclosed building, and Beth joined it, craving the proximity of many other people. She was tempted to tell everyone in sight about being followed, about the noise inside the weeping beech tree, but when she glanced around the huge expanse of gardens visible from this vantage point, she could see nothing and no one that looked suspicious. She realized what her account would sound like to these orderly, rule-following people, here in sunshine and the crisp breeze of an English spring day. Other strollers had joined the queue behind her and were indicating with their glances that they expected Beth to keep up or get out of line.

At the doorway, a sign told her that she was about to enter the Water Lily House with "specimens from all over the world." As she passed the first door and then an inner door, Beth felt a wave of moist, heated air descend onto her chilled flesh; obviously this exhibit required climate control of a special kind. Instantly, Beth's glasses fogged up from the warmth and moisture. She could barely read the sign that said KEEP RIGHT. Finding the glasses almost useless now, she pushed them up to the top of her head and shuffled along behind the other people.

The room was almost filled by a large pond; the pedestrian track around this pond was wide enough for two, at most three, people to walk abreast. The corners were filled by much smaller, tiered ponds which, on closer inspection, contained tiny, brightly colored amphibians of various kinds and goldfish. Even someone as acutely nearsighted as Beth could see the displays in the main pond. The lily pads were grotesquely large, some as big around as a dining-room table. Their flower stalks were three or four feet high, ending in radiant, lavender-colored blooms. Some smaller varieties were also evident around the edges of the pond. Beth found herself impressed with the illusion, both visual and tactile, of having been suddenly thrust into a prehistoric jungle. It was not a comforting illusion for someone who believed that she was being stalked.

As she kept pace with the people before her, many of whom wanted to pause, point, and comment to each other, Beth drew the wet air into her lungs in gulps, finally able to breathe normally when she had made about one third of the circuit around the pond. The whole building was filled with people, she now realized. She squinted across the pond at the crowd opposite her. Just to the left of center, she saw a figure partially obscured by the people in front of it, taller than most of the nearby figures, somebody in sunglasses. The man had blond, straight hair, but something in the shape of the head, the way the head sat on the shoulders, looked vaguely familiar to Beth. Then some of the other people moved and Beth saw that the man was wearing a tan jacket.

Frozen in shock, Beth came to a full stop. Someone entering the building behind her, someone who had ignored the sign and gone left instead of right, could be in that position now. She was at last able to breathe, to move. She snatched her glasses down from the top of her head, but found them still partially blurred by steam and smeared from contact with her hair. Damn it! she thought. He's here and I can't see him. And then she remembered her camera. Unless its lens was fogged like her glasses, *it* would be able to see better than she could. People were moving slowly past her as she swung the camera up from the front of her body where it was dangling and tried to focus in the direction of the man in the tan jacket. But through the viewfinder, she could just make out the blur as he began to run.

Beth dropped the camera and watched the desperate movement

toward the exit, the alarm of other people jostled out of the way. She began to run herself, back against the flow of the crowd, fighting her way toward the exit as people muttered, "Here! Watch what you're doing" or "Bloody cheek!," giving way only very reluctantly. Beth's diminutive stature worked against her here, both in terms of getting people to move out of her way and of keeping the other fleeing figure in sight. By the time she reached the door, she was already wiping her glasses against her blouse. After a last jam in the doorway, she burst out into the chilly breeze, thrust her glasses onto her face, and looked around. There was no one in sight wearing a tan jacket. No one running. No one even hurrying. In three directions, the water-lily house was only a few steps from shrubs, hedges, a sharp corner of the building itself. She was too late.

Now Beth made her way to the gate carefully, keeping close to groups of people, looking around in all directions for a glimpse of the tan jacket. Instead of turning toward the pier, she headed straight through the village to the tube stop. She knew that a District Line train would take her back into the city much faster than the motor launch, and that it would need only one change of trains to take her to Liverpool Street. Her small chin was set firmly with her determination to get straight back to Cambridge, to find Chief Superintendent Wilson's card—she'd left it on her dresser top—and to let Scotland Yard know what had happened at Kew Gardens.

Chapter **21**

Beth sat at her dining-room table
staring at the card with Chief Superintendent
Wilson's name on it. All the way back to Cambridge in the train,
she'd been thinking about what she would say to Scotland Yard about
the events in Kew Gardens and their possible connection to her break-
in and the attempt to steal her camera at Covent Garden. As Audley
End and Bishop's Stortford and Luton swept past, she rehearsed the
words. Long before she reached Cambridge, she'd begun to worry about

how it all sounded, and now she was having serious reservations about calling Wilson at all.

What could she tell him really? That she *thought* she was being followed all over the Royal Botanic Gardens, though she'd never actually seen anyone following her. That she'd hidden inside a tree and *thought* she heard a sound similar to one she'd heard in the hallway of her building one night while a wild party was going on downstairs. That she had no idea what the sound could be, of course, and, again, she'd seen no one. That a man in a tan jacket, a man she couldn't see clearly because her glasses were fogged up, had left the water-lily house, she *thought*, because she'd squinted at him and started to take his picture. That she couldn't be sure whether this man was the same man as the camera thief in Covent Garden, but she *thought* so because the jacket looked the same and the witnesses had said that her assailant was blond—never mind that there were probably thousands of tan jackets in the Greater London area, many of them worn by blond men. That the man had disappeared by the time she could get her glasses clean.

Sitting at her own table, reviewing it all, Beth was sure it would sound absurd to professional detectives; it even sounded lame to her, now that the intense *feeling* of menace had subsided. Acting on emotion was not so easy when the emotion had passed, certainly not easy for someone who had learned to discount emotion. What troubled her most was that she could think of no rational connection between these disparate events, no motive for the same man to be behind all of them. Didn't it strain credulity to imagine that a man would have followed her twice to London, taking the same trains, keeping her in view through sightseeing, subway rides, and even boat rides? And what could be the motive for such an elaborate shadowing project? To steal a camera? To—to what? What might have happened at Kew if she hadn't run from that strange sound? And if the man in the tan jacket had been the one who broke into her flat, what could be the motive for that? Nothing had been stolen. If he had been in the darkened hallway two weeks later, making that weird sound, *why* was he there?

The only reason that suggested itself to her was that someone was obsessed with her in a very sick way, perhaps because she resembled the victims pictured in all the papers. But the Scotland Yard detectives had assured her that this was emphatically not the M.O. of the strangler; none of the other victims had been subjected to prior harassment. In fact, the Swiss girl had been in Cambridge only a few days when she was murdered. So the police theory seemed the most rational: a random break-in and the coincidence of a pickpocket attack in London—two unconnected events, except that she had been the victim both times; and then there was the feeling of being followed. These events led to an increasing sense of paranoia which, in turn, had led to her imagining noises in hallways, footsteps in the gardens, menace in the wind. Beth had spent years as a scholar and teacher, years learning to value the rational over the instinctive, learning to discount superstitious "readings" of coincidence. Now she was feeling disposed to discount her own instincts, to suppress her intuition. She had been wrong about Peter Hollings, had made a fool of herself at the police station. Sergeant Evans's face came forcefully into her mind. What evidence did she have after all? They would laugh; surely they would laugh.

It was already late in the afternoon—her soul searching had been a long process—and a dull headache reminded her that the hasty departure from London had made her skip lunch; the Cornette at Westminster Pier was the last thing she'd eaten. She made a quick resolve to sleep on the day's events before deciding what to do about them. Wilson had said she was to let him know if "anything of a suspicious nature" happened and, tomorrow morning, she would ask herself again if today's events qualified. In the meantime she would see about getting some dinner. The little refrigerator was nearly empty and she was beginning to think that her modest budget was too depleted to allow for much more restaurant eating. A trip to Sainsbury's was in order and this one would not permit using her bicycle; she needed too many items for her book bag to hold. It was time for the bus, the green double-decker that careered past at irregular intervals —the buses were not as precise as the trains—and deposited her quite near Sainsbury's. A check of the schedule showed her she would have to wait another forty minutes—longer if the bus was late—but she remained confident that she could finish and get back before dark; days were longer here in late spring than they were back in Wisconsin.

. . .

At the market, Beth trundled her cart up and down the aisles, threading her way through the other shoppers; this branch of Sainsbury's was always crowded because university students regularly stopped in for snack food or soft drinks. She found herself thinking yet again that everything in England seemed made on a smaller scale than in America, even grocery carts. The one she was pushing was narrow and had the especially handy feature of rolling side to side as well as forward and backward, a feature made almost necessary by the narrow aisles and sharp corners. She picked up meat, fresh vegetables, fruit, tea, oatmeal, and a package of fresh crumpets, a British food she had come to love as a substitute for toast in the morning; with fresh peaches sliced over toasted crumpets and a nice pot of tea, she could feel authentically English.

Because she'd brought no grocery list, Beth found herself backtracking and changing direction abruptly as she remembered items she needed. And the store was so crowded that she was taking much longer than she'd planned. It was beginning to get dark when she got to the Drummer Street bus station, where she discovered that she'd just missed a bus to the Madingley Road, a bus that had left on time for a change. That meant a twenty-minute wait for the next one. She sat on the end of a bench already crowded with waiting passengers, gratefully setting down the shopping bags which had been dragging at the ends of her arms all the way from Sidney Street. She felt comforted by the presence of so many people. Each bay of the station had a crowd waiting for buses; it was that time of the day when people leave a city or cross to its other end to go home, people laden with shopping bags, tired children, briefcases.

It was almost completely dark when the bus deposited Beth and her groceries at the stop near her building. She ran across the road, the bags flapping against her legs, and hurried toward the drive that sloped downhill to the front door. As she ran, she heard footsteps behind her, running footsteps. After the events of the morning, the sound struck instant terror into her. Why had she gone out of the apartment? She should have realized there was not enough daylight left to guarantee she would get back before dark! She gasped for breath, considered dropping the groceries as she ran down the drive toward the parking lot.

"Miss Conroy," she heard behind her. "Wait a moment, please. It's only me."

She'd almost arrived at the first car in the lot before she realized that she recognized the voice. She turned and saw Constable Timothy Woods trotting up to her.

"You shouldn't be out alone at this time of night," he scolded in his nice, deep voice. "Haven't I warned you about being cautious?"

"I'm sorry," Beth gasped, almost weeping with relief at the sight of the snubby nose and the thick curls. "You're right, of course. I just thought I'd be back sooner."

"I followed you into the city by car," he explained, "and waited at Sainsbury's. When you got back onto your bus, I hopped into my car again and came back here to see to it that you would get safely inside. I don't believe anyone else was following you, but I can't just let you walk alone like this, even if someone else is watching."

"Are you just sitting around in your car waiting for me to go in and out?" Beth was breathing normally again.

"No, no," he said, and he laughed indulgently. "Not all of the time, at least. I've taken a little room in the house that's opposite the bus stop. You can just see its roof from here." And he lifted his arm to point.

"When did that happen?" Beth asked, eyeing him sharply in the gloom. "What happened to spot-checking only?"

"Yesterday," he said cheerfully. "Wilson has recommended that each of us be given a single assignment now because there are some new developments. Here, let me take those bags for you. They look heavy. I'll just take them inside. See you safely home."

"New developments?" Beth said, absently handing over the groceries. "What new developments?"

"I'm not at liberty to say," Woods said, still sounding cheerful and upbeat. "You understand, I'm sure, that the police have to keep mum about certain things. But I'm on the job full time now. Even though Wilson says we're not to be so much concerned about nighttime because this bloke hasn't ever killed anyone at night—at least not that we know of—I still don't like to see you going about in the dark. Promise me you won't do it again."

"All right, all right," Beth said. They had begun to walk now toward the front door. "Tell me something, Constable. Did you see me onto the train this morning as you said you would?"

Woods came to a stop in the center of the parking lot.

"Why, yes, I did," he said, looking down at her. "I watched from behind a news kiosk until you got aboard. No one else seemed at all interested in your activities. When the train started off, I came away. Why do you ask?" Beth felt oddly disappointed that he'd seen no one.

"It's just that I thought someone might have followed me to London today," she said quietly.

In the light from the front of the building, she could see the boyish face lower into a frown.

"What made you think that?" he asked.

"Because I heard creeping sounds all over Kew Gardens," she said, frightened again and covering it with a tone of annoyance. "I tried to catch him at it, but I never did."

"Could this have been your imagination, Miss Conroy?" he asked, and now the nice young face had the expression Beth hated, the expression that said, "There, there, little girl."

"I don't think so," she sighed. "I don't think I'm the sort of person who lets her imagination run wild. I hid to see if I could get a look at whoever it was and while I was waiting, I heard a noise, very near to me; it was the same noise I heard here in the hallway upstairs the night before Superintendent Wilson came to see me. A very strange noise."

"A strange noise?" Woods looked very interested now. "Had you told Superintendent Wilson about hearing a strange sound of some sort?"

"No, I didn't remember until after he'd left." It was Beth's turn to be embarrassed now. "But that isn't all that happened at Kew. I ran into one of the enclosed exhibitions, the water-lily building, and later I saw somebody there I thought I recognized, though I couldn't see very well without my glasses. He was wearing a tan jacket and he ran when I tried to take a picture of him. When I got outside, he'd disappeared."

"A tan jacket?" Woods asked, frowning again.

"Like the one the man at Covent Garden was wearing," Beth said. "Oh, I guess I didn't tell Wilson that either; about the jacket, I mean. The witnesses at Covent Garden said the would-be thief was fair, blond, and wearing sunglasses. That's just what the man in the water-lily house looked like. But I think the reason this man looked familiar to me, his shape, I mean, is that I've seen him here in Cambridge, seen him without knowing who I was seeing. I think he's the man who's been following me since my break-in."

"You're going too fast for me, Miss," the young man said, holding up his right hand. "Are you saying you suspect the same person of breaking into your flat, trying to make off with your camera, *and* frightening you at Kew Garden?"

"Yes, that's exactly what I'm saying."

"And you took his photo?"

"No, I said I tried to take his picture, but he started to run so I gave that up."

"And you're sure he was blond?" Woods asked again, looking puzzled, as if he hadn't expected this.

"Well, fair-haired," Beth said. "Longish fair hair. Why?"

"Never mind," Woods said, shifting the grocery sacks and smiling again. "Just double-checking. Why would this blond fellow do all these things, do you think?"

"That's just what I can't figure out," Beth sighed. "It doesn't make any sense, but I think it's related to those poor girls somehow. And you've as much as told me that the Scotland Yard people think there's a connection between me and those killings. That's why you're here."

"Well, I said I'm just following up an old lead," he said, apparently unwilling to give any more away. "But the motive for this blond person isn't clear, is it? Whoever killed those other girls has never behaved like this before."

"That's what everyone keeps saying," Beth said in an exasperated tone. "I wish I could figure out why he's interested in me in this way. Interested in my belongings, too, it looks like. That is, if he's the man who broke into my apartment."

"Well, you may be sure that I'll pass along what you've told me when I check in with Inspector Mulgrave tomorrow," Woods said, moving toward the building again. "But there may not be a connection, after all, between the incidents in London and those here in Cambridge, despite your theories. Are there any *other* men you've met recently that we should probably know about down at police headquarters, any men who seem to be trying to get close to you?"

Beth turned and squinted up at her apartment building.

"Well," she said and then paused for a minute. "There are some new tenants here who've moved in very recently. But the landlord says that's normal for this time of the year. And no one is fair-haired."

"Tell me about them anyway."

"A man named Tate has taken the flat next to mine. Says he's from Leeds University. He's dark, looks Italian or something, very dark eyes. He's been very attentive to me the past few days."

"Tate," Woods said, looking as if he were taking mental notes. The description of Tate had seemed to interest him. "Is it possible that he could have been making 'strange noises' in your hallway?"

"I suppose so," Beth sighed, coming to a stop again. "He was already living here at the time, though I didn't know it that night. He's certainly in a location where he could watch for me to go in and out, could follow me. But he wasn't here at the time of the break-in."

"Have you noticed him about in the city, in crowds near you?"

"No, I haven't. He's so dark—his hair, I mean—that he'd stand out, don't you think?"

"Oh, well," Woods said with significant emphasis. "He may just be quite clever about concealing himself—more clever than I am." And he got the sheepish look again. "Now are there any others you should tell me about?"

"Maybe I should tell you," Beth said slowly, "that I *did* sort of accidentally tell Adam Tate that I was leaving Cambridge today."

"Now, there you are, Miss Conroy," Woods said in his scolding tone. "Isn't that just what I've been cautioning you about?"

"But he wasn't the man in the water-lily house," Beth insisted. "Wrong hair altogether."

"Hullo," a voice said suddenly from the right.

Beth and Woods turned to see a figure obscured in the shadow of the fence. Beth, who was closer to the newly arrived man, could see that it was Andrew Carmichael, dressed in a suit and tie. He had apparently come out of the building unnoticed and stopped at some distance from the pair in the parking lot.

"I've been up to your flat and didn't find you home," he said, his voice sounding somehow strained. "Now I see that you're just coming in."

In the gloom, Beth couldn't read his expression, could barely see his face.

"Hello, Andrew," she said, feeling obscurely as if she'd been caught doing something wrong; she was suddenly aware that she'd cheerfully named Adam Tate as a suspect, postponing mention of Andrew. Perhaps she hadn't intended to implicate him, had unconsciously censored what she told the young constable because she didn't want to believe that Andrew Carmichael might be a suspect. Too late now.

"A bit chilly for outdoor visiting, isn't it?" Andrew said.

"Hardly visiting," Beth said quickly. "This nice young man was kind enough to help me with my groceries from the bus stop, and I was just thanking him." Then, turning to Woods, "Thanks again—Timothy, wasn't it?" And she took the grocery bags back from him.

"Yes, Miss," he said, lifting his hand to his head in a sort of casual salute. "Think nothing of it. Glad to be of service." But he looked into the shadows at Andrew with a long, searching stare before he turned and walked up the drive toward the Madingley Road.

Andrew Carmichael didn't speak
again until Woods was out of earshot.

"It may not be wise to let strangers help you with your things,"
he said coming forward into the light. Miss Chalmers was apparently
at home because the windows of her flat were ablaze, making that
part of the parking lot quite bright.

"I'm fine," Beth said shortly. "You needn't worry about me."

"I haven't seen you lately," he said, and Beth thought he might
be blushing.

"Nor I you," she responded, hearing the chill in her own voice.

"Old cronies in the city have kept me quite occupied, I'm afraid," he said, raising his hand to his mouth in that nervous gesture Beth had noticed the other night. "In fact, I've another engagement to-night."

"Well, you mustn't let me keep you," Beth said, thinking, "There's no reason to explain yourself to me, mister." She had lifted her own hand to sweep her hair behind her right ear where there was still a little tender spot from the wrenching of the camera strap. Now she suddenly realized that they were standing here making nervous gestures at each other, and the realization made her smile in spite of herself.

"You said just now that you'd been to my flat," she said. "Did you want to see me about something?"

"Yes, yes," he murmured and now he was definitely blushing. "I was wondering if you'd been to the Fitzwilliam yet."

"No, not yet. I've been busy, too, and I made an excursion to London."

"Would you like to go tomorrow?" Suddenly he seemed again the eager man she'd had dinner with last week. "I'd love to show it to you and I haven't been back there myself on this holiday, so it would be great fun for me to see it again through the eyes of someone who's never been."

Beth laughed, a nervous little laugh; she felt rather swept off her feet by his enthusiasm. And his proximity was working its usual magic. She had no reason to connect him to the man at Kew, after all; Andrew Carmichael had dark hair.

"Well, I *have* been meaning to go," she said at last. "It would be nice to have a knowledgeable guide."

"What time shall we go? I'm free for the whole day, so I can just drive us into the city."

Beth decided to draw the line at getting into a car with him. The events of the day had made her jittery again, extra cautious. And Constable Woods had been insistent about avoiding just such overtures.

"Why don't I just meet you at the museum?" she said. "I've got a few little errands to run in the city first and I don't want to drag you around to do them. Shall we say about ten-thirty?"

"That would be fine," he said, but he looked disappointed by her altering of his suggested plan, injured almost. "I'll see you then." He looked at the watch on his well-shaped wrist. "Now I'd best be dashing. You should get inside, you know; it's getting really chilly."

"Yes, you're right," Beth said, moving into the doorway. From there, she watched his car bounding up out of the driveway. On her way up the stairs she was trying to analyze her own feelings. She was glad, certainly, that Andrew had once again shown an interest in her, happy to have almost a date with him. But she felt apprehensive, too. He was so hard to figure out. He'd practically vanished for three days last week, and he'd seemed so uncomfortable when she'd seen him in the lobby on Saturday. But here he was, acting as if none of that had happened. Perhaps he was just one of those men who needed time to work up his courage again after he thought he was being rejected.

At the head of the stairs, she had to set down one sack to open the hall door, pick it up again, and then set both sacks on the hall table as she swung her book bag forward to dig out her keys. It was a nuisance to have two keys even if it did make her feel safer to have both locks on the door. As she was rummaging through her bag, she heard a door closing softly behind her. She whirled and saw Adam Tate looking at her from the head of the stairs; he'd obviously just come out of his flat. Beth was too startled to speak, and he stood for a moment longer without saying anything, apparently weighing whether to start down the stairs or to acknowledge her presence.

"Could you use some help with those sacks?" he said at last, speaking in his perfect accent.

"No, thanks, Mr. Tate," Beth said hastily. "I'm all right." She found she couldn't look directly at him while she spoke. She was breathing in shallow gasps, unable to understand why his sudden appearance had alarmed her so much.

"Oh, please call me Adam," he said coming forward into her hallway. "It seems we should be calling each other by our Christian names by this time. Can't you find your key?"

Beth snatched her hand out of her bag and placed her back against her door.

"It's just that this bag is so big," she said weakly, wondering if Miss Chalmers would hear a scream if she needed to make one. Tate was approaching her now, looking suddenly more confident than he had a moment earlier, smiling that ingratiating smile of his that somehow looked insincere, staged.

"Come along," he said. "There's no need for you to be such an independent woman. Let me help you get your things inside. One scholar aiding another, eh?"

"No," Beth said, perhaps a bit too emphatically. "I'll manage by myself, thank you. You were on your way somewhere and I don't want to keep you." And she folded her arms over her bag, indicating that she wouldn't look for the keys until he'd gone. She saw an expression of annoyance pass over his face as soon as he heard the more determined note come back into her voice.

"Yes, of course," he said coldly. "I'll be off then." And he turned abruptly to walk away. Beth waited until she'd seen the dark head disappear before she opened her bag to hunt for her keys again.

Inside, she set her groceries in the kitchen and found that her hands were shaking as she began to empty the sacks. She was wondering if Adam Tate's appearance just as she was approaching her door was simple coincidence. If he'd been watching from his front window, he might have seen her talking to Constable Woods, might have waited for her to come up the stairs so he could arrange an "accidental" meeting, try to persuade her to let him inside her apartment. "Whoever is shadowing you might try to get closer to you by striking up an acquaintance," Woods had said.

Suddenly she stopped with the package of crumpets in her hand, poised in front of the cupboard. It had just occurred to her that, of course, the same things could be said about Andrew Carmichael. He, too, could have been watching from his little box of a flat at the top of the building, could have come out on purpose just when he did to ask her to the museum, to "get closer" by intensifying their acquaintance. But surely he could have done that earlier than this evening, could have arranged to "run into" her quite naturally at any time in the past three days. That hardly seemed like the behavior of someone obsessed with her.

Of course, she had to admit to herself that her reaction to these two men tonight was instructive—or ought to be. When Andrew had appeared like a ghost in the parking lot, she'd almost instantly succumbed to his charm, agreed to go off to a museum with him without even asking him what his strange behavior of the past few days might mean. Yet when Adam Tate simply offered to carry her groceries, she'd almost panicked. What must the poor man think? If Andrew was "off the hook" for the scare she'd had at Kew, so was Tate, and on the same grounds.

She knew that if she could tell all of this to Jill Hendricks, her friend would say, "It's all in the pheromones. If you aren't picking up on the aura of those little suckers, it's 'no go,' no matter how nice the guy might be otherwise. But if you *are* picking up those vibes— ooh-la-la." How Beth wished she could talk to Jill, to all her good friends back home. She hadn't realized until this trouble in England how much she depended on exchanges with these women to guide her in coping with the world.

She heated up a can of soup, got out some crackers and a soda. At the table, she picked at the food, staring out the window at the sky, clear at last and studded with stars. It was almost impossible to believe that her family in Minnesota and her friends in Wisconsin could look up at these same stars; she felt so far away from them tonight, so alien in this land where she'd always imagined she would feel completely at home.

When the kitchen was tidied after her meager dinner, Beth went around and closed all the windows against the chill and put a few coins in the electric heater. Then she curled up on the sofa and began to "take stock," a phrase she used whenever her research had gone so fast that she'd begun to feel it was all just a jumble of disparate, unrelated bits and would never cohere into a rational whole. Sometimes, taking stock took days in the middle of a project, but the result was always worth it: With her thinking organized, she found the rest of the research easier and much more productive. Now she was taking stock of the whirl of events and feelings that had involved her since the day she'd found the door of this flat kicked in.

Five girls had been killed and she resembled them physically. Someone had been following her, but not to attack her, apparently, as these other victims had been attacked; she had the feeling that the person shadowing her was waiting for something, waiting for her to do something that he anticipated. A man had tried to steal her camera at Covent Garden, a man in a tan jacket. A man at Kew Gardens had run from her when she had appeared to recognize him, a man in a tan jacket. If these two men were, in fact, the same man, then there was a necessary connection to Cambridge and to this building because the noise she'd heard inside the canopy of the weeping beech tree was the same noise she'd heard in the hallway that night of Ramón's party; she was sure of that now. And this man could be the same man who had vandalized her flat. A man obsessed with keeping her almost always in sight had trailed her here in Cambridge and, perhaps, to London—twice. He wouldn't necessarily have to live in her building, of course—the lobby door was always open so anyone could have easy access. But living here would help him to know just when she was going in and out.

Only one detail didn't fit her mental picture of a stalker biding his time, keeping her in view without approaching her, hovering outside her door: It was the attempt to snatch her camera. Why would such a careful predator risk capture by trying to steal an ordinary camera? Unless—and now she sat straight up, her eyes narrowing in concentration. Unless the detail that didn't fit was, in fact, the key to the mystery. What if the camera was exactly what he was after, was exactly what he was waiting for her to leave unattended, vulnerable? But why? Why should her camera be a target? She remembered that Chief Superintendent Wilson had looked very interested when she'd first mentioned that a thief in London had tried to take her camera. She knew there were details the police held back from the public in an investigation; Constable Woods had said as much: "Developments I'm not at liberty to discuss." Could cameras have something to do with the Strangler case?

Now Beth actually stood straight up from the sofa as she remembered what her bedroom had looked like after the break-in: strips of ruined film festooning the rest of the jumble like bon voyage streamers. Suppose somebody thought she'd taken a picture that could incriminate him. What would he do? Destroy her films so they couldn't be developed. If he realized she might still have the film in her camera, he would follow her around and try to get the camera, or at least watch to see if she were going somewhere to have a film developed. That could be the connection she'd been looking for.

Beth began to pace now, racking her brains to remember. Had she taken her camera with her the day of the break-in? Yes, she remembered that it had been in her bag later when she'd taken out her notes. What could she have photographed without knowing she was photographing it? She'd been clicking away all over Cambridge for a month. At least two of the ruined films had been exclusively Cambridge pictures. And the film in her camera had Cambridge pictures and London pictures. But the two trips to London had come *after* the break-in, so whatever interested her stalker had to have been taken here in Cambridge before that, had to be one of the first ten or twelve exposures. Impossible now to remember what those pictures might be.

And, of course, this could mean that her troubles had nothing to do with the killings—her resemblance to the dead girls could be the *only* coincidence in all of this, a misleading coincidence that had obscured for her the other connections. She might have accidentally photographed a quite separate crime or criminal.

After another circuit of the room, she sat down again. Should she take this theory to the police at once? Just turn over the film to them? A quick glance at her watch revealed that it was almost ten-thirty. She had no idea what hours Scotland Yard detectives worked, didn't know whether she could persuade that station sergeant, or any replacement of his, to put her into contact with Wilson at this hour. There was Constable Woods, of course. She could just cross the Madingley Road to see if he was in his room or sitting in his car staking out her own building. But the thought of leaving the almost empty building to walk in the dark was very daunting. It could keep until morning, surely. She was locked safely inside and so was the film. Someone might be waiting to follow her again.

Almost as soon as she'd made the decision to wait, Beth began to have second thoughts about going to Woods or to Wilson with such a theory. If they took away the film and had it developed and there were only pictures of flowers and old people strolling across

Midsummer Common, wouldn't she look like an awful fool? She could almost hear Wilson saying, "It might be best, Miss Conroy, to leave detective work to the professionals."

But there was a way to prevent this from happening. She could have the film developed herself the next morning and look at the pictures. She'd invented some early errands to run in the city when she was trying to find a plausible excuse for not driving in with Andrew. Well, here was an errand she could run for real. If there was nothing on the film worth snatching a camera for, she was no worse off than before and no one would have a chance to snicker at her Sherlockian deductions. And if there was anything even faintly suspicious in any of the pictures, she could take it directly to Wilson in daylight hours. Yes, she told herself with a strong sense of satisfaction; that was the sensible way to proceed.

Chapter 23

"**O**, let me not be mad, not mad, sweet heaven!" That was Shakespeare. Lear, probably. King Lear was the one who went mad. Family problems. But he recovered, got better long enough to have his heart broken and then die. A curable madness, apparently, only to be done in by the larger madness—the whole world upside down, gone crazy and cruel, and the poor old blighter couldn't do a bloody thing about it. They kill you in the long run, find you out and do the one thing that will hurt you the most, murder your child, or lock you in a little room, or . . .

It was really cold tonight; even walking fast didn't help much to warm him up. And he was so tired, bone weary from almost sleepless nights, and that made the cold seem worse. But it wouldn't do to sleep too much. He had to watch most of the time because he couldn't tell when she might go out, when she would take that film out, perhaps have it developed. Only when he could see that her lights had gone out and she'd stayed inside, only then could he be sure that she'd gone to sleep. "Sleep that knits up the raveled sleeve of care." That was Shakespeare, too. He had read most of Shakespeare when he was at school, of course, and later he'd studied the major plays on his own. Shakespeare had a lot to say. But by the time she went to sleep, he was too wound up to rest, couldn't bear to go inside to the ratty furniture and the ugly wallpaper.

And he'd become too worried to watch just from his own place. She might still get out without his noticing. He'd had to find a place to watch the front door, the only door she could use. The vacated flat on the ground floor was perfect, of course, even though he could hardly bear to stay inside it. It hadn't been much of a problem to loosen one of the boards that sodding foreigner had nailed up there over the broken window. He took his Adidas bag with him whenever he went in there—just in case. But he had to be so careful because that snooping landlord seemed to be extra watchful lately. Then he could open the door of the flat just a crack—the lock would open on the inside—and see the whole lobby, the stairs, the front door. And he could feel safe, confident that she wouldn't get past him.

His teeth were hurting a lot lately, so that must mean he was grinding them more than usual. Well, what was the surprise in that? Elizabeth Conroy was driving him crazy with these trips to London. No, not crazy, not crazy. "Let me not be mad." Such an early start to the day! He'd had to wait until the last possible moment to buy his own ticket and had got on board just as the train was about to pull out.

Because he knew, of course, that someone else was following her now. Police, probably, and only the last few days. Idiots. Did they really think he was such a fool that he wouldn't notice the clumsy attempts to trap him? He'd seen the car, seen the man himself several times in the city. He could tell that Elizabeth didn't know about this fellow trailing around after her; he knew her so well by now that he would have noticed even a subtle change in her behavior. But what had made the police start shadowing her now? They hadn't done anything like this after she went into the police station that day—he'd followed her, of course, terrified that she'd developed the film, made the connection, and was taking the photo to the police, but nothing had come of it and so he'd concluded at the time that she was probably just inquiring about progress on the break-in.

When the two men had visited her flat the day after that wild party, he'd suspected they were police, though he knew she hadn't telephoned anyone—he'd watched the lobby pretty closely that night before deciding to go up to her door, and afterward, too, after he'd run out of the building. Shameful to remember that panic, best not to think about it. Maybe they had come about the break-in, had decided to shadow her because of something they had learned about that, or maybe they had some new ideas about the Swiss girl's death being connected to Elizabeth somehow. Any of these possibilities was frightening. And one thing was clear. If this new man became a problem, he would have to be eliminated. Just eliminated.

But this fellow was amateurish, not even very consistent; often he didn't stay with his quarry very long. This morning, at the station, he'd gone off as soon as Elizabeth got on the train. Stupid. But seeing him again tonight, seeing him here, that had been more than a bit disconcerting. It meant that he had to be so much more careful now, that he would have to get this feeling of desperation under control, not act impulsively. Think it out, plan, be sure. That was hard because sometimes, lately, he'd felt as if his brain was boiling, as if he couldn't stop himself from just jumping at her in broad daylight with people all around her. His arms sometimes hurt from clenching them against his sides, stopping himself.

And today had been such a fiasco! He'd thought it would be a good chance, the best chance in a long time. She would have her camera and there would be no one else watching her in London. But he'd ruined it himself. It was the jacket, the damned jacket! He'd worn the same jacket on that other trip to London when he'd made the grab for the camera at Covent Garden. The witnesses would have described the jacket; she might even have seen it herself at close range when she was struggling to raise her head. How could he have made such a stupid mistake? He ought to have burned the jacket, the way he did his other clothes when—when— Or thrown it away at least. It was just that he was getting so tired, so confused. There was so much to keep track of, so much to remember. He had stripped the jacket off right there in the gardens, just threw it down into the grass; he'd even kicked it two or three times, cursing while tears of rage rolled down his face, but cursing quietly, under his breath, because nobody must hear, nobody must see him.

Why hadn't he realized that trailing around after her, hoping for a chance to steal the camera, wasn't working? He'd only gone back to that strategy because he'd seen the other follower, the copper—if he was a copper. But it was only making him steadily more nervous and panicky. Besides, she was so jumpy and cautious now herself. Of course, that was because she knew that someone had been following her in Cambridge; he'd known that for some time now, hadn't he? But he'd hoped he could do it so cleverly that she would be lulled into complacency just long enough for him to strike.

But no. No more. Enough of this stupid attempt at a disguise; he'd always hated the wig anyway. He was proud of his own hair, thought it looked very nice, one of his best features. Whatever the risk from that stupid copper, he would have to approach her directly as he had tonight, keep trying to win her over. He could charm her, bring her to the point where she would trust him so much that he could get the film without arousing any of her suspicions. Once that photo was destroyed, he wouldn't even have to leave Cambridge. He'd hardly noticed blond girls in the past few weeks, hadn't felt those terrible things. So it *was* possible for all of that to go away, to leave him once and for all. He was sure of that now.

And he was sure he didn't want to have to kill Elizabeth Conroy. Walking along in the cold night, thinking about the whole day, he realized he wasn't angry with her; despite the panic and humiliation at Kew, he didn't blame her. In fact, the day had made him realize how easily he could love her, how much he wanted to protect her and take care of her. It didn't matter to him that she wasn't young the way he'd first imagined she was. It was better that she was older, in fact, because those traits that sometimes made him so angry at young girls were gone from her—she wasn't silly and flirtatious. She was a woman, serious and studious and very bright. He'd seen her close up, looked into her eyes, spoken to her, and he would have been able to tell if she were pretending, wouldn't he? Those lovely eyes were innocent, that smile was genuine. She could sound bossy, a little cold sometimes, he'd found out. But that was something she would get over when she felt softer toward him, when she found out she didn't have to "take over," that she had somebody to take care of her at last.

Of course, it would be a strain right now to have to talk to her again. The pretense was very difficult because he had to turn on the charm and at the same time remember the details of the identity he'd assumed; in fact he had to keep on making up details as he went along, create a character without a script. And he had to keep reminding himself of how he was supposed to sound; mustn't make a slip there, either. Of course, he was very well read, knew lots of things even if he didn't have degrees like she did, so that would help with the invention. And it would help that she wasn't British—he could claim things she wouldn't be able to contradict. It would get easier as he practiced, become sort of like second nature. He could *become* this persona, never have to go back to the other one, the one who had Father Dreadful in his life, the poor sod who had Hillary in his past.

"This is my wife, Elizabeth." He tried it out loud, under his breath, breath that was visible in the chilly night air. He liked the sound of that. They would have a home and children, very bright children. When he thought about them having children, he hurried very quickly in his mind over the business of how they would get the children. If he let himself think about that for very long, he started to have the other feelings, the bad feelings, and he didn't want to feel that way about Elizabeth. They would just have children. Then he would skip ahead in his mind to four- and six- and eight-year-old children with silky hair and big blue eyes.

And they would love their children, he and his nice wife, raise them right, the way the books taught. Never punish them for no reason, never break their hearts. When the old man died, they would have enough money to leave Britain, to travel and even live somewhere else. America, perhaps. "We've decided to live in America to be near my wife's family, as I have no family." Then she would never find out about him, about those girls. "Madness in the family." No, not anymore. It would die out. *Their* children wouldn't have the taint. If he could become this other person, the taint would be gone. If only he weren't so tired.

But Father Dreadful would have to die pretty soon, wouldn't he? No use trying to live on those paltry checks from the solicitors, not with children. Americans were accustomed to more luxuries, he supposed. And he wanted to give her a home. "My wife must have the best." Oh, how often he'd wished for the old man to die, prayed for him to die. But it had never worked, had it? Made you see early on what prayer was good for. Hillary had told him to pray when he was sad, and he'd laughed at her.

He'd told her once that he prayed for the old man to die, and she'd been shocked. That was when he was about twelve and Hillary was fifteen. "You mustn't be so bitter," she'd said in that haughty voice of hers. "It does no good to be bitter. Only poisons you and does him no harm. Besides, it hasn't *all* been so dreadful. He hasn't always been this bad." And that was true, of course, though he wouldn't tell her so, wouldn't give her the satisfaction of always being right.

He could remember the holidays in Falmouth, the walks along the water, his father singing in a rich baritone, singing against the wind that blew in from the channel. Hillary would skip ahead, poking into things the way she always did, always curious about every shell, every colored rock. But he couldn't keep up with his chubby little legs, and sometimes that big man would swoop down, laughing, and scoop him up, set him on his shoulders, and carry him along. When the old man sang then, he could feel the vibrations in his own body, in his baby hands that held onto the sides of his father's head. No, those were not bad times. But even in those days, the big face could suddenly darken into a scowl, the melody would change to a snarl without a warning. It was Hillary who could make him brighten in those days, who could distract him with her chatter, her bright little face already showing a trace of desperation.

But later, nothing could make much difference. The forced hilarity that went with drunkenness was more dangerous than the moody silences. Summoned into the room: "Come here, whelp! This is my son, my boy." The sweating hand resting on his shoulder. But later, when the others had gone, it was the deadly, hateful voice: "Sullen brat. Couldn't you speak to my friends? Shaming me on purpose. You'll have to pay for that one, little man." Pay, pay. Always something to pay. No way to predict what payment might be due for—never the same thing twice. Not Hillary. Hillary could do no wrong, most of the time, was encouraged, as a matter of fact, to join in with Father Dreadful in the game of mocking the "little whelp." And she *did* sometimes, while the old man was in the room. When he went away, she would say, "Don't mind it, Floppy"—Floppy was her own pet name for him because, she said, he had been so clumsy as a little boy—"I only do it so he'll do less of it. You see, he went right away when I started to tease you."

On her sixteenth birthday, she'd come in to dinner wearing jeans, something she'd bought secretly with some of her own money. Neither of them ever had much pocket money and they almost never shopped by themselves. Father Dreadful had by this time wholly taken over the selection of everything that came into "his" house—choice was something they were never to aspire to, apparently. He had been especially obsessed of late with selecting Hillary's clothes, buying her dresses and shoes and skirts until she had so many she could scarcely hope to wear them all. They never went anywhere socially, so she had to wear them only at home; her school, like his, had uniforms. The dresses were elaborate affairs with diaphanous skirts and ruffled bodices—not the sort of thing one saw young girls wearing. When she came in wearing the jeans, she just went to her chair and sat down, without even a glance at the old man. But Father Dreadful had gone suddenly pale, risen from his chair as if pulled upright by invisible wires. Then he crossed the room, raised his hand, and knocked Hillary out of her chair. Not one word, not one warning. Then he walked out of the room.

"Isn't this enough for you?" he'd asked after his father had closed the door. He had run to her, was crouching next to her. "Now are you ready to go away? I'm ready anytime. I've only been waiting for you to see that it's no bloody use hanging around here. He's worse and worse every day."

"Don't say 'bloody,' " she said, sitting up on the carpet and holding the side of her face where a red mark like a stain was spreading over her white skin. "And don't be so daft, talking about going away. You're thirteen and I'm just sixteen. What would we do on our own? Where could we go?"

"I don't care," he said passionately; he was crying by now. "Anywhere would be better than this. He's a brute. Even to you now, don't you see? It isn't for me that I'm saying it."

"It's no good talking like that," she said, struggling to her feet. "I can handle him. I'll be all right. You'll see." And that was all. She'd gone back to wearing the dresses and he never saw the jeans again. Probably she'd put them in the dustbin.

He shouldn't be thinking about this, shouldn't be remembering. It wasn't good for him. He had put this into the past, had closed the door on it. The doctors had told him to forget and go on, the same doctors who'd told him the name of Father Dreadful's sickness. "Put it behind you," one of them had said. "There's no need for you to blight your whole life because of what he is, because of what he's done. Don't dwell on it." Dwell on it; dwell meant "live in," didn't it? Don't live in this. How to manage that when his whole life had been inside this? But he *had* tried to follow the doctor's advice. It was just that he was so tired tonight. It took such energy not to remember.

He'd been so tired that other night, too, but he couldn't sleep then either, couldn't close his eyes in the dark. Three hours in the pantry, from two-fifteen to five-fifteen—he'd looked at the clock before he'd been pushed inside. Three hours for leaving a library book outside where the rain had ruined it. "Who has to pay for this now? It's money out of my pocket, Mister Careless, not yours." As if it were really about the money. At thirteen, you're not supposed to cry, to whimper like a baby, but he'd finally started to cry, out loud, to wail against the dark and the crushing walls. Then he'd heard the voice, calm, rational sounding: "Very well, Hillary. Since you ask so nicely, I'll open the door." And the light had come pouring in, hurting his eyes. But he couldn't get to sleep at night, had crept down the hall and up the stairs to Hillary's room. He could wake her up, talk to her, listen to her tell him not to be daft, and that would make it all right.

There was enough light in the hall so that he could see what was going on in Hillary's bed when he opened the door. The old man let out a roar when he saw the light—not words, just a bellow of rage, inarticulate, animal. Hillary sprang up, leaped straight from the bed and stood there, perfectly naked, her white body glimmering, seeming to gather all the light to itself.

"Get out!" she screamed. "You little sneak! Get out of this room."

And he had stumbled backward, not able to turn around until he'd reached the stairs. Halfway down the steps, he'd fallen, rolled down the rest of the way, banging his arms and legs against the carpeted treads. For a long time he lay on the bottom of the stairs, not moving. Then he pulled himself up and limped to his own bedroom.

She came in later, wrapped up to her chin in her blue bathrobe, and just stood next to his bed for a few minutes without speaking. He curled himself into a ball, refused to look up at her.

"It's not what I want," she said at last. "It's been going on for about a year now and I don't know how to make it stop."

He had leaped up from the bed, flung himself to the other side of the room, and turned back toward her.

"You liar!" he screamed at her. "I begged you to go away. I would have taken care of you. But you wouldn't. You want to stay with him."

"I'm afraid of him," she said quietly. "Can't you see I'm afraid of him?"

"Liar! Bitch! Whore!" He hardly knew what the words meant, only knew from the other boys at school that they were bad things to call a girl, that they had something to do with sex.

"Don't say those things to me, Floppy," she said miserably, tears on her face. "I can't help it. I don't know what to do."

"You want it," he raged. "You want this house, and nice frocks, and your bloody flower garden. And you want him to do that to you."

"Don't you dare to speak to me in that way," she cried, and now she was imperious, haughty Hillary, her rope of hair swinging as she turned. "You're a stupid little boy and you don't understand anything." And she'd run out of the room, her bare feet flashing white under the dark robe.

No sleep at all; hours of the night dragging by. Then morning light streaking gradually across the ceiling—mustn't remember, mustn't think about it. Let me not be mad. Oh, God, let me not be mad. Walk faster, think about something else, look at the stars, how many there are, how bright. Those stars are suns somewhere else, because the sun is a star, a star that's close to the earth so its light fills the sky.

The light—it was a very bright morning that morning, light flooding into the kitchen when he'd finally gone in there. The old man was sitting at the table, dressed only in his smalls, unusual for him because he ordinarily dressed so early.

"Find your sister and tell her to come in here for breakfast," the old man had said, his voice tense. Determined to pretend nothing had happened. "She's not in her room."

So he'd gone to look. No point resisting. No use saying, "Find her yourself, you terrible brute!" For that would only mean more "paying." Might as well take care of himself. Nothing else was worth taking care of. Nothing in all the world was worth getting the pantry for. She wasn't in the garden or anywhere else downstairs. She wasn't upstairs either. At last he remembered that she sometimes took refuge in the attic where all her old things were kept, her dolls and elaborate dolls' house. So he opened the door and climbed the narrow, steep stairs.

He saw her feet first, the white feet below the blue robe, the fine, shapely toes pointed toward the floor. He lifted his face into the light streaming through the narrow dormer window at the other end of the attic. She'd used the cord from the robe, strung it over a crossbeam at the peak of the house, had tipped over a chair that once stood in the corner of the nursery, when it was a nursery. Without the cord, the robe had gapped open revealing a narrow band of her white body: lower legs, the line where her thighs pressed together, the golden red pubic hair, the soft mound of stomach, the dimple at the waist, the line that swept between her small breasts up to her throat. Her head was tipped to the right, hair hanging over one cheek, the face looking straight down at him, eyes bulging out, accusing, accusing, blaming . . .

He had fallen onto the stairs, first onto his knees, and then onto his face, his mind swooning into unconsciousness. It wasn't sleep, not healing like sleep, but it was oblivion, blessed oblivion.

Chapter 24

When Beth left the building the next morning at eight-fifteen, she saw Mr. Chatterjee putting a suitcase into the trunk of his car.

"Good morning, Miss Conroy," he said with his dazzling smile. "You're off so early. So are we, of course, as you can see. We are to spend a few days with my wife's family in London. Is there anything you need before we take our leave?"

"No, thank you, Mr. Chatterjee," Beth answered. "Have a nice time."

"When one goes to relatives, Missy, a 'nice time' is not always the issue," he said ruefully.

"Well, good luck anyway," Beth said with a laugh as she began to unlock the chain on her bicycle. "You'll have a nice day for a drive in any case."

"Yes, the sun has apparently made its mind up to stay with us," he said, closing the trunk with a smart little click. "I hope your day is a good one, too."

Beth draped her bag over the handlebars and swung up onto the seat. Chief Superintendent Michael Wilson's card was in the bag. The film was in the pocket of her shirt, the pocket with the flap that buttoned. She'd carefully rewound the film and popped it out of the camera this morning, had lingered only long enough for a cup of coffee after she'd found in the hall phone book the address of a While-U-Wait photo developer—a shop that opened at eight o'clock: "Get those pics before you go to work" the ad in the yellow pages had said. As she approached the end of the drive, she suddenly wondered if she should just cross the road to Constable Woods's rooming house to let him know she was going into the city earlier than usual. But he'd told her that she was supposed to go about her normal routine; "business in the usual way," he'd said. And she wasn't sure she wanted to explain why she was going into the city so early. Not yet, at least.

It was a gorgeous Tuesday morning, sunny as the day before, but warmer, balmy and calm. Beth whizzed past the fields of the Veterinary School with their grazing flocks, past Churchill's. The sign at Churchill's reminded her of Andrew Carmichael, and it occurred to her that she hadn't heard him come in last night—dinner with old cronies must have turned into a late-night party. Of course, she had fallen asleep before midnight, exhausted from her crazy day in London, and had probably slept so soundly that she wouldn't have noticed *what* time her neighbors came home—Andrew Carmichael and Adam Tate had *both* been out last night, she reminded herself. Had Constable Woods already arranged for a check to be made on Adam Tate, she wondered, feeling obscurely guilty for having sicced the police on to a man who might be an inoffensive astronomer from Leeds. And if the police began on Tate, would they also begin on Andrew, the other new tenant? Well, it couldn't be helped. Every man *had* to be a suspect when such a terrible series of events swept around them. She hoped fervently, though, that Andrew Carmichael really was a vacationing lawyer from Birmingham.

Cambridge seemed not quite awake yet as she biked past the closed shops, along nearly empty streets, to the yellow-and-black awning of the While-U-Wait photo booth. The portly, middle-aged man who took the film from her said, "Be about forty-five minutes, Miss. You're the first of the day." Beth biked back to the Market Square and sat on the steps of Great St. Mary's Church to watch the market stalls being set up, an experience few tourists would think of as something worth seeing, but it was fascinating anyway to have stumbled across it by accident. Emptied of the merchants, the market stalls looked tawdry, squalid, almost as if this block were a bombed-out segment of the city no one had ever bothered to rebuild. The stalls were no more than wooden sheds without roofs, packed so closely together that only small paths wandered between the rows. Merchants simply took away their wares at night and rolled up awnings they had used as temporary roofs during the day.

Now Beth was watching the reverse of this process. Lorries pulled up and people, often whole families, began scurrying around, carrying boxes, pushing racks of cotton blouses imported from India, hanging necklaces from cleverly designed wooden "trees." Men and women worked together to unroll and put in place the brightly colored, striped awnings that formed the roofs of the stalls and were the hallmark of this particular open-air market. In the forty minutes Beth sat watching, the market came to life and the first customers began wandering among the stalls, fingering scarves, discussing the price of silver bracelets, holding Cambridge sweatshirts against their chests for size.

When Beth got back to the photo booth, the proprietor announced that it would be "just a tick now" and she had to pace up and down for another five minutes before she could claim her pictures. "Only thirty pics there, Miss," the fat man said as he handed over the envelope. "You could have taken six more, you know." Beth assured him that she *did* know, paid him the shockingly high fee for his speed, and climbed back onto her bicycle. She knew Auntie's didn't open until a little later in the morning, so she headed straight for King's Parade and the Copper Kettle, a café that did a brisk breakfast business among undergraduates beginning their daily rigors. Over a pot of tea and two big scones, Beth opened the envelope and took out the stack of high-gloss colored pictures.

She went through the photographs slowly, studying each one carefully: the gardens of Clare College, people engaged in lawn bowling on Christ's Pieces, young men punting on the Cam below King's Bridge, the University's Botanic Gardens, and, of course, pictures from her two recent trips to London—the Tower of London, buskers at Covent Garden, rhododendrons at Kew. Nothing in any of the pictures struck her as suspicious in the least. But she was reluctant to give up her theory so easily. She sat thinking for a moment, chewing on a scone, sipping at the sweet, milky tea. If someone was afraid she had an incriminating picture, could it mean that *he* might be in the picture, in a place or at a time that would be damaging if the police knew about it? Possibly, possibly.

So she began to sort the pictures into stacks on the table in front of her. One stack was for those pictures taken since her break-in, pictures she felt she could eliminate because the feared one must have been taken before that. One stack was for pictures that had no human beings in them, just buildings, or flowers, or animals—she hesitated here over the close-up of the squirrel reaching for popcorn from the leathery old hand offering it to him; she smiled at the memory. Surely no kindly old lady had kicked in the door of her flat or had been shadowing her across two major cities. She dropped the squirrel's picture on top of a picture of ducks sailing across a pond in the rock garden.

The last stack was reserved for pictures featuring people somewhere in the frame—a stack with only six pictures in it. Over the second cup of tea, she studied each one, tilting the photos to get the best light. Soon she began to believe that this project was hopeless. In the six pictures, she counted twenty-four people, people of all ages, in all manner of costume, engaging in many varieties of innocuous-seeming activities. Could one of the people standing around watching the bowlers on Christ's Pieces be a suspicious character? Was one of those young men on the punt in the wrong place at the wrong time? Did the man in the nice suit, who happened to be standing next to the pink-haired punk Beth had *meant* to photograph, fear exposure if it were known that he had been in Market Square on that particular day? She looked intently at every man in the pictures, hunting for that elusive impression of familiarity in build, stance, shape of head —the impression she'd had in the water-lily house at Kew when she'd spotted the man in the tan jacket. But there was no echo of it in these photos. Hopeless, hopeless.

Beth sat back, poking with her knife at the last crumbs of her scones. Could she have been wrong about the motives of her persecutor? Last night, in her flat, it had all made such clear sense. But surely no one would risk exposure and jail over anything in these six pictures. What could be learned from these photos that could frighten someone into breaking and entering, into stalking a woman for almost two weeks? An American woman who would take these pictures across the Atlantic and never connect any of these strangers with anything dangerous or incriminating? Wrong; she had been stupidly wrong, and it made her very angry. She gathered all of the pictures into one stack again, the "people" pictures on the bottom, and was about to stuff the whole lot into the envelope when it occurred to her that she hadn't really looked at her photographs as the interested tourist who had taken them—simply to enjoy the memories evoked by each of them.

So she resolutely splashed the last of her tea into the cup and started through the stack of photos again. This time she paused long enough over the picture of the ducks in the rock garden to realize that she had originally put it into the wrong stack. For there *was* a human subject in this picture. At the upper right edge, in the background beyond the pond, was a crouching figure. Beth turned the picture into the light. It was a woman, a girl really by the look of her figure and the blond hair falling forward over her shoulders. Her skirt was a bright yellow, and there was a white sweater draped over her shoulders. Her bare arms made the shape of a W with the elbows at her knees and the hands raised to hold a camera which blotted out the face. Suddenly Beth remembered, could almost feel again the warmth of the sun on her own neck as she was taking this picture, recalled the thought that had passed through her mind: "There's someone taking a picture of me taking a picture of her taking a picture. . . ." It was just as she was thinking that thought that she had swung her camera left to focus on the family of ducks, far enough left to banish this crouching girl to the very edge of the frame. There was nothing else in the picture. Nothing at all.

Beth sat back in her chair, tapping the photo against the point of her chin. What day had she gone to the Botanic Gardens? Why did the memory of the sun's warmth on that day seem to connect with something else in her mind? It had been so chilly and wet in the days after that visit to the gardens, and the damp chill was now firmly associated in her mind with fear, with menace. Could it be that the warm, sunny day had been the last time she felt comfortable and happy in England? No, that wasn't possible. It had been a whole week after that warm day when her apartment had been broken into; surely she had been confident, had felt safe, in that intervening time. Maybe it was just that she was exaggerating in her own mind the length of time she'd felt afraid. She couldn't trust her own memory anymore.

Beth swept the pictures together in an angry gesture. She was fed up, sick to death of feeling scared and threatened, of having every effort to solve the mystery of "why" turn out to be inconclusive. Perhaps, she thought, she just didn't have enough information to make sense of what was in the pictures. Maybe the police might know why photos of punters and bowlers would interest a stalker, or why the Market Square or the Botanic Gardens on a particular day would incriminate someone photographed there. Of course, she realized with a sigh, there might be nothing to her theory at all.

But she was sure of one thing: She was tired of trying to figure it out on her own. No matter what anyone else might think of her and her fears, she was going to turn over all of these photographs to the police and let them handle it. If they laughed, so be it. A glance at her watch revealed that it was already after ten o'clock and she'd agreed to meet Andrew Carmichael at ten-thirty. Well, she could at least *phone* the police before that and make an appointment. She tucked the pictures into a side pocket of her book bag, paid for her breakfast, and went out to her bicycle with a firm stride.

At the first phone box she saw, Beth brought her bicycle to a stop, fished out Wilson's card, and dialed carefully. She dropped the coins into the slot as soon as she heard the voice answer the phone at the other end.

"This is Beth Conroy," she said. "May I please speak with Chief Superintendent Wilson? He said I could reach him at this number."

"Chief Superintendent Wilson isn't here at the moment," the voice responded. "We expect him this afternoon. What is the nature of your business with him?"

"I may have some information that would interest him," she said. "It's about my break-in. He's already talked to me about it. Last week." She had begun to feel foolish as she said this; it sounded like a piece of melodrama when she said it out loud to a strange voice on the phone.

There was a pause now, and when the voice spoke again, it was much more interested.

"Can I give you to Station Sergeant Evans? Perhaps you could pass your information through him."

Beth pictured the sharp-featured Evans, the man who had found her so unconvincing the day she'd gone to police headquarters.

"No," she said hastily. "I'd rather speak to Superintendent Wilson. I'll come in this afternoon if he'll be in then."

"Well, all right then. He'll be here about two."

"I'll be there," she said and hung up.

Another glance at her watch showed that she just had time to bicycle to the Fitzwilliam Museum to keep her appointment with Andrew Carmichael. A two-hour tour of the museum, a bit of lunch somewhere, an "excuse me, please," and then the police station. All in public places. All in broad daylight. All quite safe.

Chapter 25

Chief Superintendent Michael
Wilson had spent part of his Tuesday morning
checking out a lead. A technician at a photo lab near the post office
had phoned the station saying he'd just heard from one of his customers, a photo developer, that the police were looking for anyone
who remembered processing a film with pictures from the Botanic
Gardens. Were they interested also in enlargements made from such
a film? Especially if the man requesting the enlargement was "pecul-

iar"? There was so little else to work on that Wilson had decided to follow up personally.

On the way to the lab, Sergeant Timmings drove too fast, as usual, but Wilson was too tired to protest. It had been one hell of a week for him, and he was not sleeping well. Worrying. More than three weeks now since the Keller girl had been killed. That could only mean that the killer was exercising extraordinary restraint, and therefore becoming more volatile at every moment. The psychiatric consultants had told him that control would be increasingly more of a strain for this type of criminal, that his capacity to appear "normal"—a great asset for such a predator—would be eroded as the strain grew. In the past, the talent for careful planning, the almost weirdly rational intelligence of the killer, had protected him from capture. But now he must be losing his grip, must be very near to an explosion of some sort.

One side of Wilson's mind hoped the explosion would come very soon because it would end the case decisively; the poor sod would make a bad mistake and give himself away. But Wilson realized, of course, what the cost of such an explosion could be—violence of that kind could claim several victims in one day—and that price was too high. The trained policeman knew that the ideal situation for his purposes was one of crime prevention; to close in on and capture this killer *before* an explosion could occur. That, of course, was more difficult than merely waiting for the violence and then reacting to it. More difficult, but the real heart of his job.

Yesterday, a police sketch artist had arrived from London and had spent the afternoon with Mr. Caldwell, the cranky old landlord who was beginning to take on a decided air of self-importance over his role in this investigation. It had taken three hours before the old man was finally satisfied. "I suppose that's the best we can hope for," he'd said, eyeing the artist as if he were certain that this person from London was deliberately trying to impede the capture of the Cambridgeshire Strangler by producing a faulty likeness. By nightfall, the copying machine had produced hundreds of pictures, and every constable assigned to surveillance in Cambridge was armed with a likeness of the Cambridgeshire Strangler.

Wilson's own copy was folded inside his breast pocket. Timmings brought the car to a jerking halt, double-parked on St. Andrew's Street, where his police sticker would save them from getting a parking ticket.

"There it is, sir," Timmings said, pointing at the building and applying the hand brake.

"I can see, Sergeant," Wilson growled, hoisting himself out of the car. "You wait here and move the blasted car if it seems to be blocking traffic."

The young lab technician inside looked a bit frightened at having to deal with Scotland Yard.

"Like I was saying to the constable on the phone," he said, scratching his chest in a self-conscious gesture, "I don't normally pay no attention to what's on the photos I'm enlarging. Some people take pictures of very strange things, too, I can tell you. It would surprise you the things people get up to in front of a camera sometimes. No shame."

"Yes, yes," Wilson said impatiently. "But you *did* remember this particular photo for some reason?"

"Not the photo so much, but the bloke who brought it in," the young man said, looking a little like a scolded child.

"When did he bring it in?" Wilson said more kindly.

"Well, I don't remember exactly when. But it was about a fort-night ago, perhaps more. I didn't find out until the weekend that you were interested in an unfinished film with pictures of the gardens on it. The strip of negatives this bloke gave me had only the one photo on it, at the beginning, the one he wanted enlarged; the rest were blank, never exposed."

"Why did you tell the station sergeant that the chap who wanted the enlargement was 'peculiar'?" Wilson asked, leaning against the counter.

"Well, for starters, he gave me twenty-five quid to do the job on the spot. Couldn't even wait one day. Says it's a present for his sister and he's got to have it right off. But nobody's ever paid such a sum for a hurry-up job before. Seems a bit much just for your sister's birthday, don't it?"

"Was he behaving peculiarly?"

"He was nervous as a cat. Jumpy. Trying to seem casual, but

desperate like, underneath. I don't know what he might have done if I'd refused him."

Wilson pulled the sketch from his pocket and unfolded it carefully.

"Could this be the man?" he said, placing the paper on the counter.

The technician examined the sketch for just a moment, his thick brows lifting in surprise.

"Why, yes," he exclaimed. "It looks a great deal like him, the hair especially. Perhaps the eyes are closer together than they should be, but it definitely looks like the bloke. What do you want him for?"

"Never mind," Wilson said, folding up the sketch. "Try to tell me as much as you can remember about the photo itself. What was in it?"

"It was taken in the rock garden. I've been there lots of times myself, so I recognized it. Some lovely flowers, one of the ponds. And ducks. There were ducks—babies, you know—in the middle of the photo. Quite a pretty picture, actually."

"But people," Wilson interrupted. "Any people in the picture?"

The young man furrowed his heavy brows.

"Not that I remember," he said at last. "I wasn't looking at the details, mind. But no, I don't remember any people."

"Thank you for your help," Wilson sighed and headed for the door.

Back at the car, he said wearily to Timmings, "I think it's our boy, but I can't for the life of me tell why he'd have one of Greta Keller's pictures blown up. In a hurry about it, too, as if it were important to him."

Timmings threw the car into gear and lurched out into traffic again.

"A call came in on the radio while you were inside, sir," the young sergeant said as he maneuvered around a slow-moving lorry. "By an odd coincidence, it's something about photos, as well. Evans thought we might like to check on it while we're out."

"Well?" Wilson said impatiently. "Don't always postpone the point like that. What about photos?"

Timmings smiled slightly before speaking.

"A film developer over on Petty Cury Street," he said. "He remembered we were interested in unfinished films and says he got one first thing this morning from a woman. Pictures of Cambridge and London, some pictures of gardens. And there were six unexposed frames left on the film."

"Irrelevant, I'm afraid," Wilson sighed. "We know now when Greta Keller's film was developed. Right after her death, just as we suspected. And we even know that her killer had one of her photos enlarged for some reason. But unfortunately it doesn't help us to discover where he is now or why he's so interested in one photo."

"Where to now, then?" Timmings asked.

"Back to the station," Wilson said shortly, staring out the window. "We can see if there are any messages. Something to go on. And do try to get us back to headquarters in one piece," he added as the car rocketed around a corner. "And without running down any of the good citizens of Cambridge."

"Yes, sir," Timmings said in his cheerful voice and without turning his head.

Wilson only stared out into the bright sunshine of Cambridge, his forehead pulled into a worried frown.

Chapter 26

Beth could spot Andrew Carmichael from several hundred feet away as she biked along Trumpington Street toward the museum. He was leaning up against one of the forward-thrusting platforms that flanked the staircase of the Fitzwilliam. Each platform was topped by a pair of reclining stone lions, individualized lions, one with both front paws outstretched, one with a paw curled under in that universal feline gesture of casual composure; the facade of the museum was a dramatic, almost baroque, nineteenth-century imitation of a classical temple. As Beth signaled right and watched for an opening in the traffic, she could see Andrew noticing her, standing upright, and buttoning his coat.

When she reached his side, she couldn't fail to notice how "dressed up" he was: a navy-blue double-breasted suit, a pale-blue shirt, a modest narrow tie. Had he done this for her? she wondered, feeling embarrassed that her preoccupation with films and photographs had made her rather careless about her own appearance that morning. She was wearing blue, pleated slacks, her print "big shirt" with the big front pockets, flat sandals that suddenly made her feel very short next to Andrew. He smiled his greeting, taking her bicycle from her hands and wheeling it to a rack for her. She realized that she was seeing him in daylight for the first time. His hair, which she'd formerly thought of only as "dark," was actually a lovely shade of chestnut brown, wiry hair that conformed closely to the shape of his handsome head. In the sunlight, the dark edges of his pale irises looked almost lavender. His wide smile showed to advantage his strong, irregular teeth. Beth felt a little weak in the knees standing so near to this very attractive man.

"Are you ready to be dazzled?" he said, the smile broadening even more.

"Lead on," she answered, swinging her bag up onto her shoulder and trying not to show how dazzled she already was.

Beth was surprised to discover how much she could enjoy displays of medieval armor and drawings of old masters with a guide as knowledgeable and interested as Andrew Carmichael to show them to her. He knew what each part of the armor was for, how much it weighed, how soldiers got onto their horses while wearing the armor. He explained how the horse armor—there were full-scale models of horses wearing armor of their own—was designed to prevent the worst disaster for a cavalry soldier: having his horse killed under him. Whenever Andrew wanted to direct her attention to a detail, he would touch her shoulder lightly, or her wrist, before pointing—a diffident, but somehow intimate gesture that Beth enjoyed immensely. Sometimes she would actually feign distraction so he would have to touch her to bring her attention back to what he was describing.

In the displays of ceramics and porcelain, Beth found many opportunities to return the gesture because here she was the "expert." He went along enthusiastically, smiling with real interest when she explained that the eighteenth-century Chinese *famille rose* dishes were intended as gifts and that their patterns symbolized the blessings that the donor wished to bestow.

"What a lovely idea," he exclaimed. "Sort of 'my family to your family,' eh?"

When they'd finished wandering through the exhibits of illuminated manuscripts, Beth discovered that it was already almost one-thirty. Seldom had three hours flown by so fast.

"We could do with a spot of lunch, don't you think?" Andrew said as he noticed her glancing at her watch.

"Well, it's about that time, I guess," she said with a laugh. "I think we're about museumed out for today anyway, don't you?"

"There's a great deal more to see," he smiled, "but not all in one day, I agree. Shall we have a pub lunch? You've had a British pub lunch already, I hope."

"Oh, yes. Once in London when I first got here and then once here in Cambridge at the old Fort St. George on Midsummer Common. But that's quite a hike from here."

"I know," he answered. "But I hoped I could introduce you to the Eagle, if you've never been. It's very old, very historic, and the food's not bad. We can easily walk there. It's just up the road on Bene't Street."

"Well, I suppose it's my duty as an avid tourist to be introduced to historic pubs," she said with her girlish laugh. "Don't you have your car?"

"Yes, but I left it in a car park at the edge of the city," he explained. "It's such a nuisance finding a place to park. Besides, I enjoy walking. I walk a lot."

When they left the Fitzwilliam and collected Beth's bike, Andrew took it once again and assumed without comment the task of pushing it as they walked along together. It occurred to her for the first time that day that her feeling of fear had left her almost as soon as she was with Andrew Carmichael; his very presence made her feel safe.

They had to wait a long time to cross Trumpington Street. As the crowd made conversation awkward, Beth used the opportunity to glance around. In the throng behind her, she made out a cap of brown curls and then, when some people shifted position, the freckled, snubby nose and wide-spaced hazel eyes of Constable Timothy Woods. So, she thought, he's caught up with me. Or maybe he'd been around all along, shadowing her from a distance ever since she'd left the flat.

She turned her eyes back front again, trying to assess her own feelings about having a "police escort." On the one hand, she felt relieved, of course. She was now doubly protected. If anyone should try to menace her, she would find protection only a scream away. But on the other hand, she found herself rather resenting having a chaperon on this outing with Andrew Carmichael. She was finding it harder by the moment to regard Andrew as a "suspicious character," and she felt it was absurd and very awkward to be spied on by the police as she was trying to intensify her relationship with a handsome, eligible man. And it would not do at all to have Andrew notice Constable Woods. He would remember him as the "helpful young man" who'd supposedly carried her groceries from the bus stop the night before and wonder exceedingly why this same young man should be hovering around them now in the city. "Please stay inconspicuous," Beth thought, feeling dubious about the surveillance skills of this earnest young policeman. "And don't screw up this date." A gap in the traffic finally allowed them to cross.

Just after Trumpington Street became King's Parade, they found Bene't Street leading off to the right and, shortly after the turn, a little cul de sac that held the Eagle Inn, a squat, whitewashed structure in the shape of an L sporting crude wooden tables and benches on the cobblestones of its courtyard. Beth was struck again, as she often had been before in the presence of old domestic buildings in England, by the scale—everything was small, even the doors, leading her to the realization that medieval people must have been considerably less imposing in stature than their modern counterparts. Inside, Beth chose a salad, a small sandwich, and a Scotch egg from the open buffet and then followed Andrew into the bar section to ask for a half pint of ale before emerging again into the courtyard to enjoy lunch in the sunshine.

"You know," Andrew said, spreading out his own lunch on the

table. "Crick and Watson used to haunt this place back in the fifties. They were hanging about all the time, the locals say."

Beth stared at him, uncomprehending.

"Crick and Watson?" she asked blankly.

He threw back his fine head and laughed, the first time she'd heard a full laugh from him; most of the time, he seemed more wry than hilarious in his style of mirth.

"I keep forgetting that science is not your street," he said at last. "I went to Trinity, which is fearfully proud of its Nobel Laureates in science. Has produced flocks of them, something near twenty, I think. Crick and Watson are the chaps who discovered the structure of DNA."

"I thought Trinity was famous for its poets," Beth countered, smiling in spite of feeling one-upped. "Didn't Byron go there?"

"Oh, yes," he said. "And Tennyson, too. Trinity is famous for many things. Its graduates are all outstanding blokes." And he smiled his wonderful smile again.

"Present company included?" she asked.

"Of course," he answered, and he looked deep into her eyes as he said it.

Beth knew she was blushing, took a big gulp of ale to cover her embarrassment.

"What made you take up the law?" she asked finally when she felt a little calmer.

"Oh, I don't know," he said and now he looked a little embarrassed. "A youthful passion to help the downtrodden, I suppose. Like most youthful passions, that came up against hard reality eventually. Solicitors seldom find themselves saving innocent pensioners from the gallows. Divorces and petty suits, much more often."

He seemed reluctant to talk directly about himself, had been looking past her as he spoke, in the direction of the cul de sac's opening which he was facing and toward which she had her back. From his angle, he could see the street. Suddenly, he sat up straight, frowning, the fine gray eyes losing their vague expression and focusing sharply.

"What is it?" Beth said, turning to follow his glance. The street outside was thronging with people.

"Nothing," he murmured. "I just thought I recognized someone over there."

Oh, God, Beth thought; he's seen Woods. Confound that bumbling lout!

"Really?" she said, picking at her salad. "One of your local friends?"

"No, no," he answered. Then after a pause, "I thought it was that fellow in our building, the one on your floor."

"Adam Tate?" she asked, incredulous herself, but relieved that Woods hadn't shown himself.

"Is that his name?" He looked more interested than the occasion would seem to call for. "Dark chap, looks foreign."

"That's the one," Beth said, thinking it odd, indeed, that almost everyone she knew personally in Cambridge should be in such close proximity to her at this moment. Would Wilson pop through the door of the pub the next second? Or the red-haired undergraduate? Thinking of Wilson made her remember the pictures and she glanced down at her watch. It was already after two o'clock.

"Coincidence," Andrew said, his eyes going vague again. "Seeing him here, I mean."

For the rest of the lunch, Beth debated with herself whether she should tell Andrew of her suspicions about Adam Tate, should just tell him that the police were protecting her. It would uncomplicate things, certainly; he would understand that she would have to leave now and go to police headquarters with the photographs. But she harbored some lingering doubts about this handsome stranger—and he *was* a stranger, she reminded herself. In the movies, people were always telling vital secrets to precisely the wrong person and therefore putting themselves in danger. Silence was safest. Except to the police, of course.

"I'm really going to have to leave," Beth said at last. "I've got some other errands to run."

"Oh, don't rush off," he said, looking sincerely disappointed. "I thought you were coming in this morning to run your errands. I'd hoped to show you Trinity College this afternoon. Have you been to the Wren Library?"

"Not yet," she admitted. "I could get a special permit as a visiting scholar, I suppose, but I thought I'd just wait until June when the colleges are all open to visitors again. I've been looking forward to seeing it, of course."

"Oh, do let me take you," he said, flashing his winning smile. "As an old boy, I can get us in easily. How can you pass up the chance at having such an expert guide. I'll show you the exact spot where I once was very sick after drinking too much sherry."

"How can I say no to that?" she laughed, thinking that a few hours could hardly make much difference in discovering what, if anything, the police might be able to make of her photographs.

Trinity was all that Beth had imagined it to be when she'd read about it, all that Andrew had promised. When they arrived, Andrew had convinced the gatekeeper to let them in with no other evidence than his charm that he was a graduate of the college. Beth was impressed, as usual. Christopher Wren's beautifully designed library with its spectacular windows and beautifully carved bookcases; the impressive proportions of Thomas Nevile's Great Court; the towering, double hammer-beam ceiling of the dining hall, whose carved screen sported a more-than-life-sized portrait of Henry VIII, the college's founder—all had more resonance, more meaning, with Andrew Carmichael at her side. When the tour was over, she and her guide took a rest along the long promenade, sitting up on the ledge of the wall that faced the river. They were in cool, stony shade, looking out toward the sunny riverbank; the laughing voices of passing punters drifted into the centuries-old quiet of the great square.

"Have you missed your home while you've been here?" Andrew said after a pause.

"A little, I suppose," she answered, pulling her legs up under herself. "I've sometimes had the odd feeling that I'm forgetting who I am. Maybe it's that we get so much of our definition of self from what our closest associates expect us to be—it's as if they and their expectations are mirrors where we can check ourselves from time to time. That's the good girl, good student, that my parents expect me to be. That's the 'little pest' my brother still sees in me. And that's the straitlaced professor my students expect me to be. And so that's how I define myself *to* myself. But here, there are no mirrors, so I feel a bit confused about my own identity. Does that make any sense?" She felt amazed that she was confiding this deep feeling to him.

"I think I know what you mean," he said, his strong profile shadowed by the stone arch next to him. "When I travel a lot, I sometimes feel quite different from the person I am at home. But, you know, that can be a very liberating feeling—to become somebody else." Now he turned to look at her, though she couldn't see his eyes very clearly. "Sometimes the expectations of others can define us in very limiting ways, don't you think?"

Beth wondered if he was commenting obliquely on his failed marriage.

"Sure, I suppose that's true," she agreed. "But there's stability, too, a sense of order in being sure of who you are. I'm Evelyn and Gerald Conroy's daughter, David Conroy's sister, Matthew Conroy's Aunt Beth. That's not the worst way in the world to define oneself."

"No, of course not," he said, and she could see that he was smiling now. "How old is your nephew?"

"He's eight. Sometimes a holy terror—my brother's term—and sometimes an angel. In the pictures, he looks like an angel. I don't get to see him as often as I'd like because they live so far away."

"And your parents? Do you see them often?"

"Yes, quite often. They live in Minnesota and that's fairly near —two hundred and twenty-five miles."

"Near!" He gave a snort of laughter. "You Americans have a very different sense of distance from ours. In England, two hundred and twenty-five miles is about as far as one *can* live from someone else." He paused for a moment. "Still, it's nice that you have such a close relationship with your parents that you think two hundred and twenty-five miles is just a short distance."

"What about your parents? Your family?" she asked, watching the handsome face opposite her.

"Oh," he said, looking out toward the river. "My parents are gone. Just the one sister." She saw an expression pass over his face as if something hurt him, as if he were literally in pain. "My former wife and I had no children. I feel rather sorry about that. I should have liked children."

He fell silent, staring at the river. Beth thought suddenly that he looked tired again, sensed as she had before the reluctance to talk about himself, the pulling away emotionally whenever the subject came up. He'd talked with such animation in the museum, had shared stories of the undergraduate follies of his acquaintances while they were touring the college. But there had been very little direct revelation about himself. Was this just the famous British reserve, or was it a feature of *his* particular personality?

In the silence, Beth glanced down at her watch. It was almost four-thirty. She realized that, much as she was enjoying the day, she must act fairly quickly if she was going to see Chief Superintendent Wilson before the end of this day.

"Oh, Andrew," she sighed. "I really have to be going now, but I want you to know how much I've enjoyed myself today."

"Must you really go?" She could see that he was frowning. "I was hoping we could make a whole day of it. I'd like you to have dinner with me. At my flat, I mean. I've already been planning the meal and I need only a few things from the market. We could stop on the way out of the city."

He looked boyishly eager again before the end of this speech.

"And he cooks, as well," Beth laughed. "What a paragon."

"It's not so wonderful," he shrugged. "One learns when one has to. I've got a few specialities, but the rest is ordinary."

It struck Beth that he sounded like a longtime bachelor. Perhaps this, too, was a veiled commentary on his marriage.

"Do say you'll come," he said earnestly, leaning forward into the sunshine. What a nice face he had, Beth thought.

"Well, okay," she said, pulling away to hide her blush. "But I've got to run my errands while you go shopping. Shall we say seven-thirty?"

"But I could just find a way to put your bicycle on the car and we could go together." He seemed rather insistent. "Your errands can wait, surely."

"Not one of them," Beth said firmly, wondering again if she shouldn't just tell him. "And your car is too small for that klutzy bike of mine. Just go on ahead and knock yourself out in the kitchen."

"All right," he said, looking reluctant still. "I'm not sure I like the idea of you negotiating that bicycle through all that fierce traffic, though."

Beth felt touched by this concern, more than she would have thought possible that morning.

"Oh, I'm an old hand by now," she laughed. "Don't worry about me."

As she started to get down from the wall, Andrew jumped off and helped her by holding both her hands. He didn't let go once she was safely landed. His hands were long, well-shaped and warm, and he held hers tenderly for a moment longer. Beth could feel the quickening of her breath, looked up directly into the clear gray eyes above her for a long moment. He released her then and began to walk at her side toward the gate.

"This is where I was walking when I first met Prince Charles," he said suddenly, pointing ahead along the promenade.

"Prince Charles?" she gasped.

"Well, he wasn't Prince of Wales then," Andrew chuckled. "That came a bit later when he was twenty-one. He took a history degree from Trinity, you know."

Beth had come to a dead stop.

"You went to school with Prince Charles?" she exclaimed.

"Well, not exactly," he said. "I was in my last year when he came up, so we didn't see very much of each other. Now don't tell me you're one of those colonials who's overawed by British royalty."

"Well, not *overawed*," she said, starting to walk again and blushing a little. "But it's a bit much to expect me to remain blasé when you casually mention that you were schoolmates with a future king."

"I don't know what made me think of it just then," he said with a shrug. "I suppose at that age I rather resented all the attention he got. I think he's turned out quite well, actually."

When he'd helped her to unlock her bicycle, he pointed and said, "My car park is that way."

"And I'm off in this direction," she said, pointing back into the city.

"Do be careful," he said with the same look of sincere concern.

"I will, I will," she laughed. How could she have imagined that this man might be a mass murderer? He was a lawyer, a Cambridge graduate, an acquaintance of Prince Charles, for heaven's sake. And he was so kind and knowledgeable, so modest, so charming. And so handsome, of course. She'd been in his car that night of their dinner together at Churchill's and he hadn't made any move to harm her. He'd been a perfect gentleman all day today, and the dinner invitation could hardly be construed as an effort to lure her to a secluded spot; the building they lived in had two other tenants who were both potential rescuers and reliable witnesses. No, she thought as she wheeled her bicycle away from him, it would be absurd to find any menace in Andrew Carmichael.

Chapter 27

After Beth had watched Andrew
walk away, she glanced down at her watch again.
It was so late. She'd told the policeman on the phone this morning
that she would come in to see Wilson at two o'clock. Surely he'd
passed the message along. Perhaps Wilson had waited for her, was
still waiting for her, getting angrier by the minute. She knew how
angry it made her to wait for a student who had *asked* for an appointment and then never showed up. And now that Andrew was gone,

she felt daunted by a trip across the city to the police station; the sense of complete safety she'd felt with him all day had given way to uneasiness again.

She rocked her bicycle back and forth in place, thinking. There was an alternative, of course. There was Constable Woods. It would be better, anyway, to sound him out first, to hand over the photos and ask him if he thought there was anything in them worth bothering Superintendent Wilson about. She peered into the late-afternoon throngs of pedestrians. It occurred to her now that she hadn't seen Constable Woods since leaving the Eagle Inn, where she'd spotted his boyish face in the crowd as she and Andrew were walking back toward King's Parade. There was no sign of Woods's curly head now. What was the signal he'd suggested if she wanted to talk to him? Oh, yes, left hand to the back of the head. She repeated this gesture three times, feeling rather silly to be standing over her bicycle on King's Parade petting her own head. She looked around again, waited a few minutes more. If Woods was watching her from some cover, he couldn't have failed to see the gesture.

Perhaps he'd packed it in for the day, or maybe he, too, had spotted Adam Tate in the crowds and had chosen to follow him rather than stay with her. Or—she didn't want to think it—perhaps he'd followed Andrew. In any case, he was not coming forward now. Beth sighed, feeling more and more absurd at being involved in such melodramatics. If she were ever to tell her Lawrence colleagues about this scene, they would surely think the serious and stuffy Beth Conroy had stripped her gears. "Did the damp get to your brain, my dear?" Charlotte would say.

Beth swung the bicycle around and started for the Madingley Road. She would just stop at Woods's rooming house to see if he'd gone there. It couldn't be hard to find—"You can just see the roof from here," he'd said. If she could see him, give him the photos, and find out what he thought, she would have this whole business off her hands. And there would still be plenty of time for her to bathe, change her clothes, and do something about her makeup before seven-thirty. It seemed only right that she should get all dressed up for Andrew Carmichael. After all, he'd done as much for her this morning. She could feel herself blushing at the thought of dinner in Andrew's flat, and at the same time she was amused at her own reaction. Good heavens! To be as fluttery as a girl over a date. At her age.

As she biked along the A-25, Beth could feel the warmth of the afternoon sun full in her face. Almost like summer today. Again, the sensation of warmth stirred something in her memory, just as the memory of warmth had stirred something in the Copper Kettle this morning. It was the photograph in the Botanic Gardens that had seemed connected to something else, something she had almost remembered. Summerlike warmth—

Suddenly it came to Beth and she skidded the bicycle to a stop at the side of the road, her face lifted toward the sun, her eyes squeezed shut. That sunny day in the gardens *had* been the last day she felt safe in England because the next day was the day the Swiss girl's body had been found along the river. The newspapers had said that the body had begun to decompose because of the heat and she, Beth, had thought with horror at the time that she had probably been enjoying her Sunday while that poor girl was being lured to her death. The Swiss girl had died the day she, Beth, was taking pictures at the gardens. "The girl in the yellow sundress." The phrase flashed through Beth's mind now on this new sunny day.

She snatched up her bag, grabbed at the side pocket, and brought out the packet of photographs. Her hands trembled with excitement as she searched for the picture with the crouching figure at the upper right-hand corner. When she found it, she held it close to her eyes, staring as cars whizzed past her. She had thought at first that the girl in the picture was wearing a yellow skirt, but she saw now that it could be a sundress—those bare arms, the draped sweater hiding the bodice. And this girl had long, blond hair. A blond girl in a yellow sundress.

Could this be a picture of Greta Keller? Had she unwittingly photographed the victim on the day of her death? And if she had, was this the reason someone had been stalking her for all this time? But why? Such a photo could show that the victim had been in the Botanic Gardens before the time of her death—the papers had said the police were trying to establish her whereabouts for that day, for the hours after she had left her lodgings alone. But this picture couldn't shed any light on who had killed her, could it? Once again, Beth felt stymied. It seemed such a small thing to go to such trouble over.

If this girl was Greta Keller, why would it matter so much to her killer that people might find out that she had been in the Botanic Gardens? And only *might* find out. What were the chances that an American student would identify this vague background image with the Cambridgeshire Strangler? She might not even have had the pictures developed until she was back in America. And even if she *did* make such a connection, so what? Perhaps the killer was linked to the gardens on the same day, linked in some potentially incriminating way. So he must keep it a secret that the victim had been there, that he had perhaps made the first contact with her there before he lured her to her death outside the city.

Sitting on her bicycle in the sunshine, Beth felt a sudden chill. Someone might be watching her right now, might be seeing her interest in this photograph. She looked nervously around, peering at passing cars for a few seconds before putting the photographs back into her bag. The picture of the crouching girl, however, she slipped into the pocket of her shirt, buttoning the flap firmly shut over it. This was something she would have to show to Constable Woods as soon as she found him.

Even from the outside, the house looked much shabbier than her own building: peeling paint, an unkempt lawn, cracked pavement on the drive and little parking lot. Beth left her bicycle next to the porch, took her bag, and went up to the door. Should she knock? she wondered, or just go in? A few tentative taps went unanswered, so she tried the door. It opened into a short foyer with water-stained ceiling and wallpaper. The smell of the enclosed air was decidedly unpleasant: a combination of old dirt, mold, disinfectant, and fried food. Beth swallowed a few times before starting down a hallway that displayed a row of closed doors. Each door was marked with a number but nothing to indicate the identity of the occupants. The last door at the end of the hallway had a grimy card attached to it, a card saying MANAGER in childish printing. Here Beth knocked, once, twice. When there was no answer, she pounded with the heel of her hand.

The door sprang open so suddenly that Beth jumped back in alarm.

"What the hell is it?" A woman's voice, querulous, nasal.

Beth focused on the person now framed in the doorway. She was tall, large without being fat, swathed in a floor-length bathrobe of a faded brown chenille. Her glasses were perched well down on her nose and a glittering chain draped from each bow down to her shoulders before disappearing behind the sturdy neck. Large curlers crowned the square-shaped head; the hair around them was a yellowed version of blond, the sort of color that looks dirty even when it isn't. Her age was indeterminate—perhaps fifty, perhaps sixty. Beth wondered if this woman was already dressed for bed at this hour in the afternoon, or if she had been in this costume all day long.

"Well?" the woman said, a bit more subdued now that she could see that Beth was a stranger, not one of her tenants. "What is it?"

"I'm looking for—" Beth broke off because she'd almost said "Constable Woods," and she didn't know if undercover policemen in England told their landladies that they *were* undercover policemen. "I'm looking for Timothy Woods. He does live here, doesn't he?"

"*Live* here!" the woman snorted, with a particular emphasis of scorn. "He stays here, right enough, at the moment. In number two. Back there." And she gestured with her head back down the hallway, holding on to the door of her own room as if she expected Beth to try to force her way past. "When he's here, which ain't very often."

Beth retraced her way down the hall and knocked on the door of Number 2. Another knock a few seconds later produced no response. She could see that the large woman at the end of the hall had not closed her door.

"He doesn't seem to be in," Beth called, feeling ridiculously apologetic, as if she needed to placate that large, fierce watcher.

"Could have told you that if you'd asked," the woman said. "Sometimes he leaves his car up at the top of the drive and just sits in it. Barmy, if you ask me."

"I'll just leave him a note, if I may," Beth said, watching the glint on the manager's glasses.

"It's all of a piece to me," the woman said, but she didn't close her door.

Beth dug around in the bottom of her bag, found a piece of paper and a pen. Hurriedly she wrote, "Need to see you. Beth Conroy." Then she bent and slid the note under the door of Number 2. At the front door, she glanced back to see the big woman at the end of the hall still standing in the doorway, on guard. What *did* the woman imagine? Did she think Beth was some sort of thief, someone intent on breaking into one of these seedy rooms to make off with the treasures of her tenants?

At the top of the driveway, Beth was just about to move back into the traffic of the Madingley Road when she noticed a small white car parked off on the shoulder of the road, a car pointed in the "wrong" direction for traffic, back toward the city. The car had not been there when she arrived. She walked her bicycle toward it; no one was inside. The windows were rolled up, the inside of the car was spotless, devoid of any identifying objects. Could this be Woods's car? Beth wondered, looking around at the hedges, the rail fences, and beyond them, the fields of the Vet School. He'd told her himself that he watched her building from this side of the road and he couldn't do it from his room; if he *had* a window, it would give him a view only of the sharply rising and untidy lawn outside. So he would have to keep his car up here and use it to watch from. But if he'd come back just now, while she was inside, she would surely have encountered him on the drive as he walked toward his own rooming house. Perhaps this car belonged to someone else. Beth felt immediately uneasy at the thought.

She turned her bicycle around and coasted back down the drive to the rooming house. No one was in sight outside. In the dingy hallway, she knocked again at Number 2. Perhaps Woods had gone to a back door as she was leaving. Her second knock, louder than the first, produced an answer, not from Number 2, but from the room at the end of the hall which opened sharply to reveal again the manager who was now scowling openly.

"You're back," she said, her voice hostile. "He's not there now any more than he was a tick ago."

"I thought he might have come in by some other way as I was leaving," Beth replied, feeling absurdly like a naughty child called onto the carpet by the school principal. "I saw a car up on the road, just parked, and I thought it might be his."

"I tell you he ain't here," the big woman growled.

"Could you tell me what kind of car he drives?" Beth asked, determined not to be run off by this harridan.

"What business is it of yours, anyway?" the woman asked. "Who is this Woods bloke to you?"

"I'm only asking if that could be his car up there," Beth said, injecting some of the "teacher" quality into her voice, the quality that made her students realize that they were not dealing with a "pal" their own age. "It's hardly a dangerous question. I don't plan to do any injury to the car, if that's what you're afraid of."

"He drives a Rover," the woman said shortly.

"Is that a little car?" Beth asked, again handicapped by her own foreignness in this country.

"Some of 'em are little," the manager said with a barely disguised sneer. "His is one of the little ones. White."

"Thank you," Beth said, turning on her heel to leave without bothering to see if the manager had anything else to say.

Outside, she walked first to one side of the building and then to the other, looking up and down for any outdoor areas where tenants might sit in the sun on such a nice day. No sign of any such thing. No sign of anybody around the premises. Back on the road, she paused to confirm that the white car was, indeed, a Rover. Where could he be? she wondered, looking around as if she expected him to pop out from behind a hedge. She tried his suggested signal a few times, feeling her own hand somewhat clammy against her hair. For some reason, she felt vaguely alarmed that Woods seemed to have vanished minutes after arriving here. It was silly to begin worrying about a policeman, surely. But why had he failed to approach her when she signaled that she wanted to talk to him, first in Cambridge and now here? Wasn't he supposed to be protecting her? If someone *did* try to jump her, to menace her in some way, she wouldn't be able to count overmuch on this young cop, apparently. And she seemed to have missed him by minutes just now. Where could he be?

It suddenly occurred to Beth that Woods might have gone over to her own building, either to watch for her return or to follow Andrew whom he, of course, had no reason to trust. She mounted her bicycle again, crossed the road, and pedaled the final fifty yards to the driveway of her apartment building.

There was only one car in the lot, one she recognized as belonging to Miss Chalmers. She supposed that Andrew had not yet returned with his groceries, and Adam Tate was still somewhere in the city, apparently. Even the little parking place next to the cottage was empty; the Chatterjees, Beth remembered, had gone to London. The sharp angle of the late-afternoon sun shone over an almost deserted building. Beth peered around into the shrubs, even walked to the side of the house to look into the backyard. At regular intervals, she called softly, "Constable Woods. Are you hiding around here somewhere? I'd like to talk to you." But there was no answer, no glimpse of the angelic curls. She frowned in concentration and then went back to the front of the house.

As Beth approached the front door, she encountered Miss Chalmers coming out of the building. She was an angular, tweedy person of such reserve that she had never done more than murmur a short reply to Beth's greetings on those few occasions when they had encountered each other. Beth had always accounted for the other woman's behavior by reminding herself that it must be difficult to stand long vigil over one's dying mother.

But today, Miss Chalmers spoke first.

"You've just had a visitor," she said in her dry voice—no greeting, no preliminaries.

"A visitor?" Beth asked blankly.

"I heard someone knocking and knocking, so I came out into the lobby. It was definitely at your door."

"I wonder who that could have been," Beth said musingly. "Did you speak to whoever it was?"

"No, of course not." Miss Chalmers looked faintly shocked by the suggestion. "Once I knew it had nothing to do with me, I went back inside my flat. I didn't see the person at all."

"Was it someone who walked down here to the building, do you think?" Beth asked, thinking of Woods's car parked down the road.

"Oh, no. I heard a car. Whoever it was has just missed you. Pity."

"How long ago would you say this was?"

"Not ten minutes," Miss Chalmers said, moving toward her own car. "I thought you might have seen who it was on your way in."

"No, no, I didn't," Beth murmured. How strange. Could she just be missing Constable Woods by seconds and yet never seeing him? "Thank you for telling me," she remembered to add.

Miss Chalmers murmured something unintelligible and opened the door of her car. Beth realized that she was about to be left alone—there was no way to tell if Tate was in the building, of course, but it wasn't necessarily a comforting thought that he might be. She felt a need to prolong the conversation, to establish some kinship with another woman.

"How is your mother doing?" she asked.

Miss Chalmers stood back up from the stoop she had assumed to get into her car; she stared at Beth for a few seconds.

"The doctors don't expect her to live through the night," she said at last.

"Oh," Beth gasped. "I'm so sorry."

"It's very probably for the best," Miss Chalmers said in her dry voice, but Beth could see that tears had come to her pale eyes. "She's been so ill." And she ducked inside her car before Beth could speak again.

Inside the lobby, Beth paused to sort through the day's mail which was left in a neat stack on the table under the phone. There was a letter from her mother and she hugged it against herself, thinking how glad she was that her own mother was healthy and vigorous. As she turned toward the stairs, she thought she heard a noise off to her left, a faint rustling sound coming from behind the door of what had been Ramón's flat. She froze, listening. Miss Chalmers had complained to Mr. Chatterjee of "sounds" coming from there. Beth's first impulse was to go back outside and try to look into the empty flat through a window. The shattered glass of the front window had not yet been replaced and she might be able to see inside by peering around the boards. But this impulse quickly gave way to fear. If there were someone lurking in Ramón's apartment, it would not be a good time to catch him at it. She bolted up the stairs and let herself into her own flat as fast as she could.

When she was safely locked inside, Beth sat for a moment in her living room, thinking. Was it possible that whoever had been shadowing her around Cambridge and even to London had now taken up residence of a sort in her building? Mr. Chatterjee had said that there were no signs of anyone having been inside. Was it just curtains rustling from the breezes through that broken window? Had she heard a real sound at all, or was she just unnaturally jumpy tonight?

And who had been knocking on *her* door just a few minutes ago? Woods? Andrew? Could he have come back briefly for some reason and then left again? That seemed so unlikely. But who else did she know? Adam Tate? There was no sign of another car now. She didn't even know for sure if Tate *had* a car. And even if he did, there would be no reason for him to drive in here, knock on her door, and then leave again. These mysteries were beginning to wear on her nerves. And this was a bad time to have a new mystery added to the already growing list. Should she go downstairs and phone Wilson right now? Or wait for Woods to find her message and come over?

While she was debating what to do, she heard a car outside. From her own window above the table, she watched Andrew Carmichael step out of his car and then duck his head and shoulders back inside to lift out a sack of groceries. The sight of his dark hair and strong arms, the complete normalcy of a man carrying food he meant to cook for her, calmed Beth immediately. With Andrew in the house, she was safe, she felt. She could wait for Woods without further worry. It occurred to her now that Woods might read her note and show up here right in the middle of her dinner with Andrew. Well, so be it. She couldn't help that. But if Woods returned to his car to watch and wait, if he didn't see the note, it might be later—even tomorrow—before she could get in touch with him.

A glance at her watch showed that she had less than an hour to get ready for her dinner with Andrew. She wanted to bathe and wash her hair first, so she'd better get into high gear. When she came out of the bathroom a half hour later to get some juice from the kitchen, she heard noises overhead—the box atop the building was over her living room and kitchen, but not the bedroom and bath. It made her smile to think of Andrew up there cooking. As she passed the front windows again with the glass in her hand, she glanced down into the parking lot. Next to Andrew's, there was another car as well; perhaps Adam Tate had a car after all. Odd that she'd never noticed that before. It struck her now how much the two cars resembled each other—small, boxy, light-colored. How *did* the British tell their automobiles apart? Well, now there were two men in the building, a double sense of security for her—even, she thought, if one of these men was a threat, she could count on the other for protection. She breathed deeply, less uncomfortable now about waiting for some contact with the police.

Back in her bedroom, she paged through the clothes hanging in the big wardrobe, selecting at last a pale-green and white dress she'd bought in early May at a shop in Cambridge called Miss Selfridge's. It was very feminine, almost frilly—a delicate print with a full skirt and a shirred bodice; not the sort of dress she would have chosen back in Wisconsin and certainly not the sort of dress she would ever have worn to school. From the long drawer at the bottom of the wardrobe, she took out a pair of white, high-heeled shoes, open-toed with small cutouts in a spray pattern on the lower vamp. She put them next to the dress and squinted narrowly at the combination. Some green eyeshadow, pink lipstick, the wide white bracelet. Yes, yes, very nice, she thought.

Before unwrapping the towel from her freshly washed hair, she scooped up the clothes she'd been wearing that day and began to put them away. As she was slipping the shirt onto a hanger, she thought of the photograph that was buttoned inside the front pocket, and she started to retrieve it. But then she thought better of it, gave the blouse a little shake, and hung it in the wardrobe. That pocket was as good a place as any to keep the photograph until she saw the police again.

Chapter **28**

It was exactly seven-thirty when
Beth knocked at the door that was right next to
her own in the shallow hallway. She'd slipped both of her keys into
the side pocket of her dress so she wouldn't have to take her bag with
her—that all-purpose receptacle hardly seemed appropriate for a trip
up one flight of stairs.

"It's open," she heard Andrew call. "Come right on up."

The narrow staircase had a very steep pitch, making it necessary
for her to hold on to the handrail to pull herself up. At the top, the

staircase simply emerged through the floor into the little flat. It was really just one big room with windows on three sides and a single door on the fourth side—Beth guessed this door must lead to the bathroom. In front of her at the head of the stairs was the kitchen area where Andrew was standing, smiling his greeting. To the right was a small dining table with two chairs, and to the right of that was the most open area of the room, where a sofa and an overstuffed chair formed an L shape before a small electric fireplace with a big window above it, facing the front of the building.

At the far side of the room, in open sight, were a wardrobe, a small desk and chair, and a double bed, all crowded into the corner just before the bathroom door. The wardrobe was much smaller than her own and, in fact, Andrew had apparently had to resort to using the desk chair as another place to drape some of his clothes. Like her own furniture downstairs, all the furniture here was serviceable but worn. The wallpaper was a garish floral print that clashed quite noisily with the striped curtains. "I'm not responsible for the decor," Mr. Chatterjee had told Beth when she'd first moved in. "The former owners must have had dreadful taste. When I can afford it, these flats will be ever so much more attractive."

"My, my," Andrew was saying, staring at her from the tiny kitchen. "You look just like a little girl in that frock."

"Oh, please don't say that," Beth groaned. "That's not the effect I was after."

"I thought women enjoyed looking younger than their years," he said, handing her a glass of red wine. He had changed his clothes, too, and looked much more casual than he had earlier in the day; yet the open-collared, short-sleeved shirt and dark cotton slacks were beautifully pressed, good quality.

"Most women do, I suppose," Beth said, accepting the wine. "But it's always been the bane of my existence that I look so young. People *treat* you like a child if they think you look like a child."

"Well, I promise I won't treat you like a child," he smiled. "Let's sit down for a bit, shall we? My Chinese beef with peapods won't be finished for a few more minutes and the rice is still steaming."

"Is that what smells so wonderful?" Beth asked, walking toward the sofa. "I would have thought you'd make something authentically British to show off for me."

"Oh, dear," he chuckled. "Haven't you discovered yet that most authentically British food is quite uninteresting?" He waited until she'd sat down before choosing a place on the sofa opposite her.

"I don't agree," Beth said. "I've discovered that I really like most of the foods that I'd only read about until I came here. Crumpets, for instance. I bought some fresh crumpets last night and I'm quite looking forward to having them for breakfast tomorrow."

"Certainly, we manage breakfasts quite nicely. Nothing like a good English breakfast. But dinners are usually quite grim, don't you think? Overcooked meat, overcooked vegetables, bland potatoes or heavy Yorkshire pudding."

"Well," Beth said ruefully, "I'll admit that main courses are a trifle ordinary. But desserts are really wonderful."

"Yes," he said, grinning openly. "We Brits have a notorious sweet tooth. As a matter of fact, I've got an especially delectable sweet for tonight's dessert. I bought it fresh from the bakery. Have you had Battenberg cake?"

"No, I haven't," Beth said, sipping her wine and crossing her legs so that the toe of her right shoe pointed at Andrew's knee.

"Then you're in for a treat," he said confidently. "Stay where you are while I dash off to stir things." And he sprang up with such energy that Beth jumped a little.

"Oh, by the way," she said to his back, suddenly remembering. "You weren't knocking on my door about six, were you, before I got home? Miss Chalmers from downstairs said she heard somebody who then drove off."

"Why, no," he said, turning from the stove. "When I got back from the market, your bicycle was here and there was no car at all. So this Miss Chalmers must have been gone by then. Mr. Chatterjee says her mother is ill."

"Yes, dying, as a matter of fact," Beth said quietly. "I didn't think it was you, but I'm confused because, of course, I don't know very many people in England. So I don't know who could have come to see me."

She glanced up when Andrew didn't reply and caught him frowning thoughtfully.

"Well, never mind," she said, standing up and walking to the window and back again. "It can't have been important. Perhaps it was just a mistake."

She paused at the little table next to the stuffed chair. There was a paperback book called *Tropical Fish* lying upside down on the table, opened, with about one third of it apparently already read.

"Are you a fancier of tropical fish?" she asked as she strolled toward the kitchen area.

"We used to have them when I was a child," he said, looking up from his rice dish. "I've been thinking of getting some again. Now that I'm alone." Then he seemed to feel he should explain. "My former wife didn't want pets. Too much trouble, she said."

"I see," Beth murmured. "I have two cats back home, Pip and Trabb's Boy—I got the names from *Great Expectations*. A friend of mine is taking care of them for me while I'm gone. I miss them. Lots of people don't think cats are good company, but mine are."

"I couldn't have pets that required a great deal of attention," he said simply. "I'm not at home enough. Fish are interesting, lovely to look at, but not very demanding." He stirred a dark, rich-looking mixture of vegetables and beef in brown sauce. "You would be very good with pets, I should imagine."

Beth smiled a little self-consciously. It was such a sudden swing toward the personal from a man who seemed to avoid the personal most of the time.

"Why, thank you," she said with a little laugh. "I'm sure you would be, too. Didn't you have dogs and cats when you were a boy?"

"No," he said rather tonelessly. "My father always said the city was no place for pets. Animals, he used to say, shouldn't live in the same buildings with people. He tolerated the fish, but just barely. After I was in my teens, we didn't have the fish anymore."

Beth watched the side of his handsome face. He spoke without obvious bitterness, but she could hear the undertone of regret in his voice.

"Well, that's too bad," she said. "I always had two or three pets at a time when I was a kid—dogs, birds, cats, even a gerbil or two.

I think having pets teaches children a sense of responsibility. Of course, there's heartache, too, sometimes. My brother was literally sick for a week when his dog Sparky died. Couldn't even go to school. It wasn't pretense, either. He was really ill."

Andrew smiled a bit as he began dishing up the food.

"I used to pretend all manner of exotic ailments to get out of school," he said. "Earaches were the best gambit because it was hard to tell if I was faking or not."

"Didn't you like school?" Beth asked sympathetically, remembering her own secret fondness for school as a child—secret because other children would have scorned her if they'd known.

"Not when I was little," he answered, carrying brimming plates the few feet to the table. "One of the curses of having money in Britain is that it consigns the children of the family to stuffy, authoritarian public schools—uniforms, paddling, the whole lot. You Americans call them private schools and, of course, that's just what they are. Later I got to quite like studying. Do sit down now and I'll pour you some more wine before we begin."

He held her chair for her as she sat down, then reached past her cheek to the short countertop where the wine bottle was standing. The proximity of his forearm made Beth's cheek feel very warm. She glanced at the strong wrist, the supple hand that manipulated the wine bottle without spilling a drop. Dark, wiry hair covered his forearm and even the back of his hand. When Andrew finally sat down in the chair opposite her, Beth had quite forgotten what they'd been talking about before he began to pour that second glass of wine.

"This looks delicious," she said rather lamely, but she'd hardly glanced at the food.

"Well, you know what they say about the proof of the pudding," he said, but he looked boyishly pleased by the praise.

"Did you learn to cook at your mother's knee, or is this a recently acquired skill?"

"I learned as an adult," he said and again she saw the subtle pulling away. "It's really not much. If one can read, one can learn to cook. I eat out most of the time now." His face had grown very serious.

"Your divorce was painful, was it?" Beth asked spontaneously, sure that his seeming sadness was connected to that.

He was silent for a moment, shaking out his napkin before putting it into his lap.

"Well," he said at last, looking past her. "As an experienced solicitor, I can tell you that there is no such thing as an 'amicable' divorce."

"Do you always give general answers to personal questions?" she asked.

"Is that what I do?" His thick eyebrows had risen.

"Well, I've noticed that you don't talk about your private life very much." She was concentrating on her own napkin now. "I'll back off if you think I'm being too pushy. Just tell me."

"Oh, you're not pushy," he said with a wry chuckle. "I've sometimes had a bad time of it, especially lately, but I don't feel I ought to be whining about it to anyone. We English are taught that it's bad form to complain about personal matters. I'm sorry if I've seemed secretive."

"Don't apologize," she said, blushing. "But I think it's a mistake to share only good things with people. The bad times are part of your experience, too, so they're part of you. Withholding them is showing only half of yourself."

"Perhaps," he said softly. "But I just don't want to appear to you in a negative light. Now you, for instance, are a very positive person. Cheerful, even. I appreciate that in a companion. I'd like to be that sort of person myself. I think it's one of the reasons I like you so much."

Beth was speechless with embarrassment and *very* pleased. She took a sip of wine and fiddled with her silverware before she was able to speak again.

"Well, it's easy enough to be positive when you've had a life like mine. I've got my own little neuroses, but, all things considered, I've had very little to complain about." While she was saying this, she realized that it was the simple truth, a truth she sometimes lost sight of.

"But I've known people with charmed lives who've done nothing but squander their advantages and grumble about it afterward." He looked as if he had particular people in mind. "Cheerfulness is an achievement, I think, in any circumstance."

"I haven't felt very cheerful lately, I have to admit," Beth said after tasting her first bite of dinner. "Scared, a little angry, but hardly cheerful."

"That break-in, I suppose," he said and his brow had furrowed with concern. "That must have been a nasty shock. Feeling a stranger anyway, and then to have that happen."

"Actually the break-in has come to seem like the least of my troubles. It's everything that's happened since then that's been getting on my nerves."

"Everything that's happened since?" he asked, his eyebrows almost joining together as his frown deepened.

Beth sat for a moment assessing the man opposite her. He looked so genuinely concerned, so sincere. Surely she could confide in him. It would be such a relief to talk about her fears to someone who would sympathize. She began tentatively, telling him about her sense of being followed, about the attempt to steal her camera at Covent Garden, about the red-haired undergraduate at Auntie's. She kept the account chronological, holding back any theories about how these events might be connected to each other; it would be interesting to see if *he* could see any connection, after all. Andrew hardly touched his dinner, made little clucking sounds of concern and interest as she spoke.

"And yesterday was especially scary," she said.

"Yesterday?" he asked, his eyebrows arching upward over the clear gray eyes. "You told me this morning that you'd been to Kew. What was scary about that?"

"Well, I didn't tell you *all* the details," she said with a rueful smile. "I'm pretty sure somebody followed me to London on the train and went on the boat with me to Kew, somebody who followed me all over the Royal Botanic Gardens."

"Followed you to London?" Andrew looked incredulous for the first time. "Did you actually see someone following you?"

"Not exactly," she sighed, expecting disbelief now. "But I *heard* plenty of things, noises on and off the paths. Somebody was very close to me and it was somebody who didn't want me to see him, somebody hiding behind trees and bushes. And then in the water-lily house, I saw someone who looked familiar."

"Familiar?" He was leaning toward her now, his face eager. "Somebody you knew, you mean?"

Again, Beth felt the frustration of trying to explain what she meant. If it was so hard to make herself clear to someone as sympathetic as Andrew Carmichael, what would it be like to convince Scotland Yard?

"I don't mean that I recognized the man," she said at last. "I had worn my glasses—I usually wear contacts—and the humidity had steamed them up, so I couldn't see very clearly. But I saw a man whose *shape* looked familiar—I know that sounds silly, but it's true. And this man was wearing a jacket like the one the thief at Covent Garden was wearing. When he saw me staring at him, he ran. I think that's the most significant detail. Why would he run like that if he weren't afraid I'd recognize him?"

Andrew was staring at her, his face displaying in sequence a variety of expressions ranging from surprise to disbelief to concern.

"You believe this was the same man who tried to take your camera?" he asked finally. "That would mean that you'd been followed to London twice."

"I know it seems unlikely," she said, "but that's what I believe."

"What does this chap look like?" he went on insistently. "Would you know him if you saw him again?"

"He was wearing sunglasses," she replied. "The only directly familiar detail was the color of his jacket. He had blondish hair, ordinary-style haircut. I can't really say why he looked familiar and I'm not sure if I would recognize him if I ran into him in the street."

"Not much help," he murmured, looking past her toward the windows. "But this is just appalling. Following you to *London*." He said it as if the outrage were somehow worse if London was involved. "Can you be certain that this man hasn't tried to approach you? Perhaps he looks familiar because you've already met him. Have you met anyone in England who looks like that?"

"Not that I know of," she replied. "I'm getting pretty skittish about everyone I meet. I've thought that there was something odd about the behavior of Adam Tate, that man on my floor. He's cold and shy one minute, and then he comes on like gangbusters the next."

Andrew looked puzzled by the phrase.

"That means he becomes almost aggressive conversationally," Beth explained with a little smile. "Last night, he made a big deal about wanting to help me with my groceries, to take them into my flat, I mean. It scared me a little."

"After I spoke to you outside, you mean?"

"Yes. He came out of his flat just as I was approaching my door. I thought he might have been watching from his window, might have timed it so he could encounter me. The problem is that he has such dark hair, and that's not what I saw at Kew. You said yourself that Tate looks foreign."

Andrew looked blank.

"Today," Beth reminded him. "When you thought you saw him on the street near the Eagle. You said he looked foreign."

"Oh, yes," he said, but she thought he looked slightly embarrassed, as if he'd forgotten completely about seeing Tate until this reminder. "Yes, of course." His abstracted stare changed suddenly to a look of sharp focus, just as it had done when he was looking past her at the pub.

"What about that young man who carried your groceries from the bus last night?" he asked, looking directly at her now. "In the circumstances, I'm amazed you would allow a stranger to approach you like that." And he looked disapproving, the same expression her father used to get on his face when she dated some boy he hadn't met and whose family he didn't know.

Beth debated with herself only a moment before deciding to trust Andrew with more information; it would be unkind, she told herself, to let him keep worrying. Besides, she didn't want him to think she was the sort of fool who would blindly trust a stranger "in the circumstances."

"Well, he didn't help me with my groceries," she said. "I just made that up on the spur of the moment. He's a policeman who's been assigned to protect me."

"A policeman?" He looked blank again.

"Yes, a constable," she assured him. "Apparently the local police have finally decided that my fears might have some basis, and so this young cop has been watching me for several days now. He was supposed to be undercover, even from me, but I spotted him the first day."

"It must give you a great deal of comfort to have protection."
But he didn't look especially glad about it.

"I'm not sure about that," she said. "He doesn't seem very good
at surveillance and he didn't notice anybody trying to follow me to
London yesterday. So he just stayed behind here in Cambridge. I'm
afraid he might not be around when I need him most."

"Then his surveillance hasn't been constant?" Again he looked
very curious, concerned.

"Well, I'm not sure, I guess," she shrugged. "He said last night
that he was assigned to me exclusively now. He's moved into a room
across the way and his car was parked over there when I was coming back here today. But he doesn't seem to be on the job every
minute, no."

"So then he couldn't have seen the man who ran from you at
Kew? Or the man at Covent Garden?" His face was very intent.

"No." Beth felt a little uneasy in the face of these insistent
questions. "He wasn't even given this assignment until after I told
the Scotland Yard men about the attempt to steal my camera."

Andrew squinted off into space, his expression cloudy.

"I was right to worry about you," he said. "I said I didn't like
you to be biking around alone in Cambridge."

"But you meant the traffic, then," Beth laughed.

"Yes, of course," he said, smiling briefly back at her. "But apparently there are other reasons to worry as well. It seems rather callous
of the police to let you wander about as bait for whoever is stalking
you."

"Well, what else could they do?" Beth was amazed at the ve-
hemence of his last sentence. "I wouldn't tolerate anything like protective custody. Besides, I think they must be getting closer to a
solution. That young constable told me there were 'recent developments' that occasioned his assignment. So that must mean they've
got some leads."

"Really?" he said, and his eyes had a glint of—of what? Anger?
Alarm? He was a very hard man to read. "Recent developments of
what kind, I wonder."

"Well, Constable Woods said he was not at liberty to discuss
them," Beth answered. "Those were his exact words."

Andrew didn't speak for a long moment. Beth wondered if she should tell him now about her theory, about the connection to the photograph she'd taken, to see what he thought of it. She was just about to begin by asserting her idea that her own troubles of the past weeks were connected to the series of murders being investigated by Scotland Yard. But suddenly it occurred to her that there was something rather odd in the fact that Andrew had never once asked or speculated about *why* all of these strange things had been happening to her. Wouldn't a person hearing for the first time about someone being followed, stalked as it were, naturally ask, "And why do you think someone would be doing this?" And why hadn't he reacted when she'd mentioned Scotland Yard, that she'd spoken to Scotland Yard detectives about someone trying to steal her camera? Surely the expected response to that revelation would be "Why is Scotland Yard interested in an attempted theft?" But he'd only seemed interested in whether anyone could describe the man she'd seen at Kew.

"What is it?" Andrew said suddenly.

"What?" Beth gasped, jumping a little before she realized that her face must have registered her sudden qualm pretty graphically.

"You looked so strange just then," he said. "What were you thinking of?"

"Oh, nothing," she said, pushing a piece of beef around with her fork. "I guess it's just that this subject is starting to get on my nerves. And it's going to be all right. I've got protection now."

"Of course," he murmured. "We needn't discuss it any further. I can understand why it would upset you."

And for the rest of the meal, he chatted easily about several subjects, seemingly relaxed, charming as he'd been all day. Beth began to consider that her earlier concern was misplaced. There was no need to be so suspicious of this man just because he didn't pursue a conversation in the direction she would have chosen if she'd been in his place. He was more concerned for her safety than for an explanation of why she was in danger. He would probably have gotten around to asking for explanations if she hadn't cut him off by insisting on a change of subject matter. Besides, if he was the stalker, what was this all about, this nice day in a museum, lunch, a college tour, a dinner date? Hardly the behavior of a homicidal maniac. By the time he

served coffee and the splendid Battenberg cake, she was again convinced that this man was trustworthy, harmless.

He was as good as his word, too, not alluding even obliquely to
the subject she had claimed upset her. They adjourned to the sofa to
finish the bottle of wine, and Andrew talked a little about British
politics—his views exactly agreed with hers—a little about the sort
of television he liked to watch, a little about New York City, which
he said he'd visited when he was in his twenties. He asked about her
research and listened with real interest when she described her book.
The wine was making Beth feel a little sleepy, but they were drinking
it so slowly that she felt sure she was in no danger of getting tipsy.
By the time she even thought to look at her watch again, it was already
after eleven. Perhaps she'd better check to see whether Constable
Woods might have been trying to contact her, had left some message
on her door.

"Well," Beth sighed, shifting on the sofa. "I suppose a dinner
guest shouldn't overstay her welcome. I'd better be toddling along."

"No," he said quickly. "Don't go. I don't want you to go." His
face was tender, pleading.

"Ever?" Beth said, trying to deflect his seriousness with a light
laugh.

"Well, not just yet at least," he said with a sweet smile.

All through the long evening, he'd made no effort to touch her,
had not "flirted" in any way that she was accustomed to. She'd been
rather disappointed that he *hadn't* been more attentive in that way,
so now she felt a little surprised by this sudden tender request that
she should stay on. She stood up and walked slowly toward the little
fireplace. He stood up at once, one of those polite reflexes, she could
tell.

"I don't expect—expect anything," he said softly from behind
her. "I would just like you to stay."

Beth looked back at him. He meant it, she felt sure. He was
eager to let her know that *she* could specify the terms of their relationship, that he would respect her wishes about how far the relationship would go at this stage. She smiled at him, a spontaneous and
warm smile. He was blushing a little—how refreshing that such a

good-looking man could be somewhat less than self-assured—but he didn't look away from her eyes.

"I feel that you'll be safe if you stay with me," he said, holding his position at the edge of the sofa. "It's strange, I know, but I had that feeling this afternoon, too, in the city after we left Trinity. I wanted to keep you with me so nothing could harm you. Is that very silly of me?"

"Of course it's not silly," she said, taking a step toward him. "I think it's very sweet of you to worry about me. But, honestly, I think I'd be safe in my own flat."

"Well," he sighed. "That's really only half of it. You said earlier that it might be a mistake to reveal only half of what one is feeling. The truth is that I've felt alone for so long now, even when there are people all around me. When I'm with you, I don't feel alone. You make me feel it might be possible for me to be happy." His expression was absolutely sincere, the need so naked in his eyes that it almost took her breath away.

Beth took three steps to close the distance between them and put her arms around Andrew Carmichael's waist, her face against his shoulder.

"Yes, I'll stay with you," she murmured, inhaling the clean, sweet smell of his shirt.

He paused for a second, as if caught momentarily off balance; then he closed his arms around her very tightly, lowered his face onto her hair. Beth could hear the sharp increase in his breathing rate. She slid her hands up the strong back, feeling the smooth bands of muscle under the light shirt. She began to lift her face toward his, wanting to look up into his eyes, wanting to be kissed.

Quite suddenly Andrew released her, put his hands against her shoulders, and literally pushed her away from himself. He turned from her before she could look at him carefully, strode to the far end of the room. Beth could see only his profile, but she could tell he was blushing violently, was struggling with himself in some way.

"What is it?" she whispered. "What's the matter?"

There was a long pause before Andrew finally spoke.

"It's not right," he said at last. "Taking advantage like this. It's taking advantage." The broken sentences didn't even specify who was supposed to be taking advantage of whom.

"No, it's not," Beth said, puzzled by this odd diffidence. "I'm a big girl."

"No, you're not," he said, glancing back at her with an odd expression. "You're not very big, are you? And you don't know very much about me."

"Not yet, I guess," Beth answered, thinking again that this was the most puzzling man she'd ever met.

"Yes, that's it," he said, still breathing hard. "Not yet. We should get to know each other better, before—before anything else."

Beth was thinking that this ought to have been *her* line; in fact, she had sometimes said almost exactly the same thing when a man had come on stronger than she wanted him to. She felt acutely embarrassed, almost humiliated by this rejection.

"Perhaps I'd better just be going, then," she said softly, turning away from his still-averted face.

"No!" He said it quickly, vehemently. When she looked back at him in surprise, he had turned to her and his face was pleading, humble. "Won't you stay for a bit? I have some brandy. We could have a glass and talk some more. Perhaps there are some things we should know about each other."

"Are you actually planning to talk about yourself?" Beth said, somewhat sharply because she was still feeling sore about being pushed away like that.

"Yes," he said sheepishly. "We'll sit quietly and I'll behave like a perfect gentleman while we talk."

Beth almost smiled at the irony; she emphatically did not want him to behave like "a perfect gentleman." But she returned to the sofa and sat down while Andrew went into the kitchen to fumble around in the cupboards and pour two glasses of brandy.

"Here you are," he said, handing her the glass. "Would you excuse me for a bit? I'll be right back."

He looked horribly abashed, gesturing with his head at the bathroom.

"Of course," Beth said looking away to conceal her smile. Good Lord! Wasn't this taking British reserve too far?

The brandy was room temperature, almost warm, and the glass was a big one. Normally, Beth would have sipped cautiously, but her present embarrassment was enough to make her gulp the rich, nutmeg-colored liquid. Andrew was out of the room for a long time—working up his courage to speak, perhaps. By the time he got back, Beth had almost finished the brandy.

"I hardly know where to begin," he said quietly as he settled himself at the far end of the sofa, leaving a big space between them. "I can tell that you have a strong sense of family, and that your family makes you happy. But you musn't think that all families go along as smoothly as yours."

Beth nodded, alarmed at the little buzz of dizziness that passed over her mind when she moved her head. She really shouldn't drink so fast, she reminded herself. Especially brandy. Brandy had always had a narcotic effect on her.

"Are you all right?" Andrew said, squinting at her with a worried frown.

"Yes, yes," Beth said. "Just a little sleepy. Brandy after all that wine. Go on with what you were saying. Families. I'd like to hear about your family."

"I was always quite close to my sister," Andrew said. Was his voice droning and dull, or was that just her imagination? "You see, her happiness meant so much to me. When she—when the thing happened to her that I'd like to tell you about, it had a very serious effect on me. I wouldn't be here otherwise."

Beth was feeling really dizzy now, terribly warm, very tired. Strange that the brandy was acting so fast. But there was the wine, too, of course, and she hadn't been sleeping very well lately. So worried all the time. Was Andrew leading up to some explanation of his divorce? Was that what he wanted to tell her about? What else could it be if he started by talking about families not going smoothly? But what did his divorce have to do with his sister? Why was he talking about his sister? So warm. So dizzy. Tired.

"Just put your head down right here," Andrew was saying softly, sliding toward her on the sofa. "You're so tired. This can wait until another time. Plenty of time later."

It was the last thing Beth heard him say.

Chapter 29

She would have to die now, of course. He would have to kill her. How stupid it had been to think she was different from other women. To imagine that she was pure and good. Girls were all the same, no matter what they pretended. Liars. Even if the lies didn't come from their lips, they were liars. Under the surface, they were bitches and whores. They might look and act like good women, mothers and wives and sisters, but that was only for a little while, because they *meant* to fool him, to make him believe, so they could hurt him afterward. They all flirted like that, looked into a man's eyes with that melting look, touched him that way, made him feel those things. Willing to get into a man's bed. They couldn't wait for proper ceremony, for a decent marriage. Because they were all dirty, dirty—and they made him feel dirty for wanting them, for wanting them in that way.

He wanted to just tear her apart, to rip her to pieces, to bite—but that had to be later. He had to be very careful not to think about it now because he had to stay calm; he had to get the camera, the film. Later, when he was sure that the bloody film had no chance of falling into the wrong hands, then she would have to die like the others. If it had to be here, in the building, then that's how it would have to be. He could just leave afterward, walk away, get well away from Cambridge forever, to somewhere he wasn't known at all. Australia, maybe. The solicitors could send the checks to Australia, couldn't they? And when the old man was finally dead, there would be enough money to do whatever he wanted—whatever— What *did* he want? How would he live the rest of his life? Life could be so long, stretching away into the future. What to do with it; that was the problem, wasn't it?

Mustn't fall asleep. Keeping control was so exhausting, such a terrible strain. And having to stay inside, of course. That was her fault, too. Her fault that he had to be inside almost all the time now, because he had to watch her every minute, had to keep close to her all the time. But it was terrible being inside, to try to keep control when he was suffocating. Nobody knew what it was like. Exhausting. But he mustn't let himself fall asleep. Not the way he had last night. The real mistake had been to walk for such a long time, to stay out until almost five o'clock when it was already getting light. He could finally sleep when it wasn't dark, but he'd been so worn out that it was almost inevitable that he would oversleep once he *did* get to sleep. When he woke up, she was already gone; her bicycle wasn't there in the rack, and he had almost choked from panic.

Why had she gone off so early? What was open at that hour of the morning? Not the shops. Where should he begin to look? Later, of course, he would know where to find her, but not this early. Had she taken the camera with her? Would this be the day she finished the damned film and took it out of the camera? The one day when he was *not* watching her? How could he know for sure now? Life was so damned unfair. It played tricks like that on you no matter how hard you tried to keep things in order, to have some control over things.

No use to look for her; even if he came across her accidentally in the city, there was no way of telling what she might have done in the interim. But he had to try, to get out and drive into town, because *not* to try would be too much strain. Waiting was getting more and more difficult. He ached to do something, to explode into some action, any action. Then just as he was leaving, he saw something, something that startled him, something he felt sure would lead him straight to Elizabeth. It calmed him a little, but only a little. There was still no way of telling how long she'd been gone or what she'd been doing.

It was all her fault. Why had she run off so early? They were always running off. Unpredictable. Leaving you when you least expected it. Deserting you. You count on them, learn to depend on them, and then one day, when you wake up, they're gone. Not a word, not a hint. Like Hillary. She'd left him, gone away, and he would never forgive her for that, never forgive her for looking at him as if it were *his* fault. And she *knew*! She knew what she was leaving him to, but that didn't stop her. Selfish slut! That's all she was. "I don't know what to do." But it hadn't taken her long to find something to do, had it?

They'd all expected him to go to the funeral, of course, the priest, the counselors, even the old man. Though, at the beginning, for the first twenty-four hours after—after Hillary was found, the old man had been almost catatonic, silent and rigid while doctors and police came in and out of the house. Then he'd "come to" for a few hours, mumbling about "arrangements," murmuring agreement to the suggestions made by the priest. But by the second afternoon, he was wild-eyed and rambling: "They can't have her," he kept muttering. "I won't let them have her." And that night, the house had echoed with his wailing. Bloody hypocrite! Probably expecting comfort, expecting his son to pat his poor old head and say, "There, there." Not bloody likely. He could just go to hell. With Hillary. He could have her back in hell.

When at last the old man had said he would get him a new suit for the funeral, he'd looked him square in his bloodshot eyes and said, "I'm not going to any funeral. She didn't say good-bye to me and I'm bloody well not going to say good-bye to her." And then the old man had tried to pull out all the stops, to rise up into Father Dreadful Gone Berserk, threatening, screaming. But there was such fear in the bleary eyes, terror that his only son would tell on him at the inquest—the police had said there would be an inquest. "Do you have any idea why she would do such a thing?" They were already asking the question, all of them from the outside. So it was no good the old man trying to bluster anymore. At thirteen, he was almost big enough to resist physically if the pantry was suggested, and now that he'd found his defiance, Father Dreadful was beginning to realize that his days as a petty tyrant were numbered. You could see it in the eyes.

When the funeral finally came, the old man didn't go either. He'd been drinking for twenty hours straight and was completely unconscious when the car came for them. The driver was aghast, staring at the unshaven, crumpled figure on the bed and then at the dry-eyed boy who'd let him into the house. "Well, *you* come along, then," he said at last. "You'll have to represent the whole family." "I must stay with my poor father," he'd answered, keeping his face absolutely blank. "Surely you don't think I can leave him in such a state. Tell Father Crosswaithe to go ahead with the service."

And at the inquest the following week, he *had* told. With no emotion, no hysterics, and without looking at the old man, he had simply answered with perfect honesty the questions put to him. "What happened the night before your sister's death? Do you know of anything that could have upset her so much that she would take her own life?" But, of course, he didn't tell them that she'd come to his room later, didn't tell them that she'd called him a "stupid little boy" before running out—her last words, her famous last words.

Of course, the old man had denied everything, had ranted like a lunatic, and nothing could be proven—the judge had said so in just those words—but everyone in the hearing room had looked at Father Dreadful as if they'd like to step on him. "Is there someone else you'd like to live with?" the judge had asked him after the hearing, when his father had run out of the room. "It could be arranged, I think." "Oh, no," he'd replied. "That won't be necessary. I'll be quite all right, thank you." The judge had stared for a moment, but then he'd given it up.

And he had expected some trouble at first, to be sure, some last efforts at bluster, some threats. But the troubles never came. For four days, the old man stayed drunk; on the fifth day he had to be taken to hospital, to the detox ward. When he was dried out a week later, he came back to the house looking like a different person: hollow-eyed, gaunt, and frightened—very frightened. "See to it that he takes this medication," the doctor had said. "He mustn't miss even one day."

After that, it had been pathetically easy to control the old man. Everything frightened him; he was sure that all the world had it in for him, was against him. "Your fault, you little sod," he would growl, but his heart wasn't in it; that was easy to see. He would spend hours in Hillary's room, ignoring the son and heir who stayed downstairs exclusively now, reading and going on long walks—it was the summer holidays now, no need to put on an act for the people at school. Trays of food would come back downstairs untouched; the housekeeper, old Mrs. Higgins, would shake her head and make clucking noises.

Sometimes sheer hunger would drive the old man downstairs for a meal. Then it was only a matter of waiting for Mrs. Higgins to leave the room: "Don't you think that beef looks a bit off, Dad? I hope it doesn't make us ill to eat it." And whenever the old boy tried to take his medicine: "Who *are* those doctors who gave you those pills, Father? Perhaps they mean to poison you." Oh, what a joy to see the terror in those eyes. What does it feel like to be so frightened? Do you wish someone would save you? Do you wish someone would let you out?

By July, Mrs. Higgins had given her notice. "Can't have such carryings-on," she'd said. "All that mumbling and yelling. You should get the doctors back for him, lad. I can't handle him, and neither can you." "Oh, I can handle him, Mrs. Higgins. Don't worry. But I quite understand your concern. The solicitors will send you your severance, I'm sure." And when she was gone, it was much simpler, of course, to see to it that Father Dreadful did not eat, did not take those pills. The headaches were getting worse; even the neighbors had complained about the screaming, had suggested hospitals.

Finally, early in August, the old man had simply smashed everything that would break, everything in his own room, everything in Hillary's room. By the time the police came, he was cowering on the stairs, his hands bloody, the skin scraped off his forearms; he couldn't speak anymore, could only stare in gape-mouthed terror at the uniforms, at the arms that reached for him. "Poor lad," one of the constables had murmured, looking at the son rather than the father. "Poor little lad."

The solicitors sold the house and found the boarding school for him. On school holidays, he would go to visit his father in the mental ward. People thought he was such a good boy for doing that; it impressed teachers no end. But, of course, he went mostly to see, to make sure the old man was still suffering. Drugged into a stupor, quiet as a tomb, staring blankly and uncomprehendingly at anyone who came near him. But the fear was still there, at the back of the eyes; it was still there. So it was enough. It had to be enough. Not ranting, not screaming in pain, but suffering nonetheless. And locked in. Locked in a little room with bars on the windows. Locked in forever.

Hillary would probably feel sorry for him. That's what girls were like. Feeling sorry for the people they were supposed to hate. Getting into bed with the people they were supposed to hate. And then acting innocent afterward, as if it had all never happened. Pretending to be shocked when he wanted to touch them in that way. What a joke! Why shouldn't it make him furious? Why shouldn't it make him want to tear them to pieces? They could look like the angels in the church windows, golden hair, white skin, slim bodies that didn't even look like women, not like grown-up women, not like Mrs. Higgins who had those immense pillows of breasts—like that other woman, that prostitute who'd kept him out of university. But the innocent looks were a lie. There was no such thing as innocence.

He had hoped Elizabeth Conroy was different, that he could marry her and be happy with her. It was humiliating to remember that thought now, to remember what a fool he'd been. She was sullied now. Had been a strumpet all along, probably. How could he have let himself forget that she was really the cause of all his troubles? If she hadn't been such a bloody tourist, he would be long away from Cambridge and he wouldn't be remembering all the pain of his childhood, wouldn't be reminded by being here. If he could have got that film away from her at the beginning, he wouldn't have to feel this terrible disappointment now, because he would never have got to know her, never would have begun to hope. And he wouldn't have had to linger in small rooms until he thought he would scream from the pressure in his head. It was her fault that he was so tired all the time now, so tired that he was afraid he wouldn't be able to hold onto control, to hold on long enough—long enough to— Drifting. He was drifting, and that would never do. Mustn't go to sleep. It had been such a long day, such a stressful day. Not good to start your day with panic like that. The black terror when he found her gone, when he thought she might have taken the bloody camera into the city.

Later, of course, he knew she didn't have the camera with her. If she'd had the camera, she would have taken pictures at Trinity College—lots of things for bloody tourists to photograph at Trinity. But she hadn't taken any photos at all, not at Trinity, not at the Eagle. So he was safe, for the time being. The camera, the film, must be in her flat, must be there even now. So the long, long day was only a game, a stall. And, of course, *he* had been there all day, too, the bloody fool who'd been following her lately. Almost the moment he'd seen him in the morning, he'd thought, "So you'll have to die now, too." And he hadn't even been surprised to find himself thinking it. He'd never killed a man before, but he didn't doubt for a minute that he could do it. The way he felt today, he could kill any number of people. It would give him a great deal of pleasure to choke the life out of anybody who got in his way. But there were other people in the building. What if they tried to stop him? He would kill them, too. It would be so easy. It would be such a relief to strike out, to bash people, to bite— Mustn't think about it. Not yet. It wasn't late enough yet.

Waiting was the hardest part, always the hardest. And now he realized that he should be grateful that Elizabeth Conroy was a slut, after all. It meant that she wouldn't be in her flat for the rest of the night, didn't it? He could get inside, find the damned camera, and shred that film once and for all. And then, then, then—Then Elizabeth "Beth" Conroy would get what was coming to her. If he couldn't find the camera, of course, he would need to have her alive, would just have to drag her down there and make her show him where it was, even if that meant he would have to kill anybody who might hear and try to interfere. That didn't matter anymore. Nothing mattered much anymore except for him to get that damned photograph. He felt he could eliminate anybody who got in his way; he felt that strong, that powerful. Everybody dead in his path, like a killing wind. And then he'd be gone. Just like a wind. Can't lock up a wind.

But the waiting was so hard. Waiting to kill *her* was the hardest, having to postpone that pleasure. That was the real secret, of course. That the pleasure of sex was nothing compared to the pleasure of killing. That was the secret he kept from himself most of the time, except when he got so tired that secrets couldn't be kept out of his head. So tired that he couldn't pretend to himself anymore that a normal life was something he wanted. What was normal, anyway? And who got to make the definition? It was all a pose. Everybody was acting all the time. That stuff on the telly was an act, of course— pretty homes, quiet and clean children, mother love. And *he* knew how to act, didn't he? He knew how to pretend to be the kind of man girls would like; he was good at it. But the act went well beyond himself and the small screen. It was everywhere. And behind the act was corruption, putrefaction, ugliness. The secret was that humankind loved the ugliness, craved the corruption, because humankind was no damned good.

So tired. Mustn't sleep. It was in the middle of the night that people slept most soundly. He'd read that once in a book about dreams. Dreams interested him quite a bit. Deep sleep was when people weren't dreaming at all, and for most people that was in the middle of the night. About three or three-thirty. When people were in the deepest part of sleep, it took a lot to wake them up. You could walk about in people's bedrooms, searching around in their things, and they would never wake up. So it wouldn't be much longer now, maybe another half hour. Then he would go for the camera. He couldn't think much past that, except to reflect resignedly that whatever happened then was just going to have to happen. He didn't have to imagine details. It would just be like a wind. A killing wind.

Chapter 30

Beth's eyes sprang open and she was immediately wide awake, wondering what had wakened her and what had made her come awake already afraid. Had there been some noise? Where was she? It was so dark. It took her a few seconds to remember that she was in Andrew Carmichael's flat, on his sofa. She sat up straight, her head reeling, a stabbing pain behind her eyes. Hangover, she thought.

"Andrew?" she said softly into the darkness.

There was no response.

"Andrew, are you here?" She spoke almost in a normal tone now, certainly loud enough to be heard anywhere in the tiny flat.

Again, there was only silence for an answer.

Beth peered around the room, looking for a light switch, focused on the shape of the lamp she knew was atop the small desk next to the bed. She stood up, fighting a sensation of nausea, and crossed the room. She fumbled for the switch for a moment and, when she found it, light flooded into her eyes, temporarily blinding her. When she could focus again, it took her only a moment to see that she was alone in the room. The bathroom door was open and it was apparent that no one was in that room either. Beth sat down slowly on the bed, absorbing the facts. It was the middle of the night and Andrew was gone. Where could he be?

Beth felt a terrible dryness in her mouth, a sick feeling of panic in her stomach and throat. What was going on? With a little gasp, she remembered her keys, slipped her hand into the pocket of her dress. The keys were gone. She sat there numbly looking around the room as if she expected the keys to materialize from the air. Andrew must have taken them; they couldn't just have slipped out of the pocket—it was too deep. The meaning of his action seemed suddenly clear, and Beth almost cried out in terror—she actually clapped her hands over her mouth to stop the sound. Had he waited for all that liquor to take effect so he could get at her keys, or had he somehow drugged the brandy?

She reached out to the desk chair next to the bed, meaning to pull herself up with its support. But there was a man's maroon-colored bathrobe draped on the back of the chair, its sleeves and upper half piled onto the seat. It slid away under her hand and slipped to the floor; the motion sent pieces of paper flying, papers that had apparently been stacked on the chair seat and hidden by the robe. Beth stared at the section of the floor illuminated by the lamp and then bent over to look closely at the scattered papers, touching them with a shaking hand. They were newspaper clippings, some with photos and some without, from several newspapers and several different dates; all of them were about the murders that had been frightening Cambridgeshire since Christmas. She recognized the faces of Greta Keller, of Sally Wright, of some of the other victims.

With a choking whimper, Beth stood upright and turned around in a half circle, her eyes terrified and darting. Then she began to tiptoe across the room, her bare feet coming down noiselessly on the worn carpet. Andrew, apparently, had taken her shoes off, but she didn't feel she had time to hunt for them. Gripping the railing with both hands, she eased herself down the steep stairs. The door at the bottom was standing slightly ajar, allowing a narrow strip of light from the hallway to show through. She pushed gently with her fingertips and the door swung open slowly. The slight noise of the moving hinges sounded deafening in her ears, made her begin to pull panicky gasps of air into her lungs.

When the door was finally opened enough to allow her through, Beth lowered herself down from the last step and slipped out into the hall. A quick glance to the right showed her that the door to her own flat was standing halfway open. Two more stealthy steps were enough to reveal, at a sharp angle, the inside of her kitchen, and, bent over slightly at the cupboard, Andrew Carmichael. He had his back to her, but she recognized him at once: the well-shaped dark head, the sports shirt he'd been wearing at dinner. She felt no surprise, had already been thinking what she must do to get past the hallway and down the stairs. It occurred to her that she might go to Adam Tate's door for help, but she remembered that she couldn't be absolutely sure he was there.

By running forward four quick steps, Beth made it past the angle where she would be seen if Andrew turned around. Then without pausing she made a sharp left turn toward the door at the end of the hallway, the door that led to the stairs. Thank God, it was open, she thought. Moving as quietly as she could, she made it to the top of the stairs and hurried down, heading for the telephone in the lobby. In the same moment that she'd rejected the idea of going to Adam Tate's door, she had remembered Sergeant Evans telling her the emergency number—999—and saying that one "didn't need a coin to dial from a phone box." She could quietly phone for the police and then get safely out of the building to wait for their arrival.

Just as Beth was lifting the receiver, she heard footsteps directly over her head in the upstairs hallway. There was a momentary pause—long enough for him to notice that the door to his flat was now wide open—and then more footsteps. She couldn't take the chance of waiting any longer. If he came down the stairs, he would catch her before she could complete the call. Screaming might be no use at all. Even if Miss Chalmers was back from the hospital, she would be of little use in such a crisis, and she might not even be there. These thoughts passed through Beth's head like lightning, and she was already moving toward the front door before she'd finished thinking them. She was only vaguely aware of the cold pavement under her feet as she ran across the parking lot and up the drive. The closest possibility of help was Constable Woods.

She ran down the Madingley Road on her own side to the crossing at the bus stop. There was no traffic at all, so she could dart across at once. Perhaps Andrew wouldn't know yet that she'd left the building, wouldn't see her running in the open to cross the road. If she could get to Woods's building safely, it would be all right. The little white car was parked exactly where she'd seen it in the afternoon. She found the driveway, glimmering lighter against the dark of the hedges, and raced down toward the house, barely registering the pain in her feet as she ran over the crushed rock surface at the edge of the parking lot.

The front door was open as it had been earlier and she easily found Number 2 in the dimly lit corridor. She lifted both of her hands, doubled them into fists, and began pounding on the door.

"Constable Woods," she called as loudly as she could manage, handicapped as she was by panicky breathlessness. "Open the door. Please. I'm in trouble. Constable Woods!" The last was almost a shriek.

The door remained closed; no sounds came from inside. Where could he be? What could have happened to him? The possible answer made Beth's throat close in terror. She never stopped the pounding, only drew several ragged breaths before calling again. When her hand began to hurt, she paused again, listening. Why was no one at all responding to this noise? The doors all along the hall remained closed, including the one at the end where the manager lived. Beth remembered the rollers and the robe and wondered if the large woman had been getting ready to go away somewhere. As she listened to the silence, Beth began to wonder if she was alone in this building.

A terrible chill swept up her arms as she remembered that she'd *told* Andrew about Constable Woods, had told him that the policeman had taken a room "across the way." And if Andrew had some reason to believe that Woods wouldn't be here—Beth could feel herself panting with fear at the possibility—then he might already be waiting outside, waiting for her to come out. She wanted to scream, but was afraid that the sound would get her precisely the wrong attention.

She remembered suddenly that during her circuit of this house earlier in the day, she'd noticed a side door. Where was the passageway leading to that door? She ran down to the end of the hall, looked left, and there was the narrow corridor. She darted down to the door, pushed it open gently, and stepped out into the darkness of the yard. Once outside, she stood perfectly still, considering her options. She could try some other building in the neighborhood, or she could try to make it into the city where she could find a phone. It would be hard to stay out of sight if she went back to the road, but she didn't know if she dared to risk knocking on any doors. The noise might attract exactly the wrong attention and could be fatal if she picked a building where no one was at home at all. She would have to try for the city, even if it meant using the rest of the night to make her way there, even if it meant hiding on and off all the way.

She crept to the corner of the building and surveyed as much of the lawns and drive as she could make out in the darkness. She could see the faint outline of hedges and shrubs on either side of the driveway—plenty of places for someone to hide if he meant to watch the front of the house. It would be best to skirt the property completely before going back up to the road. There was no back fence—she'd seen that earlier in the day—and the neighboring lot was screened by a high line of shrubs. Beth made her way toward the back of the yard and down a slope at an angle toward these shrubs. She ran in a sort of crouch, trying to minimize her already small size. Getting to the other side of the closely packed bushes produced some painful scratches to her hands and arms, and she almost cried out when a sharp knot of exposed roots dug into her right foot. But at last she was through and running quietly toward the road. When she emerged at the roadside, she looked right and left into the gloom, waited a few minutes until a single passing car showed her with its headlights that there was no one in sight. Then she turned right and started for Cambridge.

She'd gone only a few yards when she heard footsteps, running footsteps, somebody wearing shoes. She didn't bother to look around, but broke into a full run. Even in her terror, she didn't imagine she could outrun him; she was thinking ahead to Lansdowne Road just a few hundred feet away. She'd gone up and down this short road several times when she was first in Cambridge and had discovered it on one of her neighborhood walks. She knew there were only ten houses on Lansdowne Road, five on either side—big, "posh" houses surrounded by flowering apple trees and beautifully trimmed hedges. Some of them had low stone walls and some had wrought-iron gates. There would be plenty of places to hide and, what was more important, the road ended at a wood whose footpath, Beth had discovered, circled around to the main road again. Of course, she would have to recross the Madingley Road to get to Lansdowne, and that footpath would bring her out of the woods farther from Cambridge than she was now, but Beth didn't feel she had a choice. She had to take the chance that her pursuer didn't know about that footpath.

She watched and listened for cars as she ran, her legs flashing, the full skirt of her dress streaming out behind her. When she was across from the entrance to Lansdowne Road, she bolted straight across the four lanes of the usually busy A-25 and raced downhill on the other side. She was breathing so heavily now that she could no longer hear the running footsteps behind her, but she still didn't look around, not daring to break stride for even a second. At the third house on the left, she simply vaulted a low wall, raced around the BMW that was parked facing the entrance, and darted behind a tall stone gate-post, one of two that flanked the short driveway of this particular estate. Here, she dropped into a crouch and stopped, pulling her dress tightly around her so that no part of it would extend past the post and give her away. She drew three or four gasping breaths before holding her breath to listen.

She heard the running feet enter the top of the road and then slow; seconds later, they stopped. He's looking around, she thought; trying to spot a movement. She pulled a breath through her teeth as quietly as she could. Must steady the breathing, must be able to hold her breath completely if he should stop near her. The sound of the footsteps began again, stealthily this time and heading toward the other side of the street. Beth waited, knowing he would probably be constantly looking in all directions as he moved. She shifted her weight to the right, sank even nearer to the ground, and then moved her head just enough to look through the L-shaped space where the gate-post joined the low wall. At the other side of the road, bent over to separate a hedge, and with his back to her, was a dark shape. This was the moment to move.

She slid into a crawling position, her nose almost against the carefully trimmed grass, and began to move slowly downhill to a point where the wall ended in a towering hedge, a point that seemed to be the boundary between the two adjacent properties. She found it easier to move if she simply gathered her skirt up and tucked it into her belt; at least she was in no danger of tripping herself by kneeling on the fabric. All the while she was gliding forward, she was listening. The footsteps started again, but they were still on the other side of the street. When she reached the cover of the hedge, she was able to stand again and to look around for the first time.

There was no sign of a light in any of the houses, but she could see two other cars besides the BMW she'd passed earlier. Should she take the chance of running to one of those houses, of making enough noise to rouse somebody quickly? But what if she wasn't fast enough? What if the initial racket didn't do the trick? The upstairs windows of those houses, where people were probably sleeping, looked so re-mote, so closed up. If she couldn't get help immediately, he would be on her, could choke off any more sounds. She remembered those long, strong hands, and felt almost sick with grief to think that they could be the same hands that had touched her so gently only hours ago when he'd helped her down from the wall at Trinity. No, it was probably not a good idea to try to wake people up.

She considered going to the backyards of these properties, trying to work her way downhill toward the woods in that way, but she didn't know if the backyards were fenced. She could easily find herself trapped. She could hear the footsteps again, tentative, slow. She stooped until she could see through the little gaps in the hedge. Now she could see only the lower half of his body. He was in the middle of the road, obviously unsure about whether to commit to one side or the other. He was almost opposite the BMW now. Beth hurried along the hedge toward the place where it was punctured by an opening for the driveway. When she got there, she paused once more.

The footsteps began again, hurrying now. A glance showed her that he was moving to her side of the street, meant to look over the low wall. Just as he reached the gatepost where she had been crouching earlier, Beth stepped around the hedge, standing rigidly straight against the blunt edge so no part of her body would show on either side. Now she heard footsteps coming fairly quickly downhill, on the street side of the wall; apparently he'd decided against going inside the property. She stepped back into the yard and behind the hedge. If he simply passed the opening, he wouldn't see her, but if he looked inside—

Beth listened intently as the sounds slowed and then stopped. He was almost directly on the other side of the hedge from where she was standing. Now she held her breath altogether. She could hear a panting, gasping sound on the other side, a breathing that was much more labored than would have been necessitated by creeping slowly downhill as he'd been doing; apparently, he was even more desperate than she was. And then there was another sound, a grinding, grating noise that she recognized at once. She'd heard it twice before, she realized, once in the hall outside her flat and once inside the beech tree at Kew Gardens. What was it? she wondered. And why did it sound so creepy, so dangerous? She drew a shallow breath, then another, confident that someone making all that noise himself wouldn't hear her.

Suddenly there was the sound of running, a sound that diminished almost at once. He was crossing the road again, fast. Perhaps he thought he saw something, or even heard something, over there. Beth crept to the driveway opening again and peeked out. The running figure opposite her vaulted a wrought-iron, spiked fence and ran to the right, back up the hill toward a gazebo that graced the side lawn of that estate. Beth used the opportunity to dart across the opening in the hedge to the cover of the other side. There was only one other property now for her to get across before the woods. Her pursuer was still occupied. No doubt he was looking into and around that gazebo, a seemingly obvious place for someone to hide. When the cover of the hedge ended, Beth peered around it into the street. At first, she saw no one, but a few more seconds revealed the dark figure emerging on the upper side of the gazebo and heading back toward the fence he'd jumped over farther down. It was her best chance.

She ran now across the last lawn on Lansdowne Road, raced for the shadow of three lilac bushes at the end of the property. Once she was concealed behind them, she turned and watched the stalking form, that shape she had found familiar inside the water-lily house, as he looked around the hedge where she had so recently been hiding, then turned and moved back into the center of the street. After a pause, he headed straight toward a car parked inside a wooden fence across the road. So, she thought, he thinks I might be hiding in a car. Once he'd climbed the fence and was well inside that yard, Beth moved as fast as she could, using a few trees for hiding places, and found the opening of the footpath. A few more running steps and she was swallowed up into the dense interior of an English wood. Now she increased her speed to a full run, finding the way largely by the contrast in the hues of the trees as opposed to the path.

Gradually the path began to curve to the left and then slant uphill again. Beth paused, stepped from the path into the underbrush, grimacing at the feeling of sharp twigs under her feet, and came to a complete stop. She listened intently for a few seconds, holding her breath. Besides the pounding of her own heart, the only sounds she could hear were the normal sounds of the woods. Something had occurred to her while she was racing along the footpath. Perhaps she should just hide in the woods until morning, stay under cover until people were up and about, and then she could easily find help. The idea had a lot of appeal at the moment. Perhaps there was a natural instinct to go to ground after the initial terror of the chase. Her head was throbbing.

But almost at once, even while she was still catching her breath, Beth began to have misgivings. Waiting at full attention for hours, listening to every noise, to every nuance of sound, would be a terrible strain; she would surely begin to imagine a pursuer where there was none, perhaps panic and run straight toward him. And if he *did* find her, if he noticed that footpath into the woods and began quietly searching—the path would muffle the sounds of his shoes as the pavement had not—well, this would be the very worst spot to be found. Isolated, no help near. Just like the places those poor girls had been found. Raped. Strangled. Mutilated.

No. Hiding was out of the question—not here, at least. Beth got back on the path and began to trot again. She turned her head often now, scanning the woods behind her, searching the darkness for a possible follower, but she saw nothing except the path, the trees. The last few hundred feet of the path slanted sharply uphill and it was work to keep running. Finally she could see the opening in the trees where the path joined the sidewalk along the Madingley Road. She slowed to a walk, tucked her skirt up again in case she had to run fast. The circuit she'd made had brought her to a point only slightly below her own building, and now it occurred to her that it might make sense to go back there. Surely he wouldn't expect that. Then she could phone the police and hide outside until they arrived. Every part of the surroundings would be familiar to her. She crept forward now to the end of the path. At the last shrubs, she put her head out to look, turned her face to the left toward Lansdowne Road. No one was anywhere in sight. A car was approaching, heading west out of Cambridge. Its headlights lit up the whole road. Beth pulled her head back for a moment—no telling whose car that might be; he might have started to look for her in his car—and when it was almost past, ducked out again and looked to the right.

She found herself looking straight at a face only six or seven feet away, a face illuminated for a split second by the passing headlights. It was Adam Tate.

"Why, *here* you are," he said softly in his perfect accent, as the darkness fell over his face. But she had seen the little smile that showed no surprise at finding her here.

Chapter 31

Beth was frozen in shock for a few seconds, her mind simply unable to absorb these new facts. Then Adam Tate took a step toward her, and her numbness turned instantly into complete panic. She bolted straight into the road, running across the first two lanes without looking, across the divider, and into the path of an oncoming lorry. The blast of the horn only added to her panic as the truck passed behind her only seconds after she'd raced out of its way. Without thinking about it at all, she ran through the open gates of the Veterinary School grounds, racing along the paved drive that swept past the main laboratory buildings. So thorough was her terror that she didn't even look behind to see if Adam Tate was following her. She didn't realize that she was thus isolating herself, fleeing in open view into a place where even loud screams wouldn't bring help. As she ran, she was panting, "Oh God, oh God, oh God."

But finally her reeling brain seemed to right itself, to form a plan. She must get off this drive. It was too obvious and she was exposed to view from behind. Even as she was thinking this, she veered right onto the grass and between some flowering trees. By now she couldn't even register the feeling in her feet; they seemed to belong to someone else. What was at the end of this grassy open place? she was asking herself, because she was running almost blind in the dark—the lights from the road couldn't penetrate this far. She'd walked these grounds several times in the evenings when she got back from the library. The sheep pasture, she remembered suddenly—a fence and then the sheep pasture. And after that? She couldn't be certain because she'd never actually walked through the fields themselves, but she imagined there would be another fence to keep the sheep from—from what? What was the next thing after the Vet School grounds on the way to Cambridge? Churchill's. If she could get to Churchill's, there might be somebody there or a phone at least. There were other buildings near the restaurant, too, houses.

Beth was running so fast that she almost collided with the wooden fence that restrained the flocks of sheep whose various sizes and colors had so charmed her on her walks. But she was able to pull up in time, to catch herself with her hands against the top rail of the fence. She began to climb at once, panting, feeling sharp stings of pain as wood splinters pierced her feet. Once she'd jumped down on the other side, she paused to listen, to stop her gasping long enough to concentrate on any sounds of pursuit. She heard nothing.

The meadow sloped downhill toward a sheepfold, a rough wooden structure where the sheep could take shelter from inclement weather and could be confined for purposes of study. Beth had noticed this building on other visits to the grounds, and could now use its silhouette as a sort of guidepost to direct herself to the other side of the field. But before she got that far, she heard the running footsteps behind her. Another spurt of adrenaline made it possible to pick up her flagging pace again. When she reached the sheepfold, she darted around it and stopped, her back against rough boards. The sounds of running got closer, slowed, stopped.

Beth had hoped he would run past—she was no longer sure what "he" she meant when she thought about her pursuer. She'd been so sure it was Andrew who had followed her to Woods's building and then chased her into Lansdowne Road. But if it was Adam Tate who'd done that, then where was Andrew? What could have happened to him? Now the stalker was moving slowly in the grass—she could hear the movement on the other side of the fold. Straining to listen over the clamor of her beating heart, she tried to guess which way he was coming, because it was clear he now meant to circle the building. Almost too late, she realized he was advancing from her right. She pulled away from the boards and raced left to the next corner.

When she'd rounded that corner, she saw the flock, bunched up together in the way of sheep, lying on the grass some twenty yards away. On an impulse, she ran straight at them, dropped to her knees, and crawled in among the mounded forms. Some of the sheep stirred, but none leaped up or bleated. She hunkered down, putting her face near the earth, hoping that her rounded back would look like just another sheep. In that position, she could hear nothing except the wheezing of the sheep closest to her. She fought to keep herself from sobbing out loud, but her panic was making that harder every moment.

Several minutes passed. Had he gone on, left the pasture? She was afraid to lift her head to look. If he was near, this movement would surely give her away. The next thing she was aware of was the violent shifting of the sheep at the outer edges of the flock, followed by startled sheep sounds, a sharp bleat or two. She raised her head in time to see dark trousers moving swiftly toward her. Before she could move any farther, strong hands caught her upper arms and lifted her into a standing position.

She wrenched at the grasping fingers, swung her head to move the hair out of her eyes, managed one rather feeble scream before she focused on the face that was just above her own. When she saw who it was, she went limp with relief, just collapsed at the knees and would have fallen if he hadn't been holding her.

"Thank God," she gasped. "Constable Woods. He's up there. He's chasing me."

"Who are you talking about?" His voice was urgent, but he put his arm around her shoulders to hold her up. "Who's chasing you?"

She paused, trying to focus her thoughts.

"I'm not sure," she said at last. "I thought it was Andrew, but I saw Adam Tate when I came out of the woods. He seemed to know I was going to come out of the woods at the end of that footpath. He was just waiting there for me."

"What made you leave your building?" he said. "Why were you running in the first place?"

"I saw Andrew in my flat," she gasped, still almost completely unable to control her breathing. "I was sure he'd gone to look for the picture, and I tried to call the police."

"What picture?" Woods interrupted. "What do you mean?"

"I ran out when I heard him walking in the upstairs hallway—"

"What picture?" And he gave her a little shake to silence her.

"The picture from the Botanic Gardens," she replied. "The one I thought might be the Swiss girl, the one who was murdered. I left you a note at your room so I could show it to you. Did you get my note? Where were you?"

"I haven't been back to my room," he said. "Where is the picture now?"

"I ran to your room tonight when I thought Andrew was after me." She was almost weeping from relief as she spoke. "And I pounded on your door so hard—"

"Where is the photograph now?" he interrupted her again. "Do you have it with you?"

"No, no," she answered. "We should get out of here. Unless you've got a gun, we're not safe yet. *Somebody* was chasing me. We should get to police headquarters and—"

The shake he gave her this time was harder, making her head flop backward; his hands on her shoulders were gripping her very hard.

"Tell me where the photo is," he said, his voice quiet but very intense.

Beth concentrated now on the face opposite her. He sounded different, not so friendly, not so boyishly self-deprecating, and, surely, his accent was different, too—more upper-class. While she was registering these changes, even before she began to be alarmed by the fact that his hands were hurting her now, she heard a faint grating sound—a scraping, grinding noise like stones being rubbed together. She gasped in shock as she realized that the sound was coming from this young man's mouth, from his teeth.

"Let me go," she shrieked, struggling to free herself.

"I can't do that," he said, swinging her off her feet. "You have to tell me where you put the picture."

Beth screamed as loud as she could, but it was a short scream because Woods slammed her onto the ground so hard that her breath rushed out of her all at once. Before she could turn, he was on top of her, his hands at her throat.

"Where is it?" he said, his voice almost toneless. "Where did you put it?"

Beth tried to speak, but his thumbs were pressing down on her larynx. She was trying to breath, trying to throw him off her body.

"Tell me where it is," his voice was saying, almost like a chant now. "Tell me where it is."

Beth managed to free her right arm—her arms had been pinned to her sides by his knees because he was kneeling astride her body—and got hold of his hair. She pulled with all of her desperate strength, but he seemed oblivious, his wild eyes still staring down at her, his hands tighter, tighter.

"Don't look at me like that," he hissed. "Don't you dare look at me as if it's my fault."

Beth felt herself losing consciousness, her hand going limp and slipping from the curly hair. She would tell him if he let her, she thought. She would tell him where the picture was. There was a roaring in her ears, a roaring like the ocean, but over it she could hear the man above her cry out—"Ow!"—and then she felt his weight being lifted off her, his hands flying away from her neck. She rolled over onto her side, gasping air into her lungs, coughing, beginning to vomit. For a few seconds, the agony in her own body made her oblivious to anything else.

But gradually she began to make out sounds, thudding noises, men's voices crying out in inarticulate, wordless grunts. Finally, she heard a louder cry—"Tate! Over here!"—and then thudding again. She rolled up into a half-sitting position, her hand at her throat, and looked in the direction of the noises. There was a roiling mass of dark shapes on the ground near her. Occasionally she could see an arm, a leg, a head. There were two men struggling with each other, she finally realized. They rolled alarmingly near her and she sprang away, getting up to her knees. Then the retching sensation began again and she bent double, gasping at the pain in her throat. When she looked up again, there were three figures locked in a grim struggle, two of them apparently cooperating to subdue the third.

But they were having a bad time of it. The man in the middle was screaming now, animal sounds of panic and desperation, but he was fighting like a wild man and the other two were almost overpowered. Beth struggled to her feet, uncertain whether to flee or stay. She could at last see that the men trying to bring Timothy Woods under control were Andrew Carmichael and Adam Tate.

Very suddenly the figure at the center of the fray went limp, dropped to his knees. The others hung on for a few seconds, panting and cursing, while they tried to assess this development.

"It's all right," a clear voice said, a voice surprisingly calm. "I won't struggle anymore. You can lift me up now. I won't try to hurt anyone."

And they did lift him up. He stood perfectly still, rigid, in fact, but the other two didn't let go of him.

"Just lie down on your stomach," Andrew said firmly. "Spread your arms and legs. And don't you make another move." Woods went down like a lamb.

"You watch him, Tate," Andrew said. "Shout if he moves one limb."

Andrew turned now and came to Beth, putting his arms around her shaking shoulders. She lifted her face to him, saw blood on his mouth and cheek.

"Are you all right?" he asked. "Did he hurt you badly?"

"I think I'm all right," she said, but her voice was only a croak and it hurt to talk.

Headlights were pouring into the field from the road now, and the sounds of slamming car doors carried easily across the night.

"That will be the Cambridge police, I suppose," Andrew said. "I telephoned for them." He held Beth close but didn't take his eyes off the prostrate figure on the ground next to them.

The wobbling beams of flashlights were approaching them now very fast, five or six of them. Voices were calling, "Hallo? Carmichael?"

"Down here," Andrew shouted. "Just follow my voice. We're right over here, all of us."

When the flashlight bearers arrived, they turned out to be three uniformed policemen, Sergeant Timmings, and Chief Superintendent Michael Wilson.

"Do you need an ambulance here?" Wilson said immediately.

"No, no, I don't think so," Andrew replied, stroking Beth's hair and looking down at her in the light from Wilson's flashlight.

"Have you got him?" Wilson said, moving the beam onto the prone figure.

"Yes, we seem to, sir," Andrew answered. Adam Tate, attentive to all the talk, was silent, standing guard over Beth's assailant even now when police could have relieved him of that duty.

"Isn't he a policeman?" Beth asked, gesturing at Woods. Her voice was coming clearer now. "He told me he was a constable."

"Oh, no, Miss Conroy," Wilson sighed. "He's definitely not a policeman."

"But he knew your name," Beth insisted. "When I was talking with him, he called you by your name, and your name hasn't been in the newspapers. That's why I was so convinced. I didn't even ask him for identification." It was a long speech and it made her throat ache.

"I'd guess that you said my name first without realizing it," Wilson said. "If you think about it carefully, you'll probably remember that you mentioned me, and he picked it up at once. He's quite clever, I think."

Beth fell silent, trying to remember.

"The names of local police personnel were publicized, of course," Wilson went on. "So he probably began with those names, didn't he? Then it was fairly simple to get you to volunteer my name, to volunteer a lot of information that he could twist about for his own purposes. He's had a lot of practice getting people to believe in him."

Now Wilson turned back to Andrew, having assumed almost automatically that he was the spokesman. "What happened here, Carmichael?"

"We—Tate and I—caught up with them just in time," Andrew answered. "When I came running up, this lunatic was trying to choke the life out of Beth. I think she should see a doctor. She was gasping and being sick afterward."

"Yes, I agree," Wilson said, turning his flashlight back onto Andrew's face. "You look as if you could use some medical attention yourself, Mr. Carmichael."

"No, no," Andrew protested. "Just a few bumps and scrapes, really. He bit me, I think, here on my arm."

"And you?" Wilson swung his light onto Tate.

"Adam Tate," he said softly, his usual shyness returning in the presence of Scotland Yard. "I'm not hurt at all. Only a bit winded. Mr. Carmichael asked me to help him when he learned that Miss Conroy had run to the wrong person for help."

"I don't understand any of this," Beth was able to say at last. "Does anybody understand this?"

"We'll get the confusions sorted out once we're back in the city," Wilson said. "But right now, we need to take our suspect into custody and get you to a doctor."

"No, really," Beth said. "I don't need a doctor. I'm all right."

"No arguments," Wilson said kindly. "You and Mr. Carmichael can go with this officer. You other men take the suspect to my car. And mind he doesn't bolt."

Two of the uniformed policemen went straight to Woods and rolled him over. He jerked and tried to sit up, making a frightened sound.

"Remarkable," one of the constables said. "I think he was asleep, sir. Fancy that! Asleep."

They hauled the handcuffed man to his feet and propelled him past the others toward the road. Just as they moved past Beth and Andrew, Woods dug his feet in and tried to turn.

"Just a word," he gasped. "One word." And he turned his mad face to look at Beth, the snub nose and freckles incongruous under the wild eyes. She shrank back against Andrew. The officers dragged Woods forward, but he kept turning his head back toward Beth.

"He'll lock me in now," he called. "But you'll let me out, won't you? You'll wait until he's gone upstairs, and then you'll let me out. Say you will. Please say you will."

By the time they'd reached the road, he was screaming, the same words over and over, "Say you'll let me out!"

Chapter 32

Beth sat curled up against An-
drew in the back of the car. He'd carried her there,
murmuring, "Your poor feet. Just look at your poor feet." She was
still too much in shock to react to what had happened—she didn't
feel any pain in her feet at all. Her only sensation was of intense
relief, the sheer joy of being able to rest against Andrew's chest and
feel utterly safe.

"When I saw you were gone," he was saying now against her

hair, "I was confused at first, but when I saw those scattered clippings, I knew what you must be thinking."

"But *you* were gone first," she whispered. "What were you doing down in my flat?"

"It's going to sound so silly now," he murmured, "when we consider the consequence. I dozed off myself for a while, but then I woke up and couldn't get back to sleep. You were sleeping so soundly; I just watched you for a bit, thinking how glad I was that you were safe with me there. I was planning what I would say to you over breakfast—the rest of my confession, I mean. You fell asleep before I could get well under way. I wanted you in the very best frame of mind to tell you what I'd been up to since I met you; some good coffee and some fragrant food might better dispose you to forgive me, I calculated. You'd mentioned that you liked crumpets, that you'd bought some last night. I thought if I just went down to get them, I could surprise you when you woke up. But when I started back, I saw the door open and that you'd run out."

"Why did you have those clippings?" she asked, looking up at him in the dark. "That's what really scared me, made me run."

"I know, I know," he sighed. "And if I could have foreseen what happened, I would have made you stay awake until I'd explained everything. You see, I've been gathering everything I could find on the killings since April because the second victim, the girl in Huntingdon, was my niece. You've read about her. Jennifer Harcourt. My only sister's only child."

"I'm so sorry," Beth murmured, raising her hand to touch his face. He winced away, groaning softly.

"Oh, God!" Beth said, trying to sit up. "You're hurt badly."

"No, no," he assured her. "It's only a lump on the outside, but it's cut on the inside, and that's what smarts. It'll be fine, I'm sure. No loose teeth or anything."

"What did you do when you found me gone?"

"I ran outside and looked about but, of course, you'd run off. I remembered you mentioning that the policeman who was assigned—or rather who you *thought* was assigned—to protect you had a room in the neighborhood. I thought, 'That's where she's gone, of course.' If I was going to explain, I reasoned that I'd better find you quickly.

I called the police station to explain and to ask where their constable was staying. Of course, they told me they'd never assigned anyone to follow you, and then I realized who that chap must be.

"So I told the police on the phone that this chap was passing himself off as a constable assigned to protect you and that you'd probably run straight to him. They assured me someone would be out straightaway, but I couldn't wait, of course. I woke up Tate to help me. He was pretty confused at first, but he caught on quickly. We made a search plan, to separate so we'd have a better chance of coming across some sign of you. I was on the other side of our building, up the road a bit, when you stepped out into the road in front of Tate. He was startled when you bolted, but he waited to see where you'd gone before coming to find me. When we got into the Vet School grounds, I sent him in one direction and I went in the other. I caught up with you first, but not before that maniac did, I'm sorry to say."

"I'm very grateful you got there when you did," Beth said fervently. "Do you think you could begin at the very beginning of your involvement in all this? I'm still confused about so many things."

"Jennifer was killed in February," he explained, putting his chin down on the top of her head. "It was a terrible blow to my sister, of course—to all of us. The police weren't calling it a serial killing then. That came in April after the girl in St. Ives."

"Sally Wright," Beth said.

"Yes. The one who looks so much like you. I began to follow all the cases in the newspapers. My poor sister was just distraught that Jen's killer hadn't been caught. Finally, when I read about this Swiss girl being killed, I took an early holiday and came here, meaning to find out what I could on my own. I was at police headquarters making inquiries about the investigation that Friday when you came in to say you were being followed."

"Did you see me there?"

"No, but I heard two policemen talking about it. One said you resembled Sally Wright—the papers were already commenting that the victims resembled each other. They talked about the break-in at your flat and that you felt it was connected to the killings. They were discounting the connection, but I thought it might be a place to start.

It was easy enough to get your address off the file—they just left it lying about on the desk."

"And that's how you came to live in my building."

"Exactly. I deliberately arranged to meet you when you were coming home in the rain that day. And when I saw you leaving the house in the dark last Wednesday evening, I thought it was best to follow you. Our meeting at Churchill's wasn't accidental."

"Oh, dear," she sighed. "And I thought it was so romantic."

"It *was* romantic," he insisted. "At least it turned out that way. But I reasoned afterward that whoever was shadowing you would never reveal himself if I were at your side constantly. So, the next morning, I began following you myself. For three days, I kept out of sight, didn't even park my car at the house most of the time, and just watched you wherever you went. Yesterday when you went to the railway station in the morning, I was sure you were safe the moment you got on the train, so I came away. You can imagine how upset I was when you told me over dinner tonight that you'd been followed all the way to Kew, and that my niece's killer might very well have been close enough to you to be captured, if only I'd been there."

"That's why you kept on about it. I wondered."

"I used the day to catch up on my sleep because I've been staying up so late. But you got back earlier than I expected and then I missed it when you went out again—to buy your crumpets."

"So I *did* have a guard the past few days; just not the one I thought I had," she said, smiling up at him; the lights of the city were coming into the car and she could see him more clearly now—the left side of his face was already swollen and discolored.

"Yes, but all that following about was producing very little result. And I felt so awful about deceiving you, like such a sneak. At dinner tonight when I remarked that it was pretty callous of the police to use you as bait, I realized I'd been doing the same thing. When those safari chaps stake out a lamb to capture a lion, they don't ask the lamb if it minds, you see; but you are hardly a lamb, and you should have been consulted. I was feeling pretty ashamed of myself."

"Never mind," Beth whispered soothingly. "Then what?"

"You can imagine how alarmed I was when I looked out the

window last night and saw you coming down the drive with that curly-headed chap. What is his name, anyway?"

"He told me it was Woods. Timothy Woods."

"Well, when you told me he was someone who'd offered to help you with your bags from the bus, I got really frightened. I saw how easily someone could approach you when I wasn't looking."

"So you decided to spend every moment with me from then on?"

"Oh, you are quick." And he chuckled softly. "It wasn't just to protect you, mind. I did, by that time, want to spend more time with you, just for your own sake."

"And you didn't want me to go off by myself in Cambridge, either, did you? I mean after we'd left Trinity and you'd asked me to dinner."

"That's exactly right. But you were so stubborn. And I was worried because I was almost certain I'd seen Woods again in the city, when we were at the Eagle. I didn't tell you because I didn't want to frighten you. Then I thought of pretending it was Tate I'd seen, because I wanted to find out what you thought about him. I knew he'd moved into the house just about the time I did, so I thought he might be a suspect. I guess it just never occurred to me that anyone could think I was a suspect, too."

"Poor Adam," Beth said with a little laugh. "I suspected him, too, and he was just a shy man trying to be nice to me. I'm afraid I acted like an idiot to him. I must remember to thank him for his help."

"Yes, I think Woods might have got away from me if Tate hadn't arrived when he did. Pretty tough for an astronomer."

They both laughed quietly for a moment.

"Why didn't you tell me all this at dinner tonight?" Beth asked at last. "It would have saved lots of trouble."

"Don't think I haven't considered that. At first, when I moved into the house, I thought I might have an easier time investigating if no one at all knew what I was up to. After a few days, the pose took on a life of its own. But it made me very uncomfortable to have to deceive you, believe me."

Beth suddenly remembered something.

"You put your hand in front of your mouth when you're uncomfortable or embarrassed, don't you?" she asked.

"Yes, I guess I do," he laughed. "I'm not aware of doing it, but people have told me I do it in court when I'm bluffing. Until recently, I had a mustache, and I used to pull on that, too, they say. I must have seemed like some sort of idiot to you at times. But I was going to tell you the whole story. I was working up the courage to do it tonight, but I was so afraid you'd be angry, as I said earlier. That you would resent my using you, and think I was just pretending to like you."

"Yes, I see. How much of it was pretense, anyway?"

"Well," he chuckled. "I wouldn't normally be so socially aggressive as I was at Churchill's, it's true. I'm usually very shy, a slow starter. But the *spirit* of the whole thing was quite sincere, I assure you. And tonight, I almost swept you straight across the room into that bed. But I felt I was operating under false pretenses, so that wouldn't have been very gentlemanly."

"Oh, you are so *proper*," Beth sighed. "That's why you pushed me away, and I thought you didn't like me."

"And then I tried to confess," he reminded her. "I was trying to make it right."

"But I passed out," she laughed. "You've got a cheap drunk on your hands, I'm afraid."

"With coffee and crumpets at the ready, I would have been able to make you understand everything."

"And what about the things you *did* tell me?" Beth asked softly. "About the tropical fish and going to school with Prince Charles and about an ex-wife?" She put strong emphasis on the "ex" part.

"Every word true, I take my oath," he laughed. "I really am a solicitor from Birmingham. This really is my first holiday since my divorce, though it wasn't meant as a reunion of old Cambridge cronies. I made that part up. Except for last night. I really did have a late appointment with an old chum who's an art director for a local theater company. We ran into each other by accident last week. Do you think you can forgive me for deceiving you a little?"

"Of course," Beth whispered. "As the damsels say in the movies, you're my hero, so I can forgive you almost anything." And she snuggled closer to him as the car came to a stop in front of the emergency room door of the hospital.

Chapter 33

It was the following Monday afternoon before Beth saw Chief Superintendent Wilson and his sergeant again. She and Andrew had been treated and released at the hospital—the swelling in her feet was gone now and Andrew's face, though still discolored, had returned to its usual shape. On Wednesday afternoon, they had gone to the police station to give their statements, Beth taking with her the photograph that had started her whole involvement in the case of the Cambridgeshire Strangler.

They had been fending off newspaper people ever since, with Mr. Chatterjee's good-natured help.

The building was full to capacity now with new tenants—"summer people," Mr. Chatterjee called them, treating Beth as if she were a permanent resident. Adam Tate and Miss Chalmers were gone. Miss Chalmers had taken her mother's body home; the old woman had been the only one associated with the building to die on Tuesday night—thank God, the only one, Beth often thought. Even Ramón's flat was repaired and occupied by a couple from New York. All the new faces made Beth a little skittish—she never knew if the person in the hallway might be from the *Evening Standard*. So when someone knocked on the door on Monday afternoon, Andrew, who was in her flat at the time, warned her not to open up until she found out who it was. Sergeant Timmings answered her query and then preceded his senior officer into the flat.

"We've had the devil's own time piecing together this story," Wilson said after accepting the cup of tea Beth offered him. "At first, we thought we'd never get anything lucid from this Woods fellow. That, by the way, is his actual name. Timothy Woods. He's been using a series of assumed names, a new one each time he moved, but he told you his real name. The psychiatrist says it's part of a 'deeply buried urge for punishment.' After his arrest he behaved as if he'd had a complete breakdown. But by Sunday he'd slept a good deal and seemed better, though preoccupied with being locked up. Claustrophobia of a severe variety, I'd say."

"That's why he was asking me to let him out, do you think?" Beth asked, balancing her own tea on the arm of the big chair. Andrew had pulled over a dining-room chair to sit right next to her, and Timmings had joined Wilson on the sofa.

"Well," Wilson said after a sip of tea. "I believe he thought you were his sister at that moment. It's very complicated. She's been dead for almost twelve years, a suicide, but his mental condition seems to stem in large part from an obsession with her. And there's madness in the family, too. The father has been in the hospital since Woods was just a boy. He went to pieces after the girl's suicide—the father did, I mean. Record shows he might have been involved in an incestuous relationship with his daughter, and that led to the girl's death. It affected the boy, of course."

"Good Lord," Beth breathed. "He really came out of a snake pit, didn't he?"

"No doubt about that," Wilson went on. "But as I said, our prisoner wasn't communicating very well while we had him in the lockup. So I hit on the idea of going on walks with him, taking him from the cells—well guarded, of course—and letting him walk about outside. The weather has been so splendid lately."

"Yes, it has," Beth replied. "I'm beginning to think England has given up rain for the rest of my stay here."

"Well, after a bit, he began to talk," Wilson said. "Seemed to feel that he owed me something for getting him outside again. Seemed to trust me." Wilson paused for a moment, and Beth thought he seemed not especially happy about this effect he'd had on the prisoner. "And he was very forthcoming about his recent history. Not always keeping to chronology or even to logical connections, mind, but eventually we got most of it. One of the officers escorting the walks carried a tape recorder."

"Has he confessed, then?" Andrew asked, leaning forward eagerly.

"Oh, yes," Wilson said matter-of-factly. "What amounts to a confession. He told us details about each of the murders that only the killer could know. He talked a great deal about you, Miss Conroy, and about the photo you'd taken. Really obsessed with that picture —a fixation by this time. You see, he'd been there, in the gardens with Greta Keller, and was sure you'd taken a photo of both of them together. Wouldn't believe me when I told him he wasn't in the picture. I had to show it to him finally."

"How did he react?" Beth asked.

"He laughed," Wilson answered. "Laughed for quite a while. Doubled up there in the middle of Midsummer Common, so people passing by stopped to stare at him. Of course, he was shackled as well, so that might have been one of the reasons they were staring."

"And did he tell you about following me?" Beth wanted to know. "Was I right about that?"

"Certainly you were," Wilson responded. "He found you originally by reading your university's name on the bag you'd had with you when the Keller girl accidentally took your photo just as you accidentally took hers. We have that photo, too, by the way. He didn't destroy it, but kept it in a sport bag he sometimes carried about with him. He broke in and destroyed your films for obvious reasons. And he followed you to London, too, tried to snatch your camera. That was him at Kew Gardens as well. I think he developed some confused feelings about you along the way. Partly he identified you with his victims, who were in some way identified with his sister. His obsession with her is very ambivalent—classic love-hate thing, the psychiatrist tells me. But partly he fell in love with you, imagined you as a potential wife."

"Rubbish," Andrew exclaimed. "He meant to kill her, tried to, you know."

"Oh, yes, I know," Wilson said, turning his grandfatherly face toward Andrew. "But he was bitterly disappointed by that time because he'd seen her with you, believed in some strange way that she'd betrayed him with you. He was fiercely jealous of his sister, too, of her relationship with the father. Transferred all that jealous rage to you, Miss Conroy, on Tuesday night."

"How long did he have the room across the way?" Beth asked. "He told me it was only since last Sunday, but I guess that wasn't true, either."

"Oh, he'd been there from just after he found out where you lived—more than a fortnight. But he didn't spend much time over there lately. From what I can gather, he grew steadily more terrified that he would lose you, in every sense of that term," Wilson explained. "Afraid you might slip past him and have the film developed and take the photo to the police. But also afraid you would leave him, go away, unless he was near you all the time. He'd made friends with your landlord's dog, so he could go in and out of that flat downstairs without a disturbance."

"What I haven't been able to figure out," Beth said after draining the last of her tea, "is how he could have been so clever at shadowing me most of the time, and then be so clumsy last week at King's College Chapel when I spotted him."

"Apparently he meant for you to discover him then," Wilson explained. "He'd noticed you, Mr. Carmichael, occasionally following around after Miss Conroy. He thought *you* might be police and so conceived the idea of pretending to be a constable himself. He believed Miss Conroy was unaware of your surveillance, he said. By that time he was losing his customary caution, his usual ability to preserve his anonymity. He wanted to make friends with you, Miss Conroy, and he said he'd already caught you noticing him several times anyway—figured you would begin to put those things together in your mind unless he gave you another context for finding him familiar. But it confused him when he saw you here on Monday evening, Mr. Carmichael, actually talking to Miss Conroy as an acquaintance. He didn't know if you'd revealed yourself to her as a policeman, or if you were undercover. He hadn't tumbled yet to the fact that you lived in the building, thought you might just have been up to see if Miss Conroy was in and, not finding her at home, were coming out again."

"I find it hard to believe," Andrew said, "that Woods could have been watching Miss Conroy all that time and not known that I lived here." Beth noted with some amusement that Andrew had adopted Wilson's habit of referring to her formally.

"I think the key is precisely that he was watching Miss Conroy so obsessively," Wilson responded. "He just didn't focus on other people. And from what you told the local police on Wednesday, you and your car were often gone from here when Miss Conroy was going in and out. You were concealing yourself on purpose, remember."

"But he must have seen us together at Churchill's," Beth insisted.

"Did you go to the restaurant together?" Wilson asked, his eyes looking puzzled.

"No. Andrew came later and joined me."

"Well, that explains it, then," Wilson said. "Most of the time he waited outside the places he'd followed you to. So if he followed you to Churchill's, and he probably did, he wouldn't know whether you ate alone or not."

"But we left together," Beth insisted. "Andrew and I, I mean."

"Well, he told us that he would make judgments about the places you went. He actually uses phrases like 'I would make judgments.' If he thought you were unlikely to use your camera or make a move to get the film developed, he would go away again after you'd arrived at a place you were likely to be for some time. He seldom waited outside the library for you, for instance. He'd come to be able to tell, he said, how long you'd be there. Probably, he considered a solo dinner at a restaurant so inoffensive that he didn't need to hang about waiting for you to come out. He probably went back to his room that night —his own room, that is. I doubt that he'd moved over here yet at that time."

"Why didn't he make a move Tuesday morning, then, when he saw me go to the photo place?" Beth said; she'd been thinking about this intently for several days. "Surely that's what he was waiting for all along; that's what he was intent on preventing."

Wilson and Timmings exchanged a glance and a smile.

"It's one of those ironies that we often encounter in our line," Wilson said. "The one break in a clever criminal's concentration. He overslept. When he told us about it, he was still angry with himself for doing it. When he woke up and found you'd left for the city earlier than usual, he was at first pretty desperate. But just as he was about to leave the flat—he came in at the window, but went out of the door most of the time—he saw you, Mr. Carmichael, dressed in a robe, in the lobby to pick up your pint of milk. Then he knew you'd been living here and felt that following *you* would lead him to Miss Conroy. He was right, of course, as it turns out."

"Did he still think I was a policeman?" Andrew wanted to know.

"He wasn't so sure by then," Wilson replied. "And as the day went on, that ceased to matter to him. He was getting more and more jealous, seeing the two of you together all day, and that eclipsed everything else in his mind. He told me quite casually that he meant to kill you, Mr. Carmichael, to 'eliminate' you, as he put it."

Beth took Andrew's hand, looked up into his eyes.

"He left Cambridge before you did on Tuesday," Wilson continued. "After he'd seen the two of you separate, that is. He planned to come back here to wait for a chance to kill you, Mr. Carmichael. Because you had a car, he was sure you'd get here long before Miss Conroy. Then he imagined he would have a clear path to her. But he was badly frightened by our arrival, Timmings and mine, that is. We'd driven out here a little before six to ask why you'd been trying to contact us earlier in the day, Miss Conroy."

"Then you were the one knocking at my door," Beth said, sitting up straight. "Miss Chalmers heard you, heard your car. I couldn't figure out who it could have been." She saw Wilson's stern gaze. "Yes, I know I should have kept my appointment with you or gotten back to you later. Don't scold me, please. I've scolded myself enough the past few days."

"Never mind," Wilson said kindly. "It was just another of those missed chances." Beth and Andrew exchanged a glance, remembering other such missed opportunities. "Woods drove off again when he saw us here, left his car across the road, and crept back into that flat downstairs. Then you got back before Mr. Carmichael did, so his plans were foiled once again. He was watching from the stairwell when you went up to Mr. Carmichael's flat for dinner." Here Wilson and Timmings exchanged another glance, and Beth could almost see Wilson deciding how to continue without making indiscreet reference to the fact that she hadn't come back down from Mr. Carmichael's flat after dinner.

"When he heard Tate's car, he had to hide in the utility room for a bit," Wilson said at last. "That was very hard for him, of course. Tiny room, no light. Later he went downstairs again to the empty flat. He could get in and out easily because he'd unlocked the door from the inside and just left it open that way. Then he saw you run from the building and, of course, you know the rest very well, indeed."

"Yes, we certainly do," Andrew said, giving Beth's hand a squeeze.

"Woods was waiting outside the house across the way after you went looking for him there," Wilson continued. "He chased you until you gave him the slip on Lansdowne Road. He didn't know anything about the path through the woods that you told the local police about on Wednesday. He searched around the houses for a long time and then went back up to the main road. Of course, he just happened to be looking when you bolted across the road up here. When you'd seen Mr. Tate and misinterpreted his intention, I suppose that would be."

"Of course," Beth murmured. "And I was spotlighted for him by that passing truck."

"The only thing we can't get Woods to talk about is what, if anything, he was planning to do next while he was down in that empty flat, wide awake into the middle of the night. He just keeps saying, 'I was waiting to get the photo.' When I ask him how he meant to do that, or whether he hoped to escape after he'd done it, he just looks at me and says, 'I was waiting.' I don't think he can have slept much in those weeks following Greta Keller's death. Sleeplessness can make a mind degenerate pretty quickly, you know. Especially a mind that wasn't in good health to begin with."

"Good Lord," Beth sighed, sitting back in the chair. "To think I got caught up in all of this by simply taking a picture."

"I know it's been a nightmare for you, Miss Conroy," Wilson said with a sympathetic smile. "But if it's any comfort to you to know it, the psychiatrist is convinced that this man's obsession with that photograph and his efforts to secure it may very well have distracted him from his other ruling obsession these past weeks; if he hadn't been so distracted, he might have killed another girl before we could have stopped him. Perhaps even more, if he'd moved on, left Cambridge."

"What's going to happen to him now?" Andrew asked, a subject that clearly interested him very much.

"Not for me to say," Wilson sighed, putting his teacup on the low table next to the sofa and standing up. Timmings came to attention and sprang up, too. "Courts take over now. Our job is done, and we'll be going back to London. Woods will go to prison or to a mental ward. Either way, he'll be locked up tight, I hope, for the rest of his life. That's not vindictiveness, mind. I'm just concerned that we should all be protected from him. I don't see much hope for his being cured or rehabilitated—though, of course, that's not for me to say, either."

"There's no capital punishment for these crimes in England, is there?" Beth asked, standing up to walk with them to the door.

"No, there isn't," Wilson answered. Timmings, who had spoken no word after initial greetings, was already in the hallway. "But for this man, I really believe life imprisonment is a far worse punishment than execution would be. He has such a horror of being closed in. Says he's suffocating whenever we put him back in the cell."

"That's as it should be," Andrew said from behind Beth's shoulder. "He should suffocate every day of his life. He suffocated Jennifer and those other girls. It's no more than he deserves."

They all looked at him for a moment. It was the first time Beth had heard him express openly the rage and frustration he must have been feeling for months after his niece's death.

"Thank you for coming, Chief Superintendent," Beth said at last. "And thank you for your help all along."

"Well," Wilson said ruefully. "I didn't do very much, did I? All that forensic work and fingerprinting and police sketching, and, in the end, the case is solved almost by accident, by the criminal's tripping himself up with his own obsessions. That's often the way it happens, you know, despite the propaganda in books and films. Often we just have to wait for the bad guys to make a mistake. Then the rest is easy. But don't tell that to people back in America." And he twinkled at Beth winningly. Now that his young sergeant could no longer see his face, he seemed to relax a bit more. "Let them go on believing in the crime-stopping powers of Scotland Yard."

"Your secret is safe with me," Beth said, giving him her hand, which he held in both of his for a few seconds before turning to leave.

When the door had closed behind the men from Scotland Yard, Andrew waited for a few seconds and then spoke softly to her back.

"Now will you give me an answer to my question?" They had been in the middle of a serious conversation when Wilson and Timmings had arrived. "I've only got three days of this holiday left."

"I've already told you that I'll come to visit Birmingham as soon as my research is finished," Beth said, turning to face him. "And I intend to get it finished in a new land speed record for E. M. Forster research. What more do you want?"

"I said that you don't need to race back to America at the end of the month," Andrew reminded her. "Your school year doesn't begin until September. So why can't you just stay here until you're sick to death of this green and pleasant land? That should take at least until the end of August, don't you think? I can clear my schedule and show you the sights. Perhaps we could even go north to Scotland. I think you'd like Scotland; it's the land of my forebears, you know."

Beth looked hard at the earnest face opposite her. She realized suddenly that her recent experiences had made a tremendous change in her. Real danger, real crisis, not just imagined slights and insecurities, had been faced and routed. The Beth Conroy who had come to England would have felt locked in to the original plan of her sabbatical trip, would have felt obliged to fly home on June 30 because her ticket had June 30 printed on it. The new Beth Conroy understood clearly that airline tickets, like so many other things, can be changed. The new Beth Conroy had learned to trust her instincts.

"Answer the question, madam," Andrew said playfully, but his eyes were serious. "The court requires a reply."

"Very well, Counselor," Beth replied, taking a step toward him. "The verdict is in your favor. Tell me, is there a family tartan somewhere? Will I get to see you in a kilt?"

"If you're lucky," he said with a slow smile, and he reached out to take her hand.